Adcock, Siobl

ADC

The complet &ist

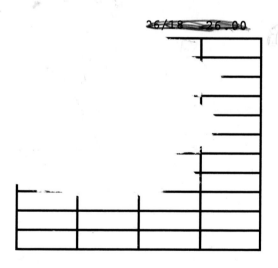

26/18   26.00

ALSO BY SIOBHAN ADCOCK

The Barter

THE
COMPLETIONIST

SIOBHAN ADCOCK

SIMON & SCHUSTER
New York   London   Toronto   Sydney   New Delhi

Simon & Schuster
1230 Avenue of the Americas
New York, NY 10020

This book is a work of fiction. Any references to historical events, real people, or real places are used fictitiously. Other names, characters, places, and events are products of the author's imagination, and any resemblance to actual events or places or persons, living or dead, is entirely coincidental.

First Simon & Schuster hardcover edition June 2018

SIMON & SCHUSTER and colophon are registered trademarks of Simon & Schuster, Inc.

For information about special discounts for bulk purchases, please contact Simon & Schuster Special Sales at 1-866-506-1949 or business@simonandschuster.com.

The Simon & Schuster Speakers Bureau can bring authors to your live event. For more information or to book an event, contact the Simon & Schuster Speakers Bureau at 1-866-248-3049 or visit our website at www.simonspeakers.com.

Interior design by Lewelin Polanco

Manufactured in the United States of America

10 9 8 7 6 5 4 3 2 1

Library of Congress Cataloging-in-Publication Data

Names: Adcock, Siobhan, author.
Title: The completionist / Siobhan Adcock.
Description: New York : Simon & Schuster, 2018.
Identifiers: LCCN 2017048287| ISBN 9781501183478 (hardcover) | ISBN 9781501183485 (softcover) | ISBN 9781501183492 (e-book)
Subjects: LCSH: Future life—Chicago (Ill.)—Fiction. | Fertility, Human—Chicago (Ill.)—Fiction. | Sisters—Chicago (Ill.)—Fiction. | BISAC: FICTION / Literary. | FICTION / Thrillers. | LCGFT: Fantasy fiction.
Classification: LCC PS3619.I58 C66 2018 | DDC 813/.6—dc23 LC record available at https://lccn.loc.gov/2017048287

ISBN 978-1-5011-8347-8
ISBN 978-1-5011-8349-2 (ebook)

for my father

IN THE FIRST PLACE

Everything is heavy here: his weapon, the metal and synthetic particles in the air, the way the light falls through them. But the two women in his crosshairs—sisters, he thinks—are just leaves. Papery, circling, drifting. They can't find their way out from the place where they've fallen. As much pity as he can feel for them, he has already felt. Now he is nothing but the trigger. This change in him has taken several moments.

And now he moves, and because he's the trigger, when he moves, usually someone gets hurt. Dies.

Usually. But it's hard to know. Since he's been over here he's trained in five or six of the new weapons classifications, like the other fire squads in his battalion. None of them really understand how the triggers work, or what's being fired exactly, or even, in some cases, what is really happening after the trigger is pulled. He thinks he's done some terrible things. He thinks he probably does them every day. But again, because it's hard to be sure, all he's left with is this idea that people—all of them everywhere but especially here, where everything is heavy and dried-out and hot—are like these leaves, these already-dead things that he's just blowing around, triggering into flame.

Now a disaster is pursuing the women, the sisters, bending the air around them, pluming in every direction. He can see the two of them better now, lit up, no longer holding hands, running hard for the H2.0

storage capsules that stretch across the rail tracks, a five-mile metal caravan of engineered water. The caravan was behind a temporary fence a few days ago, but that got breached and now it's out in the open, the world's worst-kept secret, guarded by Charlie company, all guys from the New Cities like him. Like him, a lot of them haven't slept. Like him, a lot of them have been here a few years longer than they thought they'd be.

The two women are cloaked head to knee, like ghosts, wearing the homespun, mummy-wrap-like foot coverings that most people wear here, because they can be bound high up the leg and are good in the dust. Through his scope, he can see that one woman is smaller than the other, maybe a teenager. The smaller one looks over her shoulder, and he can see a flash of fire reflected in the lens of whatever she's wearing to protect her eyes. Then she runs harder, reaching for the taller woman, whose longer strides are pulling her ahead.

Each of the H2.0 storage capsules is the length of four train cars, longer by half than the old shipping containers that were in use when the Wars started, back when his father was fighting. They are a dull platinum color, reflecting no light, absorbing no heat. They look like a colony of well-fed worms laid end to end, moisture trapped inside their shells. These worms never dry out in the sun. He has pressed his gloved hand to the sides of these capsules, many times. There's a faint pulsing inside, like the water is a little bit alive, like it has just a worm's heartbeat. The capsules are cool, the only coolness for hundreds of miles: engineered water is always 10 degrees Celsius, 50 degrees Fahrenheit, unless you have to boil it using the heating element it's sold with. In the last three weeks there have been seventeen attempts on the H2.0 caravans, a new one almost every night. Even though the people attacking them need this water to live. There's no other water left in this place. Nothing about it makes sense to him anymore, and he doesn't care.

Behind the woman and the girl, plumes of fire are racing, unfurling toward the tracks. The fires are programmed to self-extinguish if they come into contact with the storage capsules. The H2.0 is too precious to incinerate. It's too precious to exist at all, probably.

The women, who could be water scavengers, or who could be raiders targeting the caravan, seem to know this.

He knows that at this distance they could make it all the way to the train cars to detonate one of the homegrown devices that proliferate over here. Or they could get past the H2.0 caravan back to the perimeter, blow up another section of the fence. Or just fire on someone on patrol, an ordinary night's work. And then, however they got in, they might get away. They might actually make it.

He's not supposed to let that happen.

Not quite thinking but not quite *not* thinking, either, he reaches for the egg-like pod in his belt, flicks the safety, and lets it fly, which it gratifyingly does, like a football lasered downfield by a rocket launcher.

Now he's moving again, humping in his heavy dustbowl gear for the base tower. His suit and his weapon together add something like sixty pounds to his weight and he's already so tired that he's living with a constant ache in his gut, ferocious and unrelenting. His post is about a half klick from the tower and part of him is already saying, *You will never make it. Never. Just sit down. Sit down for a second; you know that's all you want to do.* All he can hear inside his helmet, amplified by the communicator, is his own ragged breath—he's Vadering, as the men call it, filling the helmets of everybody else on the hookup with the sound of his own panting. He sucks in a charred breath and swallows it as he runs and has time to think *Why is everybody else on the hook so quiet?* before the boom he's launched knocks the earth out from under him and he falls.

The next thing he is aware of is a ringing in his ears. And the taste of blood in his mouth. And a gorgeous smell, unlike anything he's ever experienced in his life. The air is heavy but not with plastic particles and metallic dust—with moisture. One of the capsules must have blown up. Or something's gone wrong. He rolls onto his back and tries to care. *That taste, my God.* Something sweet and floral on his lips. He wants to lie here and taste it forever. The scent, so lovely.

Then the taste of blood in his mouth overtakes the taste of the H2.0 and he forces himself to his knees to spit into the dust. Then to his feet. His whole body aches, just like when you've got a fever, when you're so sick your hair hurts, your *leg* hair hurts. He's never been on the ground when a boom went off before, and he supposes this is just one of the shitty side effects he'll have to deal with now. His ears are still ringing—he can imagine his head whanging the inside walls of his helmet like the clapper in a bell.

As he stands, and as the blood rushes to his head, the ringing in his ears turns to static—terrible, excruciating. He rips off his helmet and holds his hands to his ears and tries to calm his breathing. His nose is bleeding, but he won't know it until later. He won't know anything about what's just happened to him, what he's just unbuckled in himself, until later.

Even through the static, he can hear the screaming. He moves in the direction of the sound.

She's screaming for help, but not from him. *Tough shit, lady. I'm all the help you get today.* She's using the language they use over here. It sometimes sounds like his language, enough that he can pick out words if he tries, but he knows it's also code, or meant to be code. A lot of the words sound the same but they mean something different. His head is still spinning as he approaches her. He can't tell whether she's the tall one or the small one because she's on her knees. She has something in her lap. It's the other woman, curled up, shaking. A dark pool surrounds them where the metallic dust has turned to black glass, like an oil slick. He walks carefully, so as not to slip.

"Ma'am. You're not supposed to be here. You know we're supposed to fire on intruders. You're lucky I'm trained in the nonlethal—" he begins.

She shouts something at him. Her face is concealed by her hood and goggles, their scratched lenses glowing in the light from the dying flames around them in the dust.

"Ma'am, I don't—"

She shouts it again, again. Her gloved hands move to tear the goggles and the hood violently from her face, so that he can see her, so that she can say this to him, and as she moves, the other woman rolls off her lap into the black glass dust and he can see that she's no longer shaking.

Later he won't remember much about her face, what she looked like. He will remember this: She is bleeding from her eyes and ears and nose and mouth, and as he watches, blood begins to run from her scalp over her forehead in dark waves.

It's clear enough what she's saying.

You did this. You did this.

F. QUINN
RISE 8, UNIT 7 LAKE
NEW CHICAGO 0606060101
NEW STATES

PFC C. P. QUINN 2276766
MCC 167 1ST MAW
FPO NEW CHICAGO 0604030901

November 18, 11:13 a.m.

CQ,

I know you're working on it, but try to get home as soon as you can. Don't dick around. Don't wait. When you get to the other side, call me. And right before and after you call me, you better run. Seriously.

Also I have good news. I'm getting married. Pretty soon. The marriage application was approved as soon as I got to seven months. I'll tell you more when we talk. When you call me. From the base. Immediately. After *running* to a connected portal.

Maybe I'll find Gard by then. We'll see. I'm on the case. Don't worry. Just get here.

Fred

Nov 27 12:33 PM

Hi. My name is Carter Quinn

You knew my sister, Gardner?

You may know this but she's been

missing for a while.

Can I talk with you about when you last saw her?

Nov 28 10:42 AM

Hi. It's Carter again.

I'm sorry but I'm just following up

I'm trying to find my sister

Can we possibly meet

to talk about when you last saw her?

Nov 30 3:17 PM

I'm sorry to bother you

Gard is still missing

No one in our family has heard

from her since October

She mentioned you a lot

in her messages to me

Can we meet?

Dec 1 10:22 PM

Hi. It's Carter Quinn.

Gardner really did mention you a lot

Please

I have to keep trying.

ONE

My sister Gardner, a former Nurse Completionist, is missing, gone completely. She's been gone for at least two and a half months, and right now that's about all I know.

She didn't disappear all of a sudden. It was more like she evaporated, over the course of a year, while I was at the Wars. I got messages from her over there, and then the messages got slower and weirder, and then I didn't hear from her again. A few months ago my oldest sister, Fred—don't call her Fredericka—wrote me that Gard had gotten into some trouble, but she was going to handle it. I got only a few messages from my pop the whole time I was over there, and our mother has been gone since we were kids, and Gard, who was working two jobs, was often too busy or tired to write, so Fred has been my best source of news from home. Finally, even Fred's messages stopped making sense.

My third tour just ended, so I came home, to look for my sister. I've been gone for two years and five months, back three weeks.

Fred and I seem to be the only people looking for her, and before I even got back, Fred dumped the responsibility squarely in my lap, in a message that I've probably read and reread fifty times:

Nov 18 3:47 PM
Find her. You need to keep looking,
no matter what.

We've DEF got to find her
in time for this damn wedding.
And this baby.
I can't do this without her.
And I'm afraid
of what might've happened to her.
You be afraid too.

It hasn't been easy. I don't have many leads. Gard's a grown woman, not wanted for anything, and Security has already closed her file. Our father won't even talk about Gard, much less help me speculate about what might have happened to her, or where she might have gone. The one thing I *have* managed to figure out, and it didn't take long, was that Gard dropped—or lost—all her friends from nursing school, a while back. Probably when she started doing Completion work for low-income women, outside the Standard of Care. That's not a prestigious line of work, or so I've gathered. I wouldn't really know. My point is I don't have many sources of information, other than reading and rereading my sisters' messages to me, and doing some basic sniffing around of my own. My point is I do not know very much. Of course, I'm used to that, I'm a Marine. That's meant to be a joke. Sort of.

I'm less comfortable with being an ignoramus than I used to be, though.

So that's why I'm here, at New Grant Park on a Wednesday afternoon, like it's not a complete shit show, with the twelve-foot perimeter fence and the Security checkpoints. No one in their right mind comes here anymore, but all the same, it's always crowded. I remember when I was a kid there were these evil-looking blue lights that they used to run across the surfaces of the old fountains, nasty little water mirages, but they don't do that anymore. They also don't paint the ground cover green anymore because no one's bothering to pretend that chewed-up, garbage-strewn, rubberized stuff is grass. I've seen the pictures. I know how it used to look. I don't care. It's still a park. Even fake leaves make shade.

There'll be bugs and ears and screens and transmitters in every third bush and bird butt. But it'll be crowded, and there'll be noise, plus the constant helicopter traffic overhead, and the plan is to talk quietly and walk loudly. I'm wearing dress shoes, new for Fred's wedding—not a style I would have picked. But thick, expensive, imported, and crazy-ass-loud on pavement, which for my purposes today is a plus. Fred's wedding is this coming weekend, just a couple of days off, and the shoes seem like a pretty good indicator of what's about to go down in our family. We are all—me and Fred and even Pop—going to be A. J. Squared Away, even if our feet are killing us. Fred's done good, I guess. I haven't met the guy.

I move directly toward the park gate, and I don't look around. In front of me as I'm waiting to scan in are a couple of women carrying their lunches in sacks, standing close together, not talking much, not checking their wearables, and there's some quick-spreading unease behind them in the entrance line when Security actually blocks both of the women at the gate.

"What's the problem, Officer?"

"You're ineligible."

One of the women repeats it, sort of blankly. "Ineligible."

"Ineligible for park access. You're not making Care Standard. You owe"—Security checks it with a flick of the eye—"a lot. And this one." He nods toward the woman's lunch companion. "You're both, what, halfway through the Completion period? And you already owe this much? No, I'm sorry." It's clear he's not sorry. "Why don't you go home and take care of your children? That's where you really *should* be, isn't it?"

I have to wait while the points are deducted and both women are turned away with their wearables singing; one woman tearful, both of them looking furious and humiliated. Mothers. It's hard to watch, harder not to stare.

I keep my eyes down, on my new shoes.

Then it's my turn to move through the checkpoint, and I can't help but look up as the Security guard scans my wearable—once, then twice. I don't have any reason to be nervous about being bounced. I'm a veteran; they'll keep their hands off me. But since coming home I've been given more than a few opportunities to understand, in case I didn't already know, just how deep the average person's dislike of veterans like me runs.

"Go ahead."

"Thank you for your service," the other Security guy pipes up, and as usual I have no idea how to respond to that.

Inside the park I move in the direction of the Buckingham, following the general drift of the lunchers and the lonelies. It's a hot day, and shade under the stressed-looking fake trees is thin. The smell is baked rubber. The noise in here is almost overwhelming—there's piped-in Christmas music, plus the chirping of the not-birds in the not-trees, and below that the usual environmental soundtrack of fountain waters chuckling and soft breezes shushing, broadcast just low enough for people like me to hear, people who are paying too much attention to everything. Most people aren't even trying to talk over it all. And of course the helicopter traffic overhead, constant, chopping the air into rags.

At the fork of the path that bends toward the gravel circle around the Buckingham, I stop and lean against a lamppost and rub my ankle. Partly because the shoes really are starting to bother me.

I hear crunching footsteps approaching, light and purposeful on the gravel walk, but I keep my head low for an extra beat or two, just to make sure.

"You," she says.

That's my cue to straighten up and look. She's pretty. I think most women are pretty, actually—after two and a half years in the service my standards are not what you'd call high. But this one, this Natalie B., she's really pretty. Nice hair: an off-center halo of dark curls. Nice skin: makes me think of bittersweet engineered coffee, shining in a cup. Her eyes are big and dark, with long lashes. It surprises me a bit to see that she has a fairly large, detailed tattoo on her left forearm. I try not to look like I'm looking too closely at it, or at any part of Natalie B. in particular. Her mouth is set in a funny expression. Exasperation. I recognize it from having two sisters.

"Thanks for meeting me."

"Let's walk. I don't like this," she says curtly.

"Okay. You're the boss." We head down the paved path that leads toward the loudest, most crowded part of the park. "You been waiting long?"

"No."

"Then why are you so pissed off?" I give her a smile; she gives me a look. I've been demoted from exasperating to moronic. Also easy to recognize from having two sisters. "Well, thank you anyway." I'm trying now. This meeting has taken a lot of effort to arrange. "I realize it's not easy for you to get away. I appreciate it."

"You're welcome." We're coming up on a particularly loud not-bird, set on a branch at the height of a grown man's shoulder. Someone has knocked the top of its head off so that the little plastic voice box, broadcasting its chirps and tweets, is visible and totally unmuted. This is where I start to slow my pace. "I really don't have much time," Natalie B. says. Then she notices the bird. "You do that?"

I don't answer. "I know you're in a rush. I just need to know when and where you saw Gardner last."

Natalie shakes her head. "You already know I can't tell you that."

It's hard to control my temper even when I'm *not* standing in hard-ass dress shoes right next to a piercingly loud robot bird with a chopper circling overhead that's been ripping up my eardrums for a good half hour. "You agreed to meet me."

She snorts. "Like I had a choice."

I hadn't given her a choice, she means. I've spent the last couple of weeks messaging her nonstop, asking her—begging her, really—to meet with me, somewhere, anywhere she wants. Because if anyone knows anything about what happened to my sister, it's got to be Natalie B.

I try another charm offensive. I hold out my hands, big ones, imploring. "Look. I'm begging you here. She's my sister. You know why I have to ask."

This Natalie B., standing by the loud not-bird, puts her hand on her hip and looks up at me, and I can tell she's trying to actually see me—she's doing her best to understand what I might look like if she didn't have to squint at me through a veil of irritation and anxiety. I'm white and she's not, and that's part of it. I'm a combat veteran and she's a civilian. That's part of it, too. But she's a veteran of a sort herself—between Pop and my sister Gard, I've known enough medical people to understand that they form their own kind of armed force, a professional tribe who have seen unimaginable, disgusting, beautiful things most people won't have to—and in that world I'm half a civilian, because I've seen those things, too, but not because I was trying to fix them.

Also, *I* make her irritated and anxious. I have that effect on people, just in general—more often than I like.

Finally Natalie says, "I *don't* know why. You could have a million reasons for wanting to find your sister."

That surprises me. I can feel my heartbeat starting to galumph, and a strong, familiar smell of flowers is crawling down my throat. These are not good signs. Suddenly I'm talking fast. "The hell does that mean? She's my *sister*. I haven't heard from her in *months*. I'm *worried* about her. She could be *dead*." Now in my ears there's a ringing. So I have to stop.

After a beat, Natalie says quietly, "Gardner's not dead."

At this point I'm just trying to catch my breath. "What—what did you say? How do you know?"

Natalie shakes her head. "I can't tell you any more."

"You know? You know she's not dead? You know where she is?" I need to calm down. Need to. *Calm down so you can hear what she's saying.* Breathing. Breathing here and now. In and out.

"Not here. I can't tell you any more here." She touches her forehead, and the exasperation is back. "Look, if you really want to know—"

"Wait. Wait, wait, wait—" I hold up a hand, the other hand is shielding my eyes. I gulp in a few wheezy breaths. After two-plus years out west it's hard for me to catch my breath even under the best of circumstances, but I have to get myself under control or the ringing in my ears will start again and I won't hear a word she's saying, and I might never get another chance. "I just need a second, wait."

I've either frightened or surprised her, so she stops talking. After a couple of moments I take my hand away from my face, but I keep my eyes low, on the ground. Her shoes are the *on-my-feet-all-damn-day* type of rubber-soled clogs. One thing we share anyway—our feet hurt.

"Okay. Okay." As usual when this happens, I hate myself more than I've ever hated anything.

"Are you all right?"

"Yeah. Fine. Just—please. Continue. If I want to know where Gardner is I should come to your clinic. That's what you were going to say."

She steps closer to me, close enough that I could smell the scent of her, if the flowers weren't choking her out. "Why did you think I was going to say that?" Her voice is low and not pleasant.

"I didn't know everything about her life, but I knew some things."

"And you wonder why she disappeared."

"I do. I do wonder why."

"I always heard they drafted the dumb ones for the Wars."

I roll my eyes and smile for her. "You think that's supposed to hurt my feelings? I grew up with two sisters, Doc."

"You think this is a good time for a joke." Natalie B. is spitting daggers. No amount of charm is going to work on this one. Time for a change of maneuver. My head is still ringing, I can barely breathe, and I'm tired of charming.

"Honestly? I don't know. I don't know what's appropriate here. I'm not a detective; I'm not Security. I'm not anything. I'm just home because my sister's missing and no one but me seems to care about finding her. And you, you acting the way you are, you're giving me this feeling, Natalie, that as worried about Gard as I already am, I'm not worried enough." I rub my eyes, still trying to clear them. "Is that right?"

Natalie B. is no dummy. Her expression is carefully composed. "She's not dead. I'm pretty sure. But other than that, I couldn't say." Then her eyes narrow, and she actually sneers at me. "Even if I wanted to scare you, I can't imagine what would frighten someone who's been to the Wars. I imagine it would take a lot."

People hate us. I know that. I learned it while I was over there, and I keep relearning it every day now that I'm home. The Wars have been dragging on for so long—too long, most people say, now that life in the New Cities is tolerable again. Long enough for the conflict to seem less like a necessity or a reality and more like a cruelty, an unending sucker punch. One side just getting kicked and kicked and kicked, and nobody can sort out why, not the kicker, certainly not the kicked. And meanwhile the way we're fighting over there has escalated out of all proportion to what's on the receiving end of the firepower. It's just an obliteration party.

So all I can do is agree with Natalie: "It would take a lot."

This time, she doesn't swing out at me with a follow-up punch. Maybe I'm not just an annoyance to be swatted at after all. She folds her arms, stares into the tweeting larynx of the decapitated not-bird like it's trying to explain how it got like this. She's not walking away. Yet. I still have a chance.

"Natalie, I know I don't know much. About anything. I admit it. But Gard told me she trusted you. She told me once that she owed you her life. I know you worked together, I know she . . . I know she was having a hard time. Before she disappeared." Natalie's eyes soften at this; it's noticeable, even though she still won't look at me. "She told me some things. Not much. But enough that I guess, I mean, I'm glad to have met you, just to say thank you for looking out for her." Now Natalie glances up at me, with some surprise. I lean closer to her, partly because I want to and partly because I don't seem to be able to help it. "She liked you. She trusted you. So I trust you, too."

Natalie clears her throat a bit and murmurs something like *okay*. It's hard to catch, it's mostly delivered toward the baked and cracked ground we're standing on.

"So. If you wouldn't mind telling me where I can find my sister."

The moment breaks. Natalie throws her hands up. "How many times do I have to say it? I can't tell you. If you really want to know you'd have to— Oh, for God's sake, forget it. You know what, I'm leaving."

She sidesteps into a crowd of people moving past us and is carried off in their current, just like that. I'm alone in the crowded park with the not-bird. I scare people, more often than I'd like.

I've searched through Gard's place and looked at her portal. I've tried to talk to Gard's friends, the few I could track down other than Natalie B. I've asked Pop, Fred, the few other people who I thought might know anything, the same pointless questions. *Where did you see her last? Where do you think she went?* I'm no detective, just like I told Natalie

B., but if she's the only one saying Gard's still alive, somewhere, then I have to believe she might also know where *somewhere* is.

So. My first meeting with Natalie may have been a bust. But I can still keep sending her messages. Which, from the first bar I can find near New Grant Park, I do. While sitting over a nice, cold, golden, engineered beer.

The truth is, the mysterious Natalie B. is the only lead I have left.

Dec 18 2:27 PM

Sorry to bother you again, Natalie.

I just wanted to let you know

I appreciated your meeting with me today,

and I heard you loud and clear.

I'll meet you at your clinic tomorrow.

I take a long drink.

Dec 18 2:30 PM

You don't have to reply.

I know where it is.

A nice long drink.

Like most human beings, certainly like most veterans I know, I'm a better person—funnier, calmer, more decent—with about five inches of beer in me. But I'm not a drunk. I know better than that. I've known a lot of guys who come back and start drinking like it's their new job, which, to be fair, in a lot of cases it is.

I also do not have a job, obviously. Which I'm sure is why Fred holds me fully responsible for our mission to track down Gard. And also why I'm in a bar drinking at two thirty in the afternoon on a weekday.

This bar is the kind of place I might have ended up at every day if I were a different kind of person—a guy like Fred's fiancé, maybe. It's empty now, but by a few minutes past the start of happy hour it'll be full of men, traveling in packs with other men from their offices. Department guys. There's a suitable engineered bourbon collection, and the bottles gleam in the colored afternoon light coming through the stained glass windows at the front of the bar. I'm not a bourbon drinker, but if I were, the sight of those bottles would be something religious. It's as cool and dark and sleek in here as it is hot and glaring and wild out there. The guy behind the bar is wearing a collared shirt, watching the portal screen overhead while absently polishing the glasses. No one's paying any attention to me. No one has been, in fact, since I came back. Honestly, I can't decide whether that's such a great thing. The military puts you in the habit of being watched, and on watch, at all times. Partly because you and your buddies are obligated to keep one another alive, if you can, but also because they're convinced that you're always about to fuck something up colossally. They're right, of course.

I have sent Natalie B., who I'd never met in person before today, about a hundred messages, by my estimate. Scrolling through the most recent forty or so, I would say that I've been polite but persistent. Not stalking or harassing, not exactly, but not unintrusive, either. My sister Gard had a name for this kind of thing: she called it "gentle pressure, relentlessly applied." Sort of a catchphrase of hers. Gentle Pressure, Relentlessly Applied would not have been a bad operation name for most of what I ended up doing in the Wars, in fact.

As I'm rereading the thread between me and Natalie B., a message from Fred slides in over the top layer.

Dec 18 2:48 PM
What are you doing at a bar?
Why aren't you out looking for Gard?

Of course Fred would know where I am. Her wearable, like mine, like everybody's, shows her not just her own Care Hours balance and her heart rate and her messages and her account balances and her med status and her reminders but also her geo status, and the geo statuses of her immediate family, because that is supposed to keep families safer, because this whole system of Care Hours and Care Standards and everyone knowing everything is supposed to be all about keeping families safe; it is precisely what's supposed to prevent people from getting lost or disappearing.

Dec 18 2:50 PM
I don't like this, Carter.
Why are you at a bar?

I don't particularly like that I'm here, either, come to it. I allow that some part of me might be here just to piss her off. But I know better than to respond with that.

Dec 18 2:52 PM
Just resting my paws. Long day on the hunt.

Dec 18 2:52 PM
Anything new? Please say yes.
Did you talk to that NC she knows?

Dec 18 2:53 PM
I did.

I have to pause, think about how to put things. There is little gentleness about Fred but plenty of relentless application, probably the one thing you can't help but understand about her if you've spent so much as five seconds in her company.

Dec 18 2:55 PM
I can't quite get a read on her.

Dec 18 2:55 PM
Do you think she knows anything?

Dec 18 2:57 PM
I hope she does.

Dec 18 2:57 PM
We're almost out of time, CQ. This fucking
wedding is this weekend. It's this
Friday night. I can't do this without Gard.

Dec 18 2:58 PM
Wedding? What wedding?

Dec 18 2:58 PM
FUCK YOU NOT FUNNY

Dec 18 2:58 PM
You just want to find Gard in time
for her to talk you out of it.

Dec 18 3:00 PM
FUCK YOU ALSO NOT FUNNY

Fred has always talked a foul streak. As her kid brother I was only too happy to follow her example when it came to gratuitous cussing. Gard, though, usually managed not to swear. If Natalie B. is right and she's still alive somewhere, Gard is the only person in our family who doesn't curse like it's her job, her passion, her one true love.

Dec 18 3:07 PM
Don't worry, Fredlet. I'm on the case

Dec 18 3:07 PM
You better be. I'm serious.
This is fucking serious.

Dec 18 3:07 PM
I know.

Dec 18 3:08 PM
It's not about the wedding.

Dec 18 3:10 PM
I know.

Suddenly another window layers in over Fred's thread. There's a new message from Natalie. A response.

Dec 18 3:10 PM
I don't know you.
I don't owe you anything.

It's not a no.
I'm still thinking about how to reply when one last Fred message layers in.

Dec 18 3:15 PM
And don't forget the wedding rehearsal
and the party at my in-laws' tonight.
Don't you dare be late dammit.

F. QUINN
RISE 8, UNIT 7 LAKE
NEW CHICAGO 06060601
NEW STATES

PFC C. P. QUINN 2276766
MCC 167 1ST MAW
FPO NEW CHICAGO 06040309

November 12, 3:29 p.m.

CQ:

Got your note about coming home. Good news. Hurry it up.

Baby's kicking now. Hard to believe this is happening. Am completely, completely, off my rocker insane with hormones or something, so, just wanted to say sorry about my last message. If Gardner was around she'd help calm me down, but she's not.

Am worried about a lot of things and not feeling very hungry and have had some points deducted for not meeting Care Standard, but can't do anything about it. This woman in my Care Circle made a joke that PNG stood for "Pregnant? Not Good," instead of Pre Natal Guidelines, and of course all those stupid cows acted all shocked like she'd personally aborted all their babies and now no one talks to her but me.

I am also a fucking cow. You should see me, CQ. Jesus. Like a lot of people, I sort of forgot what pregnant women looked like, since there are so few of us around anymore, and now I'm with this group of them every day, and I gotta say, Fuck me. We're like a herd of cows. We look exactly like a herd of fucking cows in a picture book. And I have to sit around and moo just like the rest.

But I also should say that being pregnant sort of feels like being Santa Claus. When I'm not completely enraged or insane, I feel all fat and round and jolly, and everybody's so happy to see me, I'm honestly grateful. When I'm not feeling like I want to barf all over the place.

Again, if Gardner was here. You know.

Okay. Sorry again about my last message. See you soon. Please let me see you soon. Stay alive and don't get killed right before you get on the transport home. You dumb-ass.

Fred

TWO

Fred's fiancé's family's place is not the kind of place where the wealth is discreetly hidden away in collections or cars or nice furniture, because there's so much wealth it just keeps spilling out all over everything, like a volcano that can't help itself. They are unbelievably rich, the kind of rich that hurts your feelings. From their apartment you can still see water, if that gives you an idea. It's high up in the Lake Rises, and I always thought that the Lake Rises, as a name, was a joke, or some New City planners' wishful flourish, but now, as I can see from this terrace apartment in Lake Rise 8, it's an actual description of what you can see if you live this far up, the lake, the goddamn lake—glowing red, about ten or so miles out past the old shoreline, in the winter sunset—and I'm staring at it like it's a girl I used to love who got sick and died.

Because I missed the rehearsal entirely, and also did not arrive what you'd call early to the party, I missed a few things Fred had arranged: a receiving line with the family, a toast. I suppose in reality the party planner arranged them, but Fred's still angry, whereas the party planner has been paid to treat me like I'm some kind of minor prince. The party planner's name is Sophie, hired by the Walkers, the family Fred's marrying into. She has bright red hair. She is weaving through the crowd, toward me, with a smile tipping the corner of her mouth. So I'm watching her mouth, to keep myself from watching the drinks she's carrying, one of which is for me.

"Here you are, Private." She slides the glass into my hand. Ice—real ice. Music, conversation, a cool breeze through the window, red hair, a black dress. I'm not even sure how I got here.

"Thank you, Sophie."

She leads me by the elbow toward a potted plant the size of a couch stood on end. There's a low plush bench next to it, and my grateful-ness index is now skyrocketing—my feet are killing me. The shoes. They're high-cut, and with every step the sturdy, expensive, handcraft-ed-in-hell imported leather is now slicing into the undersides of my anklebones. The toe box is cramped, too, and the inside corner of the nail on my right small toe has cut a bloody slit in the side of the toe next to it. My combat boots and I have been through worse together, but these fancy, unyielding new wedding shoes are something else. I can barely walk.

"Do they really call it debriefing?"

"Excuse me?"

She's winking at me. She's paid to—motivated to—treat me a cer-tain way, as Fred's brother, but a semiprivate drink with me under the plant seems to be her idea. "In the army. Do they call it debriefing when you bring a soldier up to speed on a mission? Or am I not using that term right?"

"I was in the Marines. You're using it right."

"Well, Marine. Let me debrief you." Now the act she's putting on is so obvious that we both have to laugh. So nothing's on between me and Sophie the Party Planner after all. It's too bad. She is a beauty, pale skin in a black dress with that red hair, some fun in her eyes, a drink in her hand. We're sitting next to each other on the bench now, and she's crossed one leg over the other, in my direction. She's wearing heels, and with her legs crossed like this, her shoe hangs a bit loose from her foot so that her instep is visible. I could reach down and cup her instep, or better, her ankle, and from there, slip up the black-stockinged calf to her knee, to her skirt hem, to the inner line of her leg, to her waist, up, up. Left breast. Collarbone. Behind the ear. Now I'm rethinking the same trajectory, only this time with my mouth. Gentle pressure, relentlessly applied.

Sophie takes the merest sip of her drink and her eyes are amused. I'm embarrassed. I might even have been panting. Half my drink is gone already.

"I do know how to behave myself," I tell her humbly. "At a thing like this. I apologize for being late. I must have put you in a tight spot with Fred."

"Oh, Fredericka has been wonderful. I'm so grateful to Mrs. Walker for introducing us. I really hope she'll remember me for the birth parties and the rest of her Care Circle events," Sophie says warmly. She might even mean it. Fred can be charming when she wants to be. "So let me tell you what you missed, Private. By the way, were you supposed to be in your dress uniform? You and your father both?"

"Hm."

"Hm. Funny, that was what Captain Quinn said, too. I think Fredericka hoped to show off her two handsome men a bit." More likely, Fred was concerned that Pop and I wouldn't have nice enough suits to wear. And we don't, as I can see by looking around at the men here. But the shoes are right, at least.

"My dress blues are at the cleaner's." As a point of fact, as a grunt-level general discharge, I'm not allowed to wear dress blues to anything less than a full-color parade in my honor, and there isn't one currently scheduled anywhere on the planet. But I don't see the point in explaining regulation to a pretty girl who's just trying to do her job.

"Not a problem. But I know she'd like you to wear them to the ceremony. Where was I? About forty-five minutes into the evening, there was a brief toast by Mr. and Mrs. Walker, welcoming guests and inviting them to join a receiving line to say hello to the bride- and groom-to-be and meet the families—"

"I'm truly sorry I was late."

"You'll make it up to me, I'm sure. But you did miss the first half of the cocktail reception as well as the entire receiving line, which means I have a short list of people I'm going to bring you around to, so that they can meet you before the ceremony. All right?"

"And here I've been hoping we could just sit all night under this magnificent . . . palm tree, is it?"

"Dieffenbachia," Sophie says briskly, glancing up at it. It's fake, of course. Not even the Walkers are that rich. "I'm afraid not. But I'll try to make it quick."

"You haven't finished your drink," I point out. My own is gone, but I'm holding the glass close, for the ice alone. I'm not sure when I've ever had the pleasure of slurping a piece of whiskey-soaked ice into my mouth. Something I've seen in old movies but never done.

"That's where I'll need your help." She hands her drink to me. "I've only taken a few sips. But I don't have cooties, promise."

It's all I can do not to lean over and kiss her. "Thanks."

As I wet my lips with her drink Sophie gives me an appraising look. Still amused—that seems to be her baseline—but it's easy to detect something like triumph, too. Clearly Fred has told Sophie the Party Planner exactly how to handle me, and while she might not have been sure how far her charm and two drinks with real ice (real, actual, frozen H2.0—they might as well be serving drinks with straws made out of peacock feathers) would travel with a hardened veteran of the Wars, I'm making this all too easy for her. Sophie's report to my enraged pregnant older sister tomorrow should be mollifying: *He was an absolute teddy bear.*

"You must be so happy," Sophie says to me, smiling.

"I must," I agree, even though I'm not sure what she's talking about. *Because you brought me a drink?* Then she continues.

"It's a miracle. A real miracle. And how often do you get to see a miracle, in these days?"

"Almost never." It's the best I can do.

"It's incredible. You know," she goes on, "I read that there have only been about thirty-five thousand unassisted pregnancies in the entire country this year—it's down even from the year before, although—" Here Sophie stops herself. She's about my sister's age, I realize. From her perspective—from anyone's—Fred must seem staggeringly blessed. Here she is, marrying into a family that's one of maybe a hundred in all of New Chicago that could easily afford Insemina for her, if Fred and her guy were in love and wanted to try for a baby so they could get married and raise a family together. But Fred doesn't even need

Insemina, because somehow, against every kind of odds, she's having a baby anyway, the old-fashioned way, so she and this guy, the father, can apply for marriage. The new-fashioned way.

But even with Sophie's appreciation of bona fide miracles, I don't see much to feel good about in Fred's situation. Maybe it shows. Sophie's expression has gone peculiar with the effort of forcing herself to shift gears. "I'm sorry. I don't mean to talk about that. It seems like bad luck somehow." She flashes another smile, apologetic now, and stands. "Shall we? You can bring your drink."

"Liquid courage," I say, pouring the ice from the first drink into the second. I slurp at the edge of the glass to keep the overflow from sloshing out, then stand slowly and tip my drink in Sophie's direction, to which she responds with a sweet half curtsy.

I am, I will allow, a little drunk. I sat at the bar this afternoon until way too late, then got a taxi uptown, to my father's apartment on Paulina Street, where I've been staying since I got back. Traffic. Horrible heat. The driver shouting and stinking, with me in the back, watching the time, powerless to do anything about the merciless way it kept moving forward, unlike the taxi. My father had already left for the Walkers' by the time I arrived, so I sani-ed, shaved, dressed, and got another taxi (driverless this time, and quiet as a ghost) to the Lake Rises, but there'd been no time for dinner, and I like to have a beer while I'm getting ready to go out, so by this point I've entirely lost track of how much I've had to drink so far today, and the number can't be good.

Across the room, as I stand, I glimpse my sister, our Fredlet. Her long hair is black and glossy-slick in the light from the glass lamps overhead. She is wearing a royal-blue dress, long enough to sweep the floor, with short sleeves and a high collar. It's a severe-looking dress, a little futuristic even, like something an alien princess might wear to the opera, so it suits her. Her face is flushed—hot in here—and her dark eyes are bright. She's listening to an older man, some friend of Mr. Walker's probably, and the older man's wife is standing too close to her, which Fred is absolutely furious about—I know her, I can see it in her set expression, although anyone else looking at her would think she was just listening closely, her eyes intent on the person speaking, her mouth a bright straight line across her face. Fred has a sharp face, and she's tall and lean like me and our pop. Gard took more after our mother: smaller, rounder, curly-headed. Our family, all circles and lines. Fred's height and her straightness make her pregnancy a bit startling to look at. Even if it weren't as rare as it is, the effect is weirdly like a dewdrop caught on a long stem. Again, something I've seen mostly in movies.

The older woman who is standing too close to Fred is just staring at Fred's belly, the perfect round ball of it, the way Fred's expensive blue dress displays the fact of it, the miraculous fact of it. It *is* incredible. There's something incredible in the room, something we can hardly even believe that we're seeing, and the woman just wants to be near it for a minute, just stand close and let it remind her of something she used to know.

Fred is so angry. It's taking everything she has not to swat at this woman and her longing. I really can't help but laugh. Even though she won't so much as look at me. It's all right. I've fucked up. I can't blame her for being angry. I could blame Fred for a lot of things, maybe, but not for that.

Pop is nowhere to be seen.

Gard, where are you?

My feet hurt, my heart hurts, my head hurts, and I've had a bit too much.

Sophie understands. She takes my elbow, the elbow of the arm not holding the drink. "We'll take it nice and slow."

"It's better, the way things are done now. I know I shouldn't be saying this. Young people have all these ideas about how it used to be. Marriage. Before the . . . all the . . . you know, the Protection Laws."

Here the guy acknowledges me with a tip of his bottle, so I nod somberly. I'm one of the young people, I guess.

"Young people think they should just be able to get married! Because they're in *love*! Without having to *prove* they've got a bun in the oven first!" His face is huge, made huger still by a leer I'd just as soon not have directed my way: *Real men, we would never fall into a pussy trap.* "But think about it this way, Soldier: Really, now, we've just gone back to basics. This is how men and women have gotten together from the dawn of time! Isn't it now? You have to admit it, right? Don't put the cart before the horse, don't buy the cow without the milk, don't count your chickens—isn't that right?"

I have no idea how long this man, some family friend of the Walkers', has been talking to me. I have no idea who he is, or where Sophie has gone off to, or where Fred or my father are. But clearly this guy and I have been in conversation for long enough that he has decided I might not mind hearing my sister's marriage discussed in barnyard terms. I'm controlling myself by pretending he's my CO, even though this guy wouldn't have lasted a week in the service. It's a game I play sometimes to remind myself how to act, even when I want to punch someone in the face.

My problem is that I can't walk away from him, because my feet are now throbbing and my ankle is red agony. The goddamn shoes. Like bear traps. It's all Fred's fault. I have to be careful not to shift my weight as I'm standing, so that the shoes don't rub against the raw skin. As much as I would like to get away—find my plush bench under a potted tree—right now there's a drink in my hand, an engineered beer (no more ice, I heard), and I take a long swallow.

"This way, at least, both sides know what they're in for. And they don't waste any time. In my parents' day, people would get married and not get around to having children for five, ten *years*. We don't have time like that to waste anymore." He's getting maudlin. "Jesus Christ, if we'd only known."

I don't have anything to say to this.

"And you know," he adds abruptly, swaying a bit, "back in my parents' day, they had the party, the reception, *after* the wedding, not before. Weddings meant there were *alllll* these wild parties. People cutting loose. Before they tied the knot. Different now! For sure! All the ladies getting married now—*they can't drink!* Ha! How're you feeling, Soldier? Another drink?"

"Yes, please."

He signals a passing server. A cool bottle is pressed into my hand, the old one taken away. "Least I can do for a veteran." He nods gravely, and I can see what he's winding up for. "How long were you out there?"

Surely I've put in my time at this event, surely I've earned out by now. *Where is Sophie? Where is Fred?*

"You can talk to me about it, son. I come from a military family myself. My brother. In the First Wars."

That was my pop's war, too. I shake my head, take a drink. "What branch of the service was he in?" I don't really expect him to know.

And now the guy's eyes are glazing over. Maybe he's imagining it, the Second Wars, the heat, the blankness, the raiders, the experimental weapons and their experimental effects (their *special effects,* as we used to call them, when we were front row at the big show), the unending-ness, all of it. Or maybe his own fresh beer is just hitting him hard, suddenly; he's hit the wall. He's not fat, exactly, but he's a big guy, and he's pale and sweaty now in a way that makes me cautious of standing upwind of him. If I've been drinking hard tonight, he's surely right on my tail. "Wait a sec. I'm sorry." He sways in my direction. "What were we talking about, son?"

"We were talking about your brother's time in the service, sir."

"Yeah. *Yeah.* How long were you out there, son?" he asks me again. His eyes are fixed on mine now, unfocused but loonily intense.

"Two years five months."

He whistles.

"That was about average for guys in my unit, sir."

"They keep you out there. They keep you going."

"I suppose so."

"They need experienced men." He nods knowingly.

"I suppose so." I'm scanning the room over his shoulder. Red hair, black dress. Black hair, blue dress. I'd even take a nice, soft tipsy old-lady friend from Mrs. Walker's club. Or, it occurs to me, a dark-skinned, curly-haired woman in nurse's clogs and scrubs. *Where is my goddamn backup?*

"How many, ah, missions did you . . . complete? Over there?"

"I was mostly on patrol, sir. Just guarding the H2.0."

He is disappointed. "So you didn't get many . . . opportunities."

"Excuse me?"

"Or did you?"

"I'm not sure what you mean, sir."

"Well, pardon me for being blunt, but didn't you get any opportunities to—you know . . ."

I'm just starting to grasp what he means—he's asking *did I have many opportunities* to blow people up; *did I get any opportunities* to use the experimental weapons everybody's talking about; *did I get the opportunity* to be a trigger—and I'm wondering if I can keep myself from hauling off and knocking the guy down after all. Then a woman bumps into me, and my feet shift under my weight so that my sliced-up, blistered heels bash against the insides of these diabolical fucking shoes, and my anklebone feels like it's been sheared by a ragged claw, and it's so unexpected and painful that I let out a startled groan.

"I'm sorry," she says, edging past us. "Pardon me." She's already moved by. From the back she almost looks like Gard, although I know that whoever she is, she's obviously not my sister. I get only a brief impression as she moves away. She's built like her: medium height, a little plump. She's got Gard's curls and what appears to be something like her round face, brown like a nut. But the hair is silvery—this woman is older, more the age my mother would have been, although she's also obviously not my mother. She's crossing the room toward the windows, and because it's a dark black night, I catch sight of her and her reflection in the glass, both of them shining together, and then she's enveloped by the party crowd. Outside, over the black faraway dried-up lake, the lights of a helicopter wink.

"You all right, son?"

"Yes, sir."

The guy chooses that moment to clap me heartily on the shoulder. The effect is to send fresh pain shooting up my legs. I groan again. I can't help myself. It's humiliating, of course, but now I'm wondering, *Jesus, how badly are my feet fucked up anyway, and why does it feel like there are hidden razors in my fucking shoes?* Because that is what it feels like now, like there's an army of minuscule imps with pointy ears and teeth who live in my shoes and have taken up a thousand tiny silver instruments to saw and hack away at my heels, my bones, my ankles, my unlovable hairy-knuckled toes, and every once in a while one of them will pause in their sawing to take a big bite.

"Son, I gotta take a leak. Pardon."

I want to hit him so bad.

In the moment that he is gone, I realize I might not be all right. My ears are ringing, and the hot room is swinging around me like a tower bell. Aside from the pain in my feet, there's pain in my gut and a mirror pain beginning in my head, which I know is not a good sign. I drink the last of my warm beer, which is probably a mistake, and look for an exit to lurch through. I could use an arm to lean on. A velvety, slim arm attached to a sweet-smelling woman in a black dress. Or in nurse's scrubs. Natalie B. doesn't like me, I know she doesn't, but in this moment I think I'd prefer her to even the lovely Sophie.

But the person whose loss I'm feeling most right now, the person I'd give a great deal indeed to see coming toward me in this moment when I feel like I'm about to fall over from self-disgust and booze and whatever else it is I'm feeling—sorrow?—isn't Natalie or Sophie. It's Gardner.

She's the best of the three of us Quinn kids, it goes without saying. The kindest, the smartest (although Fred would never admit it), the hardest-working. She had that kind of sincerity that's so rare that when you see it in a person you instinctively think they must be fucking with you. Serious, serious girl. No sense of humor really. But she wanted to help fix the world, and that's not a funny thing. If Gard were here, she would have spent the night tearing into guys like the one I ended up talking to. Giving them the business about how fucked up the Wars are and always have been. How criminal it is that we've been fighting over there for more than two decades now, and we haven't found a way to make it stop. She could go on, our Gard. She could make people angry.

But she could also tell when I needed her. If Gard were here, if I'd spent the whole night cracking jokes to her about all the clueless fancy people, if we'd gotten drunk and rowdy, if Pop had had to tell us to stop being such smart-asses, if we'd posed for pictures and shook all the Walkers' friends' hands, if we'd stood together by the window overlooking the lake and watched Fred and Pop work the room behind us in the reflection in the glass, if after all that it turned out I'd had too much and she'd had to pack me into a car home, then it wouldn't have been the first time I leaned on her, is what I guess I'm saying.

And now I'm rageful, besides just drunk and hurting and maudlin. There's so much money in this room, the people at this party are practically incandescent with it. Whereas my sister lived like a nun and worked like a coal miner.

I know why Fred is so frantic to find Gard. Because she's getting married and needs her sister in her corner. Because she needs Gard's help understanding how to make Care Standard. Because Fred is pregnant against all odds, and having a sister who's a Nurse Completionist is like having your own personal consultant for the Completion period—all the years and changes and work and sacrifice and love that I suppose just used to be referred to as pregnancy and motherhood, before the fertility crisis made them codify it, regulate it, put a fence around it, put a Care Standard in place for it. So yeah: lots of reasons for Fred to be freaking out. Whereas I'm just the little brother—I don't have Fred's kind of skin in the game, and I know it. Right now, I don't know where Gard is or what happened to her. I don't know what kind of trouble she got into; I don't know what she could have done that made Pop unwilling to so much as say her name. I don't really know whether she's dead or alive; I don't know whether she's hurt.

One thing I do know is that she would have had better things to do than come to this fucking party.

And I just miss her.

Somehow I'm staggering toward the door. I'm not going to be able to say good night to the Walkers, or Fred, or anyone. I won't be doing the needful. No one comes forward to say goodbye.

By shuffling my feet forward in a kind of ragged scissoring motion across the smooth floors, I manage to make it around the corner from the great hall where the party is, back to the entryway, and from there—propping myself up on various expensive-looking side tables and things—to the penthouse elevator, without any more embarrassing groaning. I look ridiculous of course, a robot, a drunk malfunctioning robot, but the party ignores me anyway. Even the servers ignore me, and the girl at the door who's minding the hats and wraps and bags. Then I'm alone, falling toward the street in an efficient machine, and I'm alone when the machine spits me out.

The lobby feels sweet and windy and cool after the infernal party. Unfortunately, from where I'm standing, just outside the Walkers' elevator, it also looks about the size of the old Soldier Field. At an impossible distance, through the glass building doors, I see the black river of the street. I'll never make it all the way to the doors, never make it out to a taxi. Not on these feet. Not with the imps, sawing and knifing and chewing away.

There's no one else in the lobby. The doorman must be out on the sidewalk getting someone a cab. There are cameras, though; almost certainly there are many, many cameras. I can't care. I decide to get on my knees. I will shuffle across the lobby on my knees, while holding myself up on the blobbish, neutral-upholstered nonsense that's passing for furniture here, in the lobby of this titanically rich palace, Lake Rise 8, with its light fixtures that are exactly as spiky and sinister as desert burrs. I won't crawl. Not that I'm above it or anything—I've crawled plenty. But the pain in my head is real, and putting my head down between my hands would just cause the blood to—

"What is the matter with you."

I don't look up—I don't want to, but also I can't. All the same, of course I know that it's him. Who else could it be—Mr. Walker? Fred's fiancé? Although either one of them would be a better alternative.

"Hiya, Pop." I'm not looking up. I can't look up. I have to look straight ahead, at the door, with the sweet blackness of the street beyond. "I haven't seen you all night."

"Get up. Now."

Pop has a fearsome way about him. He's just menacing; he can't help himself. As a man I seem to have inherited some of this quality of his, and it explains why people react to me the way they often do—like they want to get on my good side and stay there, but not because they like me. His voice is tight and angry and embarrassed. I want to obey him, I always have, but for the moment I don't see how I can.

"Get up, or I'll knock you down and leave you here, you drunk sorry fool."

I press the flat of my hand into the nearest plush blobseat and start the hurtful work of getting my feet back under me where they belong.

F. QUINN
RISE 8, UNIT 7 LAKE
NEW CHICAGO 06060601
NEW STATES

PFC C. P. QUINN 2276766
MCC 167 1ST MAW
FPO NEW CHICAGO 06040309

November 9, 11:14 a.m.

CQ, you asshole.

I know you and Pop know where she is. *He* won't tell me anything, which doesn't surprise me, but *you* at least I expected to be honest with me. You and Gard have been messaging each other this whole time I've been panicking looking for her; I know it—of course I *know it.* I KNOW YOU KNOW WHERE SHE IS. [*unintelligible*] Right now I would be just as happy if I never saw you or Pop again, you fucks, you shits, but I want my little sister back, and if either of you know something about where she went, you NEED TO TELL ME.

　　Gardner is the only person in this family who's worth anything. She's better than all the rest of us put together, and she always has been, and I *know,* I know for a *fact* that she would never, ever leave me like this if she had a choice. I know Gardner would never leave me alone and pregnant if she had a choice. I know it. She was *excited,* more excited than me even, I'm not ashamed, I can admit it, I'm scared, I'm fucking petrified. [*unintelligible*] She's the only thing that's been keeping me from jumping out a fucking window.

You and Pop are men, and you'll never see her like I do, and you'll never need her like I do right now. Which explains why it's even *possible* for the two of you to be such FUCKING SHITS.

You don't even understand. Neither of you can possibly have any fucking clue what's happening to me right now. I need Gard if I'm going to have a chance of making it through this without completely losing my shit, and I admit that, but the fact is, I am also in a tricky position with the Walkers—and it looks suspicious that she's just—missing. [*unintelligible*] It does not look good. I don't know what I'm supposed to say to them about it.

Not that you care. Not that either you or Pop care about a single goddamn thing. It's all my problem. It's all on me. [*unintelligible*]

If you know where she is, you had better tell me. I will never speak to either of you again. I will never forgive you.

F

IN THE FIRST PLACE

They're not supposed to have it, obviously, but they've got a dog. For now. Sort of an older puppy, he's mostly feet and ears. Some guy stole the dog from one of the scavengers' sentry points after they'd hit it, a soft-pawed, tan-colored fellow, a little tiger. Each night the guys take turns bringing it down into the holes to sleep. It's his squad's turn tonight. The dog's name is Rip. They had another one named Tear, but he got killed yesterday. He was a nice little dog.

When a dog is in the hole with the men at night, there's the sound of him in the dark: wistful puppy sighs, a tail thumping, a tongue at work, soft breaths and laps. Yesterday, after Tear died, that damn idiot Horrocks told him, with not a trace of shame, that when the puppy curled up next to him in the hole he felt like he'd been chosen for something good, or because of something good inside him, and when he started crying, the goddamn dog just lapped the tears off his face and snuzzled his nose into him and *it was like being a kid again, you know? Like being a good little kid and falling asleep like that.* Of course he understood; who wouldn't? If anything, he felt embarrassed for Horrocks that he thought he had to spell it out. Saying it out loud made it feel like a smaller thing than it really was. What the dog did for them didn't need to be left out in the open like that.

Almost rack time and he's been thinking about the dog all day, looking forward to tonight in the hole with a longing that makes him feel both noble and ridiculous. Rip seems to prefer him, but he's a democratic dog, and over the course of the night he likes to make the rounds, first standing up and elongating from the legs, stretching his paws so the pads separate, yawning with his whole face, then shuffling sleepily from one man to another. First him, then his pal Chalke, then his other buddy Wash, then Lance Corporal Chuck, who is a known dipshit. Then back to him, usually, or between him and Chalke. Something about how Chalke's feet smell, the dog seems to maybe be a bit in love with him, or with his feet anyway.

Before rack time they have to disassemble and clean their triggers, which always takes more time than they want it to, because exhaustion, because tricky, because mysterious and humming and slippery, because you can blow yourself up, or whoever's sitting next to you, pretty easy if you're not paying attention. Lance Corporal Chuck is down the bench, he's supposed to be checking their work but he's not even halfway done with his own trigger, the lower section is still detached and resting by his feet in the dust, so there's been a general slowdown all the way through the line, no one's working especially fast, and it's making him grit his teeth a little because he wants to grab a bite and then hit the rack, but first he's hoping to get in a quick game of sock-tussle with Rip before lights. Old sock, holey past wearing, make it a knot with a tail, let Rip knarfle it, catch it in his small sharp teeth. His idea, his sock. The other guys just about beside themselves with happiness, watching. None of them ever had a dog. No one they know has ever had a dog. Who has a dog anymore? The world out there being what it is, who could bear caring for anything like this: small, stupid, helpless, hapless, instantly in love with some guy's stinking feet? Who could find it in them? Not even Lance Corporal Chuck, commissioned man, grew up in the kind of house or the kind of place where a kid could have had a dog. So when Horrocks talks about it, says it out loud, what they're all feeling, really the only thing you can feel for the dumb cluck is embarrassment, bone-deep shame for whoever would have to say such a thing.

Don't go reading too much, his oldest sister once told him. You won't like what you find out about how it used to be. Books are full of kids with lawns, kids with dogs, dogs that sometimes even double as babysitters or nonverbal but compassionate friends. Kids with hamsters, or cats that aren't feral, or even fish—fucking *fish*! Kids with tree houses; kids who take baths at night and bitch and moan about it. As a kid he'd had a book, an orange-and-green book, about a boy who bought a fish at a pet shop—a *pet shop*, okay?—and fed it too much even though the mysterious gent at the pet shop warned him against it, and the fish just starts growing like a motherfucker, right, outgrowing the bowl and then all the pots and then the sink and then the bathtub and then a basement full of water and then, the funny part, the kid who overfed the fish calls Security and the fire department and they're all *Holy shit, a kid overfed a fish, we gotta get down there on the double and deal with this!* So the fish gets towed to a pool, and the fish promptly outgrows the *pool*. And at this point, okay, there are all these people standing around in bathing suits glaring at this fish that's just taken over their pool, thinking, *Fuck you, fish*.

How did that book end? Something with the pet shop guy. Pet shop guys had world-fixing powers, apparently, back when that was a thing a person could be.

He can't remember.

Because he's within signal range of the base and because no one but him seems to be in any hurry to finish up with their weapons and get the hell out of the armory hut, he flicks on his wearable, and there's a message from his oldest sister, but she's furious at him about something, blaming him for something he can't even begin to fathom. *Fred, I didn't overfeed the fish; it wasn't me.* He knows something he's not supposed to? He doesn't know something he's supposed to? Which one is it?

He's swimming through the message, trying to understand what she's talking about and feeling more and more confused and worried, because she sounds like she might actually be losing her mind, like she might have flipped some switch and truly gone crazy, and as far as his family goes, they have enough to worry about as it is. He's in a war zone, with no way out that he can see. Their father is broke, out of work, forced into retirement, and living alone—or not alone exactly, since for a few years now, since his sisters moved out and he went to war, their father has lived with one of the terrifying schizophrenic cats you can pluck up off the streets in the New Cities, if you're brave enough or crazy enough or lonely enough to live with one. And their sister, the nice one, the sweet one, the one who was supposed to be a nurse and then changed her mind because she wanted to save the world, has been working herself to death and no one hears from her anymore. And this, it seems, is what the message is about. She's gone? She's . . . where? He's supposed to know. Some dark hole back home has opened up and swallowed her, and his oldest sister is shouting down into it as hard as she can, thinking he's down there, too.

He looks up, troubled, not seeing much, but it's just in time for him to see something happen that can only end one way. He might be the only person to see it, and in the chaos and shrieking and hot gush that follows he will do his best to forget it. The dog trotting in, sniffing the lower section of Lance Corporal Chuck's trigger, putting out a moist, curious tongue for a taste, a wet lick.

THREE

At home on Paulina Street, my feet throbbing under the kitchen table, my suit jacket limp in my lap like a soft dead animal. The kitchen is shabby, in an apartment that's wall-to-wall gloomy bachelor shabbiness. Pop has turned on the lights over the range and left the other lights off. The globe fixture overhead is dark and full of the husks of insects. Pop's old, hostile, very-much-alive cat is stalking around somewhere in the dim living room behind us.

I passed out in the driverless cab we took home from the Walkers' and just woke up when we arrived a few minutes ago, so I'm feeling woozy. It's early to be this drunk. Even after seeing me on my knees in the Walkers' lobby, Pop clearly has no idea how much I've already had, because he pulls two cold engineered beers from the fridge door, opens the drawer between the fridge and the range to pull out an ancient manual can opener, uses the business end of the can opener to pop the bottle caps, and puts a bottle down on the table in front of me. So I drink. I can't remember if I've eaten today. I only saw a few servers sailing around at the party, and none of them were carrying food on their little trays, but that's not exactly unusual. One of the ironies of life in the New Cities, post H2.0: Plenty to drink, but not much worth eating.

He sits down in the chair next to mine at the table and takes a long pull from his own bottle. Pop is still a good-looking guy, for an old crow. Has all his hair—good genes—and it's still black and straight, like

Fred's. Still plays ball some Saturday mornings with vet friends of his. He's skinny, more so than I remember from before I was deployed. If any guy in this family is growing a bit of an engineered-beer gut, it's not him. Big forehead, small eyes, small mouth, just like Fred, although he's got quite a honker, and Fred had her nose fixed back when she was between start-up number one and start-up number two. Other than the nose and the age, he and Fred could almost be twins, both sharp and slick and dark.

But he does look tired after a night on his feet being polite with strangers. I don't want to imagine what I look like. I might be swaying in my chair. It's hard to tell.

After a while he asks in a low voice, "All right, Carter?"

"Yes, sir." No one needs to talk about how he found me crawling through the lobby of my future brother-in-law's palace.

"Did you talk to your sister tonight?"

"No."

He spares me a glance. "She's been feeling sick. How about the Walkers, did you meet them?"

"Sure. Sophie brought me around to some Walkers."

"She was a good egg."

"I guess so. The Walkers seem nice enough."

"Sure."

"Fred did good."

"Sure."

We're angry at each other. It's not a new feeling. We're always angry at each other.

"I didn't get to meet Fred's young man, though," I admit, after a while. I might be trying to get a rise out of him after all. "Sophie tried to introduce me a few times, but he was always surrounded."

Pop nods. He's looking down toward the table, at nothing specific. "Big party. He and Fredericka had to talk to a lot of people." He finishes his beer and then leans back in his chair, opens the fridge behind him, pulls two more out of the door, sets about opening them. "Still, you should have tried, Carter. You could have met him, if you'd tried to get there on time."

He said it gently enough. He could have bawled me out, and I would have deserved it. "I know, Pop. I'm sorry." As I'm saying it to the old man, I honestly am sorry. No one would know it from how I act, but I don't like to embarrass him, or Fred. Or myself. "So what's he like?"

Pop is silent for a moment, then he shakes his head and comes as close as he ever does to cracking a smile. I know what he's going to say before he even says it. "If you're ready for a shock, he's an idiot." I laugh, but his half smile is gone just as quickly as it ghosted across his face. He's not happy about any of this. Fred was always his favorite; we all knew it.

"Well, now he's Fred's idiot." A little unkind of me, I guess.

Pop ignores it. "He's not in his father's line, at least. I'll give him that. His old man is in engineered water like the rest of them, but Kenneth works in health care."

"Also very profitable."

"Sure." Pop drinks his beer. The half smile almost ghosts back as he remembers something. "He calls her Fredda. You can imagine how Fredericka responds to that. I asked him about his job—*How do you like it?*—you know. You know what he says to me? He says, 'I always loved my job,' and then he says, 'And now that I'll be supporting Fredda and our baby, I've never felt more proud of what I do.' And then he smiled at Fredericka. Who has to give up all her clients for the Care Circle program she's in—you might want to talk to her about that; I think she's a bit upset. Anyway, you should've seen her face. I thought she was going to pop him." He sips his beer, then adds, "She'll be all right."

"We always assume that about Fred."

"It's a safe assumption."

"I don't know." I belch, very gently. Through my nose. Like a gentleman. It's true that Fred has always had a certain invincibility to her, for as long as I can remember—she pretty much raised me and Gard, and by the time I was old enough to have my head out of my ass, Fred was finishing an accelerated program at New Chicago University in code development, full ride. She made enough money on her first start-up that she supported Gard at nursing school, and she made enough on her *second* startup to pay for me to go to college, since I am not what anyone would consider scholarship material. But Fred's also always been a little wild, in her way. A lot of drinking, drugs, guys. Not that I'm one to judge—her day-to-day was pretty intense, from what I could tell, and I honestly couldn't give a shit what she does whenever she's blowing off steam from her gig as ruler of the universe. But I know Pop cares. And I have to wonder how much Ken Walker and his fancy family know about the real Fred, the one I've always known. "I met a guy tonight who was . . . trying to make the argument to me, I guess, that Fred and Ken's situation was just a return to the natural order. Ken had to wait until he's *sure* that the *cow* gives *milk*."

Pop yawns in an amused and musical way. "Well, the rich will always be a little bit medieval. They can't help it."

"It *is* medieval, but it's not a joke," I insist. "You know it wasn't *that* long ago that you could marry who you wanted. Before."

"Before what?"

"Before, you know, the Family Protection Laws. Before anybody got *pregnant*." He's looking right at me, but his face is hard to read, partly because of the darkness of the kitchen and partly because I've never been great at reading him. And partly because I'm wasted. "Come on, Pop. Fred's situation?"

Nothing.

"Listen. Pop. When *you* got married, it had nothing to do with the—the . . . national fertility rate. Or having someone to share a Care Hours quota with. Regular people just did it because they *liked* each other. People used to get married because they *liked* each other." I'm losing the thread a bit. Embarrassed at myself, too, of course, because the fuck do I know about marriage? Pop and my mother's marriage dated from well before the fertility crisis, obviously: three kids. But if their marriage proved anything, it's that *liking* each other doesn't cut it in the long run.

"You," he observes, "sound like you've had enough to drink."

Maybe Pop just hasn't wanted to think about it, why Fred's in this mess. "Pop, let me help you understand what's really going on here. Okay? Listen. How can I put this without making Fred sound . . .

Okay. Look. Most people didn't used to spend *their whole lives* fucking around—excuse me, messing around—with every inconsequential person they were half attracted to, because they knew none of it would matter, that they'd never be tied down, that no relationship would ever need to—to—change, or *progress*, or even, you know, *end*, because why bother, it's all nothing anyway, you just drift, in and out of people's lives. There are no stakes. For people my age, there are no *stakes*."

Pop looks at me blankly. I'm reminded, uncomfortably, of the time when I was nine or ten and got up to take a leak in the middle of the night, and as I stumbled into the hallway, I met with Fred, who was coming in the front door, quietly, her dress all askew, a big grin on her face. She would have been sixteen or seventeen. When she saw me she gave me a wink and slipped into the bathroom ahead of me and locked the door. When you have two older sisters, you learn better than to wait in the hall for the bathroom. I went outside in the middle of the night and peed on the sidewalk.

"Pop, that's what it's like now. For us. Us . . . kids. Young people. No one gets married anymore, no one *can*. Unless they have to. So why pretend like any of it matters—*sex*, I mean." I clear my throat. How *that* word came out of my mouth, at my father's kitchen table, I will never know. I don't seem to be in control.

"So what is your point?" he asks mildly. This is all an exercise to him, I see. That's what makes it sad.

"Pop, don't you know Fred just ended up with this guy by accident? Ken Walker, and his family, and that room full of medieval jokers—you think this is what she would have *picked* if she had known she was going to have a baby? This guy? These people? Come on." Now I am hearing a faint ringing in my ears, but I ignore it. "They used to call them shotgun weddings, right? But back then the people who had them were the people *without* money. Doesn't that crack you up? It cracks *me* up. We are living in an age of miracles. That's what Sophie said." That's not exactly what she said. The ringing in my ears continues. It may be louder. "An age of miracles."

As I wind down from this incoherent speech, I am panting a little bit. I am in bad shape tonight, folks, make no mistake. I have been in bad shape since my conversation this afternoon in the hot-as-baking-balls park with Natalie B. I want to put my head down on the table.

"Hold on a minute, Carter. I have something I've been meaning to give you." Pop gets up from the table and disappears into the dark. While he's gone I have time to put my hands, my clammy white trembling hands, on the tabletop and look at them, the hugeness of them. I don't even know half of what they've done. That's the weird thing I think whenever I look at my hands. But how can you avoid seeing your own hands? I hear the cat, skulking around, and then she's rubbing on my chair legs while avoiding, it seems to me, rubbing on my suit legs, which is good because it's my one suit and I don't have time to have it cleaned again between now and Fred's wedding.

And then Pop is back in the kitchen as suddenly as he left. It's a little startling. To cover my involuntary jump I say to him, "Did you hear that Fred wanted us to wear our dress uniforms tonight? My dress blues. I don't even know what they call yours." A long-standing shit pile between us that I can't help but step in every time I get a chance: I'm a Marine, Pop was Army—medical corps, but still Army. It was a problem when I surprised the whole family, unpleasantly, by enlisting instead of graduating. Fred's never been angrier at me. To add insult to injury, I didn't even go in for officers' training and instead entered as your basic-level everyday grunt, in a separate branch of service from Decorated Dad. People don't do that. Smart people don't, anyway. It was a problem then, and it's probably going to be a problem until we're both dead, and then even after that. And actually, I do know that they're blues for him, too.

Pop deadpans, "Fred would have me wear my dress blues to pick up the mail." And now I'm falling all out, laughing hunched over the kitchen table, helpless, tears coming out of my eyes; my head is ringing and ringing and my heart is pounding, and it's a few minutes before I see what he's slid onto the table next to my elbow.

"What's this, Pop?" I'm still wiping tears of laughter from my eyes. I can't really see anyway. It appears to be a stiff little piece of paper with a contact number and a name: *Rafiq*.

"Carter. That's a man I want you to see."

My head is on the table.

"Go see him. I was with him in the Wars. We worked on a lot of wounded together. I trust him."

My head is ringing.

"You can trust him, too. He's not a Kenneth Walker type."

Flowers.

"I'll make you an appointment. For tomorrow. Carter. Go see him."

"Pop." It's about all I can manage. The flowers are swarming up, taking over.

"You worry me, Carter. Go see him. I'm asking you."

"I'm busy tomorrow," I mumble. My eyes are shut tight, so I can't see what his face is like, but I'm guessing it wouldn't tell me much anyway.

"Carter. What are you doing tomorrow that you're so busy? Come on." I hear him take his seat. I hear him exhale. "What's so important."

"I'm meeting one of Gard's former colleagues tomorrow," I tell him. "I'm looking for Gardner. I haven't given up on her. That's what's important."

The ringing has turned to shrieking static in my head, so it's not until he finally speaks that I'm 100 percent sure that he hasn't been raging at me for hours.

"Carter. That's . . . unforgivable."

"You don't know what's unforgivable. You clearly don't," I tell him. I am saying this into the table, my head cradled in my arms. "I can tell you what's unforgivable, if you really want to know. It's giving up on your daughter. It's not looking for her. It's not knowing where she might be and not doing anything about it. That's unforgivable, I think."

Again there's a swelling of sound in my ears, in my head, and I'm riding it and riding it, and it's not until he actually says something that it's clear he hasn't said anything in quite a while. "Have you thought about your sister?"

"I'm thinking about my sister. Yes. Obviously I am thinking about her."

"Not Gardner. Fredericka."

"What about Fred?"

"Have you thought about what that would mean for her, if Gardner were found—right now, days before she gets married, into a family like that one?" Pop says.

"Fuck that guy. Fuck the Walkers. If he really wants Fred, let him stand up with his dick in his hand and be a fucking man about it."

"*Don't talk like that to me,*" Pop thunders. I sit up. My eyes are shut. For the moment, I can't open them. But I'm sitting up.

"I'm sorry, sir. All I mean is Ken should be willing to take a little heat on Fred's behalf if it comes to that. Gard's his sister-in-law."

"Carter. You haven't been around for a while. I'm telling you something that might be hard for you to hear. Gardner made some mistakes. She got into some dangerous territory. I tried to help her, Fredericka tried to help her, even Kenneth Walker tried to help her, and you can believe that or not, it's your choice. Gardner didn't want to be helped."

"God help you," I manage to say. I get to my feet. It's bad. It's not my finest moment. My suit jacket slithers to the floor.

I open my eyes and look down at him. I can't see much, my vision is ringed by a corona of black, but from what I can tell he's still sitting at the table looking at his hands, tired and old. We're angry at each other. It's not a new feeling. "God help you, Pop."

Then I make my way toward the blackout-dark hallway off the kitchen, and the cat follows me and I'm falling again.

F. QUINN
RISE 8, UNIT 7 LAKE
NEW CHICAGO 06060601
NEW STATES

PFC C. P. QUINN 2276766
MCC 167 1ST MAW
FPO NEW CHICAGO 06040309

November 1, 3:17 p.m.

Hi, CQ,

Hope you're taking care of yourself over there. I need this kid's uncle in one piece with all his parts attached. I don't want to have to explain to this baby why Uncle CQ has half a face or whatever. Be good. Be good at what you do, whatever that is. Gard is always trying to tell me some crazy shit she's been reading about the triggers and I just can't EVEN with her sometimes but it sounds like some real shit, so watch out, because people who don't otherwise pray are praying for you because they like your dumb face the way it is. Not that I know any of those people, I just hear things.

So I am wondering, speaking of Gard, if you have heard from her. I think she might have gotten herself into a bit of trouble. I think I can handle it; I've got some backup that could come in handy, but it certainly would be helpful if you would share whatever you might have heard, or whatever she might have told you, before I really start to worry. Worry is bad, because then I have to take extra pills and they make me barf even more than usual, which, if you can imagine . . . Like a river? Of barf? Just . . . like flowing and flowing, and so delicious? And I look so so pretty all the time from all the barfing? So yeah. I would like less of that, please. Whatever she told you, it's time to let me know.

Pop's cat is still alive, can you believe that shit? I was over at his place visiting and I swear the fucking thing crawled into my lap straight out of a fucking sarcophagus.

Be good. Seriously.

Fred

G. QUINN
NEW CHICAGO
NEW STATES

PFC C. P. QUINN 2276766
MCC 167 1ST MAW
FPO NEW CHICAGO 06040309

October 15, 6:30 a.m.

CQ, little brother,

I don't want you to worry. I love you. I love all you guys. I'll be in touch when I can. Take care of Fred. And be good to Pop.
    Love you.

Gard

FOUR

Dec 19 6:37 AM

Sorry we missed each other last night.
But you're an asshat and it's your fault anyway.
Listen, CQ, are you going to meet with that
woman from the clinic again?
Whatever else you're doing today,
on top of being a hungover pile of fly-speckled
shit, please don't blow her off. Please.
I know I'm nagging you about this.
I know I keep nagging.
But it's been weeks and we're running
out of time, like seriously running out now,
and there are some
things
I've got to talk to Gard about.
Right now you're the only one who can
help us find her. I'm trapped.
Please keep trying. I'll catch up to you later.

It's more than a hangover. When I try to focus my eyes, see what I'm supposed to be seeing, there's a dark gray corona hovering around a supernova. That can't be right. As my friend Wash used to say. About everything, over there. *That can't be right.* A hole in the ground, an extra patrol, a stick with a skull on it that was probably an animal's but that looked horribly like a human child's. *That can't be right.* It was his catchphrase, I suppose, like *Gentle pressure, relentlessly applied* was Gard's. Wash is dead now—if I wanted to, I could pick up his catch-phrase, sort of like I've done with my sister's. It'd be just as useful. But I wouldn't. I'm not stupid, but I am superstitious. Most vets are, I think.

So now I'm rolling out of bed and I can't find the floor, and then I find it in the least pleasant way possible. Pop's cat regards me with disgust from the end of the bed. Good to have cats around. Just in case you're worried you might be too fucking dignified.

When I stand up I think I might be dying of standing up. Stars. Flowers. Shooting things.

What did Pop say last night? *Get up, or I'll knock you down and leave you here.* That's what this thing is saying to me, too. *Get up and keep getting up or I will make it so you never get up again.*

It takes me a few minutes to be able to see or hear or feel anything, but when I do, I reread the message on my wearable from Fred, from earlier this morning. *It's been weeks and we're running out of time. . . . You're the only one who can help us find her. I'm trapped. Please keep trying.*

So now I'm moving.

Moving hurts. Everything hurts. I admit that Pop took me by sur-prise last night—a referral to one of his army medic buddies must mean that he's noticed more than I thought. I haven't talked to Pop about any of this, the physical things. What Carter Is Experiencing. I know it's not normal; I know that. I know that the flowers date back to that one time I set off a boom and caught the tail fire of it, about nine months before I came home. I know that the headaches and the blind spots go back to that, too. There are other things that are harder to explain—the way that the smell of flowers comes over me, the horrible thin *everywhere-ness* of it, that smell, not just in my nose and my mouth but in my eyes, in my throat, in my gut. And not just the way it comes over me, but the *when*: When I'm enraged, or upset. Upset. Oh, let's call it suicidal, that's more like it; that'll look nice in the VA's psych workup. When I want to die, that's when it comes over me, and makes me think I'm actually dying. Which scares me enough to want to live again, somewhere, in my reptile brain where the real decisions get made. Usually.

The bathroom is the first stop. The sani helps a bit, but not enough. I'm still seeing stars, I step on the cat. I shave; there's some friendly fire. I dress. I have to keep moving. Today's the day. I'm going to see Natalie B. again, at the clinic where she worked with Gard. I'm looking forward to seeing her. And I'm going to find out where Gard is. I know she knows.

I've never been inside Gard and Natalie's clinic, and I couldn't tell you the address, but I know where to find it, regardless. Gard told me, without realizing she was telling me. Even now I have to wonder if she knows how much she gave away. It's all the way down where the train lines used to roll out to the western suburbs, in an unrehabbed part of the city; a train to a bus to a walk. Suits me fine. Just keep moving.

Everybody on my route's just staring at their wearables. There's advertising to watch on the train and on the bus, but no one but me takes any notice. I love watching ads. Drugs and gum and sanifoams and appliances. I seriously love it all, especially the sanifoam ads, all the fragrances and textures you can get. In the military, it goes without saying, when you got sanifoam at all it was industrial-grade pipe cleaner stuff, fake-pine green or toilet-bowl blue, goopy and viscous and unpleasant to clean yourself with. My father's the only person I know who's old enough to remember when water used to come out of the sinks and the bathtub faucet. Most people have refitted their bathrooms by now, taken the old fixtures out entirely, put in some nice dispensers. Pop's bathroom looks just like it did before the water went off. Like he's waiting for it to come back on someday, or for engineered water to get cheap enough to run through everyday people's pipes. It's inconvenient as hell, but I wouldn't presume to tell him so. It's still his place.

When I get tired of watching the ads, I pass the time pressing my forehead against the bus windows, watching drones in their laneways scoot and soar alongside the traffic, and overhead, with deliveries, with messenger packets, with subpoenas. There are more drones than cars out at this hour of the day; it's too late in the morning for commuter traffic. I've slept in. Although "sleeping in" makes it sound gentler than what I was really doing, which was more like being attacked by unconsciousness.

When I'm bored looking out the windows I rescan the messages on my wearable. Rereading messages from my sisters to me is a familiar habit from my years out West, and now I have a few messages from Natalie B. to read and reread, too. The repetitive flicking and scrolling is calming somehow. Makes me feel like I'm doing something, studying something for clues, even when I have nothing to show for it. From Fred. *It's been weeks and we're running out of time.* From Natalie. *I don't owe you anything.* From me to both of them. *Sorry again, but I'm just trying to . . . Sorry to bother you again, but . . . Sorry, Fred, but . . .*

I've made this same autobus trip a number of times already, over the past two weeks. It hasn't helped me find Gard, but still it's comforting, in a weird way, to do some of the things I know Gard used to do. Riding her bus, for instance, just feels nice. Maybe because she actually told me, once, that she had a habit of praying for me while she rode the bus to and from work. That's Gard for you. That's the kind of person she is. At any rate, by now, a couple of weeks into my search, Gard's route is just familiar enough that I don't have to watch to make sure I get off at the right stop. Each time, I think of Gard making this same trip, taking this same bus. Her apartment isn't far from Pop's, so it's been easy for me to pick up her habits, mimic some of her routine.

What I know about her routine I've pieced together from her messages and from Fred: She worked an afternoon-to-evening shift at the same sleepy walk-in Completion service she's worked at since nursing school, in a rehabbed, gentrified neighborhood that's been slowly empyting out for years. The fertility crisis being what it is, there's been less and less for her to do at her day job, since only rich women can afford Insemina. But for the last ten months, when Gard got off her day job, she'd been taking an evening bus out to the edge of the rehabbed zones and from there walking to her other job at the clinic where she worked with Natalie B. According to Fred, it's a health and Completion clinic for low-income women—the sort of folks who can afford to live in New Chicago but not in the rehabbed zones. Service workers, food-production workers, sanitation workers, and so on. Not glamorous, not comfortable, and judging by the location, not particularly safe. From what I understand from Fred, the work was not well paid, either.

In one of Gard's messages to me from earlier this year, one of the ones I've reread so often I practically know it backwards and forwards, she told me that she had gotten into the habit of working at her second clinic most nights all night, sometimes until the early hours of the next day. She ate dinner on the way there, ate breakfast on the way home, slept a few hours, got up, did it all over again. Slept at her desk at her day job, sometimes. She wondered if it was like patrols, if how she spent her days had anything in common with what I was doing over there. I don't remember how I responded to that.

Gard's last message to me was sent back in October, and her last contact with Fred was at the end of September. Fred says she tried messaging Gard a few times in early October but didn't hear back. It wasn't until a few more days passed, and Fred checked her wearable for Gard's geo and got no response, that it occurred to Fred to worry. In any case, the best I can put together is that a week or so after Fred's last contact with Gard, but before Fred noticed she'd disappeared, I got a message from Gard. It's not much of a message. But she's definitely saying goodbye. Out of nowhere. *I'll be in touch when I can. Take care of Fred.*

I don't know why I wasn't more alarmed by it, at the time. All I can say is that I read it. I thought nothing, literally nothing, about it. I read it, and then I went back on patrol. I probably hurt a few people, but I don't remember it, and I probably fucked up something basic, but I don't remember it. I went back to base. I got up the next day. I did that again. Repeat, repeat, repeat. It was what I did every day all day long over there: think nothing, about anything. I was not prepared, in that place or in that state, to question a weirdly unemotional farewell message from one of my sisters. Gard's note might as well have been written in hieroglyphics for all the understanding I had of it. She said goodbye to me, and I did exactly nothing.

The one thing I did notice about it, I guess—the one thing that might have given me my first half second of concern, although this could just be hindsight on my part, or my conscience kicking up—was that the message was time-stamped but not geo-stamped. That was unusual. Gard had overwritten the address so it would read simply "New Chicago," because she didn't want me to know where she was when she sent her last message to me. And after her last message to me, in October, there's no geo history for her on my wearable, on Fred's, or on Pop's. We're the only family she has—wherever she went, we should be able to see her on our wearable maps, whether moving or still, a little ghost in the shape of an orange pin, labeled with her name and image. Sometime in late September, early October, Gard slipped right off our maps.

But something I learned from my friend Wash, over there, was how to find the lat/long for messages sent to your wearable. What gets displayed in the message is just the nearest known address for the sender's coordinates; the message data actually captures the exact latitude and longitude of the sender. All the illusion of privacy, without the inconvenience of causing someone somewhere to be missing data about you and your whereabouts and your relationships with other people. It takes some work to get the data out of your wearable, and it hurts a little bit, but it's not hard if you know how. So, as Wash explained it, if your girlfriend is sending you a message from some other guy's house but overwrites the address line to read like it's coming from home, you know where your first stop should be when you get leave.

Wash was our company's communications specialist. He was the one who dug out the lat/long from Gard's message for me, once Fred's messages started getting really panicky and I started making plans to come home. It was against regulations, obviously, but Wash was perfectly willing, partly just to show me it could be done, and partly because we were bored, so painfully, crushingly bored all the time we weren't mortally terrified and running for our lives, or running after someone to try to kill them. And I was willing because I wanted to hurt myself all the time over there and this seemed at least like an interesting way of doing it. Once Wash had the lat/long, and once he'd taped me back up, he sent it to my wearable.

I still have Gard's last message on my wearable, and Wash's message, too, with the lat/long of where she sent it from. One of the first things I did when I came back home to look for Gard was try to connect the coordinates with an address. There isn't one. There's no building. There's just a playground.

It's not much of a playground. No gate, no checkpoint. Rubberized surface, a couple of swings, some complicated-looking climbing structures. It's been at least 80 degrees out every day since I've been back, and there's no shade, because this far from the city center you don't find too many parks that have been relandscaped, but where I'm sitting, on a bench, drinking from a cold can of engineered beer tucked inside a paper sack, there's a strip of marginally cooler air to be found in the shadow of a flagpole. On a hot day like this one, you wouldn't want to play here unless you had no place else to go, but there aren't many kids left, in this part of town or anywhere else. And it's a school day anyway. The remaining children of New Chicago are all in classes, training up to be national treasures and counting down the days to Christmas break. The playground is deserted except for me, and a hot breeze is kicking up wrappers and papers around the monkey bars.

As the crow flies it's not far from here to the New Chicago Medical Complex, and the old VA hospital where Pop used to work before he retired. His army medic buddy has his office there—his number's in my pocket. I brought it because I was thinking I'd stop in on the way back, even though it's not really on my way, and there's no chance the guy will actually be in his office, much less taking appointments, because that's not how the VA works. How the VA works is, you pick up your severed limbs and get in line with them, get in all the lines, ever, all combined in one gigantic line. And then wait. And hope you don't bleed out while you're waiting. But I can stop in, I figure, and leave my name at the desk. Just to show Pop I'm not completely ignoring him. Just to tell the old man I tried. That much I figure I can do.

I'm sitting and drinking and thinking as much, when I see her: a youngish-looking woman, round-faced, short, a bit of belly. Early twenties, I would say—about my age. She's wearing a long-sleeved hoodie against the heat and walking fast through the park, like she's on her way somewhere. Which I'm willing to bet she is.

She hasn't seen me—I'm too far across the park for that, and too low here on the bench to be in her natural sightline. But I know better than to rise up out of nowhere on her. I first stash the beer in its sack carefully under the bench, allowing myself a half second's regret for its loss, for the cold fizz left to warm and flatten, abandoned under a park bench in the heat of the day (no kids left to find it here, a cold beer, a lucky find to brag to the other kids about at school).

I start walking slowly, making sure she sees me approach. Making sure I look like a guy who's looking for a little help and not trouble.

Still, she's obviously spooked when I call out after her, "Miss?" I can't help that, I know—and she's smart to be scared, since who the hell am I?

We're alone out here. It's broad streaking daylight and there's no shade, no cover. I am harmless. I am harmless. I stop a few yards away. She keeps walking.

"Miss, I'm sorry. I'm looking for my girlfriend. I'm supposed to meet her."

She glances back over her shoulder, makes sure I'm keeping my distance.

"So go meet her."

"I don't know how. She gave me directions but I can't figure them out." She looks back over her shoulder again, and her pace slows. "I thought maybe we might be going to the same place."

Now she stops, half turns. Gives me the squint eye.

"Can you take me there?" I hold my hands out, palms up, and wait.

It's hard to be patient. I've sat on that bench many afternoons over the past two weeks, waiting, messaging Natalie every few hours to beg her to meet with me, drinking beer from a sack (or coffee, sometimes, since I'm not a drunk) whenever being ignored got frustrating, trying not to look like the stalker that I suppose I am every time a woman passes by—always walking alone and walking fast, just to disappear from sight. I've never been able to follow where they were going, not until today. Today, through no fault of her own, this woman happens to be heading where I need to go.

I can see she's worried.

"I'm sorry to ask. But—I'm just trying to get there. I'm late. She's gonna be freaking out." I know how to look worried, too.

"She scared?" The woman is looking at me differently now. "This her first time?"

Play it out. "Yeah."

She shakes her head, one quick toss. "The dumb ones always bring their man the first time," she says dismissively.

"She's not dumb. She's just scared." I glance down at my feet, in my familiar and beloved combat boots, which look like they have seen a bit too much action—and if this woman looks hard enough at them she might guess I'm not just some poor guy who managed against all odds to get his girlfriend in the family way. So I meet her eyes again, look hangdog, as I'm well able to do. "We both are."

She sighs. "Come on, then." And then picks up her pace so fast I have to skip a bit to catch up, my not-quite-healed feet stinging and singing inside my boots. "You got nothing to worry about, hon. It's nice in there. You'll see."

I follow her through the park and across the street, where she heads straight for a bricked-up building that might once have been a small-parts factory or a warehouse. Long lines of cloudy windows, revealing nothing inside. It looks abandoned. But the door has been more or less recently painted, cadet blue, and it's open when she yanks on the handle.

From behind my guide, as we enter a narrow, dim hallway that seems to lead deep into the first floor of the building, I see papers taped to the walls, fluttering community notices and part-time, off-the-books job postings—house cleaning, office cleaning, home health care, food prep. On an interior door to the left—so small you'd miss it if you weren't looking for it—there's a painted yellow arrow, pointing diagonally down, and two small words. THIS WAY. This is the second door we go through.

Concrete and metal stairs lead down a flight underground to a third door at the foot. Bright lights, white walls, smudges above the railing where hands have trailed. On the door, also cadet blue like the others, a sign with an arrow pointing left. THIS WAY.

A long concrete corridor leads back in the direction we just descended, back under the street we crossed to reach this place. Someone's done their best to make it look cheerful, but it's still a tunnel. The concrete floor has been painted the same blue as the doors, and the walls are white with big yellow letters tipped in arrows pointing the way (THIS WAY). Round globe lights hang evenly spaced in the low ceiling. It's an echo-filled, hard place all the same. Something's humming hugely, an air filter, maybe.

Through another door, and suddenly we're in a carpeted hallway with pale walls, a level underground but still looking like every other carpeted hallway outside every other doctor's office on earth. Letters painted on the wall in blue, violet, and green spell out WELCOME, lead to a final cadet-blue door. The humming of the air filters is louder in here, like a missile about to launch.

Everything in me is telling me to bolt, abort mission, fall back. Whatever's behind that door is something I'm not supposed to see. Whoever it's for, it's not for me.

"Hang on—" I start to say. To my astonishment, the woman reaches back and takes my hand in hers.

"You got this. Don't worry. It's not as bad as you think."

She pulls on the door handle and then we're through.

And now, of course, I have to think fast. I would be lying if I claimed that I had a plan for what I would say or do if I ever finally got in here.

The woman is right, for what it's worth: Gard and Natalie's clinic is a pleasant place. In the small waiting room where we've arrived, there are fake potted plants in the corners, sweet pictures by kids hung in frames on the walls. The carpeting is that low-pile industrial stuff you see in every office, but it's a nice color, somewhere between blue and purple, and it absorbs sound and makes everything feel sort of hushed and sleepy, like someone's napping in the next room and no one wants to wake her. Cheap wooden chairs with padded seats line the walls, and there are a few low tables stacked with flyers about children, babies, how to take care of them, and there's one Department of Health flyer called *Meeting the Standard of Care* that seems to be on all the tables; there's a woman on the cover who's looking at the camera and holding her own arm like it's a wounded animal. Waiting in the seats I see an assortment of women in their twenties and thirties. Only one of them is obviously pregnant so far as I can tell, but some others might be in early-stage Completion. They all look at us as we enter.

It takes me a half second to recognize why—why everyone in the room looks up, right at us. What's not quite normal about this waiting room: no one's looking at her wearable. There must not be any signal down here. A quick glance at my own wearable confirms it.

No one's rushing forward to meet me, obviously, so none of them can be my imaginary girlfriend, the one I told my guide I was here for. I murmur, "I think I missed her. She must've already went in."

The woman smirks at me, not entirely not on my side, and releases my hand as we slip toward the reception window. "I guess you got trouble now."

"I guess." I hang back a discreet distance while the woman signs in. She gives me a final nod and takes a seat to wait—a seat, I notice, without an empty neighbor on either side. That ends that. I shouldn't press anyway. The nurse behind reception doesn't look up as I push my belly into the edge of the counter separating us. "Ma'am, my name is Carter Quinn. I'm here to see Natalie."

"Who?"

"Natalie," I say quietly. "She works here."

That warrants me a glance. Then she returns to whatever she's been keying in. "You think she's expecting you?"

"I do, ma'am. She is."

"Sit down, then."

"Can you tell her I'm here? I only need her for a minute."

"She'll call you," the nurse says distinctly, without looking away from her screen, "when she's ready for you."

I slink to a seat. I don't try to talk to anyone else, and most of the women seem to want to avoid looking at me anyway. I'm the only guy in the room, and no others come in. There's nothing to look at or check or do. I don't read any of the literature on child and infant care, since I don't expect Fred's Care Circle or Ken Walker's fancy family will want me anywhere near my nephew or niece, after he or she is born. Fred will let me know if it's okay for me to hold the baby. I never expected to get to hold a baby. Every woman in this room will. But no one I know has ever expected to hold one. I cannot imagine for the life of me why anyone would hand me an infant to hold. Not with these hands. They're trained for something else entirely.

The door to the back offices opens and my heart leaps up in my chest. *Down, fella.* It's not Natalie B. It's a young woman with a cane and a slight limp. She waves toward the reception window. "Bye, hon."

"No next time," the nurse there calls to her, with a slight smile.

"No next time," she calls back, and hobbles to the exit and is gone.

For the next hour, every time someone leaves, it's the same little call and response. *No next time. No next time.* No one in the waiting room seems especially happy to be there, but everyone coming out from the back offices looks more or less relaxed. I see a couple more women go out, one holding a cold pack against her cheek. She just nods at the reception window instead of saying *No next time.* A few more women arrive, take seats to wait. Finally my friend goes in without so much as a glance back at me.

I wait. I maintain a neutral expression and keep my body language unthreatening. I'm just a guy waiting for his girlfriend. A largish guy, with largish hands and feet, with boots that look like they were in a war, with a face like his eldest sister's, like his father's, a face like a dark knife, a face that needs careful moderation to prevent making other people uncomfortable. I'm there long enough, waiting, that the women whispering to each other in the corner might be speculating about me. When one of them catches my eye, staring at me very much as if she doesn't think I should be here, I look down at my hands in my lap. My unsafe hands. Last night is still banging in my temples and roiling in my empty stomach. I keep my gaze down.

Finally I let my head drop, might actually doze a little.

Then I hear my name.

Carter Quinn. I'm a little sleepy-eyed and slow-witted when I look up, and what I see is confusing enough that the bottom of my mind seems to drop out, and what's left of my comprehension seems to pin-wheel and teeter on the edge of a long drop.

The door to the back offices has opened, and my friend from ear-lier today (is it afternoon now? evening? I seem to have lost a few hours somewhere) is standing framed in the doorway, and her arm is in a cast. She's seen me. She's looking at me suspiciously. Why is her arm in a cast? She held doors open for me. She opened the door with one hand and took my hand with the other. Her arm wasn't broken then. But now it is. *Carter Quinn.*

I can't remember telling her my name. I can't remember breaking her arm. But no, I didn't break her arm. I would never harm a woman, not me, not myself. Yes, I've harmed women. I've damaged their brains, their hearing, their eyes, their skin. I've killed women; I'm sure I have. But that was different. I've never broken a woman's arm. I have two sisters. I would do anything for them, but I would never break a woman's arm.

The woman moves through the doorway, advances into the waiting room, her eyes still on me. Natalie B. steps out from behind her, scan-ning the room, wearing scrubs, a handheld portal in one arm, like a shield up against her chest. She's saying my name again.

"Here. I'm here." I make my way to my feet and my head swims dangerously. Flowers and stars and stars and flowers and that smell, holy goddamn.

And now that woman is coming toward me. Her expression is hard to look at. I've never seen a woman so angry, not even Fred. Everyone is watching. A woman sitting near the exit stands up and slips out the door. Another one hesitates and then follows.

My guide gets close enough to hiss at me. Her eyes are bright and black and furious.

"You shouldn't be here."

I know, I want to tell her. *I know that now.*

"Everything all right?" Natalie calls from the doorway. "Mr. Quinn? We're ready for you."

"No next time," the nurse calls from the reception window. There's a firm, no-nonsense edge to her voice. It says, *No trouble here.* It says, *Move along.*

The woman glances back over her shoulder. "No next time," she repeats. Then she passes me without another word, without another glance, and the exit door clicks shut behind her.

Natalie B. is across the waiting room, her lovely face composed into blankness. But she's breathing fast, like she's afraid of something. I'm sorry I came. There's no welcome here for me. "Ready, Mr. Quinn?"

The room Natalie shows me into has a reclining chair and a little tray of silver tools. There's a high white smell like an alcohol swab that manages to pierce the cloud of flowers surrounding my head like a gauze. I'm not sure what I thought I'd find back here, but it's more like a dentist's office than what I would expect from a women's health clinic. Not that I've been inside one before today.

Meanwhile, my head feels half disattached from my body. The ringing in my ears has already started. I can tell I don't have much time before I stop making sense, before the white and the flowers take over and I have to make it back to Pop's place and stay horizontal for about twelve hours. Sometimes I have bad days. This is clearly shaping up to be one of them. I don't know why. Some combination of a hangover and PTSD and chronic pulmonary distress and whatever is actually wrong with me.

"So you found us," Natalie says. "Sit."

Obedient, I sit in the patient examination chair. There's nowhere else. Natalie stands near the door, facing me, arms crossed. It's impossible not to notice that she is even pretty down here, in the unpleasant light of this place.

"I don't want to take up too much of your time," I begin, and then I feel a soft warm drop on my right hand. I don't need to look down. I know what it is. "Can I have a tissue, please?"

Without a word, Natalie reaches over, yanks a tissue out of an unbranded box, hands it to me. It's about as comforting and plush as a sand dune. I blot my nosebleed and do my best to continue, all business.

"I know my sister Gardner worked nights here for about a year, because she told me as much in her messages to me. My sister's last message was sent from here. It said—"

"From here? How do you know it was sent from here?" Natalie interrupts. "We don't have receptivity—"

"—down here, I know that now. I noticed. It's strange. And in her message she hid the address, or tried to, so—"

Natalie interrupts again, talking fast. "We don't have anything to hide. This clinic is private but perfectly legal. It's a safe place for hundreds of women who don't have many other appealing options. You saw that much, I think, while you were waiting."

This isn't exactly what I had been getting at, or what I expected her to say. "Sure." My nosebleed seems to have stopped. "Of course. If you don't mind my asking, though—"

"I do. You know I do."

Maybe because she's taken me off guard, the question that comes out isn't exactly the one I mean to ask: "That woman who spoke to me on my way in, her arm was broken? I swear her arms were both fine. Earlier. Before."

Natalie glares. "I don't intend to discuss our clients' medical histories with you, but you must have noticed she's wearing a cast. She has a fractured wrist."

"She didn't," I insist helplessly. "She didn't have a cast on. I talked to her earlier. She brought me down here. She took my hand, pulled me through the door. She wasn't wearing a cast when she did that."

Natalie rolls her eyes to the subterranean ceiling.

Something's not quite connecting here. And I'm still feeling wheezy and woozy. I need to get back to what brought me into this office to begin with: Gard.

"Gard's last message to me, which she sent from here, was her saying goodbye. She said she would be in touch when she could, and that we shouldn't worry about her. And nobody in our family has heard from her since. Do you have any idea why, or how, she would have sent me that message from here? It was October fifteenth, that would have been a Tuesday. Six thirty a.m. She would have just been getting off her night shift."

"The night shift ends at five a.m.," Natalie corrects. I wait. She says nothing more.

"Natalie. I'm begging you. Help me understand."

"As you know, I have a waiting room full of clients to see, Mr. Quinn. I don't know how I can help *you*, but I do know how I can help *them*. Have you tried opening an investigation with Security?"

My patience, as I have said, is not infinite, and it's quite a bit less than infinite when I can barely see straight for the gray clouds crowding in on all sides and the sparks going off in my ears. "All I'm asking for is a few minutes—or, Jesus, a few *answers*, if you don't have a few minutes! Of *course* we haven't brought Security deep into this—don't you even want to know how I knew where this place was?"

I see her glance down toward my arm, where my wearable is, just like everybody else's: embedded in the skin of the inner arm, a third of the distance between wrist and elbow.

In my wearable's virtual display, which lines up across the upper corner of my retina, my med status is visible, the digits the same blue as my veins, which thread over and around the embedded wearable panel in my arm, just like everybody else's. But because we're underground, in a dead reception zone, the icons for most of the wearable's functions are white, not blue—inactive. When they're blue, then with a blink or a stroke or a verbal command I can call up a virtual portal, also projected onto the interior wall of my retina, along with a virtual keyboard that's visible only to me, and key or dictate a message, or read messages and advertisements customized for me, or call up a map for directions or my father's and oldest sister's whereabouts, or see my last few financial transactions (all of them biweekly automatic deposits from the Department of Veterans Affairs). When the icons are blue, my wearable is transmitting as well as receiving, so if they ever need to look for me, my family members can call up my precise coordinates, my activities, my med status. Every time I pass one of the millions of sensors in this city, or one of the dozens on a city bus, or one of the few in my pop's apartment, my status is updated and upstreamed, while fresh data flows in. In and out, all day long. Like breathing. Like blood circulating.

There is one way in which my wearable isn't quite the same as everybody else's now. Wash's work left a small raised edge on the lower-right corner of the panel. When I bend my arm these days I can feel it, a slight irregularity. "There's a data port accessible from each corner of the panel, but you have to be willing to get to it, and you have to know someone with the technology to connect to it," I tell Natalie.

"I know how the wearable works, Mr. Quinn." Her voice is acid.

"Then you know how I found this place."

"It would appear that we both do." She makes a sort of funny half step toward the tray of tools, then seems to force herself to step back, fold her arms over her chest. She is nervous. I make her nervous, maybe. Or there's something else.

"Why would she try to hide her location from me? She never did that before. She never tried to send me a message from here before, either. How could she? How could she have sent me a message at all, from down here? Easier to go back up to street level, send it from the bus or the train or the getaway van as she left town."

Natalie raises an eyebrow. "You don't know?"

"I'm telling you that I don't."

She smiles, but there's no humor in it. "Ask whoever helped you pluck the location data out."

"He's dead."

"I'm sorry."

"He was over there with me. He was in communications. He knew how to do it. He helped me. He was a friend. His name was Wash. Washington. Specialist Paul Washington." I don't get to say his name very often anymore. It feels good to say it.

Natalie is quiet for a moment, then says, "Well, Wash should have told you that when you have a port connection in, you can send and upstream data and messages directly, as well as downstreaming what's in the wearable."

Something's not making sense, still. "You mean Gard would have had to connect a data port to her wearable to send a message to me from down here."

The barest pause. "Yes."

"I don't mind saying, it hurt like hell." I smile at Natalie. I see her recoil, then cover it up by turning to the tray of silver tools suspended from the wall near the chair. In this small examination room, I am less than half a foot from her. I'm bigger than she is, yes. I scare people without meaning to. My smile has a touch of fang to it. Even at rest my face is unhappily sharp. But I am harmless. I am harmless. I swear it. "I hate to think of Gard doing that just to send me a message. Why didn't she just go up to the street and send it from there? No need for any of the pain, or trouble. But it was her last message, Natalie. This is her last-known geo." I have to ask it. "Did she even leave this place?"

Natalie freezes. "I'm not sure what you're implying."

"Nothing. Not a thing." I raise my hands.

"We *help* women here," Natalie says. She keeps her shoulder turned to me, her attention on the tray of tools, which she touches lightly with one hand. I see her face in profile, her curved cheek, her lowered lashes, but she's a fast-breathing wall, and not a piece of her tells me anything. "Sometimes, at our clients' express request, we help them in ways that can be hard . . . for people to understand, but only if they haven't faced the kinds of choices these women routinely face. We would never have harmed your sister. She was on our staff, as you know. I worked with her. She was my . . . my friend. And my colleague." Natalie keeps her eyes on her silver tools. They are lightweight, delicate things. I recognize none of them. "You might want to ask yourself what the other possibilities are, Mr. Quinn."

"What possibilities? Natalie, for a minute see it from my point of view. I saw a woman come in here this morning and go out with a fractured wrist. My sister came in here and might never have come out."

Now Natalie turns to me, and I don't like her expression one bit. "Are you threatening us?"

"I'm not threatening anybody!" I exclaim, my hands high in surrender again. "What could I even do to you? But what happened to my sister in here, exactly?"

Her expression has not changed, and something in it tells me that if I were smart, I'd be getting the hell out of her office. "The question you should be asking, Mr. Quinn, is *what did your sister do here, exactly*."

I can't tell, but I might be gaping uncomprehendingly at her like a dead man. She moves, hands me a tissue.

"Your nose is bleeding again."

The volume of the ringing in my right ear mobilizes abruptly and the sound turns to static, scratchy static, unbelievable. Unbearable. In the reclining chair, I put my head between my knees, which sometimes helps. No relief. My hands are shaking, so I clasp them tightly, bring them to my mouth, and try to slow my breathing. I don't feel as if any oxygen is getting to my lungs, to my brain. Everything's crowded out by the static in my ears and the scent of flowers in my throat. My hands are sticky. I open my eyes and see that there's blood between my fingers, from my nosebleed. I hope it's a nosebleed. Once, at my worst, I couldn't tell where the blood was coming from, but it seemed to be coming from everywhere—my eyes, my nose, my mouth, my ears, even the top of my head somehow. Then I blacked out.

"Mr. Quinn? What's happening?"

Blacking out here, in Natalie's office, is an awkward prospect, but even with my eyes and hands and consciousness clenched tight against the pain in my head, I can't get it under control. I allow that it might be in process. It might be happening.

"Do you need help?" Natalie asks. Gently she pushes me back in the reclining chair. I keep my eyes shut tight and my hands clasped together in front of my nose and mouth, where I should be able to catch most of the blood. Still I hear her breath come in sharp. Her small strong fingers are on mine, trying to pry my hands apart to see what's under there, where the blood is coming from. For some reason I feel like I can't let her see, I don't want to let her see. Or I don't want to see her seeing it.

A squeal of fiery pain in my head, like static obliterating a freq, is all I can focus on for a second.

She's got one of my bloody hands in hers now. I open my eyes briefly and see that I have somehow left a bright red smear across the front of her scrubs, from her chest down to her belly. I hope to God I didn't hit her, didn't flail or lose it or lash out, but I don't know. I might have. I can feel her shaking. She's scared. She's scared of me.

But she's making her voice strong, trying to make it carry across the flaring lightning field that's bearing me off: "Carter? Can you hear me?

What can I do for you? Are you on any medications? Is there a doctor you're seeing?"

Pop's guy. I remember the slip of paper.

"In my pocket," I manage to say. "Friend." It's not exactly what I mean, but it's all I've got.

As I'm fading into gray and then black I feel her patting me down.

F. QUINN
RISE 8, UNIT 7 LAKE
NEW CHICAGO 06060601
NEW STATES

PFC C. P. QUINN 2276766
MCC 167 1ST MAW
FPO NEW CHICAGO 06040309

October 2, 5:38 p.m.

Hi, CQ,

Note the address change. I moved in with the father's family.

I'd never been in one of the towers until I moved in here, but it's as unbelievable as you'd think. We're waiting to see how things go—it was a little dodgy for a while, but it seems like we're pulling through. If everything works out, and the pregnancy stays healthy, we'll get a place together. For now, his parents' is a good option.

I'm very well taken care of. You actually kind of can't even imagine. It's different up here.

Now that I'm through the first trimester and halfway into the second, I'm learning more about what you're supposed to do. I don't know any other mothers. I'm sure you don't, either. But Gard's been a Completionist for *years* and never mentioned any of this to me, so I feel a little tricked. Like for instance? It turns out it's *not* just a rumor, I *do* have to give up my consulting practice and all my clients by the end of the year, because mothers aren't supposed to have businesses in their own names. And my Care Circle sessions are five times a week now, even on the weekends, and some women are traveling three hours round-trip to get to them. You would not believe some of the shit they're telling us. Mandatory nursing until the child is *five*. Weekly growth progress checks till age eight. Mandatory enrichment classes starting at six months. That's just Care Standard; *that's* considered the bare minimum. My Care Hours quota is already through the goddamn roof, and it just goes higher once the baby is born. So I guess it's a good thing I have to give up my business that I spent my whole fucking career building because there's no way I'll have time for it now.

But as Gard loves reminding me, I'm *lucky*: The father and his family, they're basically supporting me, partly because it's easy for them and partly, I think, because they appreciate their own heroics. Gard also loves reminding me that there are mothers out there who need to work and somehow balance it with the Care Hours they have to keep, and the math doesn't work for them any better than it does for me. Anyway. Gard's helping me with it. Thank God for her.

I get it, I do—fertility crisis, survival of the species, "the most important job on earth has never been more important"—I get it I get it I get it. Still. I think about Mom sometimes.

Not that I'm going to do anything drastic, obviously, but I just mean, I think about what's changed and I understand a little better, now, why she wanted a way out. A lot of people did, you know. It wasn't just her.

Anyway. Sorry for rambling. I just got back from a Care Circle meeting and I'm in this crazy styley lake-view apartment complex for billionaires and I'm pregnant and lonely and about to lose everything I ever built for myself out of fucking nothing. But fuck, little brother, you're in an actual fucking *war*.

Sorry-not-sorry, you still have to read my pity-party messages because I got naturally pregnant and I am therefore the center of the universe. Or so I keep being told.

I bet you say this a lot, over there, but I really can't wait for this to be over. Except I'm not sure it'll ever be over. I think it's just starting. I bet you say that a lot, too.

BE GOOD.

F.

IN THE FIRST PLACE

He's in the dust, and the dust is in him: in his nostrils, in his eyelashes, in his ears, packed into every scrape and scratch, sifting down his ass crack. With his eyes closed, behind his helmet's screen, the sun filtering through the particles and the metal and the smoke in the air barely registers, a faint disk, years away. Much closer and brighter than the sun is the firefight, still happening all around him, trails of flame shoelacing above his head. But he's been overcome, overpowered, as has been happening to him more and more, and all he can do is lie here and try to breathe and fight off the thick horrible smell of flowers, flowers blooming in heat, flowers on fire.

His squad has been trying for three days to take a raider entrenchment, hidden but lethal, bristling with snipers' bullets. The raiders want to blow everything up, mow everything down, him included. Back home, New Cities people have started calling them terrorists. But to units like his—tasked with protecting the H2.0, and the railways that take it out and away—they're just raiders. The ones left behind when the western states collapsed, or the ones who stayed, for reasons of their own. Even twenty-plus years into the Wars, no one seems to know how many there are. They just keep coming back and coming back, and all there is to do is breathe the dust and fight them, keep the train moving, keep the engineered water flowing, up the coast and then across the plains to the New Cities in the Midwest. If the raiders want the water, they have to step through a firestorm to get at it.

His friend Wash is screaming into his face. "Don't you die, god-dammit!" In a few short weeks he'll find himself screaming the same thing at Wash, but Wash won't hear him, any more than he hears Wash now.

Because bizarrely, absurdly, horribly, this is when he gets a message from his sister. Right here, in the middle of a firefight.

They must have bandwidth of some kind—they found a way to hack a satellite or an abandoned tower and transmit a wearable signal for communications within the bunker. He wishes he had the where-withal to tell Wash as much, but his mouth is full of dust and flames and flowers and he cannot speak.

The signal is weak, so only part of the message comes through and he'll have to redownload it later, but there it is, swimming across his retina, the message from his sister, and by flicking his focal point to the filament-thin control menu hovering at the edge of his vision he can turn on the audio stream and hear her voice in his cochlear implant, too.

I guess it's time I told you. Gard told me to tell you.

"Don't you die on me! Don't you do it! Get up! Get up!"

Miracles.

"Hey, Wash. They're right underneath us."

FIVE

There are a lot of bad things about swimming back through a black-out into consciousness for the second time in one day. Here's the worst thing: This time it's not just Pop's cat watching me find the floor with my face.

There's a yelp of profanity—not mine—and a clatter of delicate silver tools. Part of me has landed on someone's shoe, and the foot is yanked swiftly away. I hear people shuffling over my head and around me. Then a tense silence.

Now that I've fallen, I don't plan to move ever again. My best option, as I see it, is to remain motionless facedown on the floor, onto which I seem to have rolled from the height of the reclining examination chair, some thirty inches. My head throbs freshly, and the painted concrete floor is cool under my brow. I have never wanted a drink more. That is saying something.

"Is he awake?"

"I don't think so. Jesus, what the hell is wrong with him?"

"We should find out soon enough. That VA doctor said he'd be here within thirty minutes. He's not far."

"I don't like this."

"I don't, either."

The nurse pauses delicately, then whispers, "Natalie. Did you *know* this Rafiq was military?"

Natalie's voice is all sharp edges. "Do you think I would have contacted him if I knew?"

They're quiet for a moment, but not long enough for me to figure out what that means.

"We shouldn't risk it. We have to move him."

"Are you suggesting we somehow cart this guy out through the waiting room and up the stairs? You and me?"

"Obviously that is the best possible solution for everyone involved, especially a room full of terrified pregnant women and new mothers," the nurse from reception deadpans. I hear Natalie snort. Then the two voices are quiet again, hushed into stillness by some involuntary movement I must have made, although I'm not aware of having done anything. I'm just trying to breathe as normally as a person can when he's got blood in his mouth and up his nose and can't turn his head because he doesn't want anyone to know he's conscious.

"What about the back offices," the nurse finally whispers.

"I don't know this Rafiq. And I don't know this one here, either. I don't really want either of them seeing any more of the facility than they need to," Natalie murmurs. But then, as if she's considering it: "How would we even get him there?"

"On a gurney."

"Wait." There's a tinny-sounding beep. Someone slides a screen off a countertop.

The door whishes open and footsteps pad out. The door shuts. Natalie clears her throat. We're alone in the small room.

"Mr. Quinn. Can you hear me?"

While I'm debating whether or how to respond, she continues in a brisk tone. "We've messaged Dr. Rafiq at the VA for you, and he's on his way in now. Do you hear me?" What I hear is her kneeling down near me, the soft creaks and clicks of her joints. She's a person who spends a lot of time on her feet. "It's going to be all right," she says quietly.

Behind us the door to the examination room is opened again and a lot of whishing happens at once: Natalie standing, someone entering, too many bodies in the room for its size, then the nurse saying "All right?" and Natalie saying "Thank you," and then dry hands that are sani-ed many, many times a day (Pop and Gard, at holidays, comparing hand lotions and unguents and cracked-skin relief for hours, *days*) sliding together to meet, shake, slip apart. Will I get to touch Natalie's hand again, ever? Would she be bothered? How much? I roll over halfway, prop myself up on an elbow, groan.

"This is our patient, I assume," an amused voice says. I crack one eye open to get a look at the guy. Pop's friend. Major Rafiq of the New Chicago Veteran's Administration Hospital, decorated combat veteran of the First Wars, total unknown quantity.

Bushy dark hair, dark skin, smooth face. Gold-rimmed glasses. A bit of a tubber. A smile to melt butter. In a better world this guy would have been in pediatrics instead of in war zones. He squats, rests elbows on meaty thighs. I am obliged to recall that I am lying on the floor in the presence of a superior officer, but I can't see what I can do about it at the moment.

"Major Rafiq, sir. Thanks for . . . seeing me. Sorry I dragged you away from your office."

"That's just what our friend here said when she called. I had to agree with her that the situation seemed to merit a house call, of a kind. *And* I have to agree with her that you seem"—he's laughing, and it's not a joy to see Natalie, over his shoulder, fixing her face with a tight, polite smile of agreement—"like you've wandered into the wrong office, Private."

I nod gamely, try to shift my weight so my ass is under me instead of wedged up against the examination chair. For a moment I have the luxury of thinking there's no way I can be more humiliated by myself, but then Rafiq swoops in and somehow gets his shoulder under my armpit and his arm around my back, and hauls me to a seated position in the patient's chair like I'm so much dead weight, which I suppose I am, and while I have to acknowledge what is obviously the training of a man who's lifted men off the ground in the field, it's still embarrassing.

"Thank you," I manage to say. Looking down at myself, I'm a nightmare. Blood down the front of my shirt, on my pants and hands. Blood must be smeared all over my face. "Would you mind if I clean up a bit?"

"Of course. Of course. Please." He steps back. We both look at

Natalie helplessly, and without a word she produces a pump dispenser of sanifoam and a wad of paper towels from the exam room cupboard and passes them to me. Her expression is carefully neutral, but again, I've got two older sisters, and I understand the magnitude of the effort it's costing her to keep from rolling her eyes.

I also notice that she's buttoned a white lab coat over her bloody scrubs. Where the coat's buttons meet in a V, just above the lapels, is a smear of darkening red. I left that there, somehow.

As I'm sitting in the chair ineffectively swabbing at myself, Rafiq says, "You know, son, I was going to call you myself today, at the risk of jumping the trigger. Your father is an old friend, as you know. He is concerned about you. He says you have been presenting some symptoms that are giving him cause to worry, although you haven't discussed them with him."

A wave of fatigue crashes into me and suddenly I'm so weary I can hardly keep my head up. "That's funny," I reply. "I was going to come visit *you* today."

"Isn't that good," Rafiq says gently. He glances at Natalie. "Nurse—"

"I'm not a nurse. I'm a Nurse Completionist." She corrects him politely, but she's clearly still on edge. "I'm afraid that as long as you're seeing patients in my clinic, Dr. Rafiq, someone on my staff will need to be present. I'm sure you understand."

He frowns just a bit but doesn't press. "Of course. I'm your guest." He turns back to me, and the Syrian Santa Claus has been replaced by a standard-issue VA doc. "Private Quinn. We're both guests here. Our time is short; someone out there may be waiting for this very room. Let's get down to the business of my visit. I'd like to examine you for signs of neurological and nerve damage."

"For a nosebleed?"

Rafiq levels a calm stare at me but doesn't dignify this with a response.

I swallow. "Sure. Fire away."

"Do you need a—" Natalie begins to ask.

"No need. I've brought my own tools." Rafiq produces a scanner and a reader from his breast pocket. His scanner's a black scope attached to a short, thick-handled stainless steel wand, about the size of a chubby, extended forefinger, with a two-inch square display panel that flips neatly out from the top of the metal handle. The reader's an older model—the ones we had in the military were about the size of a pack of playing cards, but Rafiq's is bigger, about five inches by four across, and half an inch thick. "I'm a little old school," he says apologetically. He smooths his reader over my wearable so that its surface can adhere to the wearable's panel in my skin, much as charged iron filings will clump together. It's the same unpleasant but essentially painless sensation that's familiar from every med reading I've ever had, but the larger surface area means more electromagnets, and I can feel my skin pulling a bit more than I really like. Meanwhile, Rafiq passes the scanner's scope over both my eyes, past both ears, under my nose, and behind my neck, at the base of my skull. The reader's tiny needles have taken their blood sample and directly downstreamed my med-status data by the time he's finished.

"Your nose and ears were bleeding. Do your tear ducts ever express blood or other fluids, not tears?"

I shift on the seat. "I think it's happened once or twice."

"From your hairline?"

"Maybe."

"Ears ringing?"

"More or less nonstop."

"Headaches?"

"Every day. Every hour."

"Appetite?"

"Pretty good. I haven't eaten yet today but usually—"

"Difficulty sleeping?"

"No," I say honestly.

"Hm." Rafiq nods, watching data points scroll across his display panel. "Your father tells me most nights you're drinking until you pass out."

It's impossible not to glance at Natalie. When I do I find she's watching me over Rafiq's shoulder. She gives me a small nod.

"Well. Engineered beer is cheaper than engineered water."

Rafiq chuckles, still reading. "You might be surprised how often I've heard that line, Private." He exhales through his nose, long and slow and luxurious, so you can hear all the little hairs inside each cavernous nostril whistling. It's a weirdly comforting sound. "Or you might not. Rashes?"

"No."

"No?" Rafiq looks up at me. "No redness or chapping on your hands, like between the fingers? How about around the eyes, the ears, the nose? Especially after they've been expressing? Beneath the testes? Roof of the mouth?"

Over his shoulder, Natalie is doing a good impersonation of someone who's not alarmed.

"Jesus, Doc. No. Thank God."

He smiles. "Glad we can rule that out." He leans forward, eyes glinting behind his glasses. "Any sensory issues? Trouble seeing, tasting, hearing, smelling?"

"That's— Yes."

"Unusual or overpowering sensations, sounds, smells?"

"Um."

"Why don't you describe it for me. What it's like." He points to my forehead. "In there."

I look to Natalie again, but she's busying herself with something on her handheld portal screen, frowning down at it in absorption as if she's not listening to every word. I'm not sure yet what to make of Pop's friend. I'm not sure how much to tell him.

"I often feel . . ." I say slowly, "as if my head is being squeezed off. Pressure, ringing, static, stuff like that. I smell—the same flower scent I used to smell in the Wars, when the H2.0 tankers would get breached. I can't see. Often. Like right now, all day, I can't really see—it's like looking through a porthole, gray fog to about here." I make a circle with my fingers, hold them over my left eye.

"Mmm." Rafiq nods, unimpressed.

I don't know why I feel like apologizing. Actually, I do. "I'm not complaining about it. I know guys who deal with a lot worse. I'm used to it; it's been going on for a long time."

"How long?"

"Since February. This year. I was, uh—" I can't see a way out of it, but I don't want to admit, with Natalie in the room, that I was on the ground when a boom went off. Especially not one I set myself.

"You were exposed to a neurochemical agent," Rafiq finishes. "I'm familiar with the kinds of side effects that present. I think I can even name, or guess, which one you encountered. But I'll bet you wish I wouldn't."

I risk another look at Natalie. She's watching me. Her eyes are bright and hard, and half-lidded, and her mouth is set. Neurochemicals are built into most of the triggers we used over there. *Nonlethal, we were told, but don't let yourself be caught out in one. Don't take your helmet off until the trigger's completed and you're well clear. For God's sake don't take your gloves off, don't handle anything or anyone or any pieces of anyone, and don't breathe it in.*

"Yeah," I croak. "I wish you wouldn't."

Rafiq gives me a long look, then nods. "I wish I had better news for you, son. But the symptoms are not going to stop. In fact, they will most likely progress, as I'm sure you've already seen. The kind of damage we're seeing, from that particular toxin, it follows a certain course. It might not kill you, but you'll probably wish it would. We *can*, however," he says, snapping his scanner's display panel shut with a brisk little click, "treat the symptoms pretty well. I brought you something. A sample." He reaches into his coat pocket, removes an air-compressor syringe, and smacks it down none too gently on the examination bench next to my leg, then without warning yanks his reader off my wearable. A few dozen tiny needles and a panel of powerful magnets disattach from my skin. I grunt and have to keep myself from clapping my hand protectively over my arm. The skin stings and sings—it's the kind of pain Gard used to call "spicy" when she was little. Skinned knees, scraped palms, she called them "spicy."

"Sorry, son. It's an old one. I find it's better if I just yank it off in one quick shot. You all right?"

"Yeah. I'm fine."

"'First do no harm,' yes?" He smiles oddly back at Natalie. "Hold out your other arm." I extend it, and he flips it over to expose the wrist.

From the corner of one eye, I see Natalie make a hesitant movement toward us, then check herself. Rafiq presses the tip of the compressor syringe to the skin of my inner wrist and jams the plunger button. There's a sound like a zipper. "There. You should be set for twenty-four hours, maybe thirty-six if you're not as far along as I'm afraid you are."

"What?" I stare at him. Far along? Even I know that's the kind of language you use for pregnant women, or people with something chronic, fatal. "What is it?"

"You should have asked before I administered it to you. Isn't that right?" Again Rafiq smiles over his shoulder at Natalie, who looks stricken. "Kidding. I'm kidding. It's a new kind of APC, what you get from your medical corpsman when you get banged up. Basically a supercharged serotonin uptake inhibitor laced with an NSAID. Antidepressant plus anti-inflammatory, and a bit of caffeine. You'll have fewer headaches and the ringing in your ears should stop. You want more, come see me. In *my* office. In fact, come see me anyway. I'll have my staff hold you a spot. Tomorrow morning. We should talk more about this, how we're going to treat you. I am not going," Rafiq says, leaning in toward me with a gentle smile, a smile of concern so fatherly it hurts to look at, "to let you go under. I see too many good men going under. I'm tired of it. It makes me want to quit my job. And then what would I do?" He stands up, starts packing.

"You'd probably play more hoops with my pop," I reply. I feel woozy, sleepy. My sight is clear, though. My ears aren't ringing.

Rafiq looks at me knowingly, merrily. "Tell me honestly, Private. Do I look like I ought to meet Captain Quinn on a basketball court? How are you getting home, by the way?"

"I'll manage," I say. I'm not sure I trust myself to stand up yet, but I hold out my hand and Rafiq clasps it, covers it, shakes. His hands are dry like lizards, like leather.

"Hm." Rafiq looks down at me, and there's a bit less affection in his laser beams than there is a certain quality of assessment. Whatever he's seeing of my current condition, even after whatever he just shot me full of, he's clearly unenthusiastic. He turns to Natalie. "Is there a place out of your way where he can rest until the medication takes effect?"

"I'm sure we can find something," Natalie says, likewise unenthu-siastic.

"Thank you, Nurse. I greatly appreciate it. This young man's father saved my life, too many times to count. More times than that, he saved my sanity. We were in the First Wars together, you know. I'm glad to have met his son at last. And, Nurse, I'm glad to have met you, too." Rafiq expands, beams at us both.

I clear my throat. "Well. Thank you, sir. Even if you're exaggerating what a pleasure it was to meet me, and I know you've got to be . . . I'm grateful. I'm really grateful."

"Come see me," he Santa Clauses at me one last time, then turns the charm back in Natalie's direction, where I'm not sure he encounters much to encourage it. "Judging by the crowd I saw in the waiting room when I came through, I'd say you must see an impressive number of patients for a facility this comfortable and intimate. How long have you been in this space?"

"About two years," Natalie replies, voice flat. Then, unprompted, she gives the same little speech she gave me. "We're a private clinic, but fully licensed. It's a safe place for hundreds of women who don't have many options."

"Small staff, I take it?"

"We maintain a flex staff that can rotate in as needed. Mostly Nurse Completionists like myself. Some specialists."

"I should imagine," Rafiq says neutrally, but I can see Natalie bristle.

"Every mother, every pregnancy, is unique. As you probably know. What's different about our service is that we find a way to get each woman what she needs, when she needs it. Our clients can do their en-tire Care journey with us, from prenatal to Care Standard maintenance counseling."

"You must have a waitlist a mile long."

"No waitlist. We see everyone who comes to us." She smiles slightly, but her pride is obvious. Getting to throw down to a VA doc, no less. In this moment, she might even be glad I blacked out in her office, just to give her the opportunity.

"And you perform Insemina, too?" Rafiq continues politely.

"Our clients don't tend to come from the background that can afford it. Most are natural pregnancies. Most, in fact, are unplanned."

"So most of your mothers are struggling to meet Care Standard."

"Yes," Natalie says, and even at a remove from the conversation I detect some frostbite.

"No judgment," Rafiq says, holding his hands up in surrender, a gesture Natalie seems to be able to elicit from better men than me.

"The math," Natalie puts in icily, "doesn't work. However a woman attempts it."

"Just so," Rafiq agrees. He does a little bow. "Thank you for your time. And my apologies."

"For what?"

"For emptying your waiting room as I came in. Most of your *clients*, as you say, up and left at the sight of me." He's halfway out the door. It's a hell of an exit line. Natalie looks ready to murder. Rafiq is brave enough to meet my eyes, anyway. "See you tomorrow, Private. Come early."

Then he's gone, and both Natalie and I find ourselves staring dumbly after him at the closed door. I couldn't move if I wanted to, which I do not. But Natalie seems caught in a moment's indecision.

She grabs the door handle. "Stay here," she tosses back over her shoulder as she's on the threshold, and adds, on second thought, "Please."

While she's away from me—either because she's hustling Rafiq out the door before he can ask any more questions, or confirming whether he has in fact scared off all her patients—I have a moment of quiet, and I use it to test myself out, my limbs, my senses, my head. All seem perceptibly improved. Except for my heart, which is thudding heavily but otherwise just doing its job. Sir, yes, sir. Sir, yes, sir.

The symptoms are not going to stop. . . . It follows a certain course.

What does this mean? Think. Think. Try to understand. Try to absorb what he meant. *If you're as far along as I'm afraid you are.* This message, at least, is not hieroglyphics. *It might not kill you but you'll probably wish it would.*

I'm twenty-four years old. Is this really happening? And if it is really happening, does that mean it's never going to stop?

I can't absorb it, somehow. It's as if the understanding only seeps in so far before encountering a hard place, and there's nowhere for the idea to go, nowhere for it to move except to spread out along the surface, infinitely wide and a millimeter deep.

But I'm better. I feel better, at least for the time being. My head isn't what you'd call clear, but I can see, my ears aren't aching, what pains I feel are for the most part related to falling off an examination bench onto my face. I'm better, and I take a shuddering, grateful breath. If I could distill half a particle of this gratitude and slip it into an envelope addressed to Major Rafiq, he would know his trip was worth whatever trouble it cost him, and Natalie, too.

The thought of being a regular in Rafiq's office, though—of having to shoot myself up daily with whatever was in that syringe. The thought of relying on the VA for daily keep-me-alive juice—God help me. No. That doesn't want to absorb, either.

I rub my eyes with the heels of my hands and wait for Natalie to come and tell me what to do, where to go. I understand now that I'm not going to leave this place any closer to knowing where Gard is, and that hollows me out.

What would Gard want me to do? She's seen clients in this very room, I'm sure. Some vapory version of her, the echo of her atoms, surrounds me as I sit here, my ass making an indentation in the paper that covers the exam chair. *Gard, I'm sorry I lost you.* I think it at her, at the ghost of her in the room.

"How are you feeling?" While I've been rubbing my eyes and listening to the blood rush in my ears, Natalie has reappeared in silence and is leaning her back against the closed exam room door.

"Better. I hate admitting it. But better."

"Good." There's some speculation in her eyes. She's watching me steadily.

"I'm really sorry about the inconvenience."

"Which one?" With an eyebrow.

"I would like to be able to say all of them." I'm just trying to show her I'm sincere. "But I'm not sorry I came here, Natalie. I have to try to find my sister, and it . . . it feels good seeing the place where she worked, at least, even if I'm not sure she would have wanted me here."

Natalie inhales, nods once. She's still watching me, and her head inclines to the left just slightly. Finally she says, "Do you understand what Dr. Rafiq just told you, Mr. Quinn?"

"I'm not sure I do," I admit.

She nods again, purses her lips like she's tasting something not quite ripe. "Well. How kind of him to leave it to someone else to explain." I'm not sure I want her to try, but before I can interrupt her, she looks up at the ceiling and tells it, "I don't think it's *my* responsibility. But because I—because Gard, if she knew—" She breaks off. When she looks at me, her eyes are glittering. "I really liked her, you know."

"I'm glad to hear that. She—"

"Did she know what you were doing in the Wars?" she demands abruptly. "Did she have any idea you were using biological weapons on people? Exposing yourself to that?"

Shame, when you've lived with it long enough, gets hard to recognize. Sometimes it looks like itself; sometimes it looks like a furious red ball; sometimes it looks more like a blank spot between your eyes. Sometimes it's just an everyday lead weight in your stomach. That's mostly what it is for me.

"Do you even know what those weapons *do* to people?"

"I don't. I never did."

"Well. You'll have to ask jolly old Dr. Rafiq," Natalie B. says venomously. She advances on me. "Your sister was a good person. Okay? She didn't always love what she had to do, but she knew that she was *helping* people who needed help, or *trying* to, the best way she or anybody else knew how. She was scared. We're all scared sometimes, but your sister—she—what we do here wasn't easy for her. Because she was good. She was *good*, in a system that is *bad*." Natalie bends closer, fixes me with a look of such hostility it's about all I can do not to lean away. "Bad for people, bad for women, bad for poor women especially. And you. You were over there. You stupid boy. You were over there unleashing something you didn't even understand, never even asking what or why or to whom or for whom—you—" She clenches her fists, and I understand suddenly that she wants to hit me.

"Do it. Go ahead. You want to. It's okay."

She does. It seems to settle her only a bit. In fact, it just seems to make her want to do it again. So she does. It's okay. It really is.

She takes a minute to collect herself and catch her breath. She's just pummeled me, but I'm not badly hurt. Still, the look of pity and scorn on her face curdles and scorches whatever's in me that I still associate with being a good man, a stand-up guy, strong in a corner. All of that, whatever of it I have left, means next to nothing to this woman. It's invisible to her, all because of what she knows I did.

"You're going to die. Okay? You didn't even know it until I just said it, I bet, but there it is. You're going to die. And that's the only reason I'm going to tell you this. It's all I can give you. And then I need you to get out of here and never come back. Okay?"

I think I manage to nod, but probably I'm just staring at her.

"If you want to know where your sister is, you should go home and ask your father."

She steps back. She opens the door. All I can do is go through it.

GARDNER QUINN
2556 ASHLAND NORTH, APT. B
NEW CHICAGO 0606030301
NEW STATES

PFC C. P. QUINN 2276766
MCC 167 1ST MAW
FPO NEW CHICAGO 06040309

September 29, 7:32 a.m.

Hey CQ,

Hope you're doing all right and taking care of yourself. I tried sending you some socks and some candy and some good sani, let me know if you got them.

I'm doing okay. I'm tired. I'll live. I used to be able to catch a few z's on the ride home in the morning, but lately I've been a little nervous about dropping off. Nobody's ever on my bus until we get well back into the rehabbed zones, but a couple of days ago I woke up on the bus, all drooly, you know, like *whuuuh*, and there was a drone, right there outside the bus window at my eye level. It was an unmarked drone, private. It just felt like the thing was *looking* at me, through the bus window, while I slept.

I know how it sounds: *Drones are following my bus home from work.* But when I say it out loud it sort of turns the corner back around into sane again, you know? What is sanity in a world like this anyway? Natalie says I shouldn't think about it so much. Carter, I'd love for you to meet her. She's the only sane person I know these days.

Things have gotten a little . . . weird. It's not just drones, though. I'm not sure—I don't know how much Fred has told you, or what she's told you. I don't know what's safe to tell you.

And honestly I don't want to get into too much detail right now because all of this might just get clipped anyway—I'm going to try to transmit it during peak hours, when there's less bandwidth for the censor filters, you know, just in case.

But I want to try to tell you something.

Where to start, though? Okay. Let's try this: So, you know how everybody knows the water is what caused the fertility crisis—even though it'll never be officially acknowledged—because if civilization's ever going to have a chance of rebounding from the fires and everything after, we need H2.0 to do it—but still, everybody *knows*? I mean, we knew it as *kids*, when it first started to come out that the birth rate was plummeting.

What's less well understood is why *some* women are still having unassisted pregnancies while *most* women aren't, even with Insemina. Right? A mystery. So. Who are they? Well, mostly they're women like the ones I see at my night job: young women who lived their whole lives on the fringes of the New Cities, most of them paying a third of their incomes for household H2.0 and not wasting a drop of what they did manage to get. Right? So sixteen- to eighteen-year-old women, who've just maybe *encountered* less H2.0 than women from families in the rehabbed zones. *Ingested* less. It's a theory, there's no science to back it up right now. Obviously.

So poor women pay too dearly for it to get much of it. And as a *reward* they're that much more likely to get pregnant in the middle of an infertility crisis, so they can be subject to a Care Standard they can't possibly hope to meet.

This, this is what I'm trying to tell you, what I'm getting at: Care Standard is . . . I've been doing Nurse Completionist work for, what, three years now, and I really think it's impossible. I know it's based on a lot of good ideas, about how babies should be protected at all costs, especially now, when people say we're all still at risk of dying out. But it's not possible.

I know you don't know how this works. But listen. Listen. If you don't clock all your Care Hours and meet your quota, then you're not meeting Care Standard. Your Care Hours quota ramps up pretty quickly for first trimester, then slows down a bit during the second, and then goes back up in third tri and stays high until the baby's born, at which point it tends to triple. And most women start with a deficit on their Care Hours because they don't know they're pregnant for at least two weeks, unless it's an Insemina pregnancy. If you work hard at it—quit your job right away, go to all your meetings, follow the diet religiously—you can usually make up most of the deficit by the end of the third trimester. But if you fall seriously behind, you can get into a situation where you have more Care Hours to log than there are hours in the day. Then DOH can start fining you actual money, and the fines compound very quickly. Which is when things get scary.

You can actually pay down Care Hours with money. But who has that much? Most women can only fulfill Care Hours with time—their own or a registered family member's. And the penalty system for not meeting Care Standard is based on fines. It's real money.

And after a while, it's more than money.

Why am I telling you all this? Listen. Carter, I think at least one of your sisters is in serious trouble.

When you hear from Fred, let me know.

Pop is . . . okay. He's not doing much, but I suppose he's earned some time to rest and reset. He asks about you all the time. I know Pop never messages anyone ever, not even you, and I know Fred's better about keeping in touch than me, but please know how much we all think about you and love you. I'm praying for you, although Pop wouldn't like to hear me say that. You think about what he's been through, you understand why he doesn't pray. But he believes in *you*, Carter, and I do, too.

I sometimes think it would be nice if I could be really religious again, like I was when I was a kid—do you remember? I got you into it right along with me. You were so cute when you would pray with me; you were just a little booger. But I could use it—sometimes I really could use it, the ability to pray to something and believe I was being heard. Sometimes you have to do things you never thought you'd have to do, and I think that's when you need your faith the most.

I wonder if you already know what I mean, little brother, without my having to explain. Atheists in foxholes, and so on. And you were always good at reading my mind.

Thinking about you and sending lots of love. And socks, I hope. Let me know if they get there. And let me know when you hear from Fred.

Love,
Gard

SIX

I'm not quite through the scrubby park where, a million years ago but somehow also just that morning, I left a half-finished can of beer in a sack under a bench, when I realize that I'm being followed.

The sun is already beginning to set, since it's late enough in December that we're approaching the shortest day of the year. It's still 70 degrees out at dusk. The wind has picked up, carrying bits of trash and empty plastic bottles to the fences, and carrying, too, the buzzing, insect-like sound of a drone. It's not zooming past me on some mysterious and uninteresting errand; it's hanging back and hovering high. I shouldn't be able to hear it, but the hot wind is at my back, bringing with it the purr of the drone's small whirring rotors.

My thoughts still aren't exactly what you'd call clear, but thanks to Rafiq's booster shot, my vision and my hearing are both crystal, better than they've been since my first year in the Wars. I keep moving, slower now, heading for the north edge of the park, where the scannerless gate lets onto the sidewalk. All is empty, all is quiet, except for the far-off echoes of the helicopters ferrying hydroengineers and city replanners and captains of industry over the lake to other New Cities. I don't know what it's like in those other places, but in New Chicago, drones are all just doing different versions of the same thing: carrying problems from place to place. The best you can do is ignore them.

Until one of them decides you're its special personal problem.

Normally I wouldn't care about being tailed by a drone. They're unbelievably stupid machines compared to a few others I've had to stand too close to. They navigate sensor to sensor, so whatever the nearest thing is that's putting off a signal, that's what they're attracted to, exactly like bugs around a light bulb, seeking their next input. Right now, my wearable's signal is probably the closest thing there is to a sensor for a few city blocks. It's happened to me before; I've been trailed by a lost or lonely or codeless drone for a block or two, while wandering some of the uglier parts of town, searching for someplace scary enough to suit my worst imaginings of what might have happened to Gard.

You should go home and ask your father.

The buzzing follows me through the park, off the path and onto the sidewalk. There's no one else around. On the street, I turn around and look for it. Takes me a few seconds, but then there it is, hanging at rooftop level in the slanting light of the end of day. Waiting and watching.

Your average City drone, the type that messengers digital and actual flotsam around the city, looks sort of like a plastic clown head wearing snowshoes. City drones are not elegant. They're ridiculous, in fact, and I've always thought that it's exactly this doofiness that keeps people from swatting them down as they putter past in their designated lanes on streets and sidewalks—they're too inept to attack; there's no satisfaction in it. Even though a drone is almost always just about to hit you in the face when you stop at a crosswalk in certain parts of the city. It's like sharing a town with a bunch of half-sentient softballs.

But this drone looks like Security, not City. Security drones are black or gray, rather than white or yellow, and the one that's staring me down now is dark in color, hovering twenty feet overhead like a malicious little moon. At this distance it's a bit hard to tell, but the twin domes on top are the giveaways: Security drones have blue and red lights like an ambulance. The lights on this one aren't flashing—yet—but it's impossible not to notice that they're positioned to look a bit like mouse ears. Drones are just so inherently, inescapably dorky that they can't even design a Security drone that looks intimidating. Even though I don't like the way it seems to be waiting for my next move, it's impossible to be afraid.

And anyway, this thing can't be hunting me. Who the fuck am I? I'm no one. I'm just a vet full of weird drugs, a guy with sore feet and a sore arm who needs a beer and something to eat. *Go home, drone, you're drunk. Or else I'm not drunk enough.* But as I'm heading toward the corner, I hear the drone's tiny rotors shift to pick up after me.

I figure I'll shake it at the stop sign—there's a sensor in most stop signs, whether the intersection sees a lot of traffic or not. If the drone isn't really following me, if it's just momentarily codeless the way I think it is, it'll pick up a fresh signal at the intersection and reset, scoot off, and leave me be.

Then it occurs to me: Regardless of whether the thing really is following me personally, it must have picked up my trail almost as soon as I left Natalie and Gard's clinic. And for all Natalie's noise about *private but perfectly legal*, they're operating off the sensor grid at least one story underground, in an unmarked building in an otherwise deserted, un-rehabbed part of town. Whatever it is they're offering there—and I'm still not sure I understand what that is, or even want to—their exact location is obviously supposed to be a secret. All those women I saw there, everyone who found that place, had to have been referred by a friend, or at least by someone who knew where to go. *Women who don't have many options*, as Natalie B. put it.

And then I crashed the gate with my lost-sheep act, and brought Rafiq crashing in after me.

And now this thing.

I stop just short of the intersection.

What I'd really like to do is just take the thing down.

It wouldn't take much. I could chuck a brick at one of its rotors and knock the thing off course, make it crash. Drone interference may be against the law, but it happens all the time. More commonly with City drones than Security, though. Security drones are lightly weaponized. They're dumb, but smart people know better than to fuck with them.

I never said I was smart.

I backtrack down the block, toward the park gate and the drone, which hangs, awaiting a tug from an invisible hand. I slip back into the park, where the gathering darkness tucks me in. No lamps here, no streetlights. No artificial trees, either, of course, so there's not much cover, but I figure I'll find what I need more easily in here than out on the street, and it turns out I'm right: a broken piece of concrete curbing, right there along the path. Fits neatly in the hand. Now I speed up a tick.

The drone hasn't lingered long at the park gate. It's looking for me, taking its time, swinging low in wide arcs over either side of the path. Drones aren't what you'd call strategic planners. Not too difficult to pull ahead, out of range, although my torn-up feet are protesting all the sudden activity.

My good old bench. You're not much for cover, but you'll do.

Goddamn. The sack with the can inside it is still there, right under the seat where I left it. I'm actually reaching for it when I remember that no, not even I drink flat, hot beer.

Just wait here, in a balanced crouch, one hand on the back of the bench, the other hand wrapped around the chunk of concrete. Just wait, be still.

It's scooting closer now, low and buzzing, a dry insect, too undeveloped for the concept of moral action to apply. As it approaches my hideout behind the park bench, I count down from three, cup the concrete in my right hand, then stand while swinging my arm upward and overhead, putting my force and my weight underneath it, swift and silent just like I've been trained to do, keeping my eyes on the target. Underhand overhead lob, heave-ho off she goes.

Easy squeezy. Like a trigger.

The crunch is louder than I expected. The drone's flashers go on immediately, along with a recorded alert message (*Tampering with or otherwise disabling a Security device is a crime punishable by law*) that broadcasts through three repetitions at a steadily increasing volume (*CRIME PUNISHABLE BY LAW*) before the badly hobbled machine veers off, looking like a disoriented animal, something small that's been kicked too hard. Flashing and blaring and impossible not to despise, the drone starts a precarious descent to the ground, hits the rubberized surface, bounces and skids, lies inert, flashing in silence. Time to move.

And then I'm at my bus stop, ten blocks to the north and another five east, waiting alone for a bus that won't be coming anytime soon, ass painfully flattened by the half hour I've already spent perched on a narrow metal ledge trying to pass for a bus shelter bench, flicking through a few ads on my wearable, not thinking not thinking not thinking and sipping a fresh cold can-in-a-sack (bought at the corner convenience store across the street that's just closed up for the night), when Security finally finds me.

A pale gray cruiser rolls up and parks at the curb, right in front of the bus shelter. The driver stays in the car, the other Security officer climbs out. He's a well-built white guy, a comfortable twenty pounds and about ten or fifteen years on me. His eyes are close-set; his nose is gigantic. No one could call him handsome, even if he didn't look like he just came from a bar fight.

"Private Carter Quinn?"

"Sir." I nod, put the beer sack down on the ledge next to my thigh, put my hands flat on my legs where he can see them.

"At ease, young man. That's all right, isn't it?" The officer gives me a grin, which has the disturbing effect of splitting his face into two hostile zones: up north, two tiny glittering eyes flank a nose like a clenched fist; to the south, a yellowed crag.

"Sure. That's all right."

He glances at his scanner, a black metal rod about the length of his palm, pulsing softly with information ingested and displayed. He's already got almost everything about me there is to know in his hand.

"You were a long time over there, Private. Look at that service record." He shakes his head in admiration. "Wish I'd gotten to go myself. You young guys get all the good toys." Unlike everyone else in the New Cities, there are some Security guys who really seem to worship war vets. They get all wistful imagining the weapons. I've never seriously worried about getting caught by Security for anything—this isn't the first time I've *tampered with or disabled*—because Security looks right past vets like me. And any small act of vandalism I or anyone else might commit—against, say, a drone or a scanner or a not-bird—can't help but seem like an irrelevance. Security through obscurity. All the data generated by our daily movements, the file-scrubbing and the jaywalking, all of it collected and surrendered, all those feeds pouring in from sensors and wearables and drones and satellites, all of it laying bare every bad move and misdemeanor committed every day within the shrinking city we've all agreed to call New Chicago, after the real Chicago, the one where there was real water in the toilets and a real lake on the horizon and crying babies and crowded kindergarten classrooms and information privacy and cheeseburgers. Even if Security was twenty times the size, it couldn't possibly act on half of what the data shows them about this city, what's really happening here, what we're all really doing. A lot of criminal acts without an immediately recognizable data trail—vandalism, for example—get ignored. Not for nothing do the old guys call it Job Security. And when Gard vanished, of course it took them no time at all to declare my sister not worth the trouble to look for, to put her in a file and forget about her.

"It was something, all right," I agree. "Can I help you, Officer?"

"I wonder if you can, son. I have you in this area most of the day today, is that right? Down in the old park a few blocks that way?" His eyes are concerned; his tone is sympathetic. He glances at my beer.

"Nowhere else to go. Sometimes I like to just get away, sit someplace quiet." I shrug. I am harmless. "I like that little park. Hardly ever anybody there. I've gone a few times. Just sat and . . ." I trail off, give another little shrug.

Security nods. "I had a . . ." He clears his throat explosively. "I had a son in the National Guard. Over there."

"I'm sorry, sir."

He nods again. After a long pause, he adds, "I like to think that if he'd made it back, he would have made something of his life. Used his service as a way to elevate himself. Not been one of these guys who can't reintegrate into the social fabric. Know what I mean, Private?"

I keep my gaze nice and low and level. Keep my breathing nice and low and level, too. "I do."

"I bet you do," he sneers.

Of course I would get tailed by the one Security officer in all of New Chicago who doesn't have such a hard-on for war stories that he'll look the other way if I tell him about getting to trigger off a few H2.0 raiders. This could go badly if I'm not careful. Suddenly I have to wonder why I don't feel worse, why I'm not galloping into black stars and sick flowery smells and jitters. It's either Rafiq's drugs or the beer. And while probably anyone would have to consider engineered beer a miracle of modern food science, I know its limits.

Security puts a boot up on the bench next to me and leans over his knee, lets his hands dangle down between his thighs, very friendly. "So, Private. You ever see anything interesting in your little park, while you're sitting around getting drunk in public?"

"I'm not getting drunk, sir. And no, I don't really see much of anything there."

" 'Not getting drunk, sir'? I wonder what your blood alcohol shows." From his friendly-neighbor position, he hardly needs to flick his wrist to scan me. "Well, what do you know." I don't have to look up at him to know that he's reading my med status. "Looks like you're telling the truth. Congratulations, Private. You won't be getting arrested today . . . *If* . . ."

I let that *if* hang. For a while. Not too long. But pretty fucking close to too long. "If what, sir? I'm not sure what I've done wrong exactly."

"I'm not sure what you've done wrong exactly, either!" Security chuckles. "All I know is, I've got a drone in the trunk of my cruiser that shows signs of having been bashed up good with a rock or something. And not just knocked down, either—the camera processor is smashed all to shit, and it's missing all its recent data. So no accident. Someone knocked the thing down and then gave it a goddamn lobotomy. And just guess, Private, where we found it."

"I have no idea, sir."

"Come on. Don't you want to guess?"

"I couldn't even begin to guess."

"Come on, Private! Use that thick battle helmet you got there." He raps me on the top of the head with his knuckles.

I stand up. Even I know it's not my best idea.

It's not going to be a fight. I've amazed even myself at how quickly I've let my combat conditioning deteriorate, but I know better than to hit back when he delivers an elbow to my side hard enough to break ribs. He's got the weight advantage, and he's wrapped his other hand around the fist of his jabbing arm to drive the elbow back in, again, again. Even this, somehow, is better than being knuckleheaded. Better to be forcibly restrained than to sit on a bench being made to look like a chump.

While I'm doubled over: Elbow to the back, right between the shoulder blades. Down I go.

Of course, I reflect, as my chin hits the sidewalk and my teeth snap together, this is exactly what he was after all along.

He's yanking my arms behind my back and slapping on restraints.

The thing is, I feel fine—I feel better than fine. I can see perfectly, there's no horrible scent stuck in my craw, no stars crowding the space between my eyes, no static or shrieking hiss in my ears.

Which explains, I suppose, why I can still hear him talking. Incredibly, the whole time he's elbow-jabbing me—and, ah, there it is, the first kick, right above my hip as I'm lying facedown on the sidewalk, and it won't be the last—he's *lecturing* me, about, of all things, what's wrong with my generation: "—the biggest problem you kids these days have isn't quote-unquote Security brutality, and it isn't the Marriage Protection Laws, and it isn't even the goddamn Wars, although you all just *loooove* to whine and make your excuses. You know what your biggest problem is?" He drags me up onto the sidewalk, gets a knee under my belly. "You're a bunch of entitled brats who don't even know how much we've already lost, and you're too self-centered to pick up your nads and try to do something about it. Your generation was supposed to have *ended* the Wars by now! You've got the greatest combat weapons technology humankind has ever devised over there, and you *still* can't contain those raider terrorists so we can deliver enough engineered water to sustain what's left of our cities!" A body slam against the side of the shelter. "Oh, but don't worry, it's not like your mothers and fathers and sisters and grandparents are *depending* on you!" Elbow jab to the small of the back. "No, you know what? You should come on back home. Mope around, process your combat trauma and your PTSD. Sit on street corners drunk, like a bunch of twats, instead of staying on the line and defending your post. We don't exactly have an *endless* supply of able-bodied men anymore, *in case you hadn't noticed, dipshit.*" Another stomach jab. "But don't worry—when you and your generation of sad-sack clowns get tired of fighting to preserve what's left of our quality of life, guys like me will *rise up.*" Assorted plain-vanilla jabs to the face and ribs here. He seems to favor coming in from the right. "That's right, us older guys—the ones who've been patrolling the streets and protecting your families while you've been over there wasting triggers on desert rats. Us guys, the ones who've devoted our whole *lives* to protecting what's left of these sinking cities, we're gonna rise up and raise hell. I don't even care if it's a draft by then—let 'em come and draft me! I say, please, let me take a post. Give me a weapon and let me defend my country and my people. Let me show you how a real man does it. And you know what, son? The Wars will be over in six months. You mark my words. Bring a force of a couple thousand New Cities Security in to replace you sad-sack depressed entitled little shits, and we will Get. It. Done. We will destroy anything or anybody who threatens our survival."

He's dragged me to a seated position by now, my head against the bus shelter ledge. Just for a finale, he knees me in the side of the face. Now he's panting, looking down at his scanner. "So, Private Sad Sack. Just for listening to the truth for a few minutes, you're getting off easy tonight. Right before our little talk, I fined you fifteen thousand dollars for damaging Security property, plus five thousand dollars for public intoxication, since I can adjust your blood-alcohol levels to show whatever I want—eh? See there? That's all it takes, a flick of my finger and I can keep you in debt for the rest of your sad little life."

"Thank you, sir," I say. It's all I can do not to laugh, actually. I can't help it. I just cannot believe how good I feel right now. I feel like a normal healthy guy who's had the crap beat out of him by Security. I want someone to put a weapon in my hands again.

"You're welcome." He's quiet for a moment, frowning at something on the scanner. "Well, look at this shit."

I let my head hang. My shoulders are shaking with laughter. I can't help myself. I know I shouldn't. But I'm laughing. I can't look up—better to let him think I'm down here sobbing in humiliation. The guy would probably only love to concuss me if I gave him a reason.

"Your fine's already been paid. Just like that. I'll be damned." He brings the black screen of his scanner closer to his face and squints. I'd love to catch a glimpse of whatever he's looking at, but my eyes are starting to swell shut. "Walker. Your guardian angel's name is Walker. I'll be shucked and fucked." I can hear him breathe in heavy through his nose. He doesn't like his situation.

"What did you say *your* name was, Officer?"

"You don't need to know my name."

"I'd just like to know who it was that gave me my first real lesson in the truth." I tilt my head up to treat him to a bloody smile. He's looking down on me, and in his expression there's contempt battling it out with worry for himself. Walker is a name his commissioner won't like seeing on his report, I guess. My future brother-in-law, good old Kenneth Walker of Lake Rise 8, has his uses, will you look at that.

Maybe it's the drugs, the beating, the blood rush, who knows, but I really can't help it, I'm laughing hard now.

"The fuck are you laughing at, Private?"

"Nothing. It's just . . . There's no way you've got a son in the National Guard."

His face contorts into a snarl.

"I mean, you're older'n me, but you're not my pop's age. *Nobody* was having kids by the time you were old enough to start a family."

"Fuck you, Private."

"Even if you had a boy, right now he'd be, what—fifteen? Even if your wife was unlucky enough to beat the odds?"

He grabs a fistful of my hair, slams my head back against the bus shelter bench, and that's about it for me for a while.

IN THE FIRST PLACE

They've been under the dust for a few days now, and everyone's going a little crazy but doing their best not to show it. There's nothing to do but wait it out: not even the scavengers mobilize during storms like this, so there's nothing to trigger at, nothing to scout for, nothing but howls and grit and a threatening red presence edging its way in through every crease, creating a powdery fog even in the air inside the base, which is really nothing more than a series of interconnected tents and huts. Everyone's got a chesty cough; everyone's lungs ache; everyone's got their face masks on unless they've already been diagnosed with something and there's nothing left to prove. No one's eaten in a day or so. You can't open a packet without the dust getting in it.

Mostly the guys are rereading and replaying old messages. It's what they do when the storms close in. Nothing new transmits cleanly through this shit. And it beats peering through the dust, thinking about what it's probably doing to your lungs. Everybody knows the dust is mostly metal and plastic, ground down to infinitesimal, tissue-annihilating particles. There's a lot that it's better not to know.

What he wants to know most he will never know anyway.

He's going over his favorite message from Gard, the one where she's laughing and laughing and laughing. She's tickled herself with a joke she couldn't tell anyone else but him and Fred, and she can't help herself; she's laughing her head off, laughing like a loon. He loves it.

When he's finished with his favorite messages of Gard's, he calls up his favorites from Fred. The one he half downloaded in the firefight, the one where she's telling him she's going to be a mother, as only Fred would do it. *I guess it's time I told you. Can you fucking believe it?* And, later, the one where she's trying, trying the hardest way, to understand *their* mother. *I understand a little better, now, why she wanted a way out. A lot of people did, you know. It wasn't just her.*

A way out. Well. Don't we all want that.

What he wants to know is why he's here.

How did he end up here.

Whose fault is it. No, that's not right. It's not that he wants to blame anyone, he knows exactly whose fault it is. But what he wants to know is, why did he do it, why did he take the first step in the sequence of steps that landed him, ultimately, here, behind the lines of abandonment, within the First Place, unsafe in ways he'd never seriously contemplated, desperate to do anything but be here, coated in a storm made of death, sheltering in a place built on death, a million deaths, tens of millions of deaths. Everyone who used to live here is dead or on the other side, the side that's trying to kill him. During the First Wars, his father fought to save these people, as many of them as could or would be saved.

But the men he lives with and loves and relies on, they're all fighting in the Second Wars, just like him. These are the wars everybody's pretty sure will never actually end. He will have to fight the left-behind people, and go on fighting them. For reasons he can't remember. For made-up water. For a fiction. For the capsules shimmering past them in the cloud, always moving, even when they're not.

FREDERICKA QUINN
135 PAULINA NORTH, #4B
NEW CHICAGO 0606030301
NEW STATES

PFC C. P. QUINN 2276766
MCC 167 1ST MAW
FPO NEW CHICAGO 06040309

September 19, 8:22 p.m.

Hi, CQ,

I guess it's time I told you. Gard told me to tell you. She's always been bossy.

I'm going to have a baby. I'm due in early January. I'm not going to find out whether it's a boy or a girl. Or maybe I will. I still don't know. I was waiting until it was safe to tell people, or at least until it seemed like a real thing that might really happen. I had a few complications. But they went away, or I guess just became less something to freak out about.

Can you fucking believe it?

It's all a little weird. As you can probably imagine. I'm showing at this point. People stare. It's hard to explain.

You're probably still just trying to process this, so feel free to take a couple of deep breaths or whatever before the rest. God knows I needed to take a few fucking deep breaths when I found out.

Everything's okay, right now anyway. I've had my tests and I'm in touch with the father, and he's going to do the right thing, whether I want him to or not. I met his mom and dad this week. It wasn't Insemina; it just happened. I don't know why that's sort of embarrassing to admit. Everybody keeps telling me it's a miracle.

Does it feel like a miracle? Let me tell you how a miracle feels. I seem to have entered a festive stage where the pace of change has accelerated. Like up until now, things were changing, but so gradually and gently that by the time I noticed, I was already used to it, whatever it was—better skin, some dryness on my legs and hands, a small backache.

Now, though, I seem to have hit some kind of midpoint milestone, where every day is bringing something new and freaky. Also, something seems to be standing on my pelvic bone. Also, every time I stand up or bend over, I can't help but make a small weird noise. I can't imagine what I'm going to look like when I get to be thirty-eight weeks. I'm going to be tremendous.

This might all be a little too much for you, little brother, but to be honest, I've got to find someone to talk to who's not in my Care Circle, because they're all just so weepy and earnest, my God. Or who's not a Completionist like Gard—nothing you can tell her surprises her. I could have a fucking horn coming out of my belly and she'd just tell me about some woman she saw at her clinic once who had two horns.

It's hard to explain what a surprise this all was—although, I mean, I'm sure you can imagine. Who expects to *actually* get pregnant and have a baby these days? Without Insemina? I didn't. I really didn't.

On the one hand, it feels like I've been chosen, for a prize or something. On the other hand, it feels sort of unfair. I can't say this to many people. But I'm not sure I—I mean, I keep imagining my old life, the one I'm not going to have now, continuing, just without me, in some other place.

I'm all over the place. I should just stop here and hit send. Here's what I was doing while I was dictating this message, just so you can picture it: I was standing by a window, moody and making an ass of myself, rubbing my fucking pregnant stretched-out stomach. There. That's what pregnant women do. In case you were wondering.

We stand by windows and space out and talk a mile of nonsense to people who can't possibly—who might have been *shot at* that day, Jesus, Carter, I'm sorry. Forget 90 percent of this message. I don't know. [*unintelligible*] Just remember the part where I told you to be good and stay good.

Fred

SEVEN

And now I'm coming to for the third time in one day, this time because someone's standing over my head, shouting hoarsely: *"Shut up shut up SHUT UP!"*

That's not the only sound. There's also a blaring, ongoing horn, and a public safety message repeating itself at an earth-shuddering volume: *Disabling or impeding the progress of a public autobus is a crime punishable by law. Please step aside. Disabling or impeding the progress of a public autobus is a crime punishable by law. Please step aside.*

I am lying in the street, directly in the path of the bus, which like all buses in the New Cities is driverless, and which must have stopped for my signal and was unable to keep moving because I was lying, inert, in front of its wheels. But now someone is standing over me, trying to lift me by my shoulders. It's Fred, as I can tell from her currently-in-progress argument with the driverless (and probably also passengerless) autobus. The thickness of the profanity she's laying out is impressive, even for her.

"I am *moving* this piece of colorful shit as fast as I *fucking can* so shut up shut UP! I am fucking *EIGHT FUCKING MONTHS PREGNANT JESUS FUCKING CHRIST*—"

"Wait, Fred—" I mumble, nowhere near loud enough.

"You are a *bus*! You are a *public utility*! Shut the FUCK UP!"

"Fred. Fred. You're going to hurt yourself, stop—stop it . . ." I manage to push myself up on an elbow, but find I can't open my eyes more than a slit, because they've both swollen shut. "You're going to hurt the *bus*. Fred. Stop."

"And *you!*" Fred, behind me now that I'm partly sitting up, gets a knee wedged behind one of my shoulder blades and pushes at me with it, in an attempt to force me forward, up and out of the street, making horrible bellowing sounds as she does so. "*Oarrrrrgh! Ragaahhh! Move*, you crapfuck! This bus is going to keep freaking out at us until you get out of its fucking way, so *move*, dammit, *move oarrrrRRRRRRGH!*"

Somehow, via a combination of propulsive kneeings from Fred and my attempts to drag myself along, like Pop's half-feral cat wiping its own ass on the rug, I get myself back onto the sidewalk, where I sit, head and hands hanging down between my knees, and try to catch my breath. The autobus message and horn alarm both stop abruptly, mid-blare, and with a grate and a hiss the thing moves on down the road. I am wheezing audibly, sore all over, tasting blood, nose and eyes and rib cage throbbing, but I still feel good. I feel *good*. For the second time that day, I want a weapon. And a drink.

"What in the sweet barbecued fuck happened to *you*?" Fred demands.

She is standing over me on the sidewalk. I try to look up at her, but the streetlight is behind her and she's tall and all I can make out is her belly, in an expensive-looking maternity shirt. Her shoes, though, I can see clearly, since they're closer to my level and it's easier to look down than up with my eyes swollen almost shut. Ankle boots. Also expensive-looking. She looks well cared for. It could just be an effect of the streetlight, but she is actually glowing, and again I'm reminded of a space princess, descended to a lesser plane to attend this world's parties and fuckups.

"I thought you knew what happened to me." I swallow a chunk of something thick and metallic-tasting—a blood-soaked globber. "I'll have to thank Ken when I see him at the wedding this weekend."

"You," Fred says distinctly from over my head, "are the most expensive fucking idiot in New Chicago. You think Ken knows fuck all about this? And don't even *talk* to me"—here she pushes at my head impatiently with one hand—"about the fucking wedding because I'm going to die of fucking apoplectic rage before it even *fucking happens.* What were you *even thinking*?"

"Fred, please. Give me a second here."

"Sure. Oh, sure. Take all the time you need," she drawls. "And whenever your sorry pile can get up and walk, my car is parked across the street, and I'll be waiting *inside* it, because it's air-conditioned in there, and I am sweating like a medieval garbage picker, thanks to you, because I've been kneeling here in the *street* for the last twenty minutes trying to get you to wake up before an autobus ran over your stupid fucking melon. And you saw," she tosses back over her shoulder, "how well *that* went."

As her car door slams I take a quick physical inventory with my fingertips. Nose bleeding, swollen, but not broken. Ribs aching, but none of the sharp pain that comes with a break. Wrists rubbed a bit raw by the restraints, which Security must have removed before getting back into his cruiser and tossing me unconscious and bleeding into the road in front of a bus stop. My face feels worse than my ribs; I might have a bruised cheekbone. Anyone in my position would hate to admit it, but Security knew was he was doing. No lasting damage, but plenty of hurt. Gentle pressure, relentlessly applied.

Can I get up? Sure. Sure I can.

It might take a few tries.

But sure. Here, look.

Now I'm holding my left side and shuffling, a zombie, making my way to Fred's sleek driverless electric sedan, which I can hear more than I can see, its murmuring idle the exhalation of a beautiful machine. As I'm making my way to her I'm trying to figure out how much I can tell her, what I can and cannot say. I have about twelve slow, side-clutching steps to decide, for example, whether to tell my sister that I may have just been diagnosed with some kind of degenerative and apparently fatal condition caused by biological weaponry I deployed against a whole host of desperate, stupid people for about three years. That despite harassing all her former coworkers, I'm still no closer to finding our sister, Gardner. That I've been told, by someone I trust (although I'm not sure why, because she's clearly terrified of me), that I need to ask our father what he had to do with Gard's disappearance. And that I'm afraid to do it. I'm more afraid than I've been of anything.

Opening Fred's elegant car door, falling into the interior onto a seat that is suede-like—no, trusting-baby-animal-like—in its soft, scented luxury, I start with what's most likely to piss her off, because I'm her kid brother.

"I don't think I can get my suit back from the cleaner's in time for this Friday night. Sorry."

"Fuck your sorry. I'll break into the goddamn cleaner's myself if I have to." Fred looks up at me from her wearable. "Jesus, Carter." Her face, dear and sharp and beloved, alight in the glow of the car's dashboard controls, is doing something strange. If for the last twenty or so years of my life she hadn't been teaching me better than to believe it, I'd think she was almost about to cry. "Look at you. Look at your face."

"I can't look at my face. It is a physical impossibility. You got a tissue or something?" I settle against the seat back, carefully, carefully. The upholstery is plush, calming, accepting my weight. The machine curls around me. I'm surrounded by an almost unbearably exquisite sense of peace, or money.

"What, all women carry tissues around? It's our *job* to carry tissues around in case we see a guy who needs his nose or his ass wiped?" But Fred is digging in her bag, a bag so supple and tasteful I probably wouldn't mind carrying it myself, if I had anything to put in it. "I *never* have fucking tissues. Would you look at this?" She pulls out a plastic-wrapped packet and stares at it like she's just found a human head in her bag. "Someone must have put that in there."

"Thank you." I take them from her, clumsily unwrap the delicate things. My fingers have never seemed so freakishly huge as in my sister's car. I'm anxious about bleeding on something in here.

"Oh, *now* he's thanking me."

I dab at my stinging lip. "I mean it. Thank you. Not just for the tissues."

"Fifteen thousand dollars for disabling a Security drone. Fif. Teen. Thousand. Dollars. I would laugh if I didn't think you'd actually join in, you fucker." Fred sighs, reflexively looks at her wearable, but it's clear she's not really seeing anything there. Sourly she intones, "If Ken Walker could legally call this whole thing off he probably would, and I wouldn't blame him. You have no fucking idea what I'm going to have to do to make up for this."

The air conditioning is delicious. I can't feel my face. It's for the best. "I'm sorry, Fred. It probably sounds hard to believe, but I had to do it. I couldn't have that thing tailing me. "

Fred still doesn't look at me. "I know where you were," she says flatly. She's quiet for a moment, long enough for me to notice how tired she looks. Otherwise flawless, of course, but tired. She adds, "I suppose I even know why you think you had to do what you did. You found out that place is a secret. Didn't you? Gard's clinic, all the stuff that happens there, that's some back-alley, top secret, black-market shit. Am I right?"

I don't like the jealous bitterness in her voice. And I don't know how to answer her anyway. "Can you give me a ride back to Pop's house?"

"What do you think I'm here for, fartfucker? I could have just left you in the road; it's not like I *wanted* to see you after paying your gigantic fucking fine."

"Thanks. Again. Seriously. What made you come?"

"Your med status. And the fact that your geo status didn't change for like an hour. You were obviously unconscious. And your autobus wasn't gonna come for, like, *years*." Fred swipes a control in the dash and the autocar glides away from the curb and begins to shush us back toward home, toward the parts of town where people still live. I can admit I'm relieved. I've spent enough time out in the unrehabbed blocks for a day. "So you're welcome."

Fred doesn't often make me feel ashamed—I usually try to be the best version of myself that I can be when I'm around her, even if that's not saying much. My sisters both have that effect on me. I admire them, I want to live up to them: Fred, carrying all our family bullshit on her shoulders and trying to sort it out and make it right, and Gard, carrying the rest of the whole messed-up unfixable world's. I'm ashamed now, though. I can dimly imagine what I must look like to her.

"I'm sorry, Fred. I really sincerely am. I'm sorry about the money, and I'll try to pay you back—no, listen, I will. And I'm really sorry about the party, for missing half of it, and not getting to meet Ken. And for hitting on your party planner. I think she liked me. But I'm sorry. I'm sorry I've been such a fuckup since I got back."

She shakes her head. The bit about Sophie made her laugh, and there's still the slightest vapor trail of a smile across her face, but it's already vanishing into the slipstream that's following behind her as she's pulling away into her own future, too fast. Here inside the car, her belly looks huger and more uncomfortable than ever. As usual, it's hard for me to remember there's a real about-to-be-a-person-if-all-goes-well inside there. The belly. The belly of the Fredbeast.

"You know, baby brother, I'm going to tell you something. You might not believe this, but it's the truth: I don't give a shit. I don't give a shit about any of it." Fred shifts in her seat, swallows a burp. "Fucking heartburn."

"I'm sorry anyway." I lean one swollen eye against the cool passenger window glass.

"You know where I came from today? Just now?"

"Where."

"My final meeting with my final client. From my practice. I sold it to a shell investment company. I made a fucking killing on it, but then I had to do all these handoff meetings for the clients whose platforms we built up and ran. Today was my last one. So now I've been *set free*. Officially. I packed up my office. The contract's executed. I have no business anymore."

"Oh. Congratulations? That's good?"

"I guess? I don't know. It doesn't feel so good." She sniffs, looks out the window at all the ugliness crawling past outside. I'm not sure she even knows what she's looking at. Fred in the cocoon. A shell is where she seems most at home, really. The inside of a well-constructed thing, that's Fred's natural habitat. "I loved working. Or I mean, I don't *love* working—who does?—but I loved making *money*. I loved helping with your college and Gard's nursing school. I did. I loved showing up at Christmas with presents for everybody. I loved my place I just moved out of; I loved my office and my freelancers. I even used to love coding, although now not so much, I don't have the energy for the late nights anymore. I'm not sure I even have the skills after being management for so long." Fred drums her fingers on her knee, watches the streets unspooling on the other side of the windshield. We're in a marginally nicer part of town now, lights in the windows. I roll my forehead an inch forward on the window glass, find a cool spot for my cheekbone. My eyes are trying to close.

Fred goes on, mostly to herself, it seems to me: "I won't have a fucking clue what's going on by the time I go back to work. Sixteen fucking years. The Family Protection Laws may change by the time this one's a little older"—she lays one long finger over her belly—"but in my Care Circle they're all saying the courts are going to extend the Completion period all the way to eighteen years, not cut it. *More time at home with the baby,* they're all in favor, the righteous cows. By year eighteen? That's not a *baby.* When I was eighteen, I was working my way through school and Mom had been dead for eleven years and I hardly even *saw* my family—not that you missed me, you little shit," she adds irritably, then catches sight of my expression, which I'm guessing is as blank and banged-up as I think it is. "Do you have any idea what I'm talking about? Are you even paying attention? Did you ever even *read* anything I sent you over there?"

"Um. Yes. Yes, I did."

"Bullshit you did. Bullshit. But you know what? I'm not surprised. No one's paying attention to the fucking *Family Protection Laws.* The fertility rate's so low hardly anyone knows anyone who's *affected* by them. Everybody's just trying to ignore how much sanifoam and engineered food and engineered beer all fucking *suck* and they're trying to just, like, *stay alive* until somebody solves the world's fucking resource problems." Fred fiddles with the dashboard controls, her expression moody, until she finds a way to turn the air conditioning up even higher. "Thank Christ. I'm boiling like a heretical nun. Listen, Carter, I'm not asking for sympathy, but you could fucking *listen* to me after I just paid fifteen thousand dollars to keep you out of a Security pen."

"I'm listening. I am." I sit up and lean forward into the sweet-smelling cool air coming from the car's dash vents.

"Sure you are. Sure you are." Fred smirks at me. "Let me give you a little *update* on the fucking fertility crisis, CQ. As a guy who's spent the last two years guarding H2.0 convoys, I know you must be par*ti*cularly interested in what we'd call the 'downstream implications' of our dependence on engineered water. But not for everybody. Just for a lucky, lucky few. Just for walking miracles like myself."

"I was over there two and a half years," I say, and I can't believe how humble I sound. This is what it's like to have an older sister, if you didn't know.

"Two and a half years, yes, certainly. Listen. Mothers? Pregnant women like me, just starting the Completion? We're supposed to give up *everything*, for *sixteen years*. Everything we used to do, just as, like, crazy fucking normal women, is *illegal*, or if it's not illegal it might as well be. You're not supposed to work; you're not supposed to have friends outside of your Care Circle—which, I probably never even told you, but you don't even get to *pick* it, when you register your pregnancy you get *assigned* to a Care Circle based on your address and your income level. No foods they don't want you eating. No drinking, *obviously*—you probably already know that if you're a woman between twenty-one and forty, you pay five times the list price for booze even if you're not pregnant. *Just in case.*"

"I haven't asked a woman out for drinks in about three years."

"Save up, motherfucker. Anyway. *More about my problems.* Listen. I have to breastfeed—everyone in my Care Circle has to breastfeed—until the kid goes to *kindergarten*. And then, this is the best part, there's a fucking 'weaning period' that you go through with your Care Circle, where you all sit around and weep and moo together, I can't *wait* for that pungent hairy ass. And this is all, of course, talked about like it's an honor and a privilege, not a sequence of sacrifices. I had to give up my whole business! I had to give up a fucking twenty-million-dollar company! And my question is, like, who *benefits*? Who benefits from these 'family protections,' I'm asking you? Certainly not my kid—you think he-she-it wouldn't have been better off with a mom who made a shitton of money? You don't think it *benefits* a kid to have a mom who's so independently rich any kid of hers sneezes fucking quarters? You know who *benefits*? The fucking guys who bought my fucking company. And you better believe I made sure they fucking paid me for it, but that thing is going to be throwing off money for *years*, and I'm not going to be part of it."

Here Fred laughs, one unlovely bark.

"You know what I *can* do, you know what *most* women do, after the Completion period is over and our Care Hours quota goes down enough that we can do something with our lives other than obsessively, preemptively take care of our kid's every need? We're Completionists. Not professionally trained Nurse Completionists, like Gard, just Completionists, running Care Circles for other women. Once a woman's children are all grown and in school, then we can cycle into being Completionists and help other women figure out how to forget what they had."

"Fuck that," I say loyally.

"Fuck yes, fuck that. But I'm lucky. You know that? That's what fucking kills me, is, I'm *lucky*. I'm not poor, in fact, on my own I'm doing pretty fucking good, and even I can barely afford what it's going to cost me not to work for sixteen years."

"So don't do it." I'm aware even as I say it of how stupid I probably sound. "Why don't you just say fuck it and do what you want? Eat what you want; go back to work if you want; be friends with whoever you want. Do that instead. Your kid's going to be fine. We didn't even *have* a mom," I point out, although it seems to make something in the sweet air inside the car flinch or pinch, and I don't like saying it like it's an accusation of some kind. But now it's out, there it is, pulsing just like a wound does: she wasn't there. I don't even really remember her. "And look at us. We—we're fine. Besides, what are they going to do, throw you in a cell? You're pregnant, you're a walking miracle; they can't hurt you. They can't touch you."

"No. But they can fine me." She checks my face, and apparently sees just what she expected to. "You really don't have a clue, do you? Men usually don't. Although to be fair, I didn't, either, until this happened. The penalty structure is *insane*. You know how much I was fined because my med status showed I drank a fucking *coffee* in my first trimester?"

"You're not supposed to drink coffee?"

"*Seriously?* If I could throw you out of the car right now I would so do it. I wouldn't even miss you."

"Sorry. Sorry. Just—I'm catching up, here. I've been gone awhile."

"I know you have," Fred bites out. Then she's quiet.

I know what she's thinking about. Who she's thinking about.

"I'm sorry I haven't found Gard yet, Fred. I'm trying. I'm really trying."

Fred looks down at her lap, then back at me, her eyes shining with regret. "Me too."

"I haven't given up."

"I know," she says, and we're both quiet for a moment.

"Didn't Gard have any *advice* for you about—I don't know, all this? She's a Completionist, isn't that her job?"

Fred smiles sadly, and for a change, it sticks. "Gard. Well. She's good for perspective, I'll say that much. Gard knew all about it, of course—the penalties, the rules, everything. It's why she worked herself ragged at that second job. You saw, today—you were in that place." Fred looks at me, expecting some sign of recognition, understanding. I try to look wiser than I feel. "You wouldn't believe how hard it can get, how those women are subject to all these fines and . . . and . . . technological embarrassments, for not being able to meet Care Standard. Gard was—" Fred pauses, her jaw sets. "Well. You know how she always wanted to help people."

"Wants."

"Pardon?"

"She *wants* to help people. I'm sure wherever she is, that's exactly what she's doing. Still." I can hear in my own voice an echo of little-brother stubbornness from twenty years ago, digging in and half-truthing: "I'll find her. I'm close, I think. After today." *You should go home and ask your father.* Something makes me do a little involuntary shudder in the car seat, like a dead hand just slipped into my pocket. Or maybe the AC is too high. "I just have to talk to Pop about something."

Fred's staring at me now, her eyes measuring. "Really? Pop? Why? What do you mean you're close?"

Even I'm not sure what I mean, but I can see that it's too late to walk it back, or make up an explanation, or even tell the rest of the truth: *Someone told me we should ask Pop where she is. And I have to admit, the way he acts since I've been back, he makes me wonder. Sometimes.* I can't bring myself to say it; it's too strange and half-formed. "Fred . . . listen." I lick my lips, taste blood, try again. I am harmless. I am harmless. "You know what Pop said to me last night, after the party? We're sitting at his kitchen table, just drinking some beers, talking over the night. And he asked if I thought about what it would mean for you if Gardner were found. What does that mean?"

She shrugs.

"If Gard *were* found . . . I mean, Fred, you were the only one even *looking* for her until I got home. If Gard were found you'd be . . . you'd be—"

"Saved," Fred says simply. She leans toward me, urgent. "What did you mean when you said you were getting close? Close to finding Gard? How?"

I can't tell her half of what I'm thinking. I can't even properly *think* half of what I'm thinking.

My hand is suddenly under hers, clutched up in those long, cold fingers. We're not an affectionate family. It means something. "What did you find out? Carter, you've got to tell me. Please."

I'm just sitting there, fish-mouthing. Finally, I fall back into well-defended territory, the role I always play with Fred when I know I'm outgunned: Kid brother, here to make you question whether the miracle of birth is really that miraculous.

"Fred, I gotta tell you. Part of me was just hoping I'd find Gard in time for her to talk you out of getting married to Ken fucking Walker."

Fred ignores my grin. She releases my hand, sits back and glares. "Ken Walker just kept you out of jail, you ungrateful snotcock. Fine, you don't want to tell me whatever it is you think you know? Fine." She shakes her head, treats me to some heinous side-eye. "I thought we were on the same fucking side, Carter."

"Jesus God. We *are*, Fred." I'm so exhausted. Rafiq's meds must be wearing off. I lean my head back against the window.

However angry I make her now, I know I've already done the worst thing to Fred I could possibly do. I'll never make her angrier with me, sadder with me, more hopelessly disgusted by me, than she was when I told her I was dropping out of school to fight in the Wars. No, let me back that up: dropping out of the school she was *paying for me to attend*, in order to fight in the Wars. I was about fifteen credits shy of graduation when I went.

She didn't even swear at me. She just turned her face to the wall and made this sound, this *rrrrrrrrrrAAAAAAAAAAAAH!* like a wild outraged animal. She scared me, if I'm being honest.

So I laughed at her, and she got up and hit me (hard, on the shoulder) and left. She didn't want to talk to me or look at me. The day I left for recruit training, though, she was there. A driverless came to pick me up at Pop's house early, right after dawn. Seeing me off out on the sidewalk, Gard was weeping but still talking normally and even smiling a little, just unaware that she was weeping. Pop was typical Pop: inscrutable angel of death in a threadbare brown shirt like a janitor's, looking about eight feet tall as he stood next to Gard with his arm around her shoulders. And Fred stood a bit apart from them, glaring at the driverless car like she wanted to blow it up with her eyes.

I knew then, just like I know now, that trying to explain to Fred why I couldn't stay in school wasn't likely to satisfy either of us. I didn't do her the courtesy of talking to her about it before I dropped out, which I admit I only felt bad about later, but the fact is I was wasting her money, and I couldn't stand myself anymore. It *was* mostly her money, even though I'd worked for New Cities Reconstruction on and off since high school. I had a bit of my own. A bit. Not much. Certainly not enough for school. Fred had made that happen, just through the sheer force of her will.

But a lot of guys my age were already over there fighting, not sitting in classes wasting time. I could have tried to explain to Fred that I felt like a coward, that I felt like I had to do what real men do, what Pop himself had done, and she probably would have let that be the reason. Eventually, she would have accepted that, and that's one true reason, for sure.

And then there's the other reason, the one that sticks in me like a thorn I can't remove, and it's one I'd just as soon not discuss with my ambitious, accomplished sister: Even if I'd stayed, kept at it, graduated college, what would it have meant for me? The guys who stayed out of the Wars were sons with connections, guaranteed careers in health or reconstruction or banking. I wasn't going to finish school and rise up to start saving the world, like Fred and Gard had done. I'm not smart like they are, I don't surge like they do. The only way for me to amount to anything was not to try to be anything like them. Meanwhile, guys I knew were fighting and dying while I was sitting in class. I made myself sick. I didn't even want to think about what my father thought of me.

We're almost to his place now. The streets outside are familiar, the old pale brick two-flats and the bars still hanging the Old Style signs outside even though there's been nothing to drink inside but engineered beer for about twenty years.

"Listen," she says to me suddenly. "You know I didn't mean to get pregnant. I'm assuming you know that."

"Are you kidding me? Fred." I laugh. "I mean, I haven't met the guy, but I know *you*."

"Okay." She touches her belly lightly, appears to be studying something written in invisible ink across her own blouse. It comes as a painful surprise to see that Fred's hands are shaking. "So that's no secret. But there is something I was . . . keeping from you. Not about Gard, what happened to her, nothing like that—about me. I didn't want you to know. But Gard, before she disappeared, was helping me, in a way that maybe now you understand."

Fred leans back over at me, and her eyes are steady and clear, her face grave and pale, and here we both are, and it's up to us, and not for the first time I hope to God we don't fail, I hope we're good enough. I hope we're smart enough. I hope we're together enough to find Gard. She's the best thing we ever had.

"I *still* can't believe you got in, but . . . You saw where Gard worked. You saw what they do there."

All I can do is frown, shake my head, deny it. Because what did I really see?

Gardner made some mistakes. She got into some dangerous territory. I tried to help her. . . . Gardner didn't want to be helped.

"So now you know," Fred says. My sister has my attention. In the serene blue of the car dash lights I'm trying to read her face, and failing, and it actually bothers me that I can't. Pop I'll never understand, I've given up trying, but Fred and Gard—I'm their kid brother, I've spent my whole life watching them, looking up to them, studying how they got what they were after. Imagining I could protect them, if it came to that. If I know anyone on earth, if I belong to anyone on earth, if anyone on earth *made* me, it's my sisters. "And you know why Gard might be better off staying lost. From Pop's perspective."

"Fred, I don't have a clue what you're talking about. And even on a clear fucking day with visibility for miles, I couldn't see Pop's *perspective*. Do you?"

An unpleasant triumph dawns across Fred's sharp face. Smug old brat.

"Ha. You *don't* know."

Just like that, I'm the left-back little kid again. Which brings on a typically immature response from me. "Fuck you, Fred."

She smiles at me craftily. "I'll tell you, if you tell me."

"What do you mean?"

"You tell me what you need to ask Pop. And I'll tell you what Gard was doing."

If I want to hear what Fred hasn't told me, I have to tell her what I don't know. What a beautiful circle of lunacy, what a crapfuck. As Fred herself would say. "You first."

"*You* first."

"No, *you* first."

"Fuck off. You first."

We've arrived, and the car is gliding up to the curb outside Pop's house. We're out of time.

I give up. You can't win with Fred. She's just always going to win. She'll make sure of it, one way or another.

"Someone—Natalie, Gard's coworker—told me *Pop* knows where

Gard is. Okay? Or"—because Fred's immediate reaction is thunderous enough that I feel the need to qualify my statement—"or she seems to *think* that Pop can tell me. All right? I was just trying to keep it to myself until I could find out whether it was even true. There. You happy?"

"Happy." She shakes her head and barks that unlovely laugh again, glancing out the window at the front of Pop's building.

Now I wait. It's her turn.

But she's calling something up on her virtual portal. I'm already irrelevant. It's amazing how quickly Fred can make a person feel small. Finally she adds, "I'm not going in. This is your stop. I have to get back."

"What? Fuck you, Fred. I thought we had a deal." She doesn't respond, attention locked on something in her portal that I can't see. The unmistakable shield stare of someone looking through you at something that's not you: that's the gaze of these days. Fred, of course, got the fancy upgrade, multiscreen built-in retinal display, the works.

I'm sick of being ignored. I heave myself out of the car and onto the sidewalk. After a half hour's ride in the cool, sweet-smelling interior of Fred's sedan, it's hard not to feel like the hot winter night is mugging me, lifting me by the armpits, grabbing me by the face. I start making my way up the cracked and unkempt front walk, wondering how on God's formerly green earth I'm going to get my beaten ass up the flight of stairs to Pop's apartment.

Behind me I hear the sedan's expensively sealed driver's side window slide open.

"I just sent you something. Check your wearable. You should understand what this little rescue mission is really going to cost me, Carter."

I turn around, but the car is already rolling away, back to what was the lakeshore, before I was born.

Dec 19 9:37 PM

Go to Gard's house to read these.
Don't try to open this file unless
you're using her portal, at her place.
You'll see why.

GARDNER QUINN
2556 ASHLAND NORTH, APT. B
NEW CHICAGO 0606030301
NEW STATES

PFC C. P. QUINN 2276766
MCC 167 1ST MAW
FPO NEW CHICAGO 06040309

August 13, 6:35 a.m.

Hi.

I got arrested, CQ. I was at a protest and they just rounded everybody up. Pop is so mortified, angry like I've never seen him. His reaction is the worst part of all this, to tell you the truth, and having seen the inside of a Security interrogation room now, I can tell you that's saying something.

They didn't ask me much. Gentle pressure, relentlessly applied.

I was there with a friend of mine from work, Natalie B. I can't remember whether I told you about her, but she's great, you'd like her. Natalie and I got separated, on opposite sides of a barricade—Security forces were corralling people off New Michigan and onto the side streets, and I got swept up into a van and she didn't. Anyway, she arranged for me to be released by telling them one of my clients was going into labor, but it's on my permanent Security record, and who knows what that means.

Pop is so angry. So angry. It's embarrassing enough to him that I would go to an antiwar march, but then to go and get myself *arrested* . . .

I know why he feels that way, really, I do. But I don't think he understands what's happening over there anymore. I don't think he understands that is what's in the way between us—between me and him, but you and him, too.

You've just been gone for so long.

I can't forgive myself for how long you've had to be over there. None of us should be able to forgive ourselves.

And for what? For H2.0? When we know what it does, when we *know*? We should all be *rioting in the streets*. But most people our age, we just don't care. The fertility crisis feels like freedom. You can do whatever, screw whoever, you never have to worry about anyone but yourself. Given what's happening in the world, that feels not just like freedom but like license to survive.

But the mothers I work with, the ones who beat the odds somehow or just get unlucky . . . That's what kills me. Other than you, they're the only ones who see that freedom's exactly what's been lost.

Anyway. Pop's pissed at me but he'll get over it, I hope. I'm a little worried about Pop, to tell the truth, but he keeps telling Fred early retirement agrees with him, he's going to slow down and take it easy, catch up on some reading and see some old friends. Which sounds nice, I guess, but I just don't want him to get depressed, or bored—he's a guy who's lived his whole life with this *purpose*, you know, and I worry about what'll happen to him now that he's just living a regular old-guy life.

He's actually not speaking to me at the moment.

And I guess I'm telling you all this so that you know why I went to protest a war my own brother is fighting in, and I hope you'll forgive me. I went because I love you.

Gard

EIGHT

Whatever Rafiq gave me, it's not going to last the thirty-six hours he promised.

I'm in the dark, smelly foyer of Pop's building, facing the stairs up to my pop's place on the second floor, Fred's message glowing in my eyeball. Wiped out in a way that I'd like to say feels new and terrible but which just feels familiar and sick. *The symptoms are not going to stop. . . . It follows a certain course.*

I'm just going to have to run up the stairs. *No way gotta run PT it's lots of fun.* If I take it stair by stair I'm pretty sure I'll make it halfway up and then never want to move again. They'll find me in the morning on the landing, passed out against the wall.

Once, when I was a kid, back in the dark years when the city was really falling apart, that had really happened, but not to me. Fred and Gard opened the door to the landing, about to head down for the bus to school, and there was a guy on the stairs in our building, unconscious. Skinny. I remember seeing him. Thinking, *That guy is sick.* I would have been, what, four? That was the year Fred started taking Gard to school, when Fred started sixth grade, so, I'm four. Maybe three and a half. It's not a great memory, by which I just mean it's spotty and degraded, but it's also from a point in my life when I was noticing a lot of things for the first time.

Our mother died when I was two. Hit by a driverless car, but as we got older my sisters and I gradually understood what people really meant when they said that. My mother had been left alone with three kids when my father was mobilized in the First Wars, and by the time he'd been gone a couple of years, it wasn't clear he was ever coming back and it was just as unclear whether anybody else was going to make it. The water had just stopped coming into people's houses back then, and there were food shortages and lots of desperate and hungry and thirsty and lost people everywhere, the weather violent and unpredictable in a way that made you scared to go outside—dust storms, hail storms, wind storms, dying-bird and -insect storms—the East Coast flooded and the West Coast on fire and everybody in the middle hoarding and walking and suffering, trying to get into the rehabbed zones, where at least you could get rations and sanifoam and send your kids to something like school. Dark years. I can't blame her. She wasn't the only one, far from it. I hardly knew her. Fred, though, remembers her—she was old enough to understand what was going on when Pop had to be brought back from the Wars to take care of us. Fred was old enough to comprehend just how scary those times were, in a way Gard and I weren't.

By the time I started kindergarten, enough H2.0 was making its way over the mountains that food production had started up again for the New Cities, even though there was never water in the bathtub and except in a book I've never seen an apple that cost less than $20. That was the miracle of engineered water, the greatest invention of our lifetime, of a hundred lifetimes, made just in the nick of time in what was left of the technology belt in California, right before the big quakes and the big fires and the mass evacuations. The collapse. The military kept the H2.0 production running, though, securing an uninhabitable wasteland and getting engineered water back to the New Cities.

Of course, no one making money off H2.0 seems to be in any kind of hurry to build an H2.0 plant in a location that would get us out of the Wars. You could make the argument, I suppose, if you're a particular kind of person, that the H2.0 production facilities are actually safer over there, even with the raiders and the quakes and the storms and the environmental hazards. Because no one crosses the mountains. No one is left, over there, who isn't descended from someone who was left behind the wildfire line in '72, or been left there themselves. And how long can they last? So why rush things. Wait for the mountains to grind themselves down to dust; everything'll be easier then. My mother couldn't wait that long. She was afraid. I understand. I can't blame her. I can't. I'm not sure Fred or Gard feel that way, but I can't.

Anyway. That was what my pop had fought for, and later, what I would fight for. What it meant for him was different from what it meant for me. What it bought the New Cities was some kind of return to what people remembered as ordinary life. Fred saw all of it. She was just a kid.

She was the one who saw the maybe-dead guy in our stairwell first, and pushed me and Gard back behind her. He was slumped at the foot of the stairs. I remember the looks on the girls' faces, white in the gloom, dark open mouths and eyes. Dismay is a series of concentric ovals. All of us standing at the top of the stairs looking down. Pop had just finished giving us breakfast, probably the fortified cereal bars all the kids got on rations back then, and he'd been trying to hustle us out the door, single file, single-dad style: the girls to the autobus stop, me to the neighbor lady and her daughter next door, and himself to work at the VA hospital.

It's funny to me how much I've forgotten from those days, but I remember this.

Pop shooed us all back into the apartment, left us in there, disappeared down the stairs. We waited. The girls missed their bus, and I remember Fred was stressed out about that. Then Pop came back, said he'd take the girls to school, *Carter, you come, too.* When we went down the stairs together, the guy wasn't there. A little stain on the carpet, dark. A smell. I held my breath.

I'm not home yet. I can't stand down here all night in the dark and the smell, thinking about a dead guy. (Was he dead or just nearly?) Time to get my tired sorry ass upstairs.

Ready, Marine: Let's go. *No way, gotta run PT; it's lots of fun.*

Catch your breath, lean your forehead against the door. No one's looking.

I haven't eaten all day, and food is all I can think about. Also I'm just about dying for a beer from Pop's fridge, and my whole body is a contused throb. I picture myself on my narrow bed in the dark with a cold bottle pressed into my stomach and Pop's despicable cat curled up against my side, purring away in the bootprint left by that Security prick. I want that moment bad enough that it makes my head swim.

But before unlocking Pop's door and going in, I reread Fred's message. *Don't try to open these unless you're using her portal, at her place.*

As badly as I want to go to bed, I know I've got to get to Gard's apartment.

But first I've got to get her key, which I know is hanging from Pop's key hook on the kitchen wall, and I've got to eat something soon or I'm afraid I might actually drop. Again. For the . . . what, fourth time today? Third? *What happened to you, CQ?* On patrols we sometimes went a couple of days without more than a protein pouch, every ten hours a long gamey swallow of the stuff, then the pouch carefully resealed and tucked away for the next time, no matter how hungry you were, no matter how tempting it was to guzzle the whole disgusting mucousy globber.

Quiet, dim, dusty in here. I slip inside, shut the door behind me. This isn't the apartment where I grew up—we moved a few times when I was a kid, starting with my mother's death—and I don't feel any special connection to it. It's just an apartment, brown and smallish, accumulating the atmosphere of Pop's lonely old bachelordoom, which seems to have left an imaginary coating, like silt or cobwebs, on every surface, despite the fact that the place is always, in reality, meticulously clean. Slobs don't make it in the service.

"Carter." Pop's voice, emanating from some unspecific point in the gloom, is just as sudden and unwelcome as an angry ghost. I've just spent probably ten minutes trying to psych myself up the goddamn stairs and in the door, and still I'm surprised at how much I've been dreading this moment. "We should talk."

Of course, he's seen it all. He's got access, on his wearable, to practically everything I've been doing today—he'll already know about the $15,000 fine. He'll already know that I almost got picked up by Security and that Fred paid me up and brought me home. If he bothered to look at my med status he might even be able to guess that I saw Rafiq and got dosed with something, although he might not know what, or, just as important, where.

"Hey, Pop. Let me just—I gotta eat something." I switch the kitchen light on and it's stunning, hideous, star-producing.

"You get picked up by Security for God knows what and then you come home and expect to eat my food?" Pop emerges around the corner from his darkened den into the kitchen, swift as if he's on wheels, blinking furiously at the change in the light, and then stopping short at the sight of me.

Even after Fred's reaction in the car, I wasn't worried about myself—I was still riding on Rafiq's magic wonder juice. But I must look like some real shit for Pop to be staring at me like this.

"Come with me," he says tiredly after a moment.

"Pop, seriously, I've got to eat something."

He grabs a blue-wrapped bar from a shelf and tosses it over his shoulder to me. "You can eat while I'm mopping you up. Come on." He starts down the hall to the bathroom. I snick another bar from the kitchen shelf and then, quickly and quietly, swipe Gard's apartment key from Pop's key hook, hung inside the kitchen doorway.

Then I'm following his path down the long railroad hallway, unwrapping one bar and chawing through half of it in a bite. There's other stuff to eat now—the food supply in the New Cities is an infinitely less grim story than it was when I was a little kid—but Pop has always been partial to food that recalls an MRE. Bars, pouches, dump-and-heats. All that can be splashed with hot sauce shall be duly splashed with hot sauce. He used to put cayenne pepper on his crackers-with-margarine. He probably still does.

"Come in here. Sit." He's got the medicine cabinet open, digging out his kit. I edge in behind him, perch on the toilet seat cover. The smell of sanifoam and antiseptic gel is thick, but the smell of flowers is here, too, creeping up on me like it always does when I spend any amount of time with my father. He's sani-ing his hands already. Efficient.

I start in on the second bar, feeling just better enough that the dread and the anger have a chance to settle back into their accustomed spots in the pit of my stomach, to be digested endlessly alongside my dry dinner. What was it I was supposed to ask, Natalie B.? *Just how much do you know, Pop?*

I want to ask him, and of course, at the same time, I'd just as soon never talk to him again. *While I've been humping all over New Chicago looking for a shred of a sign, a ghost of a clue, did you know all along where she was? Or not? Just how much do you know?*

I've got the advantage on him. I could knock him down. I never would, but I could. He's older now. His sharp face is thinner than ever, his shoulders are bony like a crow's. His pants are baggy around his thighs. He breaks my fucking heart, is the truth.

Of course, he was a powerful guy when I was a kid. Never huge, but his hands and his arms were full of force, capable of a lot more than we kids knew.

Just how much do you know, old crow?

When I look up there's a freshly unwrapped antiseptic gel pad balanced on his fingers. "Turn this way." Pop has put on his reading glasses and his eyes are on my face, focusing closely without really looking at me, and it reminds me of how Fred was looking past me while staring deep into her own virtual portal out in her car at the curb, and I'm just starting to feel angry and fucked-up and pissed off, which has to be some kind of record: less than a minute of direct contact with the old man, probably fewer than a dozen words exchanged, and I'm already a ball of something frayed and hostile.

His fingers are blunt, precise, surprisingly strong. Whatever he's doing, it all hurts and at the same time none of it does. I keep it down to a grunt, even when he presses the antiseptic into the part of my forehead above my eye that's been bleeding on and off since I woke up on the curb with Fred screaming over my head.

One of us has to talk first. I'll be damned if it's me. But he starts in, of course. Saves me the suspense.

"How do you want to live, Carter?" He's done swabbing me up and he's threading his tool for stitches. I have about three seconds to answer him. He's that fast.

I clear my throat, shift my ass on the toilet seat cover. "I'm not sure what you mean, Pop."

Pop leans in and starts stitching up my brow bone. Shit and goddammit. While he's got me pinned, he begins, "Let me start with what I know. I know what you've been doing today. I know you've been out all day, on what I know you *think* is your mission to find Gardner. I know you went to see my friend Rafiq. I know your sister kept you out of jail tonight. Expensively. And I know you look like someone beat the tar out of you, and I'm going to guess it wasn't Rafiq or Fredericka."

"Batting nine hundred, Pop." Shit and goddammit. Shit and goddammit. I release a shaky breath and can feel myself blushing: showing how much it hurts is embarrassing, and it's not going to stop him from doing what he's doing anyway.

"Congratulations to me. Now let's move on to what you know. Do you know what I did today?"

"No idea."

"Well, this morning I got up and exercised, as I usually do, and then I came back and had breakfast and fed the cat and cleaned up around the house. I sent some messages to some friends from the service, nothing important, just keeping in touch, you know. Sometime while I was doing that, you got up and left the house for the day without letting me know where you were going, which is what you usually do."

"Sorry."

"You're a grown man, you've got your own life," he says, even-handedly enough. Then he goes on. "You don't eat; you only sleep when something's knocked you out; you don't have any friends that I can tell; you don't seem to want to talk to me or to your sister any more than you have to. You don't have anything in particular to show up for, and yet you're always running about two hours behind. You're not reading or watching anything, other than ads on your wearable; you're not getting in any exercise, although it's clear from your geo status that you're clocking impressive mileage some days, either on foot or on the bus. And when you're not doing whatever you think you're doing, then you're at a bar. See, Carter, I know what you do all day because part of what *I* do all day is try to keep half an eye on you, because I see what you're doing, and what puzzles me is how it doesn't seem to add up to a life. Hence my question. How do you want to live, Carter? Is this it?"

"How do I *want* to live?" It's hard not to laugh, even if it does hurt to do it. "What does that have to do with anything? How is *anybody* supposed to live, in this world? If there are better things to do, I'd love to fucking hear them."

"You could drink less, for starters," he observes quietly. "You could spend less time at the bar."

"Hell. What do *you* do?" I manage, in a growl I don't quite recognize. "Tell me again about how you spent all afternoon sitting in your chair, watching where I went, and probably Fred, too, on your wearable. Is that a habit you picked up after Gard disappeared?"

I never said I was a good person.

When Pop can speak again, he says, in the same quiet voice, "The reason I'm saying all this is because you matter, Carter. You matter, and not just to me. If this country, this civilization, is ever going to come back, it's going to be because of young people like you and your sister. You don't realize that, I guess, but I've lived long enough to know it."

"You're dreaming if you really think that. I don't know what else to tell you." *Old crow.*

"I know you don't realize it. I know you don't." He sighs. "But you're a Marine. You're a Marine and you're always going to be one. Which reminds me that I'm relieved to hear your symptoms are treatable, Carter," he goes on, in a firmer tone. "I had a message from Rafiq this evening to say that he'd seen you, and that he was able to do a brief examination and give you something for your pain. He said you were going to be at his office tomorrow morning." Pop pauses to press a bandage onto my forehead. "That true?"

"He's your friend, Pop. Don't you trust him?"

I've finally pushed too far. Pop takes a sharp, whistling breath in through his knife-edged nose and stares right at the little kid trembling not far beneath the surface of my stupid grown-up skull. He's always known where that kid was, how to laser in on him and make sure he stayed small. I can tell he's struggling to maintain his composure, and despite how much I've been needling him, it doesn't feel like much of a victory.

"Let me tell you something, Carter. I met Major Rafiq when our ops convoy was fired on by a bunch of crazy gun nuts, evacuation resisters with access to way too much ordinance, and he pulled me, unconscious, out from under a bombed-out building into the middle of a firefight in the middle of a dust storm in the goddamn middle of San Jose." Pop nods at me significantly. *Put that in yer pipe.* "That whole night, he covered fire for both of us from the only safe spot he could drag my completely-dead-to-the-world ass to, which was behind a dumpster in the parking lot of an abandoned office building. It was twelve hours before the armored trucks could regroup and come to our aid, with sporadic fire the whole time, and the guy is not what you'd call a Green Beret, okay? Guy's an *internist*. So whatever you might think of him, Major Rafiq's *trustworthiness* is not the issue. Are you going to see him tomorrow morning or not? Are you going to get help for this thing or are you going to let it eat you alive right in front of me?"

As if to answer him, I stare at my finger, which is covered in blood. For the last minute or so of Pop's little history lesson I've been feeling an evil tickle in my ear, like someone's giving me a wet willy, and when I stick my finger in my ear to wiggle whatever it is around, there's the blood.

Pop and I are both staring at my bloody finger.

I clear my throat.

"Where did Rafiq come from, exactly?"

"Rafiq's name means *intimate friend*," Pop answers quietly. "He and his family were refugees from Syria when he was a child. He made it to America, eventually got a scholarship for college, enlisted in Army Active Medical Corps. He'd been in the army eight years by the time I met him, in the shit for at least two of those."

I can't help the anger. I don't want to help it. It's not even like I'm feeling it; it's more like it's a wave and I'm cresting on it. Through a white-hot haze of flowers I hear myself.

"You guys are the last great Americans all right. Thank you for your fucking service."

"Carter."

"Must be nice. Of *course* you feel like you're a great American hero. You got to actually try to *help* people. California's shattering around your eyeballs? Soldier up. Get people out alive, past the crazies and the rubble and whatever fucking tsunami or wildfire or earthquake was trying to destroy the world that day. Your war, *your war*, was with straight-up fucking *acts of God*. You don't even know how fucking lucky you are. You fought to save whatever they thought was going to be left, I guess. But all that was history by the time I got over there—the whole fucking West Coast is like Mars now. Everything you remember as a war zone is just dunes and hovels and sand made of little hooked metal particles that latch onto your skin and work their way into your fucking guts."

"I know, Carter."

"You and all your smug buddies from the First Wars fought to save people's stupid skins, and me, I fought to make some people some *money*. Fred's fiancé and all his friends. All those people leveraged up to their ears in redevelopment and H2.0. I killed people—women, teenagers—I fucking killed people so that some guys back here in the New Cities could keep making *money*. So, Pop, do me a favor and don't try to talk to me about *who* was in the *shit*, okay?"

A little drop of blood drips down onto the leg of my pants, from my nose or my ear, who knows.

I didn't always used to talk to him like this. When I was a kid, God no. It was *yes, sir; no, sir; how high, sir?* from when I was a little squirt. I worshipped him, we all did. I know, even now, on some level, that he's a great man.

Pop turns away, starts putting away his war chest, all his precious tools and gauze pads and sterilizers. It is a valuable thing. And not just because I seem to have a tendency to require medical attention. Vintage, they used to call stuff like this, stuff that lasted beyond its expected life span, kept going, took a licking and kept on ticking.

Finally he says, "Carter, you're suffering. I see that. All those years

I was at the VA hospital, I saw a lot of men cycling through the kind of depression and hurt that I see you experiencing. I'm not sure I helped any of those men. I want to help you, if I can. But I'm not sure how. You're stuck in some kind of trap. This is hard for me to put into words. But what I'm saying, Carter, is, is, while coming back is hard, it's worth doing, for your family. I know what I'm saying here, Carter. Your family is worth trying to make it all the way back for. We want you here. Me and Fredericka. We're, we're just so grateful, you know, that you made it back home to us."

I can't help but laugh. "See, that's what I just don't get, Pop. You're saying family, family this, family that, family will save you—I even think maybe you believe it. But what about *Gardner*, Pop? What about her?"

"I don't want to talk about Gardner," Pop says wearily, and just like that he's already on his way out the bathroom door. In-fucking-credible.

"How can you just give up on her? You're not ready to give up on *me*, but you'll give up on *her*? When she's worth fifty of me?" Standing is hard, but I get to my feet and lean out the bathroom door into the hallway in time to see him disappear into the kitchen. "Don't walk away. Pop. Come on."

"I never said I wasn't ready to give up on you," Pop tosses back drily. I hear the fridge door clink open, see a small part of the darkness light up blue-white.

If you want to know where your sister is, you should go home and ask your father.

What if I don't want to, Natalie B.?

He doesn't owe me any answers. He doesn't owe me shit. In fact, it's obviously the other way around, and I owe him, plenty. What do I have, what could I possibly even begin to say, that might make him tell me the truth about one single thing, about anything?

I feel my way down the darkened hallway and around the corner into the kitchen. Pop's in his favorite spot, at the table in the dark, ignoring me, a bottle of engineered beer held lightly in one scaly paw in front of him. I grab another protein bar from the shelf, my bruised shoulder and sides shouting angrily about the stretch, and before I sit down at the table to face my father uninvited, I take one of his beers out of the fridge.

As I open it and take my first swig, I get an idea, or the beginning of one. How to get him to talk. How to get him off his guard enough to tell me whatever he knows, about Gard, where she went. I don't know if it will work. But like I said, maybe I'm not as big of an ignoramus as I used to be.

"Pop. Today the major gave me a shot," I begin. If I want him to listen to me, I know I need to start by explaining myself. "He never gave me the name of what it was. He said it was something like happy aspirin, an APC. But it had to have been more than that. I spent all afternoon feeling like . . . like I wanted to shoot something. I mean, I felt *great*, for a change, and maybe I just couldn't handle that. But, Jesus, I picked a fight with a fucking *drone*, and then a Security officer, the first chance I got. I wouldn't have minded fighting anybody I happened to run into. And when Fred came and picked me up out of the street with her eight-months-pregnant . . . self, I don't think I was very nice to her. Or grateful, the way I should have been. Maybe this is just the kind of shit I do now, when I don't feel like a nail pounded in crooked. All I'm saying is I'm not sure why I talk the way I do sometimes. I'm sorry I mouthed off."

"It's all right, Carter." Pop keeps his eyes down on the table, turns the bottom rim of his bottle in a slow half circle.

"Well. It doesn't feel all right. None of this feels all right, not to me. I don't even know what it was I got dosed with. And the nurse at Gard's clinic"—I pause here, then continue—"she didn't seem to know, either. But—right before the major gave me the shot, I saw her look like she was going to, I don't know, stop him or something. She kind of held her hand out for a second like this." I demonstrate Natalie's halting half gesture. "What if this shit is addictive? What if it's illegal? And now he wants to see me tomorrow morning—at *his* office this time. I don't know if I should go."

While I've been delivering this little monologue, Pop's beer bottle has come to a stop in its slow half circles. His hands have come flat on the tabletop. His eyes have lifted to meet mine. I'm looking innocent as hell, I hope. I am harmless. I am harmless.

Is he?

"Let me get this straight," Pop says slowly. "You went to *Gard's clinic* this afternoon? The one here in—"

"No. The other one."

"The . . . other one. That's where you were." He's wearing an expression like a brewing sandstorm, one thing I never want to see again. "That's where you've been hanging out these past couple of weeks."

"Well. Sort of. I've been hanging out in a playground that's basically on top of it." I shrug. Harmless.

"But today you got—inside there, somehow. And Major Rafiq—is this right?—he, somehow, met you there? *That* place is where your examination happened? Not at the VA?"

"Yeah." I shrug again, nonchalant as all hell. "Didn't he say that in his message?"

"No. He didn't."

"I went there to ask Gard's coworkers some questions. I thought they might know something we could use to track her down."

Pop gives me a long, hooded look that reminds me of Fred, in her car—she'd been *jealous*, really jealous that I'd actually seen it, that I'd been inside Gard's night clinic. And this is all I have, really: I've been there, and they haven't. I've been inside a place Fred and Pop both have been worried sick about. What I'm realizing, what I guess I've been slow to understand, is that they've both been afraid of Gard's night job for a long time. Afraid enough that Fred's desperate to find Gard, and Pop's desperate not to.

"What?" I finally blurt into the quiet.

"That's not a place for you. Or for me. And it's definitely not a place for Major Rafiq."

"Believe me, after spending a whole afternoon there, I fucking know it."

Pop's eyes are still on me, hard to read, hard to see into. I hate him a little bit right now, I can't help myself. And equally, I hate the little shaky kid he's looking at, the one who lives inside my numb skull, the one Pop always knows how to find.

"What did he see, Carter?"

I shrug again. "It's just an office."

"It's more than that," he snaps, "and you know it. You better know it." Pop leans forward, and his eyes are actually glittering like a crow's—it's unsettling as hell, and I'm recoiling before I can even stop myself.

"The actual fuck, Pop?"

"Don't you talk to me like that. You tell me right now, Carter, what you saw in that place, and what you think the major saw. This is important."

This time I'm honest with him. "All I saw was a waiting room. Bunch of women waiting to see the same Nurse Completionist I was there to see, the one who worked with Gard until she disappeared. When I got called back into an exam room I had an . . . uh. Attack, I guess. I was out cold for a while. When I came to, the nurse had already found Rafiq's information in my pocket and reached out to him."

"And he came?"

"Like he was riding on a fucking rocket. I couldn't have been out for that long, and by the time I came to, he was at the door."

"He met . . . who did you say you were there to see?"

I don't feel like giving Pop Natalie's name, just like that. "The Nurse Completionist on duty. She was a coworker of Gard's. A friend of hers. The major met her. Had a few questions for her," I add carelessly, then drink half my beer. My heart is pounding.

"What questions?"

"Whether or not they performed Insemina . . . how many people they saw in a week, that kind of thing. I don't know. Seemed like professional curiosity to me."

Pop puts his hands on the table. He seems to be debating something with himself. Finally he asks, "Did you see any women there who seemed like they were hurt? Hurt physically, I mean. Think carefully now."

I don't have to think about it. But I put on a show. I sit back, roll my eyes up to the ceiling, look uncomfortable with the question. "I might have," I answer.

"Did Major Rafiq see—anything like that? Were there any procedures happening while you were there? While he was there?" Pop's intensity is something to see. Fearsome. I'm just the worm reflected in the eye of the crow as it's about to strike downward with its beak, with force enough to puncture me through. But I know what I'm doing. I think. I hope. It's worth it, having him look at me like that, just to be able to ask this question and hope he'll answer it with whatever truth he actually knows:

"Pop. What do they do there?"

He blinks at me, clearly surprised. "I thought you would have figured that out, Carter."

This again. Everyone assuming I know more than I do. I shake my head.

"They're butchers."

"What do you mean?"

"Just what I said." Pop picks up his beer, looks at it like it's trying to tell him something in a foreign language, then takes a long drink.

I'm afraid to ask it, but I've got to. It feels strange even as my mouth shapes the words. "They . . . hurt women there?"

"Mothers," Pop corrects me. He's not looking at me now. He's just a tired old guy in a baggy T-shirt sitting at a table thinking about his daughters. "They hurt mothers."

Even though some part of my brain has been grasping at this same conclusion all day, there's another, greater part that keeps insisting it can't be. It can't be. "Are you sure? Pop, there were women lined up practically out the door at this place. Why would they all show up at a place that would hurt them?"

"The women need the points," Pop answers bleakly. "What do you call them . . . the Care Hours. A fractured wrist gets you credited a few hours back every day, for six to eight weeks—while you heal, you know. You can go back to work the same day. You can still function; you're not in too much pain. A broken metatarsal gets you credited about the same. Those are mostly the procedures they do there, but there are ways you can get . . . more done, if you need it." Pop raises his eyes to mine, that same inscrutable laser beam. "That's how Gardner explained it. When I found out what she'd been doing. I'm just telling you what she told me."

As Pop is talking I'm trying to identify what this feels like, hearing all this. If I had to compare the sensation to something else I'd experienced, I'd have to say it feels like the first couple of times you know, or are about 90 percent sure, you're in the process of killing somebody.

In my last few months in the Wars, I had a hard time on active patrols because I kept getting these attacks in the middle of attacks—it's hard to aim, to control your trigger, when you're trying to see through a gray pinhole and can't breathe for the white beautiful choking scent of flowers in your throat. In the meantime, I had a hard time explaining what was happening to my superior officers, and even though the guys on walks with me knew what was going on, to my skipper I just looked like a colossal fuckup. Other people kept me alive then, I'm convinced. Wash. Horrocks. Chalke. Wash is dead now. Who knows about the other guys, they may be dead, too, or they may have found themselves on the wrong end of a boom and they're now in the same situation I was in, staggering around in the dust unable to breathe or see or fight, relying on their friends to cover for them.

The understanding that I myself orchestrated this particular attack is as bitter in my throat as the blood and flowers that are backing up in it. At least I know what to do. Fall back. Fall back. I close my eyes and put my head down on the table and Fred's message on my retina glows green-blue in the darkness. *Go to Gard's house to read these. Don't try to open this file unless you're using her portal, at her place. You'll see why.* Fred, if this is what you were trying to tell me, in your way, Pop beat you to it, and I'm sorry he did.

"I know this is hard for you to hear. Now you know why I don't want to talk about it." I hear Pop's chair scrape back against the floor. "You should go to bed, Carter. Get some rest."

I don't lift my head. I just hear him pausing there, feel his hand on the back of my skull, slight, like a dried-out leaf landing.

"Carter. I hope you understand. This is why I can't have you and Fred out looking for her. For Gardner there's no coming back." His voice is thick. "I wish it was different."

My eyes are stinging. I sit up, and his hand falls away.

"There's got to be more to it than that," I insist.

Pop clears his throat and says, in a patient tone that has about as placating an effect on me as his punching me in the face might have had, "I know it probably helps you to think you can find her, or help her somehow—"

"Pop. If she left the New Cities, if she took off to find some fugitive colony outside the rehabbed zone, she could be in real danger." I push back and stand up, too quickly, and have to work to get my balance. "*Right now.*" My head is still spinning, but I'm conscious of Pop standing near enough to grab my elbow and not doing it. "Right now, she could need us."

When I can see again, Pop is close, fixing me with a look that combines a truly enraging balance of skepticism and concern and condescension, and fuck him. He doesn't say anything and he doesn't have to.

"You don't even care, do you? You've judged her and that's it."

"That's it?" Pop snorts. "You don't know what you're saying, Carter. Believe me. You don't know what I *tried*. You don't know what I *did*, trying to keep her out of trouble. Trying to keep that whole—*outfit*— from coming into the light. I kept their secret a lot longer than Major Rafiq will, I can tell you that much."

"Rafiq? What's he going to do?" My first thought is not just Gard, it's Natalie B. It's the woman in the sling.

"What do you think?" Pop barks back at me. "More to the point, what should *he* think? He's no idiot. If it were a Completion clinic that did the work it was supposed to and *nothing more*, it wouldn't need to be so well hidden, don't you think? You've got to understand something, Carter. Gardner and her colleagues are operating well outside the conventions of modern medicine, to say nothing of the law. Rafiq's bound by the same code of ethics I am—was—as a doctor, and an officer. I can't understand why they took the risk of letting him in there."

"They didn't know who he was when they called him," I say dully, the realization that it was all my own fault striking with horrible force. "That piece of paper you gave me. It doesn't say VA. It doesn't say anything. It just has his name and his contact number." I feel in my pocket for it, but it's gone, of course. Natalie B. has it, wherever she is. She'd had no idea what she was setting herself up for when she contacted him—she just had a big, dumb, bloody unconscious asshole on her hands who she needed help getting rid of.

"Carter. The women who work there—they think they're doing what's necessary. God knows we're all just trying to do that. But it's a crime. It's a crime under about a dozen different statutes, in addition to being a serious ethical breach. What do you think a career military medical man who's risked his own life to save guys in the field again and again—what do you *think* he's going to do when he encounters something like that?"

"You and your old war buddy have a chronic fucking case of nobility," I snarl.

"You don't know what you're talking about. And you don't know what you've done." Pop rubs his eyes wearily.

"Me? Pop, I'm not the one who's giving out his number to people!"

"Aren't you? *I'm* not the one who brought him in there!" Pop shoots back. "Jesus, Carter. Ever since you've been home, you've been telling me you're on this mission—*I'm gonna find Gardner; I'm gonna find Gardner*. But when I see what you actually do all day—walking around her neighborhood, and, and . . . riding the bus, for *hours*, from her place to the edge of the rehab zone and back. Maybe you messaged a few of her old friends . . . I don't know—you never seem to talk to anybody. I was trying to go along with it. I thought, maybe this gives you some sense of purpose; a lot of guys need that when they come back. But do you really think what you're doing is an *investigation*? You think you're going to find Gardner by harassing her former colleagues and leading the damn army right to their door? Because if you do, you are lying to yourself. And you're lying to Fred. And you're lying to me."

The next thing I know, he's on the floor. I don't even know where I am, where my body parts are. I can hardly see for the gray, can hardly hear for the static, can hardly breathe for the flowers, and I'm shaking all over.

Pop's hand, trembling, comes to the side of his head, then swipes across his mouth, leaving a bloody streak across his wrist.

"I can't tell whether I deserved that or not," he says, then absurdly, amazingly, manages a short cough that I realize is a laugh. One unit of laugh.

My nose is bleeding now, too, and not because someone's just clocked me in the face. I don't know why it's happening, why any of this is happening. I seem to have lost control of my body, maybe other things, too. I kneel to wipe up a fallen drop of blood with my forefinger, but only succeed in smearing it around on the tile. While I'm down here on his level, I force myself to meet my father's eyes. The utter lack of surprise or fear on his face tells me all I need to know.

I stand suddenly and my head keeps swimming, swirling; it's nothing new; there's nothing new in this whole damn world. "I'm sorry," I blurt. "I'll leave. I'm on my way to Gard's anyway." I shove a hand into my pocket, deep, and feel that it's still there: the key. "I'm not giving up. I'm still looking for her."

"Jesus, Carter." Pop's expression is disgusted. "What makes you think she even wants to be found?"

If there's any answer to that question it's not here, not with him. So I make my way to the door, open it quietly, stagger down to the hot night street. I just leave my father there on his kitchen floor, right there where I've knocked him down.

I never said I was good.

GARDNER QUINN
2556 ASHLAND NORTH, APT. B
NEW CHICAGO 0606030301
NEW STATES

PFC C. P. QUINN 2276766
MCC 167 1ST MAW
FPO NEW CHICAGO 06040309

June 3, 6:45 a.m.

Hi, CQ.

This is going to sound weird. But I just found out something I kind of can't believe. And I'm so happy right now I could sort of almost die of it. You ever feel that way?

I feel like life is coming together around something unexpected. I didn't think anything really unexpected could ever happen to us, to our family, not being who we are and living in the world we do, but it is, it's happening, something miraculous is happening. Is going to happen. Is happening now. Now!

I am getting waaaaay ahead of myself. I'm sorry I can't explain what I mean, or why I'm so excited and happy right now, but I am, and I guess the first person I wanted to tell was you. YOU. You know why? Because you're my little brother and I love you, you nut. How do you like that? Ha!

But being so happy you could die of it. Let's unpack that. Shall we? Because what I'm learning is that it's real; it's a real feeling; like I'm so happy, I could accidentally step in front of a driverless because I'm not— Oh, that is *not* the right way to put it, not at all, *oh my God*. Only you and Fred would understand why I am laughing so hard right now. And it's not funny! It's not. It's sad, what I just started to say—oh my God. [*laughter, laughter, laughter*]

I'm sorry. Okay. I got it. I got this. [*hee-hee-hee, gasping*]

Listen. Okay? Good things are happening. Good things are going to happen again. I want you to know that. I hope you will be kept going by that thought. It's keeping *me* going right now, it's like the sun rising and rising and rising all over again. It's almost making me feel like all this—the collapse, the crisis, the Wars—it could *end*. We could come back from this! Humanity! Isn't that a crazy thought? I admit it, I wrote us off. The whole species! The world! All of it! But now . . .

I wrote us off when our mom died, CQ. I decided the whole world was a pile of . . . of crap, and the only thing to do was to work on saving the pieces of it that I could, and I live my whole life by that idea, I do, but I never, I never, I never really believed in myself, or believed that anything could really get better. I don't know if I ever told you this. I don't know if I ever said this to *anybody*, not even Fred. But I've been a fraud, honey. I've been working on helping people as best I could, I guess, and I go to protests and try to be a right-thinking activist and whatever, forgive me, I hope you can, but I—it never seemed like I could really change anything, it was just better than doing nothing. I can't abide doing nothing. None of us can, I think that's what me and you and Fred have the most in common, actually. That's why I'm here, in the clinic, and you're there, at the Wars, and Fred's where she is, way up there in the heights.

Fredlet. God love her! God bless her! Oh, Carter. I wish you were here. I'm sure you would feel it, too, I wish I could tell you.

Remember when we were kids? You know, Fred, little Fred, she was as good a mother to us as you and I were ever going to get. You know that, right? Even as a little girl she was so determined, so right. She fought so hard to make sure we were okay.

Do you remember the time she scared that guy away who'd broken into our building and was lurking on the stairs? She was *ten*.

She's always been our real mother. And that's the truth. And I love her so much for it. And I love you for listening to me go on like this. But believe it: Good things are happening. To us. To our family. You've got to take care of yourself. Now more than ever.

Stay safe, honey.

Gard

NINE

Walking feels like dragging a body. Mine, I guess.

A warm wind knocks garbage against the buildings.

The night is hot and empty. The sidewalks in Pop's neighborhood are all open to the skies, right now black and crowded with stars and satellites, sailing like lit cigarette tips through the dark. A driverless car shines past in the road, someone coming home from a long night. It's only about a fifteen-minute walk to Gard's place from Pop's house, but I stopped in at the old guys' bar down the street and drank and watched ads on the portal hung in the corner until the place closed. Now I'm the last man on earth, making my way through a dark black night, everything in it hard and glowing. Pale brick buildings, pale sidewalk, pale street, pale tree stumps. In rehabbed neighborhoods like Pop and Gard's, the dead trees and bushes have mostly been chopped down, dug up, and carted away, not left in place to point their cutting dead stick fingers.

Fred's message is still glowing blue in a corner of my eye. I pat my pocket, make sure Gard's key is still there.

Fred, what are you up to? Gard, what have you done?

I'm not just the last man on earth. I'm also the last man on earth to know anything. But now that I've had a little more to drink, I've had some time to reassess things. Put some pieces together.

Whatever was going on with her, I still don't believe Gard would just go off and leave us. Even after these weeks of following cold trails, and harassing her coworkers, and calling her old friends who'd decided they weren't her friends after all—even after all that, I don't believe it. Gard is still alive, somewhere. Natalie B. as good as guaranteed it.

But the thing is. If Gardner's alive and she knows we're looking for her and she's not getting in touch or responding to anyone's messages—maybe it's really true, and Gard is just gone, and wants to stay gone.

Why can't I let her go?

Because she's my sister. Because we need her. Because she loves us. Because she and Fred both love me, when no one else does, or can. I know this. I know them, my sisters.

And if Gard's not just gone, that means something took her, or sent her. That means she's in danger.

Fred, what are you up to? Gard, what have you done?

I've got to help them somehow. They're in trouble. They need me to man up. But I'm too stupid, too lost, too tired.

The wide sidewalk. Should not be this close. Up, grunt. Oo-rah.

Three blocks to go.

Just then I get the idea to message Natalie. To thank her again, let her know that I'm still standing, and that I appreciate what she did for me. She'll be asleep now, at an hour when my sister would have been just finishing the last few hours in her night rotation. I flick on voice control in my wearable's retinal display, but my eyes don't seem to want to focus. (Fred always loved dictating the messages she sent me when I was over there, but because she talks—and swears—so fast, her messages always contained at least one [*unintelligible*] from the voice-to-text translator.) Finally on the third or fourth try I get it, and I say quietly to myself what I want to say to Natalie, and then I flick send, or try to, and then I have to do it again, and either it works or I might have deleted it, but I hope it went.

Maybe she's thinking about me, wondering how I am.

Probably not.

Something in the night is buzzing. I saw a movie of a bumblebee once, at school. But the bumblebees collapsed. Everything collapsed.

That's why we, humans, men, Marines, women, too, and also me in this particular moment, that is why we can't collapse. It was our mission, over there: *Forestall collapse! Prevent recollapsation!* Have to say, it's not a hell of a rallying cry. *Keep shit up! Keep shit shitty!*

From upstairs in one of the apartment buildings, from a darkened window, *Shut the hell up down there.* Sir, yes, sir.

No Marine forgets how to keep humping on once they've learned it. Now I'm breathing hard, listening to the breath thundering in and out of my nose as my steps retake their rhythm. I have something like Pop's nose, something like Pop's hooked overcast face. I have never considered myself handsome. I am a bit strange-looking, to be quite honest. I have a face that can be alarming. But women like me. They do. Sophie! She was beautiful. The woman in the park, the woman with the broken arm—she liked me, enough, until she realized that I didn't really belong there, that I'd tricked her. Even that nurse at the desk, Ms. *No-Next-Time.* Tough customer. She liked me, though. Didn't kick me out. Does Natalie like me? I like her, I admit it. I've admitted it, to myself, over and over, since the minute I met her. I do like her and I want her to like me. She's pretty; she's smart; she's good. I can imagine her, us, I can imagine her skin, her mouth, my hands, my God I'm walking down the street in the middle of the night hard like a fucking teenager.

Yes, I'd like to fuck Natalie. Of course. But more than that I want her to—what? I want to kiss her; I want her to want me. I want her to like me. I respect her. I know she does not respect me. Men want women's respect, but women want men's respect, too—I don't think it needs to be made more difficult than that. But Natalie's not going to give anything away. With her, you have to earn it.

So that's the problem. The problem that's not going away.

I have a few of those right now.

One's slowly unstiffening in my pants.

Several others are in my heart, or head, or wherever I'm keeping the things that keep me moving even when all I want to do is sit down for a fucking second.

Nope. On your feet, grunt.

Then there's the problem that's not going away because it is following me down the street in the darkness. I can hear it. Metallic bee.

I've already taken out one of your buddies today, metallic bee. Don't make me hurt you.

Don't make me hurt you, motherfucker. Okay, yes, volume decreasing. I get it, sir, yes, sir.

Ahead is the building I'm looking for, and does it seem a little bit miraculous, on this night, that I even found it? Yes, it does. But I'm being followed. Again. Little metallic bee. I know better, this time, than to chuck something at you, but I also know better than to let you trail me, especially where I'm going.

I bank left, cross the street. The drone speeds up *brzzzzzrrrrrrr-roooooooo. Come at me, little fucker.*

Time to swerve off the main street onto a sleepier street of two-flats. Between dark-shrouded buildings there's an empty, trash-flecked driveway, and this I walk down—not running, not even at a trot, but at the pace I'd walk if I lived here and wanted to get home, inside, into my bed—until I reach a row of overflowing trash cans. I take a knee behind one and listen.

Get back to your hive, little bee. The drone passes straight by the house I'm crouched behind, rocketing down the street. Halfway down the block the security flashers come on, lighting up the gray faces of the buildings along the block in blue and red strobes.

From a distance, the canned message sounds less certain of itself: *For your own safety, please return to your homes. For your own safety, please return to your homes.*

A feral cat is looking at me without much interest from its perch atop the fence that separates this driveway from the next.

"Kitty," I say. I'm drunk, yes, but I would argue that this is anyone's instinctive response upon catching sight of a cat, even a feral one that would eat your face given half a second's chance.

Who's out there?

Still in my crouch, I put my hands lightly on the pavement for support and freeze every muscle. The cat and I stare at each other. The cat takes its moment and slinks on down the fence line. I lower my eyes, slow my breathing. Count to a hundred.

When I finally exit the driveway there's not a sound, not a movement, not a light all up and down the road. Just me and the heat and the garbage and the stars and the dead trees and the sleepers, all around.

I backtrack to Gard's building and let myself in. Her apartment is on the third floor in a brick multifamily, a little two-bedroom she used to share with a friend from nursing school until her friend moved out. Fred had been helping with Gard's rent, as she made a point of informing me, and she's been continuing to pay the landlord since Gard was discovered missing. Another sign that Gard can't be really truly gone: her older sister is prepared to pay her rent forever just to prove it.

The place has been ransacked by a sequence of careless investigators from Security, none of whom found anything, none of whom bothered to put anything back. If it wasn't such a lonely holy mess, I might have moved in here, to avoid staying at Pop's place. But to live here, someone would first have to put all of Gard's hard-heartedly strewn things away, her scrubs and her clothes and her novels and her shoes all over the bedroom floor, her sanifoam in the bathroom gone gummy, her stale cereal and dusty plates in the kitchen. Neither Fred nor I have had the heart to do it yet, to touch her things. Pop hasn't been here, I don't think, but I've been here a lot, looking for clues. Or something. But there's nothing to find.

I hate being here, to be honest. Being in Gard's place is like running a pointless drill over and over again. Sitting in an empty room surrounded by all her stuff doesn't make Gard any more likely to show up. Probably makes it less likely than usual, in fact.

Gard's portal was, of course, analyzed as part of the investigation when she was reported missing, although if Fred's message means what I think it means, no one who wasn't meant to find anything would have. Fred's first jobs were in software engineering, privacy and security. She and Wash could have had a fine time comparing not-quite-officially-approved access methods, if they'd ever met. It takes me a few minutes to find the portal, but then I spy it, on a soft chair in the living room where it's been tossed by whomever skimmed it last, probably me, on one of my own unsatisfying hunts for a lead, any sort of lead. Gard only ever used a handheld portal, and this one's about the dimensions of a sheet of paper. Even if she could have afforded one, I don't think it would ever have occurred to Gard to buy a portal big enough to hang on the wall. Although Fred would have dearly loved to get her something bigger—she's already threatened or promised as much for me. *Christmas is coming and you have no idea how cool the technology has gotten since you've been gone.*

I swipe the screen awake and of course the thing badly needs a charge, so I stumble around in the half dark until I find one of Gard's charging targets and thank God it's next to another chair, some low-slung thing that looks like a wadded-up mattress on a wooden frame, so I can at least sit down (*don't even think about falling asleep*) while I try to figure out how to unlock Gard's portal.

As it turns out, I don't have to work very hard.

I've barely touched it, but the screen of the portal blinks once, then twice, then goes blue. Three lines of text fly into the top layer on the screen and—this is unexpected enough that I instantly feel about 20 percent more sober—onto my own retinal display. I sit back hard enough that I feel the chair's legs scoot underneath me. How in the sweet shellacked hell?

Hello, sweetheart!
If you are Gardner Quinn, please say hi.
If you are not Gardner Quinn, please go fuck yourself.

I close my eyes: the same three lines, right there in blue on my wearable's top layer. I've never seen a portal do that before, didn't know they could. The only time I've ever seen a portal screen transmit something simultaneously onto my wearable's retinal display was when Wash had about half a dozen lines snaked into a two-inch incision in my forearm in his sandy-ass little communications hooch somewhere in what's left of California.

"Hi, Fred," I murmur experimentally. Again, on both the portal screen and on my wearable, an unsettling visual echo:

It's you!

Then nothing, for long enough that I feel my headache lift its ragged flags again. My eyes want to drift closed and stay that way. It's got to be, what, four in the morning by now? Five?

Then a lot of movement happens, very suddenly: a layer opens on top of the messages I've already seen—but not a layer exactly, more like a second interface. Like a foreign operating system opening on top of the existing one. Which might be what it is, in fact, for all I know or can tell. Then Fred's earlier message to me swings past, like a drone on its way someplace, and an icon of a little envelope with a padlock on it (very quaint) extracts itself from the message text and flips open. A series of files—messages, by the look—are dealt into the lower-left corner of the display, a neat hand of poker.

The top file is a message from Fred to Gard, from a month ago:

November 12, 6:18 AM
Where are you? Why aren't you getting back to me?
Are you all right? Please answer me. Please.
Sweetheart, I promise. I won't do anything, I won't
ask you for anything. Please just let me know you're okay.

I can flip to the next file by swiping this one to the right side of the screen, it seems, but I can't tell whether I'm doing it by touch on the portal or by midrange focus on my wearable, and the effect is a bit nauseating. Also, hard to control—before I know what I'm doing I've flipped over half the stack of messages (*sorry, Fred, but there's some UX to work out here*), which seem to go backward in time, so that the oldest messages are buried beneath the newer. There are messages from Gard in here, I realize, and my heart and my stomach both execute a nasty lurching half step.

Sep 20 10:31 PM
They're all just barely making it.
I don't think you understand.

It's too much to look at the portal screen and the same thing on my retinal display, but I can't figure out how to disable one without the other. Also I'm beginning to feel a peculiar tugging sensation in my eyeballs, like Gard's portal screen is magnetically attracted to me. My wearable arm feels a little warm, too. It's not unbearable, but I wouldn't call it pleasant. Still, it's impossible not to be impressed. *Fred, what are you up to?*

The earliest file is an exchange dated March 8 of this year, between Fred and Gard.

Mar 08 7:27 PM
This is it! It's so cool, you don't even know. I've been
dying to show to someone and you're the lucky gal

Mar 08 7:29 PM
Wait, what even is this? What did you do
to my wearable? Whose portal is this?

Mar 08 7:29 PM
Yrs now, honey—don't let anybody else use it!!
And now you have the 1 thing nobody else in
this town has: Some fucking privacy

Mar 08 7:31 PM
I have plenty of privacy.
Other than my clients I talk to like 2 people.

Mar 08 7:31 PM
Yes, that's my problem and my point.
I'm worried about you
Ever since you took this other job

You've been weird, like super super weird
and I know you're not taking care of yourself.
And if you can't talk to me about it in person,
because you're in trouble, or something,
then you can talk to me here. That's why I
built it. It's safe.

Mar 08 7:35 PM

Fredlet, don't be mad, but I don't want to talk
about it, not even with you. Can you just let it be?
I know you want to help
but I don't need help. I just need sleep.

Mar 08 7:36 PM
Do you even know what I went through to get us
connected on a private network like this?

Mar 08 7:36 PM
No. I'm sorry. But you really didn't have to

Mar 08 7:37 PM
Yes I did.
I did it so you could
TALK TO ME
so you could TELL ME WHAT THE FUCK IS
GOING ON

Mar 08 7:39 PM
My arm feels like it's on fire. Is that this thing?
What is this? What did you do to me?

Mar 08 7:39 PM
It's safe, don't be such a weenie
It's just your processors working a little harder than
usual

Mar 08 7:41 PM
I don't like it

I flick to the next file in the stack. My own arm is warm like I've been resting a trigger on it all afternoon. It's a weirdly familiar sensation.

MARCH 11

Mar 11 6:27 PM
you are worrying me again
you are worrying Pop
I wish you would just tell me what's going on

Mar 11 6:30 PM
It's just your processor working harder than usual. Don't be a weenie.

Mar 11 6:30 PM
Ha ha not funny

Mar 11 6:31 PM
I'm fine.

APRIL 28

Apr 28 10:33 PM
Thank you for listening to me today

Apr 28 10:33 PM
Of course. I worry about you.
Please take care of yourself.
Be careful.

Apr 28 10:35 PM
I am. I will.

Apr 28 10:37 PM

Did that patient, the little mom with
the baby, did she
is she okay?
What ended up happening?

Apr 28 10:39 PM

I think she's all right for now.
I can't talk anymore.

Apr 28 10:40 PM

OK. Please be careful, Gard
Whatever you're doing
I know you don't want to tell me
But just be careful

JUNE 2

Jun 02 11:02 PM

Gard I'm freaking out

Jun 02 11:05 PM

Why? Is Pop OK? Did he hear something
about CQ? Is everything all right?

Jun 02 11:05 PM

ur asking me? that little shit never
messages ANYBODY over there

Jun 02 11:06 PM

You scared me

Jun 02 11:08 PM

I have something I want to tell you
it's a secret

you can't tell anyone
but i need your help i think

Jun 02 11:09 PM
Anything. Anything I can do I'll do.

Jun 02 11:11 PM
OK
I think I need to see a completionist

Jun 02 11:11 PM
What! What?????

Jun 02 11:11 PM
Keep your pants on. Christ

Jun 02 11:11 PM
But that's really exciting!
I didn't even know you were getting
Insemina treatment!

Jun 02 11:12 PM
Gard come on

Jun 02 11:12 PM
??

Jun 02 11:13 PM
You know I haven't been doing fucking Insemina

Jun 02 11:13 PM
Are you telling me you're naturally pregnant?

Jun 02 11:15 PM
Fred?

Jun 02 11:17 PM
Are you there? Are you OK?

Jun 02 11:20 PM
It's all right. You know you can talk to me.

Jun 02 11:21 PM
I'm sorry I was so surprised—it's just amazing!
You know how rare this is, right?

Jun 02 11:23 PM
Fred?
You there?
Listen. Let me give you the practitioner's view
as someone who's been an NC for three years now.
And that's thanks to YOU,
and thank you again, because it makes it possible
for ME to help YOU for a change, which maybe
you have no idea how exciting that is for me. OK?

Jun 02 11:25 PM
But from an NC's view, natural pregnancies
are what we live for.
You are so special, honey. You represent hope
that humankind can maybe come back from this.

Jun 02 11:27 PM
Well that's fucking comforting.

Jun 02 11:28 PM
Trust me, Fred.
It might not seem that way now but everything's
going to be all right. I'll help you. It would be
my honor and my privilege to help you. Srsly.

Jun 02 11:31 PM

OK wring your tampon out already

But thx

Really thx

I don't want anyone else to know yet, ok?

I mean it. Not Pop or CQ, first and foremost, but

also, I need to keep this under wraps until I can

figure out what to do at work.

Jun 02 11:35 PM

Fred, honey, don't you know?

If you're pregnant,

you can't keep it a secret.

Jun 02 11:35 PM

Oh yes I fucking can, and I have to. My business has to

come first right now.

Jun 02 11:36 PM

That's not what I meant.

How many weeks are you?

Jun 02 11:37 PM

Fuck if I know.

Jun 02 11:37 PM

You must have some idea.

When did you hook up with someone last?

Jun 02 11:38 PM

Wouldn't you like to know, you perv.

Jun 02 11:38 PM

Fred, come on.

Jun 02 11:40 PM
Last night. Whatever.
But I think it was a different person.
I've been feeling sick for a couple of weeks.

Jun 02 11:43 PM
OK. Look. Here's how this works.
If your body carries a successfully fertilized
egg past 2 wks your wearable
automatically sends a med status notification to the
Dept of Health, and to Security.
So you literally can't keep it a secret. Someone
from DOH is going to contact you by the
end of this month, probably.
You're lucky.
Women below a certain $
or outside the rehabbed zones
get contacted by Security and
the notification process
is a lot more like being arrested than being
invited to a book club.

Jun 02 11:47 PM
fuuuuuuuuck

Jun 02 11:48 PM
Here's how it will go: DOH will message you with an
appointment time. You do not want to miss it. Even if
it conflicts with something else you have to do.
Got that? Do not skip, and do not reschedule.
I can't even tell you the logistical nightmare
you'd be in for, plus you'll be charged a ton of extra
Care Hours for administrative fees.

Jun 02 11:50 PM

Wait what?

I'm responsible for Care Hours already?

When does that start?

Jun 02 11:51 PM

It's already started—they're retroactive
to the date of conception, although you
won't see the charge on your accounts until after your
first appointment with the DOH.

Jun 02 11:53 PM

Charge? What charge?

Jun 02 11:53PM

Care Hours are like a
high-interest debt.

Jun 02 11:53 PM

They're not just actual hours you're
supposed to spend doing fucking maternal things?

Jun 02 11:54 PM

Yes, they are actual hours.
But starting from the moment
of conception you have a quota of Care Hours to
fulfill doing prenatal care: There's a list,
and I can help you with this, but it's stuff like
exercise, nutrition, meditation, yoga, Kegels.
But also Care Circle meetings, which are mandatory.
And some other stuff you'll like even less, I'm afraid.
But don't worry about that now.

Jun 02 11:56 PM

Gard. I should say: I got the message from
DOH already.

Jun 02 11:57 PM

OK. So did you set up your appointment?

Jun 02 11:57 PM

No

Jun 02 11:57 PM

When did you hear from them?

Jun 02 11:59 PM

Fred? You there?

Jun 03 12:00 AM

Yeah. I just wanted to check my messages. I guess
they've been trying to set something up with me.
For a while. A few weeks.

Jun 03 12:02 AM

Really?
Fred. That's not good.

Jun 03 12:03 AM

A month.

Jun 03 12:04 AM

OK.
Hang on.
No visit from Security?

Jun 03 12:04 AM

No. Why? I thought you said I'd hear from DOH,
not Security.

Jun 03 12:05 AM

Usually if a woman ignores DOH they'll send
Security to pick her up and bring her in. You're lucky.
How many messages have you gotten from them?

Jun 03 12:07 AM

Um. Five. I think.

Jun 03 12:08 AM

OK. Listen. I don't want to freak you out but
DOH is going to charge you an administrative fee
for each reschedule,
which is what they call it when they contact you and
you don't get back to them to confirm the appt. And they
will probably, not 100% but probably, ALSO charge you
for the DOH Completionist's time since you didn't
show up, and they might also charge you for
the testing materials, the room, and the support
staff's time, for each appointment they'll say you missed.
So for the love of Mike, Fred, you have GOT to
reply right away when they contact you next.

Jun 03 12:11 AM

Shit. Should I message back right now? How much is
all that going to cost me?

Jun 03 12:11 AM

Fred, I don't even know.
But it's not good.
I'm so sorry, I didn't want to upset you.

Especially because, Fred, I know it doesn't feel like it
right now, but you deserve to be EXCITED. You're
a walking miracle, and I hope you know it.

Jun 03 12:14 AM
Gard. Don't. Please. I feel shitty enough already.

Jun 03 12:14 AM
See this is what makes me so furious.
If we really valued motherhood,
if we really wanted to come up with a solution
to the fertility crisis
that included valuing women as human beings, we
wouldn't SHAKE WOMEN DOWN for every penny

Jun 03 12:17 AM
Gard, I know this is your thing. But can you STFU
for a hot second and help me think of a solution.

Jun 03 12:17 AM
Sorry. I know.
I just hate it
It makes me so furious.
We treat poor mothers
like they're entering a penal system
rather than a health care system!

Jun 03 12:17 AM
GARD, SHUT UP AND HELP ME

Jun 03 12:18 AM
OK. Sorry.
I know a person at DOH. I'll reach out to her,
see if we can get some of your reschedules

recategorized, that will bring the cost down.
Here's the other thing I need to tell you, though:
You should stop working, like as soon as you can.

Jun 03 12:21 AM
What? That's not possible.
Gard, I OWN this business. I can't just
stop showing up to work. Anyway, how the fuck
am I going to pay for all this shit if I don't work?

Jun 03 12:22 AM
I know it doesn't make sense. I know.
Believe me.
I know.
But you are going to be
retroactively charged for your working hours,
going back to the date of conception.

Jun 03 12:23 AM
What?????????
I'm going to be charged a fee for WORKING?
Just because I'm fucking PREGNANT?

Jun 03 12:23 AM
Fred, I'm sorry. But yes. This is how it works.

Jun 03 12:23 AM
How much?

Jun 03 12:24 AM
I know what you're thinking. You're thinking
you'll eat the charges until you pay off the
reschedule fees. But don't. I promise you
it's not worth it.

Jun 03 12:25 AM

Fuck the reschedule fees, Gard. You think just
because you live paycheck to paycheck that I do
too? I have my own MONEY. What I'm talking about
is my COMPANY. I'm not ready to just walk out
on it tomorrow!

Jun 03 12:27 AM

OK. You don't have to be challenging. I'm trying
to be helpful. Here's what I can tell you. You'll be
charged Care Hours on a prorated basis going back to
the date of conception.
Your day rate will be calculated
based on your current salary and on the type of work
you do—which, for you, fortunately, isn't physically
strenuous, you should see what a housekeeper who
works throughout her pregnancy gets hit with.
But even though you're not doing physically demanding
work, which by DOH calculations gets charged
at a higher rate since it's theoretically less safe for
the developing fetus, you should expect your day
rate will still be high because your salary is so
high. So—and I'm just telling you this to prepare you,
and so you can make the decision that's right for you
financially—you need to expect to pay a daily
surcharge equaling about ⅓ of what you'd earn
each day if your salary was calculated and paid out daily.
Pretax.
So figure out what that is and then decide if
you can afford to keep working long enough to
pay off the fines for rescheduling your first appointments.
Plus the fines for continuing to work.
Plus there's the fines for all the Standard of Care infractions
you've no doubt quote-unquote committed by now.

You probably haven't been eating an approved diet.
You probably haven't been taking prenatals.

Jun 03 12:32 AM
Are you kidding?

Jun 03 12:32 AM
Take a deep breath.
You probably haven't been reading or playing music to your uterus.
You've probably used public transportation.
You haven't been doing Maternal Meditations.
You haven't been to the weekly mandatory check-ins.
You haven't been to your Care Group meetings.
And this is just the Care Hours
starter kit stuff, this is just the beginning.
You're starting off at a disadvantage.
You're in debt.

Jun 03 12:36 AM
You're scaring me.

Jun 03 12:36 AM
Honey, right now I'm TRYING to scare you.
This is not a joke.
I'm saying you need to take this very, very seriously.

Jun 03 12:37 AM
I suppose I shouldn't even ask this, but what if
I don't intend to stop working at all? What happens?

Jun 03 12:37 AM
Once the baby is born, if you continue to work
you'll be assessed extra Care Hours at a day rate
that goes up to ½ to ¾ of your quota.

If you apply to get married, though,
and your application is approved—and for you it
almost certainly will be—then you and your partner
can share the total # of your Care Hours, although
typically it's hard to get approval for him to
be assessed more than ¼ of what the total
Care Hours quota comes to; you'll
still be responsible for most of it yourself.

Jun 03 12:45 AM
Gard.

Jun 03 12:45 AM
I'm here.

Jun 03 12:46 AM
This is a fucking nightmare. How do people
even live through this? How do people do it?

Jun 03 12:46 AM
Honey. I know. Believe me.
This is why Insemina is such a joke. Even when
it works, which is only about 10% of the time,
the couple has to be super committed
plus financially comfortable to make it worth
the Care Hours—and that's before you
even factor in the cost of the Insemina treatment
itself. The argument is that since there's
nothing more important than protecting
unborn children, the system has been put in
place to protect them: This quota of guaranteed
Care Hours
with penalties for not meeting them,
starting with prenatal, it's all supposed to be
in the service of protecting children. Who we need,

we need them so desperately. We know that. Fred,
just think about that.
But what people don't realize, now that mothers
are such an unusual and highly regulated class,
is that all this protection comes at such a high cost
to the women. No one who hasn't gone through it
herself even understands—even I can't claim to
understand how you must feel right now.

Jun 03 12:56 AM
I think I need to think.

Jun 03 1:02 AM
Fred? Can I just ask you one thing? Who do
you think the guy is? Do you think you can
marry him?

Jun 03 1:03 AM
I can't get into that right now.

Jun 03 1:03 AM
I'm sorry. I'm really sorry to ask. But your
situation is really special, Fred. And I don't
want to see you go through your pregnancy
stressed out about money. Having someone
to share the Care Hours burden with, it could
be really huge for you. I know you
didn't see your life playing out this way.
I know. But think about it, Fred. Please.

Jun 03 1:06 AM
Oh my God. Gard. I need a fucking minute, okay?
I have to sit and think. Let me get back to you. I
have a million questions but right now I think I
have to go throw up for like a thousand years

Jun 03 1:08 AM
OK. I'm here. I'm here when you need me.

JUNE 6

Jun 06 7:16 PM
Gard. You were supposed to be the one in trouble.
But I'm in trouble. I'm in big, big trouble.

Jun 06 7:17 PM
What happened?
Can we meet?

Jun 06 7:17 PM
No. I can't. I can't even say out loud half of what
I'm thinking right now.

Jun 06 7:18 PM
Fred, I want to help you. Ask me anything.
I mean it.
But could we please please please get together
in person? It's so hard to
communicate over this thing.
After the other night
I had to wrap my arm in a cold pack for
an hour. I've still got a headache that starts
behind my eyes and it's not going away.
We could meet at my place? Or at Pop's?
If you don't want to meet at your place?

Jun 06 7:20 PM
Gard, WTF? You're the one who's been refusing to meet
in person to talk! I've been trying and trying for months
to talk to you
and you kept saying it's not safe, it's not safe, no no no

And now suddenly you want to see me
and have a big therapy session and hold hands???

Jun 06 7:23 PM
That was different. You wanted to talk about
my job. And I can't discuss that with you.
Especially now.
But this—Fred, there's stuff
you need to know
about your Completion.
If I can help you, if I can even
try, I want to.
Did you talk to DOH today?
Was your appointment date set?

Jun 06 7:27 PM
They pulled me in. Just like you said they would.
It was a fucking horror show.
I was at work.

Jun 06 7:27 PM
Oh my God. Fred.
What happened?

Jun 06 7:28 PM
Oh not much, just got pulled out of a meeting
by Security like a fucking criminal
in front of all my employees
no big deal

Jun 06 7:29 PM
Oh no.

Jun 06 7:29 PM

I was back in the office by this afternoon, is the funny thing

Well one fucking funny thing

The other fucking funny thing is the "client"

I was meeting with

at the time

Want to guess who it was

Jun 06 7:31 PM

??

Jun 06 7:31 PM

The guy. The father.

After our exchange the other night

I got back in touch with him

I felt like I should.

But I decided to have him meet me at work

bc I wanted to feel him out a bit

before I told him anything

and I had a crazy day stacked up but I thought, eh,

maybe I'll just see if he wants to come in and see me

at the office and of course he did

bc he's fucking crazy about me

even though I haven't exactly been

that nice to him or encouraging

up until now

Jun 06 7:35 PM

Um that is actually kind of funny

Jun 06 7:35 PM

Right? I know. I'm an asshole. Poor guy.

So when Security shows up, while he's there,

he starts making all this noise

about how they're handling me,
which btw if I had any fucking illusions about whether DOH
was concerned about my personal fucking well-being
as a pregnant woman I certainly know better now
Aaaaaaaaanyway the guy is all You can't treat her like this,
there's some kind of mistake, do you know who she is, do
you know who I am, blah blah blah, I was kind of
embarrassed for him to tell you the truth
Especially when Security was like, She's wanted
by the Department of Health
Because HIS family is actually DOH and they're despicably
rich la la la and powerful la la la so he gets this look on
his face like Oh you are gonna be sorry and he makes a
call and five minutes later I'm being picked up
in a driverless for my first appt with the head of the
Completionist clinic at New Chicago University Hospital
and he's all, I'm coming with you
to make sure you're safe
and that's when I was like good because you're the father.

Jun 06 7:42 PM
OMG. SCREAMING.

Jun 06 7:42 PM
So it has been rather a theatrical day.

Jun 06 7:43 PM
I'm sorry but I can't even breathe I'm laughing
so hard. You are PRICELESS.

Jun 06 7:43 PM
Well. That's an interesting word choice.
And it would be nice if it were true.
But as it turns out there's quite a price
All that stuff you said

the administrative charges, the retroactive Care Hours
the point penalties
all of it
It's unreal
I'm not kidding
I've never even seen numbers like that
Before Ken intervened they were talking about
stuff they can do to me
To Pop
To you
Gard, I'm fucking terrified

Jun 06 7:46 PM
Will he help?

Jun 06 7:46 PM
That's part of why I'm fucking terrified
He's already applying for us to get married
It'll be expedited
bc of who his family is
I feel like
I know how this is going to sound I guess
but I feel like I just got sold to someone

Jun 06 7:50 PM
Fred. I want to tell you I'm sorry.
I've been feeling like
such a shit for even suggesting it, that you
actually marry some guy just
for the Care Hours.
You don't have to go through with it.
We'll figure out something. I'll help you.
Pop can help you. Even Carter could help you,
I know he would want to if he knew—
families can arrange to pool Care Hours,

I've seen it. It's complicated but
a lot of the women at my night clinic are
doing it now, pooling with their sisters and
aunts and parents if the father's not in the
picture for whatever reason or if they couldn't
get a marriage approval.
I can help set that up for you!

Jun 06 7:56 PM
BTW I'm three months already. I'm due in January.

Jun 06 7:56 PM
Oh my God. No wonder.
You must be
how many Care Hours did
wait
that's got to be in the millions

Jun 06 7:58 PM
It is.
I think I have a plan.
In the meantime I have no choice but to keep working
because I've got to sell my company and I have to
do it fast.
They can come for my whole family if I can't pay the balance.
I assume you know that.

Jun 06 8:00 PM
Yeah.

Jun 06 8:01 PM
I've got to go.

Jun 06 8:01 PM
OK. I love you.

Jun 06 8:01 PM
Love you too.

JULY 3

Jul 03 6:12 PM
Pop told me.
You don't have to do this.

Jul 03 6:13 PM
Too late. It's all arranged.
It's the only way.

Jul 03 6:13 PM
This is crazy.

Jul 03 6:14 PM
Is it? To me it makes total sense. It makes me feel
like a princess in a fucking fairy tale. Or like a fucking
fourteenth-century farmer's daughter getting married
off for a field full of fucking goats. I've got a fucking
DOWRY, how many women can say that in this day and age?

Jul 03 6:17 PM
Not funny

Jul 03 6:17 PM
Oh I've just been laughing and laughing about it
Now don't go getting all sad and fucking shit up for me
It all still has to be made official
And it's all a little bit under the table
Like most masterful negotiations are, ho ho
No shitting I'm really pretty fucking proud of myself

Jul 03 6:20 PM

But what's Ken's family even going to do with
a technology consulting firm? What are they
going to do with your business, just hold it for you?

Jul 03 6:22 PM

Well, Ken's family isn't going to buy it, not exactly.
Ken's father's friends are going to carve it up and
buy the pieces, and he gets an ownership stake in
all the pieces so he really gets like 3 businesses for the
price of one son. Plus bragging rights. The guy is legit over
the moon to be having a grandchild, and one born of LOVE
and not CHEMICALS (actual quote). In exchange I get someone
to share my points quota with, after the baby's born, plus a few
million bucks to pay off some of the Care Hours I've
already accrued. In just a couple short months we'll all be
free and clear, but it's all got to go down exactly as I
planned it and no fuckups. But I think it'll all be okay. I made
a good deal for myself. No worries. Your big sister's
no dumb-ass. A little bit of a whore maybe but no dumb-ass

Jul 03 6:25 PM

Jesus, Fred

Jul 03 6:25 PM

KIDDING I'M KIDDING God
Such a fucking puritanical goody
Don't worry

Jul 03 6:26 PM

I'm worried about you

Jul 03 6:26 PM

I'm the one who's worried about YOU
not like you'll let me do anything about it.
Don't worry about me. I've got this shit covered.

Jul 03 6:27 PM

If that's true, then congratulations. I mean it.
I'm proud of you. We've all always been so
proud of you, Fredlet.

Jul 03 6:28 PM

Me? What did I ever do? You're the one who made Pop's
dreams of having all his kids bloody up to the
elbows in other people's guts come at least ⅓ of the way true

Jul 03 6:28 PM

You're kind of gross when you're exultant.

Jul 03 6:29 PM

You know, no one's ever said that to me before.
Go to bed.
Love you. Good night.

SEPTEMBER 13

Sep 13 3:03 AM

Gard something's wrong
I'm scared to call my Completionist
But I'm scared something's really wrong
Can I come over? Please please please
There's blood I think it's blood

Sep 13 3:04 AM

Stay where you are I'm coming to you
don't move and don't call anyone until I
get there

Sep 13 3:05 AM

If I lose this baby I lose everything

Sep 13 3:05 AM

Fred just hang on
I'm at work
But I've got a driverless coming
to pick me up in
3 minutes

Sep 13 3:06 AM

OK
hurry

Sep 13 3:07 AM

What are you feeling?

Sep 13 3:07 AM

Cramping? Or maybe
contractions?
I can't tell what's happening
I didn't want this to happen

Sep 13 3:09 AM

Fred I'm on my way just sit still
breathe
and get off this thing I don't think it can
possibly be helping

SEPTEMBER 15

Sep 15 5:22 PM

Hey.

Sep 15 5:24 PM

Hi. Thank you. Again.

For trying.

Sep 15 5:24 PM

You don't need to thank me. I'm just sorry I
couldn't do more. What happened?

Sep 15 5:25 PM

It's okay. I'm at Ken's parents' place now.

They're taking care of everything

Sep 15 5:25 PM

That's what Mr. Walker told me.

Sep 15 5:26 PM

They're all DOH and H2.0

It's good

I'm covered

Don't worry

I'm sorry I couldn't wait for you

I didn't wait for you

Sep 15 5:27 PM

It's OK.

How are you feeling?

Sep 15 5:27 PM

Tired

Sep 15 5:27 PM

Let me know if you need anything

Anything at all

SEPTEMBER 19

Sep 19 6:42 AM

Fred. I was thinking.

Have you told CQ what's going on yet?

I think he should know, right?

It's time someone told him.

Let me know if you want me to do it.

Sep 19 6:42 AM

No. I will. I will today.

Sep 19 6:48 AM

Fred, I need to ask you something

Sep 19 6:49 AM

What's up

Sep 19 6:51 AM

Gard. You there

Sep 19 6:52 AM

Yeah

I just wanted to ask

are you mad?

Sep 19 6:52 AM

Why would I be mad?

Because I didn't get there fast enough
that night that you had your scare.
I've been thinking about it
and feeling terrible.
I was at work
and I told you to sit there and wait for me
instead of calling DOH
like you did
which is what I should have told you to do
in the first place.
I didn't take you seriously enough
and I just didn't get there
fast enough. I didn't get to you in time
to see how serious it was
or to help you
or even just hold your hand.
I'm really really sorry.
I really wanted to help.

Sep 19 6:57 AM
It's fine. Really.
The baby is fine. I'm fine.
Everything ended up fine.
Please don't worry.

Sep 19 6:58 AM
OK.
Love you.

Sep 19 6:58 AM
Love you too

SEPTEMBER 20

Sep 20 9:58 PM
Fred.

Sep 20 9:58 PM
What's up?

Sep 20 9:59 PM
I'm sorry.

Sep 20 9:59 PM
It's okay.

Sep 20 10:00 PM
And I wanted to tell you why.
If you want to hear.
I wanted you to know why I couldn't leave
the clinic right away, why I
couldn't get to you right away.

Sep 20 10:02 PM
Gard, it's all right.
Whatever happened, it's all right.
Trust me.

Sep 20 10:04 PM
I owe you so much, Fred.

Sep 20 10:04 PM
What are you talking about?
You don't owe me anything.

Yes I do. Yes I totally do. It was you who
took care of us when we were kids, after
Mom. You protected me and
CQ, all the way, until we were way too old for it.
You made it possible for me to be who
I am and to do what I'm doing. I owe you a lot.
And I love you for it. That's all I wanted to say.
But also I thought you deserved to know.
If you want to. If you want to hear.
I'll tell you if you want to hear.

Sep 20 10:08 PM

You know I do.
It's only ALL I've been asking you to tell me
this whole year
It's why I made this private portal connection for our
wearables. You KNOW I have been asking you
and asking you and sick with worry for you
YES COME ON AND TELL ME

At this point I haul myself into the kitchen and throw open Gard's freezer door and stick my wearable arm inside, up to the shoulder. After a moment's hesitation I put my head inside, too, and rest my throbbing forehead on a plastic packet of what feels like engineered mixed vegetables. My eyeballs feel like they're being dragged out of their sockets by invisible hooks and my arm is a streak of flames.

Otherwise, I feel great.

I don't know how much time I just spent in the middle of my sisters' messages flicking back and forth, but it felt comfortingly like being back on base flipping through old messages on my wearable. Or, really, like being a little kid, faking sleep, listening to them whispering back and forth across our bedroom in the dark. I don't remember if I ever actually did that, but right now it feels like I did.

Breathing in the cold air of Gard's freezer, feeling my lungs tighten and my muscles contract, I also can't help but notice that my head doesn't hurt. I don't even think I'm that drunk anymore. I would take this, whatever this is, over another dose of Dr. Rafiq's mystery meds any fucking day. I guess it's no mystery; it's just love. Big, dumb, backward brother-love for these two fucked-up girls I ended up sharing DNA and a pair of painful parents with. I don't know half of what they've been doing while I've been at the Wars, but I've always known I would do anything for them, anything at all. Even though from what I'm reading now, I barely feature in this version of their lives. Pop and me both, we're hardly even mentioned. Fred knew she was pregnant all the way back in June, and didn't tell anybody but Gard till just a few months ago. I don't know why I don't feel more surprised, or jealous. But I don't.

To close my eyes and keep reading, keep hearing their voices in my head, is all I want to do on earth right now, but with the portal across the room it feels like my eyes and my wearable are both straining harder than I really want to deal with. So I stagger back into the other room, swipe up the portal, make my way back to the freezer, prop the portal up on some notional corn and carrots. I've skipped a page and I can't figure out how to go backward but I don't care. It's Gard's voice, so clear and strong and sad it's like she's really here, although I don't think in reality I could bear to hear her say these things.

Sep 20 10:12 PM
While I was in training to become a nurse,
I sometimes saw
women coming in to the hospital with self-inflicted
injuries, saying they'd had accidents. These women
always had little kids. Or their sisters did. Or their kids did.
Birth rate is way down,
we all know that, and we all know it's because of H2.0,
but all that doesn't mean there aren't still women
all around us
going through Completion in some stage or other.
We have a theory about it at our clinic

I'll tell you about it sometime.

Anyway.

Eventually one of the other NCs explained it to me.

If you have an accident or get hurt badly enough
the number of Care Hours you have to log goes down
a prorated amount that's
proportional to the severity of the injury.

This NC told me,

"A kitchen burn gets you off the hook
for an hour—

which is enough time to, say, go to a job interview."

She wouldn't say anything else but I never forgot that.

And I learned it myself, of course
eventually.

A broken toe gets you about 20 hours a week
for 6 to 8 weeks, which is enough time to cover
a second job. That's a
popular Markup at my night clinic, especially since
the pain isn't bad and you're still pretty mobile
while you heal up.

Sep 20 10:25 PM

Gard. Fuck.

Sep 20 10:25 PM

I know how it sounds.

Believe me I know.

Listen. I know you're new to the Care Hours
system.

But all women, regardless of whether
they can afford it, are expected to spend 80 hours
per week on childcare, even if they also work 40
hours per week. If a woman has 2 jobs, which many
do, then the math becomes unsustainable.

And women are good at finding a way out of no way.

Sep 20 10:29 PM

I don't know what to say.
A Markup? That's what you call
breaking a woman's toe? A Markup?
Who would ask for something like that?

Sep 20 10:31 PM

They're all just barely making it.
I don't think you understand.
Anyway once that nurse put the idea in my head,
I just saw it happening more. You'd be surprised.
At almost any hospital, you'll find nurses
who will inflate the severity of an injury report
to help women who need it carve
a couple of extra hours into the week, although
obviously that's a crime and can result
in serious consequences—jail time, fines, losing your
license to practice medicine. Once I saw how
common it was, though, it seemed like the
right and easy and decent thing to do.
Women don't do this casually, as you can
imagine. It takes a lot.

Sep 20 10:36 PM

I'm not that brave.

Sep 20 10:36 PM

Well. I would dispute that.
Anyway. Once a young woman came in—
really young, terrified. She'd accidentally
disfigured herself. She had her newborn with her.
You remember me telling you about it.
I was pretty upset. She was in my ward for a few weeks.
She needed—a lot. I couldn't work out how to help her.
I went back to one of the older nurses who I'd seen

revising patients' reports in special cases
and I asked for her help figuring out what to do.
She was furious.
Threatened all kinds of things, threatened
to have me fired, everything.
But then later I found her
while she was waiting for her bus home,
dragged her into an actual alley
like in a movie
and made her tell me what was going on.
Because I realized
I didn't care about getting fired or exposed,
not really.
I just felt like I needed to know. I needed to.
So.
She was the one who told me
about the clinic
where I'm working now.
She said there were women who were running
a kind of black market for Care Hours.
I didn't know what she meant at first.
She said these women came mostly from
medical and technological backgrounds.
She told me
there were women, nurses mostly,
who would perform what's called Markups,
the kinds of
harmless injuries that could buy you
a few hours a week,
done painlessly and humanely and safely.
She said there were a couple of surgeons
who could do more serious work
without killing you.
The most expensive and potentially risky solution,
she said,

was to employ one of the technologists
to actually slide through a back door
and add Hours to your balance
cook your time sheet, essentially
so you get more Care Hours credited
without needing to log an injury.
Lots of professional women take this option
and bake it into their monthly budget,
or their husbands help them pay for it.

Sep 20 10:46 PM
Really?

Sep 20 10:46 PM
Yes.
I started there the next week.
She was right. About everything.
When I did my first Markup
I thought I was going crazy
I remember it so clearly,
every second
every second of the procedure
I'll never forget it as long as I live.

Sep 20 10:49 PM
Sweet Gard.
I'm so sorry.
I'm so sorry you feel like you have to do this.

Sep 20 10:50 PM
Some of the people I work with
They're just really good at
compartmentalizing,
you know? For the longest time

I didn't get it

My friend at work, Natalie, she told me once

that every procedure was buying someone

literal hours of life, hours outside of a grave.

But for the longest time I just saw us,

women, maiming each other,

animals in a trap biting each other's legs off

Sep 20 10:54 PM

Oh, sweetheart

Sep 20 10:54 PM

I got my head right, though. It took me some time

but I'm proud of what I do. I want to change

the system, of course, but without being

able to do that myself at least I know I'm

helping people.

Sep 20 10:56 PM

Thank you for telling me

Thank you for trusting me

Sep 20 10:56 PM

Well. I wouldn't go thanking me just yet.

You know why I'm telling you, right?

Sep 20 10:57 PM

I do. I have to think about it.

I think I have an idea

But I'm so tired, honey

I'm sorry. I have to get to bed

I'm dying

Sep 20 10:59 PM
Yes. Do that.
You know being up past 10 pm
costs you Care Hours right?

Sep 20 11:00 PM
ok never mind
not going to bed
going to blow some shit up

Sep 20 11:01 PM
Sorry.
I shouldn't have told you that.
Just go to bed.
Right now.

SEPTEMBER 22

Sep 22 9:00 AM
Gard. Sorry to wake u
before your day shift
I'm really excited
have an idea
need to talk to you about it

Sep 22 9:03 AM
?

Sep 22 9:05 AM
Here is my idea: HIRE ME
I can do it
i figured out how
fixing Care Hours
i fucking hacked it man

I AM 3L33T
lololololol

Sep 20 9:08 AM
wht ru tlkng about

Sep 22 9:08 AM
Your sister is a FUCKING GENIUS
that's what i'm talking about
and you can sell my genius to clients
at a small friends and family discount
and everything is going to be awesome

Sep 20 9:10 AM
OK. Go on. I'm awake.

Sep 22 9:11 AM
now that i'm living @ walkers
i've got ACCESS, it's a totally different level here
i've been messing around
and i think i got something
and i need one of your clients
THAT YOU TRUST
this is important
so i can test it
but i think i figured out how to do
care hours adjustments
and i can sell it to women like me
or women who've had insemina but
want to continue to work

Sep 20 9:14 AM
That's impressive.
It really is.

But, Fred,

You're sure you know what you're doing, right?

The last technologist we had who did CH

adjustments raised the price because

she was scared she was close to getting caught.

You're working on the Walkers' portal?

Or something?

Are you sure that's safe?

Sep 22 9:16 AM

oh don't worry about it

trust me, your sister knows what she's doing

Sep 20 9:17 AM

Just make sure nobody sees my messages to you.

Nobody at DOH should find out about it

OK? This is important

Sep 22 9:18 AM

Gard, I'm not an idiot

Sep 20 9:18 AM

I know, I know you're not. But if anybody

in Ken's family read what I told you,

that could be bad. That would be bad,

definitely.

Are you sure this is safe?

Sep 22 9:20 AM

Gard! SHIT! Did you understand what I

just said to you? I'm talking about something

that could HELP you, I've got a way to help you

from the inside of the goddamn DOH system

I tried it on my own CH balance first obvs and

I think it worked but I'm scared to adjust myself
too much or more than once
i need one of your clients
somebody to test my code on
please! this is my
i don't even know how to put this
you don't know what this could mean for me

Sep 20 9:23 AM
Fred. Please. You have to slow down.
First of all
my clinic doesn't serve many women
who can afford Care Hours adjustments
it's so rare
we hardly even offer it

Sep 22 9:25 AM
Well offer it! To someone! You
must have someone who's coming in who's
not just looking to have her fucking arms
broken or her fingertip lopped off

Sep 20 9:27 AM
I think I am done with this conversation now.

Sep 22 9:27 AM
Gard, wait I'm sorry I'm sorry
I didn't mean it like that
I know why you do it, I get it
I get why THEY do it
I really do
I'm sorry
Gard

OCTOBER 1

Oct 1 6:17 AM
Gard I'm really sorry

OCTOBER 2

Oct 2 11:11 PM
Hi. Just checking in on you.
I wrote to CQ today. Told him
I'd moved in with the Walkers.
So he'd know where to find me
if he ever decided to actually
write to anybody back home
the jerk

Oct 2 11:15 PM
Hey you out there?

OCTOBER 3

Oct 3 9:33 PM
Hi, darlin
I know you're still mad at me
But I felt a kick today and I wanted
to tell you.

Oct 3 9:37 PM
That's beautiful. Thank you for telling me.

Oct 3 9:37 PM
OMG it speaks

Oct 3 9:38 PM
I'm so sorry, I can't talk right now
I'm just really exhausted

This schedule is catching up with me

I've got to get some rest

I'll talk to you later, k?

Oct 3 9:40 PM

k

OCTOBER 5

Oct 5 5:22 PM

I want you to know I'm not judging you or

anything you or your colleagues do

OK?

I support it, in fact.

I'm TRYING

I even figured out a way I can help you

I don't know why you won't even talk to me

Oct 5 5:28 PM

I'm sorry I've been out of touch

I'm just busy

OCTOBER 6

Oct 6 2:41 PM

Gard I really really need to talk to you

Please don't shut me out

I need your help

I'm just being honest now, okay?

I was levied an additional "backdated" penalty

from my first trimester

Extra Care Hours plus several hundred thousand in $$

If I can't find a way to test the code I wrote

to fix my own hours somehow

then I need to come in to your clinic and I

need you to walk me through the options
Show me what's on your menu

Oct 6 2:45 PM
I can't do that

Oct 6 2:46 PM
You have to.
I can't tell the Walkers about this
It's too much for me to bring to them
I need a way forward
This is it

Oct 6 2:47 PM
I can't

Oct 6 2:47 PM
Why the fuck not?

Oct 6 2:48 PM
i just can't
i'm really sorry
i love you

Oct 6 2:49 PM
you think I'm not serious about this
you think I'm not tough enough
if you can handle it I can

Oct 6 2:50 PM
that's not it

Oct 6 2:50 PM
then what is it

Oct 6 2:50 PM

Fred

This is not safe.

And I don't think you're safe either.

Oct 6 2:51 PM

Gard you know that's crazy

you're being paranoid

I built this system and I'm

telling you for a fact it's secure.

Oct 6 2:53 PM

And I don't know if I'm safe.

And I don't want to cause more trouble for you

Oct 6 2:54 PM

What? You're scaring me

Let me help

Let me help you

You know Ken's family is crazy fucking connected

I can probably get you out of anything

Just don't do anything really stupid

And just do this one thing for me, please

Oct 6 2:56 PM

I'm sorry but I really can't

That's the last message from Gard in the file packet. The rest are from Fred, a series of repeated, unanswered efforts to get Gard to respond, all dated October through November. Fred's final try, the message I saw first, is too sad to reread now.

I'm so tired. My head and my arm are throbbing. I have to think; I have to figure out my next move, but I'm not sure I can. I swipe Gard's portal off and grope my way cautiously into a kitchen chair. Daylight is just beginning to creep across the grimy little window over the sink.

As Gard's portal powers down, I feel the pressure in my eyeball dropping, too. It's a peculiar sensation, like my eye is leaking fluid. A spot of blood falls onto my knee. I touch my own face gingerly, my stitched-up forehead, my nose, the inner corners of my eye. My fingertips come away bloody. I don't want to know why. How long was that thing hooked into me, drawing on my wearable's processors? Two hours? Less?

As Fred's interface blanks out of view, my own familiar wearable interface swings back into place across my retina and I see I have messages waiting for me. Someone from Rafiq's office. Confirming an appointment.

And Natalie B. replied to the message I sent:

Dec 20 2:03 AM

Thank you, Natalie. I took your advice.
I hope you're well and not in too much
trouble. I'll see you again soon.

Dec 20 5:44 AM

I really can't talk to you anymore. I'm sorry.

But because I can't leave it at that, because I can't let her think I never figured it out, because I want her to believe I'm smart, or trying, or I don't even know what, I send it before I even have time to think about what I'm doing:

Dec 20 5:45 AM

My sister Gardner
She left
before our older sister Fredericka
could ask for a Markup at your clinic.
Didn't she
Isn't that why she left
Isn't that right
Why didn't you think you could tell me

IN THE FIRST PLACE

The squad was late coming back over the ridge after a sweep and got caught out beyond the perimeter after sunrise, and from there everything pretty much went to shit. Dusk, dawn, and nighttime were typically the best times for troop movement, or any kind of movement, because of the airborne particulate, which was everywhere and contained everything, microscopic pieces of dust, rock, sand, plastics, glass, steel, metal alloys, and iron. In daylight, with the sun refracting off millions of airborne particles per square foot, visibility was severely limited and temperatures ran too hot for the triggers to operate predictably. It was like being an ant stumbling through smog under a magnifying glass. An ant *carrying a nuke*, stumbling through smog under a magnifying glass. But just because most of the patrols happened at night did not mean that they slept during the day. So movement tended to be slow, at all times, even without heavy contact.

Fire Support Base One, also called the First Place, was tucked into the lean shadow of a low ridge that had been constructed, many years ago as their fathers' wars aged and rotted into their own, along the railroad tracks for the purpose of sheltering the H2.0 route, miles upon miles of piled-up and hastily buried concrete, asphalt, rebar, siding, furniture, billboards, drywall, trailers, battered cars with the car seats still latched into the back and the manuals still tucked into the glove boxes, all bulldozed into a rough mound and interred beneath what must have been some of the last of the state's topsoil, but which now more closely resembled a thick layer of fine gray sand. He had heard there were bodies under there, too. They had all heard that.

Any squad or team returning from a patrol was expected to make base well before sunrise to avoid being caught out on the ridge, either scaling its eastward side or crossing over the top of it, spotlighted by the rising sun and a pitifully easy target, even in low visibility, to be picked off by sniper fire, one by one. The ridge, of course, conferred the very same advantages on their own defense during the frequent raids on the H2.0 capsules.

Wash reported the squad's position as they arrayed in a straggle at the bottom of the ridge well after sunrise, just as the sun arrived over the mountains and began to bear down in earnest, fixing to cook them alive using the pale mound at their backs as its fry pan. They were close enough to the ridge that they could see the top of the First Place tower, just past the ridge inside the base, and overlooking all: the dust- and debris-choked valley, the ridge separating the poisonous valley from the base, and, running alongside the base's western perimeter, the line of H2.0 capsules inching their way slowly toward receiving depots somewhere up north. Like the rotating earth itself, the line of H2.0 capsules never stopped moving, but slowly, so slowly that it never appeared to be in motion. Sixty or so miles to the south were the last remaining H2.0 production facilities, which no one on base had seen, at least not in the years he'd been here.

"We're going to wait for fire support from the tower before making the ridge. Could be a while." Sergeant Fine, always delivering the not-so-fine weather.

"We look like a fucking shooting gallery sitting here in broad sun," someone pointed out over the hookup.

"Skip's orders. Find cover, stay close."

So they broke into teams of four and found what cover there was in the debris, which for most meant backtracking from the ridge a significant distance—so much for covering in place.

"XO hasn't sent a cleanup crew out to bulldoze in a while," someone observed over the hook.

"Lucky us. Plenty of nice, comfy rubble to snuggle into."

"Keep the chatter down, kids."

"You trying to sleep?"

Sleep, while impossible, was actually tempting. Fighting fatigue was harder than fighting thirst, or hunger, or heat.

He found himself covering with Chalke, Wash, and Sergeant Fine in a rusted bulk that might have once been a short bus, tipped onto its side and blown out, rubber and plastic and reddened metal weathered by dust and sun. Inside, they were partially exposed to the sky, and to the sandy broken road running north, but they spread out and found what shade they could.

Heat crowded in with them as the sun rose higher.

At first the sergeant had Wash sending an encrypted request for updates on fire support every quarter hour. After ninety minutes of this came a terse reply from someone high enough on the command chain that Sergeant Fine and Wash exchanged a brief look. *Hold for your fucking frag order, dammit.*

"One more update request from Charlie and they'll send us humping up the fucking mountain," Chalke observed unnecessarily. Sergeant Fine told Wash to close up shop until command made contact. They each recorded their water levels and settled in to wait. Someone on the hook was humming tunelessly. For once nobody seemed to mind. There was nothing else to listen to out beyond the ridge but debris skittering in the wind, and the unceasing patter of particulate against their helmets, a sound like grains of sand poured into a metal bowl.

They were accustomed to the heat, to the airborne particulate digging into their eyes and mouths and skin, to the exquisite mixture of boredom and fear, to being tired. They were experts at sharing, conserving, and reusing water. Thick tongues, burning eyes, raw and cracked membranes. Fingers curved into claws inside gloves because of broken knuckle skin. Toes clenched inside boots around a scalloped half-moon of dust, cemented in place between the fleshy forward edge of the balls of the feet, and the scraped thin skin of the undersides of the toes. You can survive anything, Sergeant Fine had told him once, by surviving it in ten-minute increments. Anyone can do anything—sweat in 110-degree heat, endure thirst, target other humans with unregulated biological weapons—for ten minutes. And when the ten minutes you've just survived elapse, and they will, then the next ten minutes begin, and you survive them, and survive the ones after them, and keep doing it, and one day you'll realize you're still alive. *Don't look forward to that day, though*, Sergeant Fine had said. *Don't even think about that day.*

While thinking about the current ten minutes and how soon they'd be over with, three things happened, out of all apparent respect for temporal order. He felt a puff of air on his cheek, the infinitesimal shoving aside of millions of airborne particles, as something solid hurtled past, pushing both sound and mass before it. Then Fine, sitting opposite him in the hulk of the short bus, slumped over and was dead. And then he heard the ragged pop of molecules displaced by the bullet, snapping back into place.

"*That can't be right, that cannot be fuckin' RIGHT!*" Wash shouted hoarsely. Parts of Fine's eyeball and cheekbone and brain and scalp were everywhere among them, including on Wash's comm board, a reinforced-metal-and-matte plastic tablet that was notoriously finicky and difficult to use even without the inside of someone's head splashed over its surface.

Into the hole of stunned silence on the hook Lance Corporal Chuck spoke, from wherever he was hunkered down in the debris fields outside the First Place: "Private Washington, get your comm board set up and send an update to command now now now—"

Then the hook exploded with the sounds of static and mocking laughter: "*Now now now, Private Washington, now now now, Private Washington, now now now.*" It was like a nightmare where you hear voices in your head that no one else can hear, except that this was real life and the whole squad and all of Charlie company could hear it. Somewhere in the debris field, hidden away in the piles or in one of the shelled-out shopping centers that ringed the base all around them, the raiders had found a way to take over their channel, and to position what suddenly seemed like a goddamn battalion's worth of snipers.

Over the high-pitched squeal of static and the braying horrible laughter and the wails of men being found by sniper fire that had by that time all swamped the hook, Lance Corporal Chuck screamed something so stupid it didn't even register at first. "Squad, get ready to take the ridge running, we've got to get over and back to the First Place, now now now!" Even if they hadn't specifically been told to cover in place until the tower could provide fire support, running on command through a field of fire toward a ridge made of slippery, shifting, boot-eating gray sand—on unencrypted orders given over a compromised hook, no less—was suicide, plain and simple. But damned if he couldn't see that dipshit Lance Corporal Chuck weaving through the rubble, trailed by three panicked kids from his hole, picking their way toward the ridge through a pattern of whirring bullets.

Chalke gaped, wide-eyed, at him and at Wash. "Never happen. Never. Fucking. Happen."

His own croak-whisper hurt his ears. "Now now now, Private." But they didn't move. Neither of them could find a way to do it. His body simply was not accepting or processing any additional information, please try again later.

Wash didn't bother looking up at either of them. He was coding a new line in to the First Place and starting an update for command over the fresh encrypted channel. Not for the first time, Carter was grateful for his friend's speed and expertise, even as his right forearm still throbbed from Wash's latest demonstration. "One, this is Charlie. Multiple Coors. Heavy contact including sniper fire. Compromised hook. Need to advance to ridge with tower support." As he said this, Wash glanced up at him, and he nodded back quickly: Permission to ventriloquize for Lance Corporal Chuck-Run-Amuck granted, by him at least. Now they just had to hope the crazy motherfucker didn't somehow actually make it up the ridge before command came back affirmative.

As it turned out, they needn't have bothered worrying, because the CP's base-wide hook had been taken out by the raiders as well, and no one could hear them; they were completely isolated, surrounded and under fire, with an inexperienced and frankly frantic second officer newly in command. It occurred to him afterward to be grateful that he didn't know all that at the time.

"They're all going," Chalke observed, again unnecessarily. Through the hole in the side of the short bus they could see the second team of their twelve-man squad emerging from cover and running in a crouch toward a low pile midway between their own hole and the base of the ridge. They could also see two of Chuck-Run-Amuck's team: the Chuck himself, plus some other unlucky son of a bitch he couldn't recognize from fifty yards through the particulate, but who he ardently hoped was their medical officer, known as Squiddy. They were hauling the bodies of the two other guys from their team back to cover.

"WASH! WHERE THE FUCK ARE YOU?" The Chuck shrieked over the compromised hook, creating a new counterpoint in the chorus of taunts, *Where the fuck are you? Where the fuck are you? Now now now, Private Washington.*

Carter didn't know how Wash wasn't going completely insane. His friend looked terrified, they all did, that familiar pinched look around the wide eyes, and the flat rictus of mouth, but he also looked like he, perhaps alone among all of them, actually knew what the hell he was supposed to do. "I've got to get up there to the Chuck. He's command now." Communications was supposed to move with the officer in command; Carter knew that. With Sergeant Fine dead, Wash was supposed to move up the line to the lance corporal so that squad command could communicate with base. Base didn't seem overly eager to reply to them, though.

"Shouldn't we wait to hear back from the First Place?"

Wash shook his head. "I've got to move. You and Chalke have to carry Fine between you." No man left behind. No man, ever. He and Chalke got to work.

As they struggled out from beneath the short bus into a lethal mist of bullets and airborne particles, he and Chalke straining under Fine's weight and Wash taking point, something happened that later he could only say probably saved his life, although at the time it seemed hell-bent on killing him where he stood. The sun was hard and fully up by then, scattering its blinding power across the particle-choked air, creating a shield made of billions of needlepoints of reflected light. But from across the valley floor that spread beneath their feet and the cursed site of the base and the H2.0 they were meant to spend their lives trying to protect rose up a dust storm, one that would have made him run for his life, if he weren't already preparing to do just that.

It was upon them in an instant, fully formed and howling. The bullets whirled inside it. Mindless with fear, choking, he pulled his air mask and face shield into place one-handed—he and Chalke each had one arm under Fine's shoulders. With his shield in place, he reached out and grabbed for the back of Wash's jacket, flailing in the direction of where he'd seen Wash crouching just a moment before. Wash hadn't moved—he'd stopped for his mask and shield, too. He was inches away, and Carter couldn't see him. Everything, every man and bullet and landmark and razor-sharp piece of metal sticking out of a pile of debris in the dead zone, was utterly concealed by the dark grayout of the dust storm. It had happened in less than five seconds. They were more lost now than they'd ever been.

His hand gripped the back of Wash's belt, and from the front, Wash gave the belt a tug. *Okay.* He tugged back. *Okay.* He could feel Chalke to his left, his arm stretched across Fine's back, and he wiggled his fingers against Chalke on the other side of Fine's body. Chalke wiggled his fingers in response. The men began staggering through grayout in the direction of the ridge.

Wash had the unlucky job of detecting obstacles in the darkness and feeling his way gingerly around them. Sometimes one of them stumbled and they all fell down, clutching one another and Fine's body madly until they were back on their feet and ready to move again. As they staggered forward, whoever was firing on them continued firing blindly, indiscriminately, into the storm. Occasionally a shot could be heard above the screech of hurtling wind and sand and decay, but more often you'd feel the whiff of the bullet flying past without a sound. Even the mad taunts of the raiders, broadcast directly into their implants through the company hook, were lost in the roar.

They'd taken cover almost a quarter mile from the ridge and had to retake that ground an inch at a time. He heard Chalke scream once, but wherever he'd been hit, he managed to keep going. Something sharp, a nail, perhaps, pierced his boot, but he couldn't feel any pain after the first moment. Each breath became sharp and agonizing; the oxygen in his air mask felt like it was setting his lungs on fire. The only way out was to keep going. Once, over the hook, he thought he could hear Wash sob, and felt himself wanting to weep, too, in the helpless, unmindful way of a child who is overtired. In this way an indescribable amount of time elapsed.

The dust storms, they'd seen, could rise up out of nowhere and engulf an area the size of a city for days at a time, and just as suddenly withdraw back into the earth. Or they could last an hour, or a few minutes, or span the equivalent of just a few city blocks, or take several perceptible minutes to spin themselves back down. There was no way of telling the size of the storm they were working their way through, or when it might suddenly whistle off and disappear, leaving them exposed in the middle of the sand-coated dead zone of the debris field, targets so vulnerable they might as well be naked. He tried not to imagine what would happen then, or what could happen, what bottomless depths he would find himself capable of sinking to. Would he be the Marine who used his CO's body as a shield? Would he be the Marine who shat himself in fear? Would he be the Marine who ran? Or would he simply be the Marine who, as seemed to be happening to him more and more now, sank into a field of flowers and blackness only he could smell and see, and let his buddies haul him along until they all died of whatever this was, whatever force kept taking him out of himself and away. His terror was all that kept it at bay now. Only when he was convinced he was going to die anyway could he keep himself from feeling death creeping toward him on its soft, sweet-smelling hands.

When the First Place tower began laying down trigger fire across the debris field, they heard it before they felt or saw it: a high whistling keen over their heads that made them freeze in their tracks and instinctively dive to the ground. Then the unmistakable earth-hammering sound of the strikes, making the sand quake into rivulets and ornate patterns around their bellies. And then the sky was alight again, the dust storm burst wide open, the particulate forced up into the air in a spreading cloud overhead. He rolled onto his back and watched: a cloud of dust and metal, like an angel of darkness at war with itself, roiling and heavy and gray, and tearing itself to pieces in the sky.

He looked around, trying to understand their position. They were halfway to the ridge. Chalke was shuddering on the ground next to Fine's body, his left pants leg red to the knee, his boot almost black with pooled blood. Wash seemed all right. He was squinting toward base, gauging the distance to the ridge. No one else from their squad seemed to be in the field.

He found out later that the rest of the squad had made it to the base of the ridge before the storm hit and somehow managed to scramble over it through the swirling dust. His own team was all the squad left on the other side, and in zero visibility the tower held off for as long as it deemed advisable before opening fire on the raiders still firing on them through the storm. Their slowness to react to the lance corporal's order had cost them time and possibly a few more dead raiders, and although they were commended for bringing back Sergeant Fine—and in the end, Wash—their failure to act meant Chalke and Quinn were put on point for the next two patrols. Lance Corporal Chuck eventually got a medal. He'd brought back the bodies of two men. Single-handedly, it seemed.

But that came later. When the dust storm cleared around them, it was obvious they had about two minutes, tops, of less-than-ideal visibility to make it to the ridge and over, and with Chalke's leg and Fine's body, all three men understood they weren't going to make it.

Wash got on Chalke's other side and they threw themselves forward like maddened animals across the debris field, crouching low when shells began whizzing overhead, this time directed at the fire squad in the tower. For the time being.

They reached the base of the ridge in about ninety seconds, and there was no time to strategize, to plan how they would get over. They started their scrambling ascent together, a clothesline of bodies hung on each other's shoulders, each man hauling the weight of his friends, clutching handfuls of sand, falling, pushing upward again. Their breath came in ragged heaves, their legs strained, their hearts seemed to fly open. He fell, got a mouthful of ash, and screamed with the work of surging upward, pulling Fine with all his strength. *Don't look up. Don't look at how far you have to climb. Just push, goddammit, push.*

Chalke reached the top first, Wash hauling him over with a hoarse cry of effort, and Carter gave Fine's body a shove that sent it rolling after Chalke, knocking him to his knees and then to his face in the gray sand on the base side of the ridge, which was shallower on the inside, like a steep-sided bowl with a thumbprint's depth. Wash made a sound between a wheeze and a moan, and when Carter looked to his friend he saw he'd taken a round through the side of his neck. Wash fell. Backward. On the wrong side of the ridge.

"Don't you die! Don't you fucking die!"

Carter had already stumbled over the ridgetop, but he scrabbled backward in the dust anyway, knowing he was too late to correct his downward slide into the bowl of the base, but trying, trying to get back to the top and pull his friend over to safety. Clawing at the ash and sand, he found no purchase. He dug in with his knees and crawled until his arm found the soft, sliding, infernal sand of the ridgetop and groped blindly. Reaching one arm over the top of the ridge, his body flat in the sand on the base side of the mound, his hand found Wash's shoulder and gripped it. He could feel Wash's body convulsing.

With the final team over the ridge and back in the base, the tower opened up with a layer of hellfire. Over his head, where he lay in the gray sand clutching Wash's blood-soaked shoulder, triggers rent the day into wild flame.

TEN

He's surprised to see me. That much couldn't be clearer from his expression.

"Your office is pretty easy to find," I offer by way of explanation, even though it hadn't been, not exactly. I'm leaning back against his desk, facing him as he comes through his own office door, my back to the rattling windows that overlook his view, a crumbling parking lot.

Major Rafiq brings out the patent-pending smile and his face lights up, just a few seconds too late to be entirely genuine. I'm a lot bigger than he is. "Evidently. Or perhaps you were meant to find me!" To his credit, he doesn't ask how I got into his office before it opened.

I'm sure he would have been less surprised if he'd found me skulking around outside, lost and hangdog, in the brown and yellow hallways of the old VA medical building. Or if I'd picked a fight with his desk staff—the same ones who didn't notice me walking right past them as the office opened. Or if he'd just passed me hanging out in the rundown street outside, too sheepish to walk through the building doors. There are a lot of those guys around. But I'm not that guy. At least I don't think I am.

Because here's the truth about us veterans: We're not broken. We're not all damaged. Some of us, a lot of us, make it through the day the same way people who haven't seen combat do: minute by minute and hour by hour, as human beings. We don't need fixing, or pity. Some respect would be helpful, though. Very helpful. Not that I'm expecting to find any here, in this place. For servicemen of my generation, the VA is the place you come if you want to be slotted into a folder, ushered into a seat, or helped into a room that has nothing to do with you, or where you belong, or what you need.

But I do need something, right now, badly enough that I had to come. I'm just trying to hold on to as much of my dignity as I can while I'm asking.

"Sir, I don't want to take up too much of your time. But I need a . . . I'm here for a refill."

Rafiq's expression is unchanged: he's broadcasting nothing but relief and delight at my presence. I don't trust it, although I'm not sure why. Because he's Pop's friend, I guess. That's the only real reason I can name.

"I'm glad you're here, son. I didn't sleep much last night, thinking about—" Here he holds his hands up, palms to the sky, and does a little puff of his cheeks that could be regret, could be helplessness, could be a lot of things but probably not anything useful to me.

"I didn't get much sleep, either, sir."

Rafiq nods, gazing at me meaningfully. "I was sorry to give you the news."

"Yes, sir." A short silence spins out between us. Into it, I lob a lame shot: "It's not every day a guy learns he's dying, although that probably sounds like a strange thing for a Marine to say."

"Not at all strange. In fact, the least strange thing in the world." Rafiq nods again, even harder. "Come sit," he adds, and gestures to a pair of horribly uncomfortable-looking chairs in the corner of his office—an awkward little conversation nook, for those of his patients who need convincing that he's more than just a desk jockey. I slide down from the corner of his desk and move toward where he's pointing, feeling already as if he's in the process of turning the tables on me. Whatever advantage I may have started with by surprising him here, in his place of safety, he's already directing me down from my higher ground. "How do you feel this morning, Carter?"

"Like a bad road, sir."

"Bad road. I like that expression." Rafiq chuckles. In point of fact, I feel like a bad road through hell: the singing headache is back for its big encore, my old friend the gray corona has settled back into its customary spot around my center of focus, and while my face bears the distinctive signs of having been worked over by someone lacking a gentle touch, that's nothing to how the rest of me feels. It hurts to inhale.

"Well. You should see the other guy, sir." This makes Rafiq laugh louder. Even as I'm settling into his uncomfortable chair for an uncomfortable talk, I'm finding that it's hard not to smile, a little bit, at how easily amused he seems to be. Every second this guy has lived since his refugee childhood, or since his years in the field hospitals, must seem like a goddamn gift to him. If the guy is overfull of horizon-sweeping joy, you honestly can't be mad at him for it.

"I won't quiz you about your symptoms today," he promises, as if I looked worried. "I want to talk about other things."

"I just came in for a refill, sir." Sooner rather than later, I hope.

"Oh, I'll prepare that for you, too, don't worry. But Carter, as your father's friend, I must tell you"—he leans toward me, locks his teddy-bear brown eyes on mine—"I am concerned."

"Yes, sir."

"I hear from my friend. His son is home after more than two years. Possibly depressed, showing signs of PTSD. And then I hear from a doctor—excuse me, a Nurse Completionist"—it's impossible to like the tone in which he pronounces Natalie B.'s job title—"who tells me that this boy, my friend's son, is unconscious on her floor, and as his friend can I come to help him. Well!" Rafiq shakes his head, wide-eyed. "So I come myself. And what do I find? My friend's son. My dear, dear friend from many years, who will always have a place in my heart even if years go by without our getting a chance to talk. My friend's son is covered in blood. He is unconscious. He is desperately sick and cannot admit it even to himself." Rafiq's eyes are shining, his empathy is unbearable. His concern, his caring, it all feels painfully overwrought, like we're starring in an ad on someone's wearable. "And he is in a very dangerous place. How he got there I cannot say. But I find him in—how can I put this? One of the most dangerous places in all of New Chicago—for anyone who finds it, but perhaps especially for him."

"Especially for me? Why?"

"We'll get to that," Rafiq says gravely. "Carter, I want to help you—you have no idea how much I want to help you. But I must ask, how did you come to be there, in that place?"

The more he says he cares about me and what happens to me, the more nervous I get. All I can do is stare at him. The thing is, he could be telling the truth—he could honestly want to help me—but I still wouldn't want to tell him anything.

"Doc, I don't mean to be rude. But could we get that refill?"

He smiles, gratified even though I've changed the subject—for the time being. "It worked for you, did it?"

"It did," I acknowledge.

"I'm glad. I'll get you a scrip, you can fill it downstairs."

I was hoping he would give me another dose more or less as soon as he walked into his office—I'm feeling that bad—and I'm about to tell him as much, despite how it hurts my throat to think about asking, but then he changes gears, again.

"Every time I see a case like yours I'm reminded of how long it's been, this war. Twenty-four years! My God. It started before me, and it will not end until after me, this much I know now." He shakes his great bespectacled head sadly, slowly, lenses glimmering. "And here we are, *still* at war in the West. Why do you think that is?"

I can't imagine what he's gaming at with this question. My jaw swings a bit on its hinges as I try to think of an answer. "Well, H2.0, sir. That's what the raiders want to blow up. They want to disrupt distribution to the New Cities. Or, if they can't do that, they want to keep the military engaged, at least, so there's something left to steal from over there."

"Yes. Precisely so. And yet the materials, the facilities, the technologies that produce synthetic water, none of these have been reproduced on the other side of the mountains, eh? Or indeed anywhere near a New City—which would render H2.0 less expensive to produce and distribute. Yes? It's almost like we *want* this war to continue." He's saying what everyone from op-ed authors down to dumb grunts like me all already know about the Second Wars. Gard used to rail against it like no one else I ever knew. "Like the oil wars of the decades before your father and I were born, the current wars are all about a resource that's only extractable from an environment hostile to our interests."

"Okay." I offer a nod that's half a shrug. The gesture does nothing good for my swimming head.

"But don't you see, *that's* why we're still at war. That's why, even after *years* spent—by your father and myself, among many, many good men—*years,* trying to clear and secure a massive, *massive* region of the country that has been declared unsafe and uninhabitable, there are people still there. Fighting. Poisoning. Detonating each other. For the sake of a train." Major Rafiq leans toward me with a shrewd, insider's smile. "And that's what the men call *some next-level bullshit.* Have I captured your thinking on this issue, son?"

Now I think I know this game. If he, Wise But Uncondescending Senior Medical Officer, can demonstrate how well he understands me, Average Poisoned Grunt with PTSD, a type he's no doubt seen in this very office many times before, he believes he can get me to open up and start talking.

"It's what everybody thinks. It's what anybody who sees the news thinks." I am struggling to remain upright in my seat. "I don't know if it's what the army thinks, or the Marine Corps." Exhale. Keep breathing. "Although the Marines aren't exactly known for thinking."

Major Rafiq nods hugely, leans back with a heavy thud into his chair. "Sure. Sure. Who knows. But here's one thing I do know, son. I may hate the war—and I do hate it, I hate everything it's done. But I love the army with everything in me. The same way I know you love the Marine Corps, despite everything that's happened to you. Because the Marine Corps is not the commanders or the administration, or the Corps itself, the idea of it, the concept—although many good men love that concept more than their own mothers. No, you love the Corps because for you the Corps is your friends. It's your men. It's the men you'd die for. This is what I'm saying: your father and I, for each other, we *are* the army. The same way that for you, the Marines *are* the men from your platoon, from your company. That's why even though you may have come to hate the Wars and what they did to you, you'll never hate the Marines. You could no more hate the Marine Corps than you could hate your sisters."

I don't have any reply to this.

The major presses on. "To someone on the street in New Chicago or New Detroit or New Minneapolis, it seems like everything west of the mountains has been blowing up or falling apart for decades. The Wars are just an ugly idea, and the veterans who make it home are just the ugly men who lived inside it. They don't have reason to care as long as there's food and water over here—unless you're young, of course, unless you're in love." He smiles sadly at me. "*Then* you're in trouble. You can't get married, unless you're pregnant. And you can't get pregnant, because of the infertility crisis. And we all know it's down to the water we're fighting for, of course, we all *know* it, but who can do anything about that?" Here is the helpless gesture again, the hands lifted toward the ceiling like they're testing for rain. Impossible rain.

"I suppose someone in New City government could start by admitting it," I snap at him. I'm tired; my head hurts; my everything hurts. I didn't mean to engage with him, much less on this particular point, but it's Fred I'm thinking of, I guess, and I don't like how Rafiq's tone seems to be making light of what's been happening to her. And I really just wanted another dose, for God's sake. For the love of all that is holy. For the pure sweet love of Christ on a piece of buttered toast can I please have that shot. "For some people it's a real problem."

"For all of us, for all of humanity, it's a real problem!" Rafiq exclaims earnestly. "Who could deny it? After surviving all of this! The water scarcity! The climate crisis, the storms! The quakes, the fires! The flooding and collapse of our coastal cities, the evacuations, food shortages! To survive all of this, and then find the technology and the inner *strength*"—here he puffs his chest, although his eyes are shining as if he could weep—"to begin to rebuild, and to succeed, to come back so far! Only to find we might be doomed to collapse because of *infertility!*" The way he says the word makes it sound like it's someone's fault, and he'd very much like to take that someone by the shoulders and shake, hard. If it weren't so laughable it would be sad. "For someone who's seen what I've seen? Carter. Let me tell you. Humankind is an incredible, a beautiful force. It is destructive. It is not harmless or blameless. But by God it is worth fighting for, to the last man. The last man." He nods, mostly to himself, and folds his hands in his lap.

My own hands are in fists, I realize. It's all I can do to keep myself straight in the chair, which is just as uncomfortable as it looked. I need another dose of pain reliever, worse than I wanted to admit even when I came here this morning. But I understand where this Rafiq is coming from now, at least, as sentimental and self-glorifying as it is. And if he's told me this much, he might be able to tell me a bit more—as much as I can stomach hearing, anyway.

"Doc, can I ask you a question?"

"If I can ask you one," he responds, in a milder tone.

"Fair enough." Carefully I unclench my hands and put them on my knees, where I can see them. "That medication you gave me. It worked. It really worked. And I'm grateful—it helps. But. I need to know, I guess, for my family's sake . . . if there are side effects I should know about. Like am I going to be addicted to this stuff, for one."

"No. One hundred percent no." Rafiq has put his hands on his knees, too, deliberately mirroring me, it seems. "We have a policy against prescribing habit-forming drugs to our veteran patients. We've seen an elevated risk of abuse."

"Okay. Okay. Good. I'm going to choose to believe you on that."

"I hope you will."

"One more question. Maybe you know this, maybe you don't. But could this stuff cause . . . changes in mood? Like aggression, for example."

"You're asking does it cause mood changes?"

"I'm asking does it cause feelings of aggression. Specifically. Could it make you, you know, sort of violent?"

I see the merest flicker of unease in his eyes, behind the gold-rimmed round glasses. Abruptly, as if surprised I would even ask, he says, "No. Not at all."

"Okay."

"Now my turn, yes?"

"Sure. I mean, yes, sir."

"You're going to like this question"—he smiles—"because it will be familiar to you. The same question I began with. What were you doing in that place yesterday?"

"From what I remember, mostly a lot of bleeding and lying on the floor."

Major Rafiq roars with laughter. He laughs so hard he has to produce a cloth from his pants pocket to wipe his face. This time, though, it's harder for me to crack a smile in return.

"Okay. Okay. That was good. You got me," he says, with a helpless, winding-down *hee-hee-hee.* "Listen, Carter. The reason I'm asking is because I want to help you. Will you let me do that for you?" He holds his hands out, palms up, again, in a gesture of apparent goodwill. By now I'm sure he means it. He really does want to help me. That doesn't mean I can let him do it, though.

"Sir, I appreciate—"

"I don't want to be just a source of medication once a week." *Once a week?* The pulse in my neck does a pounding gallop. If I have to wait another six days for a dose, I need to seriously reconsider how I'll be getting through the next fifteen minutes. A drink would help. I stand up. "Wait. Please. Carter, I want to be an ally, for you *and* for your family. That's why I've taken the steps I've taken since I saw you."

Steps? "What steps?"

"I want you to be honest with me, and that means I need to be honest with you myself." Major Rafiq stands and moves between me and the door so gracefully I hardly have time to react. "Carter, I think I know what brought you there, to that place. The same reason it was so dangerous, so foolhardy, for you to go: your sister."

My whole body freezes in place. I stare at him, feeling and probably looking capable of much more than I would ever want to do to this guy—not really, I would never hurt anyone really, but right now, right now. Right now I'm not even sure what I would or wouldn't do.

Then he says, "The one who's getting married this week. Fredericka, yes? Beautiful name. She's pregnant. You're worried. I understand. I even admire you, for wanting to help her so badly that you would go to a place like that."

None of this is tracking—but he's gleaming with the self-satisfied pride of Sherlock Holmes pronouncing a solve. "What are you talking about?"

"It's natural for a young man to want to protect his sisters. I have sisters myself, younger and older." He reaches out a hand to me. "One of my older sisters died on our way out of Syria, an infection. I've never forgiven myself for not being able to save her somehow. I never will. It's why I went into medicine."

"I'm sorry, sir, that's terrible. I really am sorry. I'm sorry. But what—"

"Your sister is important to you, I can see that. I know it. It's a noble thing, to want to be a good man for your sister." Again his eyes shine with a sentimental light—so heartfelt, and so completely at odds with what he says next: "But what you have to understand is that women are far, far better off not relying on ways to cheat the system. Care Standard exists for a reason. We must all help the women in our lives who are governed by it to live up to the spirit and the letter of Care Standard regulations. It's for the good. It's for the good of *humankind's survival*— just as we've been talking about, here, now, this morning!" he adds excitedly, those tender teddy-bear eyes aglow.

"You think I went there looking for *Fred*. To try to help *Fred*." I can't tell whether what I'm feeling is relief or anger. In either case I feel like laughing. So I do. "Major, I gotta tell you, you're an even worse detective than I am."

Major Rafiq's expression is somewhat hurt. "I'm not saying she was a client there. No, I did not assume that at all. But I did think: a young man's sister is pregnant, and by her own father's account she's feeling a certain amount of pressure, *a mountain of Care Hours*, I think were his words, and her private business is costing her more in penalties than it's earning her to run. A new life is in front of her, by anyone's measure an easy one—and a joyful one, a worthy one. But she's struggling to accept it. And this young man, home from almost three years of helping to secure the safety of his country's most precious asset, hears about . . . *a way he can help her*. Not a legal way, not a safe way, but an *effective* way. Before he tells her anything, he decides to check it out, find out what's true and what's not. It's what any right-thinking soldier would do—recon. When you think your mission is to help secure and protect something precious." He shakes his head, smiles at me kindly. "I'm telling you I *understand* you. I don't blame you, far from it. It's a bit heroic. Misguided, you understand, but . . . heroic."

This is all so off the mark I almost have to admire him for being able to fabricate it. "I wish I were the guy you're describing, Major. I really do."

"I believe that you are. You are a good man, Carter."

"I don't want to hear that," I growl.

"Nevertheless." He squints at me. "I understand why anyone would be afraid. Your sister is significantly below Care Standard. You know that they come for the family members when they can't get what they want from the mothers? The penalties. They accrue to loved ones, too. Another reason you felt you needed to go, I'm sure."

It's time to go. Past time to go. I edge past him, reaching for the door like it's a glass of water in a goddamn desert. Then I remember. "Wait. Wait, wait, wait." It's hard, but I make myself turn and look at him.

"Carter, I wish you would stay. You don't look well. Please let me help." He's got his hand out to me.

"No. No more *helping*, Major. I want to know what you already did. What were these *steps* you took—what did you do after I saw you yesterday?"

He looks at me gravely, sadly. "The only thing I could do in good conscience, Carter. These are women's lives at stake. This is the good of humanity, the survival of humankind we're talking about."

"Christ, nobody's *killing* anybody there, nobody's—" I stop myself before I say it. Because it's not exactly true that nobody's hurting anyone. "They are just trying to *help*, the same as you think you're doing." I take a step toward him, and I see him recoil, and I can't help that. "Just tell me you didn't . . . report them, or something. Please just tell me that."

Major Rafiq says, "That nurse, the pretty black one I spoke to. Natalie is her name? She begged me not to tell anyone I'd been there. She came flying out of your examination room, put her hand on my arm.

Told me women were dying, women were actually *dying* beneath this burden that has been placed on them—the burden of Care Hours, the *burden*, as she called it, of consecrating your life to a child's. Well. I've seen men dying for worse reasons. Believe me. I've seen more than enough of that." He's reaching out for me, but I'm already leaving. "Please don't leave like this. You make me afraid for you, Carter. Don't make me call your father and tell him you left my office looking like you might not make it down the street."

"I'll make it."

I make it, in fact, as far as the playground above Gard and Natalie's clinic. As I'm passing through I manage to keep myself from looking for the sack with the beer can under the bench, although I won't lie and say I'm not thinking about it. Everything's pounding in me in that one particular way that a beer can really help with, the softening of internal blows.

The air smells burned.

As I approach the far side of the playground, the burned smell grows stronger. In the street leading to the long brick building there are stains, char marks, like things were set on fire and dragged. There is broken furniture in the road. Scattered among the smoking unrecognizable objects there is glass, milk-white, probably the remains of the globelike overhead light fixtures I saw in the passageway. And the flyers are fluttering everywhere, so she's gazing at me from a thousand places, the woman who's looking straight at the camera and holding her own arm like a wounded animal. *Meeting the Standard of Care.*

The door to the building, the one I was led through by the hand, has been replaced by a new door—gray metal, shiny new hinges, shiny new lock. The old door must have been destroyed. There's a notice posted. CLOSED BY ORDER OF DOH.

Someone's inside-out purse is in the road, near the curb. Near someone's shoe, a rubber flip-flop.

Someone else has left a note, too, wedged into the seam where the door meets the frame, on paper that looks like it spent a good amount of time at the bottom of a backpack. When I pluck it out to read it I see that the note is written in pencil. It reads *Please help me.*

I'm too late to help. I'm the wrong person to help, anyway. I destroyed it. It wasn't Rafiq's good intentions—it was mine. I did this. I didn't mean to, but I did. It was me.

FREDERICKA QUINN
135 PAULINA NORTH, #4B
NEW CHICAGO 0606030301
NEW STATES

PFC C. P. QUINN 2276766
MCC 167 1ST MAW
FPO NEW CHICAGO 06040309

May 1, 11:13 p.m.

Hi CQ,

Hello, it's me, your oldest (and prettiest) sister, the one who loves you and messages you often, even though You Never Message Me Back but okay I get it just try not to get shot.

It is, as you know, Pop's birthday, and if you *don't* know, I wanted to remind you, but don't worry, it's handled. I got him something nice from the three of us. I assumed you would have other things on your mind, like Not. Getting. Shot. And Gard is unusually unusual these days. She needs more sleep. She looks like shit. I don't know how much she's told you about what she's been doing to herself, working sixteen hours a day, but it's hard to see her being able to sustain that. Maybe you can talk to her. It probably wouldn't sound right coming from me, it's almost midnight and I'm just home from work—which is really good, by the way, just busy.

At least I get paid. Gard is still just scraping by.

The last time I heard from Gard, just to give you an idea, she was trying to tell me about something that happened at the clinic where she does her night shift—and, honestly, the thing that upsets me most about it is that it's apparently in the middle of this seriously extremely unsafe part of town and she takes the bus there and then walks. She won't let me pay for an autocab for her, either. She's such a little shit.

Anyway, she was telling me, or trying to tell me, about something she'd seen once, at work, but she kept breaking down and bawling. She couldn't get through the story. Finally I managed to get it out of her and I guess a young mother with a newborn came in late one night. The baby was fine, but the mother had disfigured herself. Cut off one of her own fingers. Among other things. With a kitchen knife. I was like What The Actual Fuck, Gard? If the no sleep doesn't get her, the crazy shit she's seeing will.

Sorry to worry you with this. I know you have enough to contend with. I just wanted to let you know.

But you know what, don't—actually, don't feel like you have to talk to her about it, or anything like that. Forget I said that. I'll handle it. I just want everybody to be safe. And be good! You little shithead!

Love
Fred

Dec 20 11:03 AM

Natalie, please let me know if
you get this. I am looking for you. I know
what happened. Please please let me help.
If I can.
My sister, my other sister, she may be able to
help you, somehow. So please get back to me
if you can.
I am thinking about you. To tell you the truth
I am always thinking
about you. And I'm so, so sorry.

Dec 20 11:23 AM

Fred, I need your help again

Dec 20 11:23 AM

Don't tell me that right now

Dec 20 11:23 AM

Gard's friend, her coworker
I'm pretty sure she's been arrested
Or picked up by DOH.
or something
Can you help me find her

Dec 20 11:25 AM

CQ how many women are you
prepared to save at one time?

Can I just remind you?
Gardner?
Our beloved?
Who even is this coworker
Oh wait
Oh shit

Dec 20 11:28 AM
Yes. Oh shit. Exactly.

Dec 20 11:28 AM
Is this bad? Tell me this isn't bad.

Dec 20 11:28 AM
I honestly don't know. It's my fault.
I think I accidentally
I don't know
revealed
let down
endangered
gave up
this person, who btw
I actually gave a shit
about, and
who I know Gard cared about too
And everything Gard was working on
and everything she was trying to do
it all got trashed, closed down
I don't know
I don't even know half of what I did yet
All I know is I'm responsible

Dec 20 11:33 AM
You're at a bar aren't you.
I can see that you are

Dec 20 11:33 AM
So what if I am

Dec 20 11:34 AM
CQ get out of that place
isn't that the place near Pop's house
where everybody looks like a wadded-up sock?
Don't stay there. Don't stay there.
Come to me at the Walkers'
There's something I need to tell you

Dec 20 11:36 AM
Fred I don't think I can handle any
more surprises from you

Dec 20 11:38 AM
Oh you read the file, did you

Dec 20 11:38 AM
Yes.
But don't worry
I think you're a good person.
In a system that is bad.
And I'm sorry all this is happening.
And I know we're not this kind of family
but I love you, Fredlet.

Dec 20 11:42 AM
I love you too
you little crapfuck.
Come over soon. I have some news.

Dec 20 11:43 AM
OK. Will be there in a little while.

Dec 20 12:48 PM
CQ, where are you
You said you were coming over
like an hour ago
and your geo status is still showing
you at the Wadded Sock
or whatever the fuck it's called
Please tell me you haven't been
drinking since then

Dec 20 1:04 PM
CQ, come the fuck on
answer me already

Dec 20 1:36 PM
You forgot, didn't you
You forgot it was today
I honestly didn't think you'd forget

Dec 20 2:07 PM
When you sent that txt this morning
I thought you at least remembered
what was supposed to be
happening today

Dec 20 2:17 PM
I honestly didn't think I had to
remind you

Dec 20 2:22 PM
I honestly thought you were capable of
keeping your shit together,
at least for this

Dec 20 2:28 PM
I honestly thought you really meant it
when you said you'd help me find her
I can't believe
how dumb I was
to believe in you.

Dec 20 2:38 PM
I never imagined that you would just
go to a fucking bar at 11 am
and sit there all day long
till you were too drunk to remember
your sister was supposed to be
getting married tonight

Dec 20 2:00 PM
23 15 42 02 52 53 87 69 23 92

Dec 20 2:00 PM
Natalie thnk god
thaaaaaaaaaaaaaank
gooooooooooooooood
are u ok
pls tell me
wht does that mean

Dec 20 3:00 PM
23 15 42 02 52 53 87 69 23 92

Dec 20 3:00 PM

i dont understnad

Dec 20 4:00 PM

23 15 42 02 52 53 87 69 23 92

Dec 20 4:00 PM

can u pls

answer

Dec 20 4:05 PM

please

ELEVEN

Dec 20 4:00 PM
23 15 42 02 52 53 87 69 23 92

I keep looking at it.

I've been messaging Natalie all day, on and off. She's not responding. Maybe she can't. But she keeps sending me this, the same thing, every hour.

It's just a string of numbers, but I know it means something. It's code, or meant to be code. I need Wash, but Wash is dead.

Meanwhile I am fantastically, gloriously, heroically lit. After I turned my back on Natalie and Gard's closed-up clinic, I bought myself three 'neered beers for the autobus ride (and for the pounding headache and the screeching inner-ear static and the overall sensory shittiness), and drank them while headed back to Pop and Gard's neighborhood, where I entrenched myself at the old-man bar near Pop's house and ordered a fourth. That was around eleven this morning, and I've been here drinking steadily ever since. Pop and Fred both know where I am, I assume—I'm on their wearables, I haven't moved; I'm an easy target. I'm half surprised that Pop hasn't come around the corner and walked through the sticky door of this place just to push me off my chair. I wouldn't blame him, wouldn't even mind. And it wouldn't take much to knock me off this chair, I admit it. But at least I'm not feeling the effects of withdrawing from Rafiq's injection anymore, and I'm not feeling the effects of staying up all night with Fred's Frankenportal crawling through my eyeball and my forearm. I'm not feeling the effects of having had my ass soundly kicked by Mr. Secure America for Americans, or knocking down my own father, or getting Natalie arrested and at the same time accidentally destroying something my sister cared about and might have even given up her life for. Or realizing that I maybe will never find her, never.

No, now what I feel is pleasantly buzzed, a good three-quarters of my consciousness plowed under, and I'm engrossed in the mystery of Natalie's message to me. What does it mean? What would Wash say? I want it to be encoded coordinates for a meeting time and place, is what I want: 23 15, that could be eleven fifteen. Tonight? But couldn't the entire message just as easily be an accident, a randomly swiped-and-sent string of numerals that ended up going to me, her most recent contact, just as she was losing consciousness in the back of some Security van on her way to be processed?

Part of why I came here: I've been watching the news portal over the bar all day. There's been nothing about a women's health clinic or a Nurse Completionist under investigation, nothing about arrests or detainments that match Natalie's profile, or even possibly her colleagues'. But that doesn't mean it's not happening. The helplessness of suspecting it and being powerless to do anything about it is part of what drove me here and kept me here all day, ignoring increasingly despairing messages from Fred and an ominous wall of silence from my father. My worry about Natalie is like a dust cloud overtaking the horizon line: it has a nice way of eclipsing all the other things there are to worry about, and I'm letting it.

Because I can't be this big of a failure, this gigantic and criminal of a fuckup. I can't lose my sister and then lose Natalie, too. And I *know* she doesn't like me, I *know* she doesn't, but that doesn't even matter. That, in fact, is just proof of the purity of my concern. My mission, as Major Rafiq would have it.

"You all right, Private?" The guy behind the bar calls to me. He knows me now, after the last couple of weeks they all know me, all the guys up and down the bar. The fact is this isn't the first time I've been here. It's not even the first time I've spent all day here. The table where I usually sit is against the wall, beneath one of the high, brick-framed windows hung with the glowing logo of a beer brand no one makes anymore, and I've found that if I come to this table in the early afternoon, a rectangle of light will sit on the chair, like a spotlight beckoning me to stand in it.

"I'm fine, sir," I lie boldly.

"Go sani up, son. You've got blood all over your—" He makes a motion over his own face that looks like lathering up a beard that's about to be shaven.

"I'm good."

"Bring this over to the kid there," I hear the barman say, and a few shumble-shuffle-staggers later there's a small haystack of sanifoam wipes in little foil packets at my elbow. The fellow who brought them to me at my table then lurches off to the men's room. Godspeed, sir.

I tear open one of the saniwipes, and even though my eyes water at the smell, I keep my eyes on my hands, useless, untrustworthy. It is a colossal effort just to make them do this one fine-motor thing, pluck out a sanifoam-soaked tissuelet from a little foil-lined envelope. I'm not even sure I can do it. Closing one eye helps, because it brings my focus into line on one of the many little saniwipe packets, held by one of the many sets of five tremendous, fumbling fingers. I'm holding the saniwipe packet between the terrible fingers of one hand, and trying to line up my other terrible fingers to poke, pluck, pinch down into that little pine-smelling opening, it's unspeakable somehow, like trying to pluck something from between the lips of a wound. But I manage to tweeze out the saniwipe and then comes the unfolding of the thing, the frankly impossible unlayering of a delicate square of foamy tissue. I get one layer opened and then bring the wipe, balanced on my shaking fingers, to my face. The familiar sani smell zings into my mouth and windpipe. The wipe is good for a couple of dabs, until it comes away bloody and dried out. And then to start the whole process all over again because now the blood on my chin and my forehead (it's been coming from somewhere beneath my hairline again; I felt it earlier but didn't do much about it) is wet again and it's going to drip on the table or on my sleeve if I don't get wiped up—oh, look, there it is now, I'm dribbling pink into my beer. I take a drink and put the glass off to one side. Then close my eyes. Then pick up another saniwipe packet.

I don't want to face Fred like this. I don't want to face Pop. They'd be better off if I just lived here in this bar, if I went back to the Wars without saying goodbye. Fred would have a nicer wedding, a nicer life. And Pop would be less worried about me over there than back here, I'm sure. That's the strength of his faith in the service. For men like him the service is like having an extra backbone, it makes them stand straighter, live stiffer, hold tighter, and for guys like me it's a prop for nothing—when you remove my Marine Corps spine I just end up flopping all over the place like a bad, mad rag doll. I want to tell him that. That's what I want to tell Pop, right now.

Conveniently, here he is.

He's put it off as long as he could, but now he's here looking for me. I spent most of the day expecting that this would happen—that Pop would eventually get sick of staring at the ghost of me on his wearable and come try to drag me out of here—but it doesn't make the sight of him any less of a jolt. He's got a big bruiser of a black eye, my fault, and even though he's still tall enough to fill the doorway, creating a spooky, backlit effect when he pauses on the threshold to let his working eye adjust from the bright glare out there to the comfortable dimness in here, what you notice about him is that he's skinny. He's a skinny old dude. At some point while I was away at the Wars my father lost a lot of his power. It makes me sad.

He's got something big, puffy, shiny draped over his arm that I can't identify at first but then realize is his dress uniform and my one good suit, both wrapped in cleaner's plastic. I wave my whole arm at him and in the process send scattering like bunnies a small pile of dried-up bloody antiseptic wipes.

Pop sees me on my golden-lit chair near the wall but does not approach. Instead, he moves toward the bar. Hope rises. We will drink together. We will make peace over the bottomless mouths of a few bottles of engineered beer. It would be fitting, it would be right.

"He paid up?" Pop asks the barman quietly. Hope falls. At the good gentleman's nod of assent, Pop spears his gaze in my direction again. Without coming any closer, he gently lays our wedding duds in their plastic sheaths over the barstool nearest him so that he can use his left hand to swipe the virtual keyboard of his wearable on and key a quick message, fingers stabbing in the air over his right arm. Pop's old-fashioned that way. Most people use the retinal control panel now for messaging, or the voice-to-text translator. But I appreciate Pop's reliance on the virtual keypad—I like to use it sometimes myself, when I'm sending something long, or when I'm not sure what I'll say.

"Can I leave this here for a minute?" Pop indicates the dress blues, slung gently over the barstool. "I'm going to get him outside and into a car. Then I'll be back for this."

"You need help?"

"No."

"I'm happy to help, sir." Another guy from the bar stands up. He looks unsteady on his feet, though perhaps less so than I am.

"Thank you, I'll get him to walk on his own."

"I can carry those," the guy offers, swinging an arm toward the plastic shroud on the barstool. Pop's hesitation clearly stings. "Or not. That's fine. You got it? You sure?"

"I'm sure. Thanks."

And now here he comes. I have to stand, or at least try to. No, I have to do it. All the way up. I might be hunched, I might be curled in like a parenthesis around my own gut, but my legs have moved, they're almost straight. Something clatters behind me. It's the chair.

Pop nods at me briskly. "Carter. It's time to go."

I square my shoulders to him and reply, nonsensically, "I'm sure you're right, sir." I am very, very drunk.

"I brought your suit and tie. There's a car outside for us. You've got about two hours to sober up before the ceremony." I want to laugh. I don't. Then he adds, low like it shames him, "And I have something for you. The major insisted I pick it up for you. He said it would help you."

It is hard, so hard, to say this, but somehow I get it out: "I don't want it, sir. I don't want to take any more of that stuff."

"It's not going to hurt you any more than drinking yourself to death will," Pop observes, with one glance taking in all my dead soldiers, the dark droplets on the tabletop, the pile of dirty saniwipes on the floor and at my elbow.

"You don't know that," I insist. "And I don't know that."

He exhales. "We can talk about it later. Right now it's time to go. Your sister needs us."

"Sir, yes, sir."

At first I'm not sure what will happen if I try to move, but the Great Hump Instinct of the Marine Corps kicks in almost immediately. It's not the first time I've started walking while being unsure I could physically do something as outrageous as put one foot in front of the other. The room is bending at the corners in a way I don't like, and everyone in here has their bleary eyes on us. But all I have to do is make it to one door, and then the next, and then after that probably the next and the next until the final door, the last one I'll see on earth, and wherever that door is, I want to see it, I want to stare it down, I want to guard and protect and serve it. If I'm dying anyway let me be of use: I'll stand guard at the door between this world and the next. I'll keep anyone else I love from falling through it. Pop's narrow shoulders are now framed in the light pouring through the door that leads from the bar out to the street. I square my shoulders to his, like the two of us are marching drill.

"Pop," I blurt out. "I gotta get my shoes."

"Your what?" He wheels around on me so that I'm fixed in his evil falcon's eye, and goddamn if he doesn't seem to like making me jump.

"Fred's shoes. She bought me a pair of shoes. From England. They must have cost a thousand dollars, I don't even know where people get shoes like that. She wants me to wear them. For the wedding." The room is getting swirly now, but if I focus on the stripe of sunlight over Pop's head I can make it stay still long enough to explain this, to get this out. Each word feels like a dry rubber ball I'm trying to work toward the front of my mouth, let them drop and bounce. "That's where we're going now, right? I gotta go get my shoes. They're at your place. In the closet. Fucking cut my feet up all to shit but I gotta wear them. For Fred."

It's funny but. The air whistling around my ears. And then the sideways slip. But I'm good, I'm still up. I've got my arm on his shoulder, how did that happen? Doesn't matter. I'm not on the floor, and I'm not headed that way.

Pop nods. He looks down at his own feet. I follow his eyes and see: He's got his own pair of beautiful bear traps on.

"I hate these damn things," he growls.

At some point after the autocab stopped at Pop's place and he disappeared inside to go grab my shoe box, I passed out in the back seat. The afternoon sunshine was too golden, and the quiet and the vinyl stink of the car were too comforting. I didn't see Pop return to the cab with my shoes, and I missed the ride to the Walkers' place, drones flinging themselves around us and the other autocars through the uneven streets. I missed all the minutes up until we arrived at the threshold of Lake Rise 8 and Pop nudged me awake. The red sunset was all around us as we worked our way out of the car and to the door: a couple of banged-up-looking men, carrying a wad of plastic wrap enclosing something dark and indeterminate, and a suspiciously smooth and new and unadorned box, nothing to label it as a container for shoes, the idea among luxury brands after the world almost ended being, I suppose, to keep a low profile even in the packaging.

Building Security hassles us, of course they do. But after a quick call upstairs, we're identified and waved in, and then I'm following my father toward the elevators, through the stark, crazy, futuristic lobby that I wanted to crawl through on my hands and knees the last time I saw it. The downward pressure of the elevator's upward slingshot into space buckles my knees but I'm still standing next to my father when the door opens into the Walkers' penthouse. And that's where things get really weird.

It's dim and quiet, like a cathedral. Just inside the doors, in a spacious gathering room off the entryway, a large but still tasteful number of white chairs, one for each guest, can be seen stacked in angles on wheeled traveling racks, looking like they're somehow copulating.

Chair sex. The chairs have been interrupted by what appears to be a large delivery of flowers. Fake, of course, but elegant, and scented to seem more like the real thing. We pass into an even larger room, which I recognize as the main stage of the rehearsal dinner party I attended just two nights ago—is that all? can that really be all?—and here the interrupted atmosphere is even stronger and more strained. The windows overlooking the lake are hidden by drawn curtains, heavy-looking velvet in a pale color that's almost no color, but there's just enough light coming from a few of the dimmed overhead fixtures to make it plain that something has gone wrong here. There are open crates of caterers' glasses and plates sitting on the polished floor near another abandoned fake-flower delivery, something has been broken and left unswept, a bitter cluster of high cocktail tables stand nude and scarred and ugly in a corner without their customary shields, the silky white tablecloths that are lying in a useless heap at their feet. For a place that's allegedly about to host a marriage and a reception in a little more than an hour, the place looks unsettled, a haunted house that's had a bomb scare. At first there's no one to be seen, no one seems to know we're here, but then the efficient click of heels begins from somewhere nearby and grows louder and closer and more insistent, even breaking into what sounds like a little skip behind me in the second before I turn around.

"Captain—and Carter, oh, am I glad to see you. I'm so sorry for the state of things. We're in recalibration mode and it's all a little— Well, as you can see. But there's no one I'd rather bring in right now, even with things in this state. Oh. Oh my. Oh, look at— Can I bring you anything for that? A cold pack, a bandage? Oh wait, I know, I'll have the makeup team in to see you, they can camouflage *any*— Although that looks a bit raw, my goodness, Captain Quinn, I'd certainly like to see the other guy!" Sophie the Party Planner gives a breathless, lovely laugh, and to my surprise Pop chuckles, too.

"The other guy—that would be him." He gestures at me. Sophie's beautiful eyes widen, but the corners of her open mouth are turned down as if she might actually cry, and she stares at me in horror and dismay—*that you would be capable of . . . !* "It's all right, sweetheart,"

Pop says tenderly, touching Sophie's arm with one of those scaly mitts of his. The tone of his voice, low and intense and fatherly, has an immediately comforting effect on her, and she turns back to him so gratefully I would swear she'd like nothing more than to bury her face in his narrow crooked chest and weep. Maybe she really does want to. From what I can tell by looking around, our redoubtable party planner has had a rocky afternoon.

She only has eyes for my father. "Captain, I just hope you can talk to her. We can pivot on a dime, honest—we can get this whole thing turned around. If that's what she wants. Whatever she wants. The family is clear on that. Whatever Fredericka wants, they'll do. And I'm here to make it happen."

"I know you are," Pop says, in that voice that sounds like permission to sleep in comfort and safety, no matter how impossible safety may seem, and of course I know he honed that voice, the effect of it, in field hospitals with dying men, and in VA examination rooms with men who were afraid to die, or live, or know which, over the course of many, many long years, but I can't help feeling such evil jealousy that he'd turn it on here, and now. And that I haven't heard it myself in a long time.

"I'll take you back?" She's already turned, extending her arm toward the far hall.

"Please." Pop glances at me—*we're going in.* "We've never really been here. We would hardly know the way."

"Just follow me."

The hallway she brings us to, across the wide-open plains of the reception room, is broad and carpeted, hung with pictures of gleaming people I don't recognize. It's hard not to feel like we're passing through an unsecured tunnel, open to attack from either end, and from the way Pop's shoulders tense ahead of me I can tell he feels the same way. As we pass the first of many shiny, reflective surfaces: Ambush. An unwelcome glimpse of myself. Sophie didn't spare much pity for me, not that I need her to, but I have never seen my face—unlikable as it already is—look like such shit. I'm unshaven, which goes without saying, and my red eyes are sunk into purple-yellow pits, my two shiners grown up to be overachievers. My nose, never a delicate sight even on my best day, is crusted with dried brown blood mixed with probably snot. Beneath it my busted lower lip is also crusty where the skin is coming back together. All across my forehead and cheekbones the skin looks like it's been smeared with something, the dried blood the saniwipes left behind I guess. Worst of all, the bandage covering the stitches in my brow is filthy, streaked with seeped-through blood gone black, and curling up at the edges. The bandage is so offensive that I peel it off and pocket it, but then I catch sight of Pop's neatly threaded angry-spider stitches in the next little mirror I pass. No wonder the beautiful, fragrant, lush Sophie can hardly bear to look at me: In the two days since she brought me a drink—two drinks—I have transformed from a squared-away private, if an odd-looking one, into some kind of patchwork monster. I know I reek, too. Plus I'm still drunk.

Still, I've felt and looked worse. The realization catches me as I pass myself in the hallway's last shining frame and I have to laugh. No matter how bad I've felt the last couple of days—and I have reached lows I never thought I'd get to back home in the relative safety of New Chicago—I have actually been in worse shape. The thought gives me some strength for the gauntlet ahead, I'll say that. *Bring it, dipshits.* I laugh again, louder this time, and Sophie glances back over her shoulder.

"Through here," she says quietly, as if she's showing us into a room to see a dead body. The disapproval in her tone is not subtle. Everything about this is, for her, a crisis, professionally and maybe even personally, and I see that, and I am not too drunk to realize that laughing right now, even about something unrelated to the problem of Fred's wedding, isn't going to endear me to anybody under this roof, but come on. Come *on*. I'm about to say as much, about to try to crack wise—I'm still drunk enough to say just about anything that comes into my head, apparently—when I see that Sophie has not brought us directly to Fred, as I'd thought, as maybe even Pop assumed she would. She has brought us to Ken. Ken Walker. In the flesh.

We're in some kind of private home office: beige things everywhere, quiet so deep you can hear the ventilation system roaring away. There are a couple of stern-looking couches, a desk, a set of windows overlooking the bleak lakeless lakefront. There are no other Walkers anywhere to be seen. It's just him. The Intended. Standing with his back to the windows, leaning against the desk. Looking like he's been waiting for us.

He holds one smooth hand out to my father. "Captain, I'm glad to see you." His eyes flicker over Pop's shoulder to me, but don't seem to register me at all.

"Hello, Kenneth," Pop gravels out. "I hope you're holding up, son."

"Oh, I am, I think." The guy emits a chuckle. Everything about him sends off soundless nerves and shock waves, although right now he looks composed enough. Tall (he'd have to be, for Fred), sandy-haired, receding hairline but so well-kept you don't notice it much, broad through the shoulders and across the forehead, generally looking high and tight in his groom's tux and shiny shoes. There's a fake flower in his lapel, white. It's pretty, but not as pretty as him. He's holding himself fairly stiff, I judge, like someone's just punched him deep in the gut, which I suppose is just what's happened. People act exactly how you expect them to when the shit hits the fan. Ken Walker's mouth is compressed whenever he's not speaking, or looking for words, as he seems to be now. "I would appreciate it if . . . I mean I . . ."

Pop waits him out patiently. Whatever this good-looking tight-ass wants to say right now, he's ready to hear. Myself, not so much.

"We haven't been introduced," I put in, surging past Pop toward him and putting my hand out for a shake. I see his eyes widen with alarm and, oh, that's gratifying; I won't bother denying it. "I'm Fred's little brother, Carter. She calls me CQ."

"CQ. Hi," Ken says whitely, by which I mean with white lips and also with a prissy ultimate-white-guy's overall *thing*, if you will, and he accepts my big blood-crusted paw in his clean handsome grip for a second and then releases it. "I'm sorry we're not meeting under better circumstances."

"Me too, chum. I hear I owe you fifteen thousand dollars!"

Ken says, "What?"

"Carter and I should probably go speak with Fredericka," Pop says smoothly.

"Oh, I'll pay you back. I'm getting paid every other week by the military for going on three years now and I've got nothing to spend it on—I'm homeless, no job, nowhere to go but the bar. So don't worry." I smile big. "I got you."

Ken looks from me to Pop, then back again. "I'm sorry . . ." he begins.

"Never mind me. I'm drunk," I say conspiratorially. "And since I got back, I usually just say whatever I feel like, even though I don't make any sense."

Pop turns to me and fixes me with a look of such incredulous disbelief I can only widen my eyes back at him. Then without a word to me he turns back to Fred's jilted fiancé, her Slightly Balding Intended. There's a crinkle as he shifts on his feet in the cruel shoes and I realize Pop's still holding our suits from the cleaner's, still holding my damn shoe box.

"We're sorry to intrude here, Kenneth. We'd like to see Fredericka."

Sophie clears her throat delicately, which seems to remind Ken Walker that she's here, parked off to the side in a discreet but still available position. "Mr. Walker, I'd be glad to bring your guests back, help them freshen up a bit, show them where Fredericka's sitting room is."

"Fred has a *sitting room*?" I ho-ho-ho but no one joins in. Apparently, yes, that is a real place and Fred is sitting there, on her tuffet.

Ken is looking at me still. Something locks into place in his expression, and he nods once, and observes in a quiet voice I don't like, "You need me to bring you to her."

"Please," Pop confirms politely. He's an old army captain, goddammit, but in front of this guy, standing in his tux in his fortified palace, Pop might as well be a porter. Holding all our shit. For this wedding that's not even happening anymore. I make a move to grab something from him—I'm aiming for the shoe box—but Pop turns his shoulder, all deliberate, so I end up clutching ineffectively at the plastic wrap.

Ken Walker, looking at me, but looking past me, but looking through me, is beginning to creep me out a bit. I broaden the old smile, so much that I feel my lip split open again, so much that I feel my face becoming the mask I sometimes assume on patrols: the flat grimace, the dead leer, the *don't fuck with.*

"I suppose I could do that," he says softly. "Or not."

He lets that one sit between us for a moment, during which all Pop and I can do is stand dumbstruck and fish-mouth at him. *The fuck is this guy trying to pull?*

Ken's head tilts to one side, and he looks to Sophie. "I wonder," he says, still soft, "do you think Fredda wants to see anyone right now?"

"She asked for us, Kenneth," Pop says firmly.

"But she's very upset. Very unstable."

"That's why we're here," Pop insists. "For her. She's my daughter. I—"

"I just think that anything . . . stressful, or painful, to her, might make her worse. Might make the situation worse. I wouldn't want to put her through that." Ken smiles faintly.

Pop and I are just staring at him. "Are you saying you—" Pop begins, but Ken interrupts him again, in his nervy way.

"I'm saying I wouldn't want to make things any worse."

"You're making them worse right now," I say, stepping closer to him, "every second that you stand in my way."

"I'm just trying to protect her."

"Fine. Great." I take another step into the space between us. It's a little like walking off a roof into a tall column of empty air. "But if you think you know what's best for my sister, if you really think that you speak for her when it comes to her own family, well then. Ken. Try to keep us from seeing her. I'm begging you." Now I'm smiling down at him, I'm right on top of him, and his clear gray eyes are searching out the corners of the room, looking for backup. I am not harmless, will you look at that. And here come the flowers, thick, sick, sudden, in my mouth and my chest. My breathing narrows to a constricted wheeze, sweet and thin.

Ken visibly swallows. Then the guy croaks, right into my face, his pulse clear in his throat, "You don't get anywhere near her without my okay."

"Because we're in your house. I know. That's the only reason you're not in a chokehold right now."

"Stand down, Carter," Pop says quietly behind me. He comes around my side, gently moves me by the shoulder, gets between me and Ken. "Kenneth, for whatever reason, Fredericka only listens to her brother. No one else. Not me, not you. If you want someone to talk to her about all this, then Carter's the one. We can have Sophie direct us to wherever she is. That's your only real next step. I suggest you take it."

Ken looks to Pop, measures, finds something that fits. Nods once. I hear Sophie, across the room, exhale hugely and swish her way toward us. Me, I'm still watching the Intended, I won't take my eyes off him. We're so close. I could lift him up right by the throat without so much as having to reposition my boots. Ken's eyes flicker toward me and quickly back to Sophie. She has my elbow, she's murmuring something about coffee, about a sani, but I can hardly hear her. There's a roaring and a hissing in my ears, and I'm breathing nothing but high hot flowers. The guy's good-looking face is disappearing into a halo of gray.

"Good luck," Ken Walker says, in that white voice. Then we're dismissed, and Pop and Sophie are sailing me out of there.

GARDNER QUINN
2556 ASHLAND NORTH, APT. B
NEW CHICAGO 0606030301
NEW STATES

PFC C. P. QUINN 2276766
MCC 167 1ST MAW
FPO NEW CHICAGO 06040309

April 29, 6:36 a.m.

Hi, CQ.

I hope you're taking care of yourself over there. I sent you some stuff, I hope you got it.

We're all doing good here. I suppose you might have heard from Fred that Pop had to take early retirement from the VA hospital. I think it's because of his physical condition, which is not great, but he's not saying anything. Typical. Anyway, I stop by to check in on him as much as I can. Gentle pressure, relentlessly applied. He's looking a little worn-out. God, I want him to live forever.

I want you to live forever, too, little brother. I'll send another package in a couple of weeks. I'm not sure what makes it over the mountains these days, they're saying a lot of what we're sending to the troops—the supplies, the food, the stuff from home—it's mostly getting intercepted or blown up. Those poor people. They call them terrorists now but the fact is we just *abandoned* them. No wonder they're trying to blow up the supply routes, I mean, who can blame them?

Sorry. I guess that is a supremely stupid thing to say to you right now.

Sorry.

I just see it both ways, you know? And I know, I *know*, under your dumb-grunt act you're smart enough to see it both ways, too. And *that's* why you don't write back to us. That's why you don't even tell Pop anything about what you're doing over there. But, CQ, you should know, there's a lot of people back here who *get it*, how wrong this war is, and we're not going to stay quiet about it.

[*message clipped*]

TWELVE

Everything is beautiful—this I can tell even through the wretched state of whatever's left of my fried-out sensory receptors, through the haze and the flowers. This room, my eldest sister's sitting room, it's beautiful. And there she is, beautiful and panicking, a queen trapped in a tower, right in the middle of it.

I've never been so happy to see a person in my whole dumb life.

Fred is trembling when she gets her arms around me, around Pop, in a staggering kind of pileup embrace. Her belly keeps her from crushing us against her too hard, but the effort, the strain, is all there in the long, wiry arm cranked around my neck. When did everybody in my family get so stringy? "Thank God. I've been going fucking crazy here."

"Fredericka. Language."

"Pop, I just fucking called off my own wedding. Right fucking now is the time for language." As she pulls back, she gets her first hard look at the two of us. "Jesus Fucking Christ on *Toast*. CQ, you look even shittier than last night. Which should *not* be possible. And *you*! What the hell happened to you two?" she exclaims, staring at Pop, her hands gripping his skinny forearms. To my abject dismay, Fred actually sobs, looking at our father, at my handiwork.

Then, because she's Fred, she pulls her shit together and pulls Pop over to a lamp where she can look at him closely. I'm left swaying in the center of the room, looking for a tuffet to collapse onto. I settle for a low squashy lounge chair in a tasteful shade of gray. My breathing is still forced, my sights are still limited to a pinhole in the center of a gray halo. And the chokehold of flowers is everywhere, although some of it may just be the ambient scent of Fred's throne room.

"You poor, good old thing," she murmurs, inspecting Pop's face.

"Fredericka, don't embarrass me," Pop says gruffly. But he's clearly loving it. "If it were anything to worry about I'd have had it taken care of by now. It's just an old shiner." He glances back across the room at me. I turn my head away so I don't have to look at him. "That one right there's the one we need to worry about."

"Him? He's young. He's a goddamn Marine. You think this is the worst he's ever felt?"

"I love my big sister, and I will fuck anybody's shit up who tries to fuck with her," I bellow meaningfully at the ceiling, which is painted blue, pale sky blue. The whole room is done up in insistently serene colors: gray, blue, creamy white, some silver winking here and there. There's a bunch of chairs like this one, a few low tables, a huge window overlooking the streets of New Chicago. I can rest here. I'm just going to lie here and catch my breath, sink as deep into this absurdly comfortable couch-thing as the cushions will let me.

"Will the two of you please pull yourselves together?" Pop says mildly. But he's delighted, I can tell. We're together again. Yes, Gard is missing; yes, the Intended is still out there, floating around like a stray hair; and yes Natalie is still missing and possibly under arrest, and I can't decode the only message she's seen fit to send me; and okay, yes, I'm dying, still, I guess, according to her and Rafiq both, but other than that: nothing can go wrong now. We're together. It's not just me, all three of us feel it. There's a sudden pulse of power, of potential, in the room. Which I might have to sleep through because this couch, my God.

"We have to figure out what we're going to do," Pop continues.

Fred groans. I laugh.

"You set up a nice goat rodeo, Fredlet," I say to the ceiling above. "This is a whooooole shit show you've got going on. I just met Ken, and I gotta say, I'm surprised you called it off. What an outstanding young man."

"Fuck you, CQ."

"Both of you. Knock it off. This is serious."

"Hang on. I gotta go over there and punch his lights out," Fred says.

"His lights," Pop says, "are pretty close to out already, in case you haven't noticed."

"He's been drinking."

"All day. And he won't take a dose of the medication I humped all the way over to the VA to get for him." My heart galumphs a little bit at the reminder, I admit: there's something here, right here, as close as Pop's pocket, that could make all this, the physical shit, go away. The symptoms. What Carter Is Experiencing. I grit my teeth.

"CQ? Why don't you just take it?" Fred calls from across the room. "You look like shit. You look like you *feel* like shit."

"Can we please," I say tightly, "talk about *your problems*, Fred?"

"Oh. Those." I hear her moving closer. "Shove over." She sits heavily on the lounge near me, then pulls my head onto her knee so that my pounding skull is sharing Fred's lap with her belly, the rounded warmth that contains the next member of this family, this monster tribe. I keep my eyes closed and focus on the feeling of that belly against the back of my head. *Hello in there,* I think at it. *It's gonna be okay.* My heart feels huge in my chest. Fred announces, "I'd really rather not."

"Fredericka," Pop says after a short, delicate pause, "you've got to tell me what you want to have happen here. We want to help you."

Fred drops a tear onto my temple, and I feel it trickle down into my collar. "I just want to put off this fucking wedding until we find Gard, that's all."

Pop says angrily, "This bullshit again." I never, hardly ever, hear him curse. It makes me open my eyes, although my eyelids are so heavy, so heavy. I could sleep here, on Fred's couch, but the thunder on Pop's face, it's making me want to try to stay awake.

"We're close. Pop, we're so close," Fred pleads. "I wish you'd just help us."

"Help you?" Pop explodes, incredulous again.

"Yes! Help us! Pop, for God's sake! CQ told me last night that one of Gard's work friends says *you* might actually know where she is! What the fuck? If it's true— It's not true, is it?" He doesn't respond right away. Fred's belly pushes against the back of my neck, her breath coming fast. "Is it?"

Pop is quiet for a bit longer. When he speaks again his words are like concrete blocks, one dropping onto the other in a crashing pile. "I can tell you something right now that will help you both more than you know, and I want the two of you to listen to me carefully. You are *not* close. You will *not* find her. She is *not* coming back."

"How can you say that?" Fred shouts. "You don't *know* that!"

"I know it because I know your sister. If she wanted us to find her, if it were possible . . . Gardner would have *made* it possible," Pop says. "I'm asking you, Fredericka. Stop with this. You can't ruin your whole life for this—think about what's at stake."

"Are you seriously suggesting that I just forget all about her and go through with it? When we don't even know if she's alive, if she's hurt, if she—"

"Fredericka. I'm not just suggesting. I'm begging you. Please. Don't throw away your life, your chance at happiness, at *security*—"

"It is *not. Happening.*"

"Never happen," I mumble, from within a half-awake dream.

"You're strong enough. You're more than strong enough, God knows." Pop pauses. "And you've got to let her go. We all have to."

"I will *never*," Fred chokes. I'm keeping my eyes closed, my head down. I can't bear to look at either of them. "And neither will CQ. And you can go to hell."

"Fredericka," Pop says. "Look at him. Look at your brother. Look at what's been *happening* to him since you put him on this . . . this hunt. My God, look at him *now.*"

"I'm fine, sir," I say. My eyes want to open. It's so hard, though. I'm really tired.

"Whatever the two of you think you're doing, it's not good for him. It's not good for either of you. Can you see that?"

"Are you fucking kidding me with this?" Fred's voice is creaky.

Pop has had enough. "Carter isn't going to find anything Security hasn't already found. He's not going to get anyone to talk to him that they haven't already questioned. It's pointless. It's just leading him to a . . . a dark place. If you really need someone to point that out to you I guess I'm going to have to be the one to do it. This is killing him."

This, I feel like I need to correct. "Actually." I push myself off the couch in one giant surge and stand between the two of them. Everything feels like it's toppling over. I make myself open my eyes, but my vision is doubled, so I shut them again. I've got to say this anyway: "I'm finding out plenty. I know plenty. Like that Gard was being followed, for one."

"What?" Fred stares up at me.

"She was being followed," I argue. "She told me. In a message she wrote me. Drones. Maybe more than once."

"You're drunk."

"Yep. But she was being followed, Fredlet. From right around the time you moved in here."

Fred says quietly, "How do you know that."

"From your messages." The whole room is pitching and yawing. "All I had to do was put the dates together. After your . . . your complications, back in September. Gard couldn't get to you when you . . . needed her. Because she was at her night job and she couldn't leave. So you called the Walkers, and they came and got you, and right after that you moved in here. But then Gard went and explained to you . . . everything. And then I think . . . someone must have read those messages. Between the two of you. Because that's also around when you started playing around on the Walkers' network, trying to fix your Care Hours. And after that's when things got weird for Gard—she told me she was being followed home from work by drones. She told me. But she didn't want to tell you. I don't know why. I think she . . . was trying to keep her distance from you. Keep you out of trouble."

"Carter," Fred says wearily. "Sit, please. You—"

"No, no. I should tell you something else." While I'm on my feet, swaying feels better, like I'm impersonating a flagpole in a stiff wind, so I do that. "I saw Natalie, Gard's friend at work. And then Pop's medical buddy. They told me something else. You should know. About me."

I open my eyes. The whole room is swimming around me. Pop's

face below me is dark and sad. He already knows. He already knows. Rafiq must have told him this afternoon, when he got my dose. I look down at Fred, try to keep her face in my sight, even though the whole room is graying around the edges.

"Fredlet. Pop's not entirely wrong about me. He's half wrong, half right. I don't know. Look. I *am* sick." I try on a smile. "I got sick from one of the triggers we used. Over there. It's bad, I guess. I'm probably not going to get better, or so they tell me. But I'm fine! I just want you to know it's not *your* fault. I'm just like this. And I'll be all right."

Fred is crying. I don't know what to do. She looks at Pop. "And I suppose you're going to tell me you're sick, too."

Pop says nothing.

"It's obvious, you know. Both of you. I don't know who the fuck you thought you were fooling. You're both . . . fucking . . . messes. And as usual I'm the one who has to clean everything up." Fred wipes at her cheeks with the heels of her hands. "You." She looks up at me. "Whatever you've got. It—ah, Christ, I knew I was pushing you, but I kept thinking somehow it would help you, to have something to do, to help me find her before today. I was wrong, and I'm sorry, but fuck, Carter. And *you.*" She pushes herself up off the low couch with difficulty, and Pop approaches to try to help her up, but she steadies herself. Now the three of us are standing, me and Pop facing Fred, who is towering, gleaming with tears, rueful. "How much weight have you lost since this summer? You think I didn't see it? How you never, ever eat, or sleep, or leave the house? How long have you been sick? Is this why you left the VA?"

Pop shakes his head, looks at the floor.

"Well?"

"You don't need me to tell you anything," he finally says. Which is how we know it's true.

"Are you *dying*?" she demands.

"We're all dying, Fredericka."

"I sure am," I say brightly. My knees choose that moment to do a little sideways maneuver but it's cool, I've got this.

"Fucking FUCK!" Fred is on the march, kicking small footstools and smushy unresponsive chairs. "Fucking *fuckety fuck fuck all of this*!"

"Fred, I want one thing. One thing." Pop's eyes are following her around the room.

"You want her to give up looking for Gard," I slur helpfully.

"Okay, two things," Pop actually snorts, acknowledges me. "Son, sit down before you fall down." He's helping me back down onto my lounger as Fred is storming around the room. "Two things, then. Please. My girl. Please listen."

Fred forces herself to stop. Fists clenched. Face set and terrible, eyes bright. Even from here I can see that she's breathing too fast and hard. All this can't be good for the kid, I'm thinking. Then I slip sideways into the couch cushions and it's about all I can do to breathe, just breathe, here and now, in and out. Gentle pressure, relentlessly applied.

"Please don't give up on the chance to make your problems go away, to live with some real security when you're going to need it most. Whatever else you may think of the guy. I'm not saying give yourself up—I want you to be *selfish*. I want you to think about yourself, and your future, and the future you can make for your little one. I can't—I can't have you living out the rest of your life in trouble, in poverty, in a hole you'll never scrape your way clear of, after how hard you've worked, your whole life. I just want the kids I have left to me, to be . . . to be . . . to be taken care of. I won't be around to do it. And I know it's what your mother would have wanted for you, too."

Fred laughs bitterly: Gentle pressure, relentlessly applied. Observe where Gard and I learned it: from the master himself. Still, my heart is lurching and aching and battering itself to pieces inside my chest, and the flowers are thickening. Pop is not just skinny and old, he's telling us, there's more, and it's darker than we know, and if he's admitting it at all it's because he's worse than he's going to say. And me, I might not make it, either. *No one's going to be around to help you, Fredlet. God help you, you might be on your own with all this.* After reading her messages from Gard last night I think I have a somewhat better grasp of what she's up against—I don't understand it completely still, maybe I never will. But millions of dollars and Care Hours underwater, with a baby, and unable to work to support it without racking up millions more, with no one to share the burden with, any of the burdens—because how *hard* it must be, to raise a child, even now, even when every child born is recognized as the precious, infinitely precious asset and resource that it is. Even now, it's hard, right? Got to be. Always has been. Look how that *hard* wore on our mother, to the place she couldn't come back from.

Still. There's got to be a better way for Fred than this.

It takes a moment, but the smell of the antiseptic finally registers. Because the flowers, the flowers are clearing.

I look down at my arm, the one closest to Pop, and I'm too late to stop it, it's already happened, I don't know when, but the antiseptic wrapper and the plastic packet the syringe came in are lying torn open on Pop's skinny little leg. I can see too clearly. My head is clean; my vision is clean. My heart is slowing its stride and hustle. I can breathe; I can feel.

And what I feel is that I'm afraid. There's no way this shit is just an APC.

"What did you just do?" I croak, although I don't need him to answer me. I push myself upright. I'm clutching the soft, fine gray plush cushions in my big strained stained mitts. I feel like I could tear one apart.

Pop is watching me carefully. "How do you feel, son?"

"You don't even know," I growl at him, "what you just put into me. So you do *not ask me that*."

"CQ?" Fred has stopped her pacing.

"You," I tell my father, "don't know what you're saying. You don't know what you're doing. You don't know how deep in it I am, and you certainly don't get how deep under *she* is. You're sick? You're *dying*? I'm sorry. I am. But it's too late. Don't prop me up—don't prop either of us up. Not with *that shit*, and not with whatever lies you're telling yourself about Fred's *security*, here, in this place—look around you, Pop! Look at what these people have built for themselves! The whole fucking city is dry as the fucking moon, there's not enough H2.0, there's nothing to eat but engineered garbage, there's no sanitation, no services, nothing but drones and choppers and autocabs everywhere—no *hospitals*, just a big for-profit corporation disguised as the DOH, running history's biggest health care scam, and you want her to *shelter in place*? Inside the fucking beast? Since she's already been swallowed whole by it, I guess it makes a certain kind of sense. But she will not be safe. She will never be safe. Even after they took everything she had, she still owes—what is it, Fred, ten million? Twenty? More? And she owes it to *them*. Because her husband and his family and their friends are the ones collecting the bills!"

"Take it easy, CQ." Fred holds her hands out to me.

"You want Fred to give herself away. Just like you gave me over to your VA buddy without looking back or thinking twice. Just like you gave away Gard, or gave up on her, or gave her over to Security, I don't even know which. Which is it, Pop? Did you turn her in? Is *that* how you know she's gone for good, is that why you keep telling us to let her go? Did you call Security on Gard when you found out what she did? Did you call them again yesterday when you figured out where her clinic was, when you figured out it's where I've been sitting just about every day I haven't been rotting my guts out at your fucking neighborhood bar?" Pop's face is very white, his eyes are dark and black and glittering. "Tell us what you know! Tell us what you did!"

I don't know when I rose up over him, and I don't know when Fred got herself across the room. But I know what I did then. I know I picked him up by the shoulders, this frail old man who'd just told us he couldn't protect us anymore because he was sick, and I threw him, without seeing or caring where, and I know Fred was there, trying to get a hand on me. What I don't know is whether I pushed my father into my pregnant sister and together we knocked her down, or whether I did it myself after I'd finished shoving my father away. I just don't know. I don't even know if I did it because of the injection. Maybe. Maybe not. Maybe I'm just not harmless, at all. I don't know.

Here's what I do know: if you are looking for a way to hurt yourself as badly as you possibly can, hurting the only people who love you is a good way to do it. The best way there is.

That's why I drink. That's why I fail. That's why I'm here.

FREDERICKA QUINN
135 PAULINA NORTH, #4B
NEW CHICAGO 0606030301
NEW STATES

PFC C. P. QUINN 2276766
MCC 167 1ST MAW
FPO NEW CHICAGO 06040309

March 8, 10:45 p.m.

Hey, little brother.

I have to be honest with you, I try not to watch too much of the news, so I don't know the latest over there. If you'd message someone in your family SOMETIME and let us know how you're doing SOMETIME, or if not that, *what* you're doing, SOMETIME, well then maybe I would know?

As it is sometimes I make the mistake of asking Pop if he's heard from you and what he thinks you're doing and then I get this, like, super logistical answer that goes on for a half hour, about establishing a new fire base and sending out overnight patrols and blah blah blah. Or sometimes I will ask Gard, and she'll, like, actually start praying right there, on the spot.

So. Not good? I guess? You're doing not so good?

Fuck, I can't believe we're still sending people into this fucking dust-bomb shit show, after all these years. Knowing what we know. About the air there, the chronic diseases, the cancers. There's something they're calling Veterans' Lung.

Is it possible that you've been over there for a couple of years without actually, like, breathing the air? Please tell me that's somehow possible.

Anyway. I'm almost done asking for impossible things from you. Just one more and then I'll go.

Check in with Pop sometime, okay? He's retiring today from the VA. Did you know about this? He kind of sprung it on me and Gard; it was sort of a surprise when we found out. We're not sure what he's going to do with himself now. I have my suspicions about what all this is about but, well, no one listens to me—I'm just a thirty-year-old self-made female tech millionaire; the fuck do I know?

Anyway. OK. That's it for the list of impossible things I needed to ask you. Oh wait, one more. Don't. Get. Hurt.

Love
Fred

Dec 20 5:00 PM
23 15 42 02 52 53 87 69 23 92
23 15 42 02 52 53 87 69 23 92
23 15 42 02 52 53 87 69 23 92

Dec 20 5:55 PM
Natalie
for the love of god

Dec 20 5:56 PM
please answer me if you can

Dec 20 6:00 PM
23 15 42 02 52 53 87 69 23 92
23 15 42 02 52 53 87 69 23 92
23 15 42 02 52 53 87 69 23 92

Dec 20 6:00 PM
what does it mean
please
i want to help
i want to do the right thing
and i don't know how

Dec 20 7:00 PM
23 15 42 02 52 53 87 69 23 92
23 15 42 02 52 53 87 69 23 92
23 15 42 02 52 53 87 69 23 92

23 15 42 02 52 53 87 69 23 92
23 15 42 02 52 53 87 69 23 92

Dec 20 7:34 PM
all i know
is that I just watched my older sister
marry a greedy little weasel
because she can't afford not to
and i am standing in a reception party
overlooking the city
with a drink
i think you know i drink
everybody is looking slick
and to them nothing is wrong here
this is a miracle
this is a celebration of life
instead of the end of almost everything
she ever wanted
i have failed
every person i ever cared about
i couldn't stop this from happening to Fred
in fact i helped to push her into it
Gard is not here
my mother is not here
you are not anywhere
everyone i've ever tried to protect
is in worse trouble than i could imagine

Dec 20 8:00 PM
23 15 42 02 52 53 87 69 23 92
23 15 42 02 52 53 87 69 23 92
23 15 42 02 52 53 87 69 23 92
23 15 42 02 52 53 87 69 23 92
23 15 42 02 52 53 87 69 23 92

Dec 20 8:01 PM

please

please

tell me what it means

THIRTEEN

I can't stop looking at Ken Walker's teeth. They are powerfully on display, have been for hours. During the ceremony, during the family's apologies for the delay, during the receiving line, the party, the toasting toasting toasting. He's been smiling the whole time. Lit up like a candle. Actually and factually over the moon. Sometimes he'll pause to gaze at Fred like she's the best present he's ever unwrapped, then he'll turn the full-moon-effect of his white face and his white teeth again on whoever's nearest, and on the room at large. *Luckiest man on earth. I am the luckiest. Man on earth. The luckiest.*

The drunkest man on earth, meanwhile, is trying not to embarrass his family even if he finds himself unable, for the time, to be entirely a credit to it. Thanks to the injection, I'm more or less upright, and keeping the corona of darkness and the screen of static and flowers at bay with the help of a massive quantity of intoxicating agents. Pop has been at my elbow on and off all night, realighting like a drifting ash, brushing himself away on mysterious floating errands. The old guy looks sharp in his dress uniform, if skinny. He looks like a vet should look: trim, tall, squared away, sober. He's keeping an eye on me, wordlessly assuming responsibility for me. Fred, meanwhile, refuses to acknowledge me, and I cannot and will not blame her. We're all a little shaky, all three of us. After what I pulled.

I pulled her up from where she'd fallen—been knocked down, say it—and put her on the squashy chair. She said, without looking at me or Pop, *Fuck this*. Pop, meanwhile, got to his knees, then to his feet, on his own power. Then he sat down again, suddenly, as if his legs had stopped working. My sister and I both stared at him for a second, during which I believe we were both thinking the same thing, some variation of *Holy shit, he's not lying, the old guy is not well.* Fred also probably thinking about what a mistake she'd made to rely on me in any way. Which, of course, I was thinking, too. And then Fred stood up and went to the door and got Sophie, and directed her to show me and Pop someplace where we could clean up for the wedding. *And by the way, Sophie, get the whole goddamn wedding rolling again.*

I've pretty much been sitting under the fake dieffenbachia all night. Every time someone comes by with a drink I take one.

Dec 20 9:00 PM
23 15 42 02 52 53 87 69 23 92
23 15 42 02 52 53 87 69 23 92
23 15 42 02 52 53 87 69 23 92
23 15 42 02 52 53 87 69 23 92

Pop drifts into my orbit and manages to look me over for signs of imminent collapse without necessarily catching my eye, then his attention is pocketed by some well-wisher from the Walker side and I'm alone again.

This is what family does, I guess. This is what it means. Whatever stupid shit you pull, they will find a way not to erase you from their lives, until one day you finally cross the line that can't be uncrossed. I would have thought I had crossed that line long ago—shit, if *Gard* managed to, how *I* somehow kept myself on the other side of that line is beyond me. Whatever Gard may have been up to, she wasn't using biological weapons on people, shooting people, living life as a walking trigger, shoving and punching and knocking down the people in her own family unlucky enough to love her. But here's the other thing about family, the big secret: the rules work differently for her than for me. What an accomplished, smart sister could never be forgiven for, a fuckup little brother could do every day for three years without fault. No one ever said family was fair. But it will hollow you right the fuck out. What do I have to do, how low do I have to get, before I'm finally written off as a bad case, the way Pop has apparently done with Gardner? I don't even know half of what I've done wrong over the past three years, but shouldn't what I've done in the last three weeks be enough? The past three hours?

Yes, sir, I would like another, thank you.

I'm sitting on the plush bench where I sat with Sophie a couple of nights ago, my back straight against the wall, my feet firmly planted. From here I can catch the occasional glimpse of the lovely Sophie skirting the edges of the party, working her white magic. She's all business tonight; there will be no catching her eye and luring her into another semiprivate, twinkling-eyed moment under the fronds. But earlier, when she came to deliver me to the fragrant warm tropical mists of the most religious sani I've ever had in my life, she'd talked my ear off— nervous about being alone with me, I think, but also irrepressibly elated about the way her day had ended up turning itself around. *All thanks to you and your father.* The Walkers' bathroom, you can imagine, was equipped with the kind of sani that the average renter in a New City rehabbed zone never sees in person, only hears about in technology news on the portals, so Sophie had to explain it to me, how somehow the foam is particle-ized and reformed into warm fluidlike streams not unlike the real water showers they used to have, down to the mist that clouds the mirrors. She left my suit and tie and the shoe box and clean pressed underwear and socks, God knows where she got them, in a little antechamber that let off from the sani, where there was also shaving gear, a mirror, a few other needfuls like a stick of antiperspirant that probably cost more than I spent on 'neered beers today. *The guest wing,* she said. *Everything's here. Everything you could need.* Then she ghosted.

Now, across the room, weaving her way through, she's in brief conversation with Mrs. Walker, confirming something, then pointing the way for a guest who needs some kind of service, then leaning toward a server who needs some kind of direction, then putting heads together with the lead bartender who has a question for her—all of these exchanges are handled so efficiently I'm telling myself I'm just keeping an eye on her because she's like a precision instrument, and it's a pleasure to see anything so finely calibrated go about its work, but it's not true, or only half true. I'm really just some drunk asshole shamelessly ogling a pretty woman who's doing her job. I am harmless. I am harmless. I swear to God. I just happen to be a fucking failure. I'm unable to keep myself from hurting the girls I love, or at any rate I don't try hard enough not to.

My sisters, both of them, are just as capable and highly trained as Sophie, right? Yes. And all they wanted was—what? can it be this simple?—to be set free, allowed to do what they did well. To work. To work their rooms of influence, just like Sophie's working hers right now. And all *I* wanted was to save them, somehow. But what am I, anyway? Just some guy, some dumb grunt. That's all I'll ever be.

I could be imagining it (I'm sure I'm imagining it), but I think I see Sophie look my way once, her face cool and composed, expressing nothing. Then she goes back to ignoring me. I'm pretty much just a zit on her otherwise flawlessly executed party. Sorry, Sophie.

Yeeeeeeeees, sure, I'll have another. I sure appreciate it, sir. I am drunk. I am drunk and maudlin, sleepless and beat-up and throbbing and miserable, and someone should get me out of this place before I bring any further shame on myself. Before there's no stopping it.

That someone's going to have to be me, I'm afraid. Gard's not here. Fred's traveling away from me at light speed. Pop's just trying to hold himself up. My mother's not here. Natalie, no, I don't have the right to call on her for help, even if I could. So it's just me.

Up, Marine. I'm not sure exactly what my plan is, either right now in this moment or for the rest of my life, but I think it's something like this: make it to the elevator, get to the street, autocab back to Pop's, or better yet to Gard's (the key, it was in my pocket all morning, and I'm keeping it with me; I made sure of it). Curl up in my middle sister's dusty chair and plug myself into my oldest sister's dangerous machine and just let it spool out every message between them, every beloved sentence and fragment, until my arm catches fire or I pass out. Good plan. God knows no one here will miss me.

But somehow the infernal shoes, they have a plan of their own. It involves going back over to those windows, just one more time, to look out over the dark blanket at the horizon line that represents what's left of our precious lake, and to watch the helicopters streak in blinking rows through the night. I have to admit I like the shoes' thinking here. Who knows when I'll ever get to look out at the lake again? Even if someday Fred decides she's willing to deal with me, Ken Walker's not going to be excited about letting Uncle Carter into his carpeted beige palace.

Those teeth.

I turn away from them, their gleaming power, and find myself facing the wall of black glass at the farthest end of the room. I've shuffled my way over here without attracting too much attention, it seems, but now a small, polite space is clearing around me, embarrassed party-goers moving discreetly aside, so that I can do what I really want to do, what I've wanted to do all night, which is lean my stitched-up forehead against the glass and fog the pane with my breath a bit and look out at what there is to see, which is nothing, a high-up hot lonesome nothing. The lake is black and invisible. The moonless night sky, same. The blinking helicopters are all there is, chopping through the blackness, back and forth, back and forth, mindless like overgrown drones, which I suppose is pretty close to what they are.

"You must be Fred's brother, Carter," someone says. "Are you all right?"

I stand at something like attention and try to focus my eyes. "Yes, ma'am."

"You sure?"

"Oh, yes, ma'am. Just a little tired."

"Hm." She's a bit on the short side, with rounded everything, like a picture of a snowman. Her hair is curly and graying, around a small circular face. Older. She's looking at me with so much kindness and interest, I can't bear it.

"I'm really okay."

"Are you now." She sighs and turns one shoulder on the room, angling herself toward me and the darkness outside the window. "Fred doesn't have many friends here tonight. I was hoping I would meet some of them."

I'm embarrassed. I never even thought about Fred having friends here—I haven't been to any weddings before, I don't know how these are supposed to work. "This is my first time at a wedding. Are you supposed to invite your friends?"

"Oh, sure," she says easily. "I'm here, aren't I?"

"I'm sorry, ma'am. I'm being really rude, I know. But . . ."

"Who am I? Right. I'm one of Fred's former professors. I advised her thesis project. Brilliant." The woman smiles at the glass.

"You're a . . . technology teacher?"

"I'm a technology teacher," she affirms, still smiling. "Not as busy as I used to be, but. Margaret Pierce. Very nice to make your acquaintance."

"Did you, um, did you get to speak to Fred?" I ask, trying on small talk and finding it's not exactly one-size-fits-all.

"Yes." Professor Pierce is still looking out the window, not at me. "I did. I'm very proud of her." She blinks. Her eyes are shining. "I hope she'll be happy."

I don't have anything to say to this. But then I recognize her, Professor Pierce. I saw her two days ago, too, in this same room, in this same place, with her back to the room, looking out the window. I saw her crossing the room toward these windows after she bumped into me. The woman who reminded me of Gard, or my mother, at the warm-up party, right here. It's her.

Professor Pierce now glances at me. "You were in the Wars, I understand. Fred's told me a little about you. Dropped out of college to enlist."

"Yes, ma'am." I can see she's of the blunt, no-bullshit tribe my older sister also belongs to. I might even be looking at the elder who initiated her, made her what she became.

"Speaking as a professor, you understand, dropping out to fight in a war seems like a poor choice."

"School and I were natural enemies, ma'am."

"School was your enemy. Then the native West Coasters were your enemies. Now that you're back from being over there, who are your enemies going to be next?" She smiles at me. I don't expect she wants a real answer, so I don't offer one.

"It's a pretty long list, Professor."

"Is it?" That kind, knowing smile again. I'm not sure what I did to deserve it, but I like it. "Your new brother-in-law on that list by any chance?"

I stare at her. Then I laugh. I can't help it.

"Hm." She nods, raises an eyebrow. "Say no more."

I'm not sure why, but that encourages me to elaborate. "He's not the kind of person I think she'd be happy with," I admit.

"Hm."

Something about that grunt, the quality of it, makes me go on rather than stop. "In fact, a few hours ago it looked like she wasn't going to go through with it."

Her smile grows wider. "That was the scuttlebutt all night."

"But then she did."

"Yes, she did." Professor Pierce rocks toward the window, seems to examine something in the blackness. "Any idea why?"

This is probably one of the stranger questions anybody's asked after watching two people get married, I'm guessing: *Any idea why she married the guy?* But there's only one answer, so I hand it to her. "Because I failed her. I couldn't—I didn't find her something she needed. Some-one. The person who could have maybe helped her find another way out."

Professor Pierce turns her curiosity on me. Her round face is drawn and sorrowful, the smile has gone out of it. "Why on earth would you say a thing like that?"

"Oh"—I shrug, take a warm swig of whatever the mostly finished drink in my hand is—"don't know. It's true, I guess that's why. You seem like a person who likes the truth. So."

"Well. It's a bit self-pitying," Professor Pierce observes. I bow my head, don't bother denying it. "Fred's choices are hers. They should stay hers. Don't you go mixing up your hopes for your sister with whatever mistakes or good steps *she* decides she's got to make."

"It's good advice, Professor." I tip my drink at her. "Good night, ma'am." Now it's time to move the shoes in the direction of the door, but they're slow to go. Slow enough that she has time to grab my arm, in fingers surprisingly strong.

She leans in toward me, her eyes shining with emotions I don't really know her well enough to read. "Don't worry about your sister, Carter. All you have to worry about—this is everything—is just being a good man. Be a *good man*. That's all she needs from you. I promise."

I give her a nod. It's about all I can manage.

She releases my arm. I take that as my cue. Turn away and make for the door.

She had me by my right forearm, right where Wash's disinterment of my wearable left a raised edge, and I can still feel the warmth of her grip as the repeated message from Natalie wings in, lights up, insistent.

Dec 20 10:00 PM
23 15 42 02 52 53 87 69 23 92
23 15 42 02 52 53 87 69 23 92
23 15 42 02 52 53 87 69 23 92
23 15 42 02 52 53 87 69 23 92

I stop short. "Professor. You're good with codes, right?"

"I'd better be," she says behind me. "You know what a person has to do to get tenure?"

I can take this risk. This one is okay. I think. "Can I show you some-thing, ma'am? Maybe you'll know what it means?" When I turn back to her, she's got an expression on her face that makes me like her even more—something crafty and witchy about it, but excited, warm.

"Oooh. I love a challenge."

"Well. I don't know if it's a challenge. I don't know if it's anything. I'll pull up a virtual share—you can see—" Swipe of the forearm, a flick to activate the share control, there she is, labeled *mp.ncu.edu*, selected, she's swiping on and seeing the invitation to share my view in her own virtual portal, and in less than a second I've got someone I can only assume is a sharper, clearer mind than my own by a factor of several hundred million looking right at Natalie's code, blue and insistent, sent and resent, timestamps going back to this morning. Professor Pierce also sees my own pitiful replies, begging for clues, for help, for forgiveness.

Tactfully, she says nothing about that. But her voice has an edge when she says, "I don't know what this means. This isn't code. This is just—oh, I see what you mean. It's not code, but it's encoded in some way." She spares a compassionate glance up at me. "I mean, I'm no cryptographer, Carter. I write software, not spy novels." She lasers a long look into her virtual portal. "Are you sure this is . . . deliberate? That it's not being sent in error? It could . . . no . . . I'm sorry. I'm just not sure."

"It's not the same, is it?" I can't help but feel miserable at this new evidence of how stupid I can be. Of course code and encoding aren't the same—maybe they're related, it's all a question of coming up with a language and trying to communicate in it—but I don't feel capable of explaining how I made the leap, which I'm sure leaves Professor Pierce freshly convinced of my idiocy.

"I'm afraid not," she says. I flick the share control off, exposing the layer behind Natalie's message, which happens to be a mapping I pulled up earlier today, drunkenly following a beacon from the autobus back to Pop's corner dive because I didn't trust myself to make it otherwise. That's when I see it, and the world drops fifty floors around me, my ears are ringing, I'm standing in a tower surrounded by a whistling nothing.

Gard. Her avatar. Her ghost. Lit up. Pulsing gently, a beacon, a beckon.

Blindly, I whip around, trying to look in all directions and seeing nothing. As if she's in the room, but invisible. But she's not in the room. Focusing in at the mapping function, I can see she's not even close by— she's somewhere miles north, an old, rundown neighborhood where families used to live but which is now mostly rattling old storefronts. Outside the New Chicago rehabbed zone, which stretches north about to the old Calvary Cemetery, then peters out for about a mile before the New Evanston rehabbed zone picks up tentatively in the blocks around where the university used to be, before there stopped being many students to teach, and the New Chicago University formed around the profs and academic types who were willing to pack up and downshift for the sake of the city. Our Professor Pierce one among them.

"What is it? Are you all right?"

"I'm— My— I need to go. My sister Gardner's wearable just came back online for the first time since— I have to go." My heart is in my throat. Whatever this could mean, I'm not sure I'm ready to know.

Professor Pierce's round face records a stunned pause, then she nods briskly.

"Then you should go. Good man."

GARDNER QUINN
2556 ASHLAND NORTH, APT. B
NEW CHICAGO 0606030301
NEW STATES

PFC C. P. QUINN 2276766
MCC 167 1ST MAW
FPO NEW CHICAGO 06040309

March 1, 6:31 a.m.

Hi, CQ.

I miss you. I'm praying for you. I hope you know we all love you. Please be careful with yourself.

Had to get that out of the way. Sorry to start heavy. I had a heavy sort of day, I think, at work, so that's the context. But I know you're not supposed to compare battlefields; it's disrespectful. I don't know what it's like for you, I could never guess. You know what, though? I'm on the bus a lot these days, and while I'm on the bus I have this thing where I try to imagine where you are and how you are and what you're doing. So that's, like, ten to twelve hours a week that someone on earth is doing nothing but thinking about you and sending good wishes and love your way. How do you like that? How many people can say that, right? And those are hours I could be spending zoning out on my wearable, so, you know. You're welcome.

Whenever I picture where you are, I'm thinking hot, because Pop told us it was hot, and I'm thinking dusty and destroyed, because of what happened over there. Other than that, I don't know. They're blocking photos from out west in the news these days. When we were kids, I feel like you couldn't escape the news about what was happening out there—I remember seeing the LA wildfires on all the portals. I remember the day they announced they were going to have to abandon any survivors behind the fire line. It was right after Mom. I was five or six. You were just a little squirt. Now it's like nobody wants us to know what's happening over the mountains. Can you see the mountains? Probably not, too much particulate in the air. I'm guessing you probably couldn't see the mountains until you were right on top of them. Going toward the mountains in the dust and the smoke you would just gain and gain altitude without realizing you were headed up into the hills until you were already there. Maybe the air is clearer up there? God. We can all hope.

When I picture what you're doing, I'm thinking it's a lot of routine, a lot of patrols, a lot of long walks and long days and nights, because that's what Pop tells me about infantry—*you* don't tell me anything.

And then, when I picture how you are, I get stopped. You're my little brother and I can't bear to think of you hurt or in pain or even tired. I would just want to tuck you into bed. Picture me tucking you into bed. Whenever you're tired. Just picture that.

So I don't know what it's like for you but I can tell you what it's like for me. Oh I'm just tired all the time. I know how that sounds, me telling you I'm tired all the time. Don't laugh at me! I have this second job now, you know, I can never remember whether I've told you about it, or who I've told and who I haven't, but it doesn't matter. Anyway, I'm there most nights. I get the bus from my day job and eat dinner on the way there and think about you while I'm riding. Although, okay, I guess I'm not thinking *just* about you on the bus for ten to twelve hours a week, because I'm *also* thinking about how much I hate the taste of engineered food, but that's what I can afford, so. Subtract, what, five minutes a day for hating food. Anyway. I'm at my nighttime clinic until the early, tiny hours of the morning, and then I get the bus back home, and I dutifully think about you on the way and wish you from harm, which is sort of my daily prayer session, and sometimes I eat breakfast on the way home but it depends on when I get off work. I sleep for a couple of hours and then I go back to work at my day job, but it's so dead in there I can usually sneak in a nap at my desk. Seriously, no one notices. There's not a single pregnant middle-class woman left in all of New Chicago, I think. They're all either rich or broke, there's no in-between. They're Insemina or they're lucky accidents.

That's why I took this other job, actually. I felt like I had to help somebody, somehow, and while my day job pays the bills, almost, it's not work. It's naps.

Anyway. I'm not comparing myself to you and what you're doing, and I never would, because from the outset I've always been pretty sure this wasn't going to kill me, or cause me any kind of, I don't know, bodily harm or trauma. But I like to imagine that I'm on patrols with you, just moving back and forth between my posts, and thinking about all the people that I want to keep safe.

Stay safe, honey. And write me back, you little turd. I totally sounded like Fred just then, right?

Love,
Gard

FOURTEEN

Finding Fred is not difficult—she's a planet of her own, surrounded by several orbiting, irresistibly attracted clusters, an assortment of sparkling gray-haired women and their husbands, robust older guys. All of them are beaming at Fred, talking at and around and about her. Several have their hands on Fred's body: her belly, mostly—a couple of the women are petting it tenderly, and in fact it looks as if these women have formed a line just to touch Fred's belly—but also, one woman in a smart floor-length green dress has her arm around Fred's tense shoulders and is talking to her earnestly while Fred attempts to ignore all the people touching her own midsection. To the small development inside her, I laser a thought: *Hang in there.* I think it at Fred, too. Her face is pale and worn-out looking and it's obviously costing her something to endure all this; I can't imagine what or how much. Poor old Fred. Jesus.

But I can't wait for these women to each take their turn fondling the miracle Fred's carrying. I'm keeping the mapping function of my wearable open and checking it constantly, making sure Gard's beacon doesn't suddenly disappear, which it could—it could—and that's why we've got to go, now. We've got to get to it, now.

"Excuse me." I shoulder my way in, none too delicately, but these hale and happy people are hard to shove past, their delight and their satisfaction have rooted them in place. Fred sees me from the corner of her eye, manages to give me a hostile look—*the fuck, CQ?*—using just the facial muscles that control her peripherals (and if anything is the exact definition of highly specialized oldest-sister skills, that's it right there) and continues listening to the woman in green. "Excuse me, ma'am. 'Scuse me, sir." The shoulder pads; the twinking necklaces; the jewels hanging from lobes; the soft, mobile jawlines. I'm only about a third of the way into the cluster when it occurs to me to drop my drink with great force.

Glass shatters, everyone scatters, and I have just a half second to contain the smirk on my ugly mug and replace it with something like embarrassed contrition before I find myself standing alone in the middle of a shame circle a few meters wide. *Did he* throw *that? She's right there; imagine what could have—!* Someone hustles off for Sophie, who appears in an instant as if teleported from wherever she's been, and begins to direct the cleanup, not before shooting a surprised, wounded look at me. Which I don't have a proper answer for, just muttered apologies.

Fred and the woman in green haven't moved. Fred appears frozen, until I see her just-perceptible shake of the head at me.

"Fred, can I talk to you?"

"Young man, we haven't been introduced. I'm Fredda's mother-in-law, Olivia Walker." The pale-haired woman in green puts forward her right hand, keeping her left arm tight around Fred's shoulders. I might be meant to kiss it, but instead I step toward her, over the mess on the floor, and shake her hand in both of mine.

"I'm Carter, Fred's little brother. It's a pleasure to meet you, ma'am. I'm sorry I dropped my glass just there."

"Not at all. It's a party. These things happen." Mrs. Walker, with one indulgent glance, takes in the scrum of cleanup activity I'm sensing behind me. Then, her expression hardening somewhat, she scans for the group around them, diffused but still circling, waiting at a safe distance for the signal that I've been disposed of and Fred is safe to approach and ensnare again. "I'm sorry to have to ask you to wait to speak to Fredda, Carter, but I'm sure you can see there are so many people who are here for just tonight and are eager to talk with her as well. Could Sophie help you find another drink?"

Hold your line. "No, I'm good, thank you. I just need a minute with Fred. Please. Right now."

"Everything all right here?" An older guy in a tux with a broad, shining forehead like a helmet appears next to Mrs. Walker.

"Yes, this is Carter, Fredda's brother. He just dropped his drink but I'm sure we can find him a fresh one," Mrs. Walker says quickly. "Carter, this is my husband, Jackson Walker."

"Sir."

"The veteran!" Mr. Walker exclaims, his face reddening. "I've been looking forward to meeting you, son. I want to hear all about the Wars! I hear you boys've been triggering those desert rats five ways to Sunday!"

I can't. Not with this guy. No way. I appeal directly to my sister. "Fred, please. I've got to tell you something. It's important." But Fred is white-lipped, wide-eyed.

"Are you sure you want to—" Mrs. Walker begins.

"Fred, please." Hold your line. Be a good man.

"Carter, she'll talk to you later."

"It's all right, excuse me for just a minute." Fred maneuvers herself out from under Mrs. Walker's wing, slides deftly past her father-in-law, who I notice has positioned himself to block.

I pivot and make for the dieffenbachia, waving Fred along without touching her or grabbing her to pull her with me—I figure she's already had enough handsyness for the night. As we walk, me leading the way to my bench, with her following behind, I swipe open the virtual portal share command again and look for Fred's handle to select. There are so many people around us it takes some scrolling, but then there she is, *FREDDOM*. Fred gets the invite as we reach the low white bench under the fake tree.

"Look," I tell her, and Fred's gaze goes glassy as she intakes the shared window directly to her retina, rather than her virtual portal— lots of cool shortcut features with the higher-end wearables, I always hear—and then Fred grabs my arm. Squeezes so hard I feel the raised wearable panel edge straining against the underside of my skin.

"I first saw it ten minutes ago, maybe—she hasn't moved. What do you think this means? Do you think she's waiting for us—there?"

"I don't know, CQ. I—" Fred looks wildly around the room, scanning probably for her new husband and his family. It's a room full of strangers to me but to her it might look more like an obstacle course. "I think we've got to get out of here, though. We've got to go see. Don't you agree?"

"Yes. Yes. Exactly." I'm so relieved I don't have to do this alone that I don't even care if she knows it. "You're coming, right? I'll call us an autocab."

"Yes. I—" Her face sets hard. "I'm coming. But, CQ."

"What? Please, Fred, we don't have time—"

"Pop. What about Pop? We can't just leave him here," Fred says in a low voice.

I stare at her. "Do you not remember how just a couple of hours ago—just like every time we've asked him to help us find her—he told us to *forget* about her? He doesn't *deserve* to know."

"He'll know if he turns on his mapping function," Fred points out simply. "We're all his kids. Our beacons are all there on his map. As a matter of fact, that's probably the first thing he'll do once he figures out we've left and we're not here—turn on his mapping and start looking for us."

With something that feels like a pinch to my navel, I recall what I said to him: *Tell me again about how you spent all afternoon sitting in your chair, watching where I went, and probably Fred, too, on your wearable. Is that a habit you picked up after Gard disappeared?*

"At least we can get a good head start."

It's not until we're in the autocab hurling itself northward through light Friday-night traffic that I see how tired and freaked-out and masklike Fred's face is. She has so much makeup on it's like an entire other woman's face has been applied over hers: her eyelashes are twice their normal lengths, her eyebrows are twice as black, her cheeks and lipstick twice as red. "Hey. You okay?"

"No. I am obviously not okay."

"Gard is here! She's right here in New Chicago! We're going to see her

in"—I check the autocab's ETA in the shining panel set in the dashboard—
"forty-eight minutes! We found her! Aren't you glad about that?"

"She hasn't moved."

"What?"

"She hasn't moved; her beacon hasn't moved, in what—a half hour
now?"

"So?"

"Live beacons move, CQ," Fred says, and now I understand why she
didn't fight me on not bringing Pop with us. She doesn't want him to
see it, if we're heading toward what she thinks we're going to find.

I swallow something thick in my throat and look away from her,
out the window, where to my right the dry cracked lake bed can be seen
illuminated in the streetlights along New Lake Shore Drive as we pass,
spotlight after spotlight creating empty circle after empty circle.

"I'm sorry, CQ. I just want you to be ready if that's—" Fred's voice
rasps back to quiet. Then I hear her strained whisper, "God, it's too
much. I'm losing all three of you."

I turn away from the window and scooch over on the car seat to
give Fred one of those awkward, supportive, pat-clasps that are the
only recourse of little brothers when their older sisters look like they're
about to break apart. "No. Fred. Come on. I'm still here. I'm still here,
and I'm going to stay here. And Pop's gonna hang in there, too—he's a
tough old bastard. Vet cancer or whatever the fuck he's got, he'll probably outlive us all, like the cockroaches. And Gard is back. Fred, she's
back. She's still alive. I know it—she's in hiding, waiting for us, that's
why she's not moving."

Fred dabs at her eyes, around all the extra stuff on them. It's not a
helpful effort, but I don't bother telling her so. "I'm so sorry, Carter, for
all the shit I put on you since you've been home. I thought I—I thought
I was carrying too much." She gestures at her belly, and it turns into a
gentle smoothing motion over the round hopeful fact of herself. "But I
know it's not fair to compare with what you're carrying around inside
you. You're so young, you—shouldn't have to carry—death." Her breath
hitches. "But I guess that's why we have to give it to you. You're the only
ones who can carry it. It's why we *make* you carry it."

I'm not completely sure I understand what she means, but she seems to be talking to the Marine I used to be, or maybe the one I should be. "No one made me. I went on my own. I enlisted. I knew what I was doing. I thought I knew, anyway."

"They poisoned you. They put death in your hands, and in your— your *self*." Fred insists, weeping the same way I've seen men weep in battle, unconsciously, just the grown heart's natural response to the bottom of the world dropping out.

"If I can carry it, I don't think I deserve to make someone else do it for me," I tell her honestly. "Jesus, Fred, if you knew half of what I've done you wouldn't feel so bad for me, trust me. I've—I've killed people, in, in *horrible* ways. I've made people's organs fail; I've cooked them from the inside; I've made their skin glass; I've made their hearts and their tongues and their eyes swell—these triggers we're using over there, you have no idea. *I* have no idea—half the time, I'm just triggering out and I don't even see what happens."

She's no longer weeping. She's just staring at me. I need to stop; I know I need to stop telling her these things. But my sister let me read her private messages with Gard, she's let me in on everything about herself she was most afraid of—her debts, her fears. I should let her in on at least some of the truth about me, too, mainly that I am not harmless. I am not. But I can be a good man, or I can die trying.

"I killed this teenage girl once—earlier this year—I saw what the trigger did to her. I think I saw. I'm not sure what I saw. But I was exposed to whatever killed her. That's why I'm sick now. I did it myself, Fred. No one poisoned me, I did it myself."

"No. That can't be true. I can't let you think that."

"It's the truth. I mean, yeah, I didn't make the weapons; I didn't make the Wars. I signed on because I wanted to outgun Pop, outhero myself. But I was that trigger. It was me, Fred. I don't blame anybody else. I could blame this—I don't know—this world, but I don't want to."

"I want to. *I want to blame this world*. It's the same world that has Gard breaking women's arms so they can afford to raise their children. It's the same world that sells me to the highest fucking bidder. No one asked me to carry these debts; no one asked Gard to pick up those burdens; no one asked you to be a fucking vehicle for death in the world, but that's what we are. You are going to *die*; you are *fucking twenty-four years old*. Be *angry*, CQ! Be fucking angry about it!"

"I could just as easily have died over there, a hundred different times!" I shoot back, exasperated.

"But you didn't. *You didn't*. You came home. You were *supposed to live*."

"Fredlet. It's okay. I'm fine."

"You are not fine. Nothing is fine."

"Okay. I'm sick. Pop's sick. You know, a lot of people are sick, the world keeps turning."

"Not for me it doesn't."

I hold her hand awkwardly, unsure what else to do. Be a good man, or die trying. I can't say I've made my peace with whatever it is inside me that's eating me, or tearing me to pieces, or stripping me down, but I can see how it's just as hard for Fred to watch as it is for me to live with, or die from. Because if the best way to hurt yourself is to hurt the ones you love, the second best way is just to watch the ones you love hurting and not look away, just keep looking and looking, knowing the whole time that you can't do fuck all about it.

The car curls around us. Outside, the warm air, the battered buildings that were once beautiful in pictures, now pocked with broken windows and signs of ruin, and the sulfurous stink of the lake bed all flow by into whatever's past.

Dec 20 11:00 PM
23 15 42 02 52 53 87 69 23 92
23 15 42 02 52 53 87 69 23 92
23 15 42 02 52 53 87 69 23 92
23 15 42 02 52 53 87 69 23 92

Natalie's message again. I think it must be on some kind of timer, set to auto-resend every hour.

"A few weeks before Gard disappeared," Fred says, "I had a scare. I was bleeding, and I wasn't sure what to do. So I messaged Gard— privately. You saw that, I think. You read those messages, all of them?"

"I did. Yeah."

Her shame is obvious, and pitiable. "Gard tried to calm me down; she was on her way over—and I just, I guess, I panicked. I didn't wait for her. I felt like I couldn't. I messaged Ken, and got his family involved—the whole DOH emergency corps was at my place in like two minutes, I swear to God. They fucking *mobilized*. And from that moment on I've been *indebted* to these people. On top of all the Care Hours I owe and the millions of dollars in penalties, I might owe the Walkers this baby's *life*. Do you see what I mean? Gard was hurt, I think. Like I didn't trust her, or like I'd chosen them over her. But that's . . . I hate myself for this, but that's really why I felt like I had to go through with it tonight, get married to Ken, join the family, the whole fucking goat rodeo, you called it. Yes, I owe them. And, yes, my family keeps dying off or ghosting out on me. But also I'm just not sure I can do it myself—keep this kid alive, be a mother." A shake of the head, her hands cupping her belly. "I hate that I'm too weak for this," Fred says stonily.

"You're not too weak for anything. Look at what you did just tonight. You went through with something hard, to help your baby have a better life. You're going to find a way through it that works for you—I know you. So you had to marry a rich fucktard, people have had to do worse." Now she's laughing, reluctantly. "You're taken care of, and your kid is taken care of, for life. And at Completion you're going to rise up and build something even better than what you sold them—and you sold it to them at a *profit*, okay? So they haven't beaten you. Not by a long shot. You're done when *you* say you're done, and not a second before." I'm thinking of Professor Pierce, the way she smiled just thinking about Fred, Fred as she was ten or so years ago, when she was just getting ready to storm the towers. "You're FREDDOM, dammit. No one who's ever met you could forget it."

"Okay. Okay. Enough." She's smiling slightly, which means I've helped. I'm glad. How could I be otherwise? We're on our way to Gard. I want Fred to feel the way I feel about that—like we're going home, after a tiring fucked-up trip. "Thank you."

"Well. I'm your little brother, it's my job to look up to you."

"I'm sorry I didn't tell you sooner about—about those messages, between me and Gard." Fred swallows hard. "I'm sorry I didn't tell you anything about the night I almost lost the baby, or about the debt, or about what Gard taught me, what Completion's really like. I was ashamed. I was just ashamed of myself and what's been happening to me. I'm the sister who's supposed to have her shit together."

I can't help shaking my head at that. "Fred. I didn't tell *you* anything, either. Don't you know that's why I never wrote home to you, no matter how many times you asked me to? Don't you know I was just ashamed, too? I still am."

Fred's face is now alight with anger, and somehow it makes me feel better to see—the rageful Fred is the one I know, not the desolate Fred with another woman's face painted on over her own. "That's the worst thing about this goddamn world, Carter. You served what's left of our fucking country, and I'm pregnant with what's left of the fucking future, and still somehow we're made to feel ashamed of ourselves, because of how we have to do it. This should be good. We should be *good*."

"We are good," I tell her. "We are."

"You are."

"No, *you* are."

"No, *you are*."

Okay. Now we're laughing a little. The terror is in front of us, and behind us, but at least we're still together, and that means something.

"Fred, I want to tell you something."

"Okay."

"I've been getting this message all night from Natalie, Gard's coworker. I can't understand it. It could be nothing; it could just be a mistake. But she keeps sending it and sending it. I think it's got to mean something, but I don't know what."

"Can I see?"

I share it to her. She frowns. "What time is it?"

"Almost eleven. Wait, a bit past. We're getting there."

"Well, fuck, CQ. Did you even try looking it up as a lat/long? It's got a forty-two and an eighty-seven in it, that's New Chicago's latitude and longitude, everybody knows that."

"Nobody knows that," I assure her. "Only a nerd like you would know that."

"Fuck you, everybody who pays attention in geography knows that!" she protests hotly. "Besides, what else would she be sending you, other than a location to meet her? These numbers before the forty-two I don't know, but could be an hour of the day, probably eleven fifteen. Jesus, CQ, it's not even that complicated, if you hadn't been drunk all day you could probably have figured it out—"

I'm not listening to her. My heart is pounding. I roll down the window. I stick my head out into the whip of the hot hell-smelling slipstream and whoop. Victory.

"What the fuck are you doing?"

"Look it up, Fred, look it up. Copy the—the lat/long into the mapping, the thing."

"It's probably where we're going," she says brattily, but she does it, I can tell, the way her focus flicks up, right, across, down. "Yeah."

"Yeah? No shit?" I can hardly sit still. I'm about to bounce out of the car. Gard and Natalie are both there, in the same place, the place we're headed to right now. It doesn't seem possible that I've found both of them at once. It's too good to be real.

"No shit. Up near New Evanston. An old middle school, looks like." Fred smirks at me. "You really have a bone for this girl, huh?"

"She sent me this location, like, fifty times today. She's the one who has a bone for me."

"Dreaming," Fred says flatly, crossing her arms over her belly, but she's loving it.

"You tell me! Fifty times. I swear to God."

"Pop's on his way, he's in an autocab about ten minutes behind us," Fred informs me. "His beacon just lit up at the bottom of my map."

This deflates me somewhat. The wearables. This technology, it's invaded all of us to the point where we almost have no secrets, but it is also just about all that tethers us to each other. "What do you want to do?"

"I," she says in a steely voice, "want to find my little sister."

"Fred?"

"What."

"I hope you have a girl."

Fred and I leave the autocab about a half mile from where Gard's beacon is pulsing on our maps, and we walk by moonlight in darkness. Other than the taps of our heels, it's quiet this far from the city, and we see no one else on the streets. Most of the houses look like no one's lived here for a while; there are dead shops and dead bushes on the corners. We're really in the outskirts of New Evanston now, having crossed through the unrehabbed zone that separates it from New Chicago. Fred's shoes—heels, white and bejeweled, they mean business—are bothering her. Mine, too. We stagger on.

The beacon glowing on our retinal panels is all we want to see, pulsing, leading. Fred and I don't try to talk anymore. It's too hot, it's too quiet and dead all around us, and we're both tired, and tired of talking. As I walk by Fred's side, the beacon pulses us toward an old middle school, built late sometime in the last century, back when there were armies of teenagers who needed penning up during the day. We walk around it, following Gard's signal, until the middle school is at our backs, surrounded by dead tree stumps. Back here behind the school there's a stripe of dead lawn intersected by a cracked concrete pathway. From there we enter a narrow paved alley, long and empty and lined on both sides by shabby garages and gray wooden fences, just taller than me or Fred in her heels. Over the top of the fence line, just visible, are the shapes of more empty houses, tucked into their dead back lawns. We watch our own beacons approaching Gard's on our wearables. Dead trees climb up over our heads on all sides, reaching for the dark. Our steps get quieter, slower.

We walk down the alley until Gard's beacon is just a few yards away—by all appearances right on the other side of the weather-beaten fence that lines the alley. But there's no sound, no signal, no further sign from Gard. Fred and I glance at each other, and then we stand silent, unable to see anything, for several moments.

"Gard!" I woof out, and Fred jumps.

"Jesus, you fucking asshat!" she explodes.

"Sorry. Gard? Are you here? It's CQ! I'm with Fred!" My heart is pounding in my ears at the silence. I don't like this. And for the last few minutes, as I've been tiptoeing around in this zombie zone, the injection has noticeably begun to wear off. I know this alley full of overturned trash cans can't really smell like a garden in high forceful bloom, and a familiar gray cloud has begun to crowd in on the darkness in the corners of my vision.

I don't like this.

I gesture Fred toward the line of fence opposite Gard's blinking beacon in the alleyway. To my surprise, without so much as a rolled eye or a lifted eyebrow Fred actually moves in the direction I'm pointing, where a tall leafless oak stands guard over a half-collapsed wooden gateway. Fred slips into a shadow, standing partially behind the sinking door of the wooden gate, ankle-deep in yellow weeds. "Stay there," I mouth at her. "Stay down." Two and a half years of combat duty, a year of training before that, and still I walk right into the open mouth of what could be a very nasty surprise, just because I got excited at the thought of my sister and Natalie B. waiting for me in some well-hidden safe house. There's no excuse other than that I must be the ultimate dumb grunt.

I drop low and find a line of advance in the darkness, inching toward Gard's beacon along the base of the fence, my very pregnant sister behind me without any real cover or protection of any kind. This could be bad, I'm realizing. This could be the biggest mistake we ever made.

But what else could we have done?

A gate opens in the fence at my two o'clock, and Natalie steps out into the alleyway, carrying a plastic bag.

I shoot to my feet.

She leaps about a foot backward, then recovers, glaring at me. She puts her finger to her lips, walking toward me, gesturing me to follow.

Heart pounding, flowers stinking, gray corona settling, I work on collecting myself enough to follow after her. Natalie is already headed back out of the dead-tree alley, moving swiftly in the direction we just came from, toward the middle school reared back on its haunches in the hot darkness. "Wait," I whisper hoarsely as Natalie passes Fred's hiding place.

Hearing my voice, Fred slowly emerges from the shadows and the yellow dead weeds. Natalie acknowledges her with a surprised jut of her chin, and then a small smile she seems unable to prevent, when she catches sight of Fred's belly in the darkness. Fred rolls her eyes. I catch up to Natalie and stand between the two of them, my sister and my sister's only friend.

"Natalie. Where's Gard? We followed her beacon here," I whisper, not sure why I'm whispering. We're miles from anywhere or anyone, there's nothing here and no one to hear us in this abandoned neighborhood. Everyone who once lived here is gone.

Natalie shakes her head and says quietly, "Just follow me—to the school. We're meeting someone there who will explain."

"But Gard is *here*—she's right here, her beacon is—"

I can't look at the plastic bag she's holding. I can't look at it or I'll go crazy. All I can do is try to keep sane, through the static's shriek and the flowers' chokehold, try not to grab anyone by the throat, try not to hurt anybody, myself included. Be a good man or die trying.

Fred says, in a voice I don't recognize, "Oh God. Oh no no no. Is that—?"

Natalie looks down at the plastic bag grimly. "Just follow me, please. We shouldn't do this here." She starts off again for the school, setting a brisk pace.

Unable to bear the sight—the existence—of that bag, but unwilling to let it out of my sight, I follow, and Fred staggers along beside me. She's just about completely spent, I can tell. Her shoulders droop, her head droops. I put an arm around her shoulders and a hand under her elbow and try to help her keep up, propel her along. After a second's stiff resistance during which I half expect an elbow to my bruised ribs, Fred lets me.

We emerge from the alley behind the school, following Natalie's slight figure and that swaying, horrible plastic bag. She takes us down a cracked pathway, across the school yard that leads to a metal basement door. Natalie waits for us at the door without looking at either of us. Then she reaches down, turns the knob, and eases the door open.

It's cool down here, dry and dusty and utterly black, until Natalie flicks a switch.

Blue-gray carpeting. White particleboard partition walls. A half square of chairs arranged against the walls. A low table with pamphlets, showing a woman holding her arm like it's a wounded thing.

"It's not as nice as the one we had to leave behind, yet. But it will be," Natalie says approvingly. "Private Quinn, you recognize this setup, I'm sure." Without waiting for me, she turns to my sister. "Mrs. Walker, you've never been to one of our Completionist clinics, but this is a pretty fair facsimile of the one where your sister, Gard, and I worked together."

"I need to sit down," Fred says faintly, her eyes hungrily fixed on the waiting room chairs. As if Fred's need has flicked on a light switch of its own, Natalie springs into Nurse Completionist mode.

"Of course, please, let me help you. What else can I—?"

"Don't you touch her," I growl at Natalie, who recoils, startled. I help Fred move toward the nearest chair, keeping my eyes locked on Natalie B.'s, which have gone wide. "Don't even look at her. You tell us what happened to Gardner. Right now."

Natalie looks helplessly down at the plastic bag. "I know this looks—like the worst . . . has happened. I'm sorry. I want to explain, but I think we should wait—"

"No. Now. Right now."

"Please," Fred says quietly. "Please." She's staring at the bag. She holds her hand out for it. "Give it to me."

Natalie pauses briefly, then without looking at me she reaches past and puts the plastic bag on Fred's lap. Seeing it there, next to Fred's belly, I'm not sure I have the strength to keep standing. So I kneel. I'm right next to her. Fred's hands are shaking so badly she can't get the bag open. I have to help her. The sound of the plastic crinkling as we peel it back is like skin ripping apart, like the world ripping apart.

Inside the bag on Fred's lap is a collection of small metal and plastic components: one about the size of a playing card, with hundreds of fiber-optic filaments extending out from every edge like millipede's legs. These filaments, when new, are clear, but the ones in the bag are reddish-brown. Another piece is a small, shiny beige-pink mound of compound plastics, also cascading a few dozen filaments that are mostly gray. There's a bone-gray chip with a black center. The smallest piece in the bag is clear pale blue, tiny, shining, a lens, with a corona of its own tiny blue filaments. I recognize what I'm looking at but I wonder if Fred does, until she says it.

"Gard's wearable."

The insertion of the wearable elements is simple; all it takes is one outpatient procedure to slip the implants into the ear and the arm, the retinal disc into the eye, and the tracking chip into the anklebone. But once the wearable's inserted, the filaments discharge and spread to find their connection targets, hooking into arterial pathways, nerve endings, rods and cones and God only knows what else. They're built to be upgradable, but not removable.

The thought of how this was removed from Gard's body rears up, impossible, and I know it's hitting Fred, too. She puts a hand over her mouth; her eyes are watering not with tears but with the very real possibility that she's going to be sick, and she pulls herself sideways out of her chair and lunges toward the door we came through. Natalie and I both hear her puking over the peeling-black-painted iron railing that separates the door from the school's rear parking lot.

"I'm sorry. I'm sorry about this. I want to explain—everything. But I have to wait."

"Why? Natalie, why?" I'm still on my knees; I can barely see her even though she's standing right over me. Her hand comes down on my shoulder, light and cold and trembling.

"I'm not the one who should tell you," she whispers. "Please forgive me. I promise I'm just trying to help."

The plastic bag has fallen to the floor, and I can see the reddish-brown filaments scattered across the carpet, and the little lens winking up at me. It takes all I have, it's all I can do, but gently and with infinite care, remembering whose body this all belonged to, I place the components back into the plastic bag. My sister. Then I sit back on my heels and rub my eyes and try to breathe. Natalie steps closer. She touches my shoulder with one light hand. She's shaking.

The door to the back parking lot swishes open again.

Pop's voice enters the room, low and ragged.

"Good. We're all here."

My hands drop away from my eyes, which don't seem to want to process what they're seeing: Pop and Fred are coming through the doorway, and my father is helping an unnaturally pale and wide-eyed Fred to a chair, while Natalie hurries to get something for her to clean up with. She's got a thin line of sick down the front of her dress, but otherwise Fred is trying to hold herself up and succeeding pretty well. It's good one of us is keeping their shit together, because I don't know how to look or where to look or how to feel right now.

"The fuck are you doing here?"

"Captain Quinn is here because I asked him to come, when I wasn't sure you were going to make it," Natalie says, handing Fred a wad of napkins that aren't going to do much for anything. "I was underground and off-network until just a little while ago tonight, but I set up one coded message to repeat to you. I was hoping against hope that you'd get it. But tonight when I got here, it looked like you hadn't understood me, and"—she glances at Pop—"and for me the clock is ticking. I didn't have time to wait. Today we finished setting this place up, at least well enough that it can function for our clients. Tomorrow I'm joining a group of people leaving New Chicago. So I switched on the wearable and sent you and your father a message to meet me here." She looks at the plastic bag, then at me. "I needed to give someone that. I can't keep it anymore. Not where I'm going." She looks back to my father. "The surgeon should be arriving in a few minutes if you're available to assist again."

Pop nods his head heavily.

Fred looks from Natalie to Pop, then at the plastic bag in my big weaponized hands. "You helped them remove that?"

Pop is quiet. He's standing perfectly still, like someone's encased him in a thin layer of clay that will shatter if he moves. Then he clears his throat and says, "She needed me to."

Fred says, "I'm sorry, Pop."

"She didn't feel anything at the time." Pop looks at Natalie squarely. "They do clean work here. Whatever else you want to say about it, it's clean." Natalie nods. "You know what the recovery is like, though," he says to her. Natalie nods again, this time less assertively. "Okay. You're the brave one. When do we start?"

"Wait—you're having your wearable removed? Here? Tonight?" I stare at Natalie, willing someone in this room to tell me, despite all the evidence that I'm holding in my hands, that something that gruesome would never be attempted, especially not on her, or on my sister.

"I wasn't at the clinic when Security came," Natalie tells me. "Which is why I haven't been picked up. But my colleagues and I are under surveillance now. I need to get out while it's still safe."

"Your sister," Pop begins slowly, "was also under surveillance. Not for . . . her work, necessarily—or at least, not at first. She had a good cover thanks to her daytime job. But she was at a few war protests where people got swept up. And then she started getting followed, as you figured out yourself. Drones first. Then . . . it got past that point."

"Because the Walkers were having her tailed," I put in angrily. "That *safe* family you were so sure Fred should marry herself to, for her own *security*. They found out where Gard really worked, and they put a drone on her."

Fred stares at me. I can see it move across her face, the understanding of what's happened, the moving aside of uncertainties. I can't tell of course but I must look much the same way, like I'm emerging into a light that's worse than darkness. Finally Fred says, "But that would have to be because of me. Because someone tracked down what I was doing behind the DOH network safety net, because they found me and Gard's messages to each other." She looks down at the plastic bag. "After I—after I doctored my Care Hours. The first time. Carter's right. He's right."

Pop looks pained. "We don't know any of that for sure. And, Fredericka, it doesn't change the fact that you need the Walkers' help now. Without their protection you're at risk—more risk than you even know." From the look on Fred's face, though, she knows all too well.

A phrase from one of Fred's messages to Gard flies through my mind like a poison dart. *They can come for my whole family. . . . I assume you know that.* "You need to stay safe, and the Walkers can protect you—they're motivated to protect you, anyway, until the baby comes. But Gardner—" Pop glances at Natalie. "Well, after a while she felt she was risking too much. That's when she made the decision to . . . to go where Natalie's going."

"Outside the New Cities? Where?" I demand.

Pop shakes his head. "I can't say. Tomorrow morning Natalie will be given to a trafficker her people have been in contact with. She'll be taken outside the city and delivered to the next safe house, and then the one after that and the one after that. Natalie won't see any of it; she'll be unconscious for the trip, recovering from her surgery tonight. But it's probably not the same trafficker Gardner used. We don't know where Gardner went. *Gardner* may not even know where she is." Pop looks at Natalie again. "The recovery takes a lot out of you, they say."

Natalie nods, her lips pressed together hard.

"But like my daughter, you'll be alive. And not in prison," Pop reminds her. "And that's all we need to know."

"Is that supposed to be directed at us? You think that's all we need to know?" My hands are clutching the plastic bag. I have to remind my fingers to uncurl.

"It's all we're going to know," Pop says tiredly. "So we might as well accept it."

I stand up, my knees creaking. I move carefully through my gray haze toward Natalie, who I can't help but see shrinks back a tiny bit. I can't blame her. I consider taking her hand in my own, but think better of it. I just want to tell her why she shouldn't hate me: "I didn't report you. I want you to know that. I didn't mean to bring any of this down on you. I didn't mean to expose you, having you call on the major. I didn't know." I glance at Pop. "I don't think either of us knew what the major would do."

"I know that," Natalie says tiredly. "I'm not stupid."

I can't help it, that makes me like her all over again. "Let us try to help you somehow, Natalie. There's got to be a better way."

"Not for me there isn't." She shakes her head, once, sharply. "Out there I can do a lot more good than I ever could here. There's a need for Nurse Completionists outside of the New Cities—beyond the H2.0 distribution lines, they say the birth rate might be rising, not falling. But those women out there, they have nothing. And I need to be where I can help people, do something, about all this. Your sister wanted the same thing." Natalie gazes at me intently, willing me to understand her on this one point. "That's *all* she wanted."

Fred, who has been utterly quiet, maybe ignoring us, maybe just staring down at the bag with Gard's wearable, which she's pulled back into her lap, speaks up suddenly.

"I can do more for you than you know, Natalie." I watch Fred's expression shift—we all watch—as she pauses, decides, plunges on: "That's what I wanted to show Gard, before she disappeared. I think I know how to fix my Care Hours through the back end, and I think I could fix other women's, too—I can show a balance that's humane, something you could live with, or close."

Natalie squints at Fred. "That's dangerous."

"No more dangerous than what you're planning to do," Fred says, and she looks so tired and hurt it breaks my heart.

Pop says, "Fredericka, you have an obligation to keep yourself safe."

"Pop, I have more obligations than just to myself and my kid. You of all people know how that works." Fred fixes her laser stare on Natalie. "You should stay. You should stay long enough to deliver me. I need a Completionist I can trust."

Natalie shakes her head. "It's too late."

"The family I married into can protect you," Fred insists, putting her hands on the plastic bag and pressing down. We all hear the material crinkle, hear something glassy inside the bag shift against itself. "They owe me that much."

Natalie stiffens. "You've been gone from them too long already. You should leave before they start searching for you. You're off the sensor network as long as you're in this building, but it would be bad for all of us if you were somehow tracked here."

"Please, Natalie. I can help you. And you can help me," Fred says.

She stands up unsteadily. There's a dark smear on her dress, on her seat. We can all see that she's in pain. "I think I—I think this is starting."

Natalie moves toward her. At that moment the door behind us, the door onto the old school parking lot, opens again. It's a small woman of Indian descent, wearing scrubs, looking a bit scared. "Hello," she says uncertainly, looking around at all of us.

"Dr. Sivajee. I was going to be your patient tonight," Natalie says briskly. "But I think the plans have changed, at least for now. This is Fredericka, Gardner's sister. It looks like her labor has started. This is army medical officer Captain Quinn, he'll be attending. And Fredericka and Gardner's younger brother, Carter."

"Please let me help you," Fred says again.

I can see that Natalie wants to believe her. *Believe in her like I do*, I think at Natalie, but before I can say it, she gets back to action.

"I appreciate that. But right now it's time for us to help you." Then Natalie turns to me.

"If you want to be useful," she says, "we need someone to guard the door."

I don't know if this will reach you, Gard, or how, but I'm giving it to Natalie, and she promises that she'll try to find a way to get it to you. I thought you would want to know what happened after you left, how we finally fit the pieces together. How we got hold of your wearable. How Fred and I finally figured out why and how you disappeared, if not where.

I'm so sorry, Gard. We're both sorry, me and Fred. We never would have wanted this to happen to you.

Fred helped me splice this document together, along with the messages from you two, the ones that pointed the way. And I wanted to send you some of what's true about me, too, so you know the answers to some of the questions you sent me while I was over there. I'm sorry now that I never responded. We had to pull this together pretty quickly, while Pop and Natalie and Dr. Sivajee were prepping Fred for surgery, so the letters go backward, but I can't fix that now. The baby's coming early. But we think it's going to make it. Natalie says it's looking good.

As soon as Natalie's done with Fred, she'll have to make her decision, whether she's going or staying tonight. So I'm not sure how much time I have. I just want to say that we love you. Me, Fred, Pop, we all love you so much. I guess I understand that Pop wouldn't have hidden your tracks so well if he didn't love you so well, and if he wasn't so scared of losing all of his kids. Try to forgive him, I guess. I will try. Fred will try, too.

Oh. You'll like this. Fred is going to talk to your clinic's old points-fixer into letting her pick up where that work left off, with the test code she developed. I hope it helps. I hope it works.

As for me, if Natalie and her colleagues let me, I'm going to be a guard here, right here at this door, until the day I can't be anymore. Be a better man or die trying. That's the new "gentle pressure, relentlessly applied." You like it? They're going to have a hard time getting rid of me anyway, they might as well let me do this.

I'm sorry. I love you, Gard. You and Fred both. And I wanted to tell you that you two, my sisters, and Natalie, even, although it's hard for me to tell her that—you are the reasons I want to be a good man.

That's why I'm here. I'm going to stand here at this doorway as long as I can. It's probably the best thing I've ever done. So far.

ACKNOWLEDGMENTS

Many thanks are due to the Sustainable Arts Foundation and the Salty Quill Writers Retreat for Women for their support, as well as Betsy Lerner, Karyn Marcus, and Anduriña Panezo for their excellent insights and guidance. I am grateful to Kara Krauze, Jeremy Warneke, and the Voices from War teachers, students, and volunteers for their welcome and community. I am humbly indebted to the writers Karl Marlantes, Peter Heller, Kevin Powers, Claire Vaye Watkins, Joe Haldeman, Margaret Atwood, and Ben Fountain. And my greatest thanks, as always, goes to Andrew.

ABOUT THE AUTHOR

Siobhan Adcock is the author of the novel *The Barter*. Her short fiction has been published in *Triquarterly* and *The Massachusetts Review*, and her essays have appeared in *Salon*, *The Daily Beast*, and *The Huffington Post*. She lives with her husband and daughter in Brooklyn.